ACID
TEST

ACID TEST

Ross LaManna

BALLANTINE BOOKS • NEW YORK

A Ballantine Book
Published by The Ballantine Publishing Group

www.randomhouse.com/BB/

Library of Congress Cataloging-in-Publication Data
LaManna, Ross.
Acid test / Ross LaManna.—1st ed.
p.   cm.
ISBN 0-345-43992-9
I. Title.
PS3562.A149 A65 2001
813'.6—dc21   00-052941

Text design by Holly Johnson

Manufactured in the United States of America

First Edition: May 2001

10   9   8   7   6   5   4   3   2   1

For Lynn, Kathleen, and James

Acknowledgments

This book could not have been written without the generous assistance of the following people:

General (ret) James P. Mullins, USAF. Former commander Fifteenth Air Force; former commander Air Force Logistics Command. For making me aware of the existence of the U.S. Air Force Office of Special Investigations when I was searching for a fresh dramatic hero, then answering hundreds of questions about life in the Air Force, its bases, procedures, personnel, and equipment, as well as geopolitics and governmental procedures. Also, for what I consider his finest accomplishment: a fabulous daughter, to whom I'm married.

Colonel Don Reid, AFOSI Headquarters, Andrews Air Force Base, for his kind hospitality in allowing me to visit with the people at OSI HQ, see what they do, how they live, and ask them innumerable questions.

Lt. Colonel Napoleon B. Byars, Office of Public Affairs, Secretary of the Air Force, The Pentagon. Aside from a fabulous personal tour of the Pentagon and much encouragement, a special thanks for the invaluable information about hypersonic aircraft, new weapons, and air-defense systems, as outlined in the fifteen-volume Air Force publication *New World Vistas: Air and Space Power for the Twenty-first Century.* They were a great help in creating the fictional weapons and hypersonic aircraft described in this book.

Lt. Colonel David B. Morrow, Chief, Computer Crime Investigations and Information Warfare, AFOSI Investigative Operations Center. For letting me witness some of the amazing work being done in the OSI

Computer Lab, considered to be the best of its kind in the Department of Defense.

Major R. Steven Murray, Director of Public Affairs, Headquarters, AFOSI. My official tour guide at Bolling and Andrews. He also answered dozens of questions via phone and e-mail about the OSI and the newly formed Washington Field Office.

Howard A. Schmidt, Director of Information Security, Microsoft Corporation. Former director, Computer Crime Investigations, AFOSI Investigative Operations Center. Also for a tour of the lab, some great war stories, and much fascinating information about stegography, biometrics, computer security, and related topics.

Special Agent in Charge Robert H. Hicks and **Special Agent Nelson J. Fink,** AFOSI, Detachment 110, Los Angeles Air Force Base. For sharing with wit and enthusiasm what it's like to do their job, and for proving that OSI agents are definitely heroic.

Mr. Charles Davis, United States Air Force Motion Picture & Television Liaison. For arranging visits to Bolling and Andrews, for information about the history of the OSI, and introductions to the special agents at Los Angeles AFB.

Gina Centrello, President and Publisher, Ballantine Books. She bought this novel. What more can I say?

Joe Blades, Vice President, Executive Editor, Ballantine Books. For his terrific editing work, and even more for his unflagging enthusiasm.

Gary Brozek, Editor, Plume. Former Editor, Ballantine Books. For his assistance and insights during the difficult early revisions process.

Lisa Erbach Vance, Aaron M. Priest Literary Agency. My literary agent, who handled the selling of this manuscript with enormous skill and continues to be much more helpful than I could've ever hoped. She also spent an inordinate amount of time educating a new novelist in the ways of the publishing world.

Drew Reed, Head, Story Department, Artists Management Group. For helping me and my Los Angeles agents compile a list of potential representation in New York, and for introducing me to the Aaron Priest Agency.

Jim Gosnell; David Saunders; Jim Kellem; Steve Fisher; Caran Sealey; Art Rutter; Jewerl Ross, Agency for the Performing Arts. My film and television agents, who have kept me busy enough to afford to write a novel.

Keith Fleer, Esq., of Counsel, Loeb and Loeb. For his world-class legal work.

Catherine Boyer. One of the sharpest development minds in Hollywood; nothing passes under her red pen without being much improved, including this book.

Jim Bannon; David R. Black; Joseph Burgo, Ph.D.; Diane Drake; and William D. Goldstein. For reading the manuscript and their insightful notes.

Stephen Cochran, city planner based in Washington, D.C., for sharing his encyclopedic knowledge of the capital city.

Thomas M. Heric, M.D., Ph.D. Neurologist and raconteur, who advised on certain passages dealing with things medical.

Lyman M. Dally, for his illustration of an LSD molecule appearing in this book.

Curt P. LaManna. For his expertise regarding arms and ammunition.

James and Rosella LaManna, my parents, for not laughing when I said I wanted to be a writer—or telling me to consider a real job.

Lynn L. LaManna, Esq., mediator, arbitrator, judge pro tem for the County of Los Angeles. For her notes on the manuscript and advice on legal issues therein, for putting up with the general irritation of a husband writing his first novel, and for all the sacrifices, great and small, that allowed me to actually sit down and do it.

ACID TEST

One

The American hadn't moved. Barely breathed. He'd been crouching on the cold desert ground for nine hours and forty minutes, and a light film of khaki-colored dust coated his boots, jeans, leather bomber jacket, even his hair and face. Just like the bloody aborigines, thought Major Edward Linden of the Australian Defence Force—he'd seen native hunters stay in that same intense, trancelike state for hours, even days.

As the first shafts of sunlight touched the rock mountaintops in the distance, reflecting pink and gold onto the salt flats below, Special Agent Matt Wilder snapped off the tiny infrared video monitor at his feet. His sudden movement startled Linden, who had cramps in his legs and back and needed to piss so bad he could taste it. He wondered how Wilder had remained so focused. They were both thirty-three, six feet tall; they could almost pass for brothers. Although Linden considered himself a fucking *specimen*, Wilder's feat of concentration vastly exceeded his endurance. Turning, he spoke into the bullet-sized microphone clipped to his collar:

"Stand down, mates."

Six young Defence Force troops in camouflage fatigues—two sharpshooters, an electronic surveillance expert, and three strike-force Commandos—appeared from behind the scruffy vegetation to groan and stretch. Two more of Linden's Commandos—big, tough bastards—were inside a cluster of windowless, bunkerlike concrete buildings. He'd put them there as a greeting party, in case anyone managed to slip through the outside perimeter. In unison, the men outside lined up to relieve themselves along a twelve-foot-high chain-link fence separating the buildings from the salt flats. Some passed around cigarettes while others took vacuum bottles of coffee from their packs. Linden pissed and smoked by himself, apart from the enlisted men, and he scowled when Wilder walked over to them.

"Morning, sir," a Commando said. "Cup a coffee?"

"Yeah, thanks."

Having arrived yesterday, Wilder's body was still on Washington time—fourteen hours behind local time. He scooped a handful of water from a fifty-five-gallon metal drum next to the fence and sniffed it. Satisfied at its relative purity, he submerged his entire head. The Australians looked at each other, amused—the Yank was definitely not your typical officer. Wilder held his head under water until the fog of fatigue lifted, then ran his fingers through his hair and took a plastic cup of lukewarm coffee from the Commando. He smiled and listened to the Defence Force kids laughing and joking; after the long, uncomfortable stakeout he appreciated their lively camaraderie and the new light of dawn. Remembering his first years in the Air Force, he wondered what the men did while off duty. The choices had to be limited being dead-center of nowhere: 78,000 square miles of the undulating plateaus, salt flats, and low vegetation comprising the Woomera Prohibited Area of South Australia.

The concrete buildings on the edge of the Island Lagoon flats were part of the Woomera Instrumented Range, the most private location in the world for space, air, and ground weapons testing. For the past year designers from a joint U.S.-Australian hypersonics team had been leasing the range. Experimental aircraft components—low-orbit thrusters, cold-burning stealth engines, and combo air-breathing/solid propellant boosters—went from blueprint to prototype in the buildings, then were moved to the testing area on large, specially modified semis.

"Back out at sunset, looks like," Linden said, walking over to Wilder. He didn't look forward to another night in the desert.

"Next time you should tighten the perimeter," Wilder said. "Put some additional surveillance on the back of the buildings."

"Look, Wilder, we went over this last night. They're concrete. Solid. Anyone wants in, they'd have to go in here, or up there." He pointed at the front entrance and at the roof.

Wilder understood Linden's resentment—the American and Australian brass made it clear the U.S. Air Force Office of Special Investigations would do nothing more than observe this operation. Although

American personnel first detected the earlier infiltrations, and the proto-types at Woomera included some sensitive new technology from the States, the Aussies had home-turf advantage. They would plug the secu-rity leak.

Linden turned to his men. "Get to the jeeps." Then he radioed for the two Commandos still inside the building. "MacGregor, Ahearn; let's hustle."

The men outside began walking to their jeeps, hidden near the test area, but Wilder stared expectantly at the building's doors—the other two should've come out by now. He shot a look at Linden, who was thinking the same thing. Linden tried the radio again.

"MacGregor? Who copies inside?"

No answer. Wilder pulled his nine-millimeter Sig Sauer P226 from its holster and started toward the entrance. The men instantly fell silent.

"Two by two, follow me," Linden said, then turned to Wilder. "You're bringing up the rear."

Wilder snapped the safety off the Sig. AR-15s set to three-shot bursts, the platoon moved cautiously, single-file, toward the buildings. Linden held his hand up to halt their movement, then made sharp move-ments to the left and right to indicate they spread out. He crawled knees and elbows the last ten yards and paused at the orange-painted metal door. Listened. Nothing. He reached up, tried the handle. Locked. No surprise—he'd bolted it himself nine hours ago. He glanced over at Wilder, who shrugged: It's your show, bro.

Linden slipped the key into the lock and turned it. A tall Commando everyone called Farm Boy, with Clark Gable ears and an overbite, stepped forward to assist. Linden pushed the door open a quarter of an inch and they heard a whoosh of air—the building's air supply was filtered and the atmospheric pressure kept slightly higher inside than outside to mini-mize dust contamination. While Farm Boy held the door in position, Linden took a dentist's mirror from his belt kit and ran it along the cracked door, searching for tripwires. Satisfied, he took the handle from Farm Boy, gestured him to step back, and opened the door. No explo-sion, so they went inside.

Except for a few halogen task lights on the desks and worktables, the windowless building was dark, and nothing seemed disturbed since last night. Linden gestured to proceed and the Commandos came forward in pairs. One pair checked the offices and cubicles to the left, one went to the large assembly area to the right, and one stuck with Linden. No one spoke.

Wilder, entering last, immediately sensed something that gave him the creeps. A smell, he decided, sharp and coppery.

"Oh, Jesus!" A startled, shit-scared voice, coming from the assembly area.

Wilder and Linden were the first ones through the double doors. The voice belonged to Farm Boy. He and his partner, a short, tough Tasmanian with black hair and thick, connecting eyebrows, stood paralyzed at the edge of a twenty-by-forty-foot room with a high ceiling. Around the perimeter were long metal construction tables supporting prototype jet engines in various stages of completion.

In stark contrast to the white linoleum floor, a twenty-foot-wide russet puddle slowly expanded toward the feet of Farm Boy and his partner. It came from MacGregor and Ahearn, the two Commandos positioned inside. They'd been bound back to back and hung by their ankles from a block and tackle used to move jet engines. A small, neat slit had been made in each of their jugulars, right below their ears, and with each pump of their hearts thick ribbons of blood spurted from the holes. Normally, such a wound would be fatal in moments, but being upside down gravity continued to supply blood to their brains. Their bodies would have to drain dry before they lost consciousness and died.

"Mother a God, get 'em down, quick!" Linden shook with fury.

The Commandos moved forward to help their comrades, walking carefully on the linoleum floor made slippery from the blood.

Wilder, saddened and disgusted, remembered how he'd sat next to Ahearn in the jeep during the ride from base and the kid had excitedly told him about his upcoming marriage.

"This just happened, maybe five minutes ago," he said to Linden. "Any longer they'd be bled out."

Wilder looked around the room, spotting faint bloodstains on the floor beyond the big blood puddle. Footprints. *One* pair. It made no sense to Wilder: How could a single man overpower two armed, highly trained Commandos and hang them up like this? He followed the footsteps, slowly. Another prickle of danger nagged at him.

Farm Boy, meanwhile, stood motionless at the edge of the bloody pool, his eyes locked with MacGregor's. His friend tried to speak, but could manage only a garbled, hissing gurgle.

Four men linked their arms and gently lifted MacGregor's and Ahearn's heads up, while others pressed squares of gauze to their wounds. Everyone knew it was too late, but they weren't going to let their mates die hung up like pigs.

Wilder paused from tracking the bloody footprints on the floor, noticing MacGregor still trying to communicate something to Farm Boy—urgent, a warning. Linden crossed to the wall panel and lowered the block and tackle so the men could lift MacGregor and Ahearn off the hook.

"Wait!" Wilder yelled, just as they freed their feet.

A small, metallic ping was the last thing most of them heard. As they disengaged the hook, they simultaneously pulled the pin from an M-33 "baseball" antipersonnel grenade hidden between the men. Wilder knew that sound. He dove for cover behind a metal table, tackling Farm Boy as he went, then a fierce, fiery explosion enveloped everything. A jumble of blackened arms, legs, and torsos flew from the epicenter of the blast, thudding against the walls and ceiling. The explosion slammed Linden against the wall, breaking his back, and a millisecond later the heat wave hit him. Behind the table, Wilder and Farm Boy were spared the direct results of the concussion and heat blast, although the sudden, violent increase of pressure in the airtight building felt like immense hands around their bodies, intent on crushing them to death.

Woozy, Wilder tried to get to his feet, but the wind had been knocked out of him. If he'd been injured beyond that, he couldn't tell. He saw Farm Boy curled up beside him, knees to his chest, scared but alive. Horrified, he stared at the carnage, feeling utterly helpless, then crawled over to Linden, who was muttering something about getting to his boys. Wilder's ears were ringing so badly he couldn't hear him. Linden tried to pull himself toward the center of the room, but Wilder gently stopped him.

"Lie still."

He snapped a partially melted telephone handset loose from its cradle. No dial tone—either damaged in the blast or the Infiltrator had cut the phone wires. More likely the latter. The guy was thorough, Wilder thought, going to a lot of trouble to be as ruthless and cruel as possible.

He turned back to Linden, who looked at something way beyond him and, with one resigned breath, went there. He closed Linden's eyes, crossed to Farm Boy and helped him up. Together, they limped out the front door. The sudden sunshine, fresh wind, and vast wilderness came as a shock to Wilder's senses. It seemed so clean and benign; he felt as if he'd been inside that goddamn building for a year. Shading his eyes, he scanned the area but saw no evidence of movement. The numbness and disorientation from the explosion slowly began to fade and was replaced by a growing, gut-deep rage. He looked up at the edge of the low, flat roof.

"Boost me up."

It took a moment for Farm Boy to respond. Wilder knew the kid was freaked, but right now he needed him.

"Can't, sir. Gotta sit down. Gotta sit."

Farm Boy repeated it over and over, so Wilder shoved him against the side of the building.

"He waited till dawn to string your friends up, wanted us to find 'em alive, still bleeding, just to fuck with us. That means he's not far. You want a piece of him or not?"

Farm Boy blinked and nodded. The hope of ripping the heart from his enemy brought a little life back into his eyes. He knitted his hands together and held them at crotch level so Wilder could step up onto the roof and take in the panorama. Behind the cluster of buildings stood a sheer rock wall—the base of an enormous mesa rising suddenly out of the flat landscape. Safe to say the Infiltrator neither came nor went from that direction.

In front of the buildings lay a twenty-one-mile-wide salt flat. On its far side, to the north and west, were the rugged, bare mountains that he first saw illuminated by the dawn, seemingly so long ago. He squinted at the featureless, tawny wasteland, wishing to hell he had binoculars. After a moment, he thought he saw something, far out on the flats, almost beyond his range of vision. Or did he? It was too early in the day and too temperate for mirages. No, it was real: a low spiral of dust from a moving vehicle.

"Out on the flats! Halfway across!"

More pressing than his desire to catch and punish the fleeing Infiltrator, Wilder needed to retrieve any top-secret information taken or photographed. He looked around for transportation, but the only candidate seemed to be the canvas-covered jeep they'd come in, parked behind the modified semis used to move the test units from the assembly area. He jumped down from the roof and ran for the jeep. Farm Boy ran along with him.

"Never catch 'em, sir. Once he makes it to the hills, he's gone. Million places to hide out there."

"I'm not gonna stay here blowing him kisses."

The test area was about half the size of a football field, empty except for some equipment at its edge and four steel-reinforced concrete pilings in its center, designed to anchor a jet or rocket engine while it ran at full throttle. Test engines and tanks of fuel sufficient for a measured burn were attached at the assembly room to two-inch-thick steel plates; one such unit sat on the flatbed of a unibody semi, its metal slab bolted to the truck bed the same way it would be attached to the pilings.

Farm Boy crossed to the troop jeep but Wilder ignored it. An idea had occurred to him—along with a hundred reasons why he should not even consider it. He knocked on the fuel tank next to the prototype engine atop the flatbed. It had fuel inside it, but he couldn't tell how much. Not until Wilder jumped into the semi, started it, jammed it into gear, and turned it around to face the salt flats did Farm Boy realize what he planned to do.

"Bloody insane, sir!"

Wilder replied by turning the truck's motor off and putting the transmission in neutral.

"Hook up the power pack. Turn it over, then jam the throttle open."

Farm Boy helped him connect a cable from the power pack to a receptacle on the side of the engine. Starting a jet engine is not much different from starting a car: Power applied to a starting motor in conjunction with the regulation of a fuel supply gets the thing going.

As they worked, Wilder relied on his pilot's training to make some calculations. The engineers would've put exactly enough fuel in the tank for a test burn, but standard tests can run either three or four minutes. At an estimated speed of 350 miles per hour, or almost 6 miles a minute, fuel for a three-minute burn will take the rig about 17 miles out, leaving enough room—maybe—to stop before hitting the boulder-strewn foothills, 21 miles away. It was easy to do the math on where fuel for a four-minute burn would put it: inside a rock.

Wilder climbed back into the semi, Farm Boy flipped a switch on the power pack, and the huge jet engine on the back of the truck whined to life. He didn't know what he'd do once he reached the fleeing Infiltrator; he'd worry about that when he got there. Farm Boy shoved the fuel throttle control all the way forward and leaped out of the way. As the semi lurched forward, Wilder started the stopwatch on his Rolex to count down three minutes. The acceleration inside the cab jammed him against the back of the seat and he found it nearly impossible to keep his hands on the big, almost-horizontal steering wheel.

Trying to keep the semi on course reminded him of flying the early versions of the F-117A stealth fighter-bomber. Its nickname back then was the Wobbly Goblin; pilots complained of it being the sloppiest aircraft they'd ever flown. When the semi tore through the chain-link fence and hit the salt flats at two hundred miles per hour with a terrifying slide and yaw, Wilder knew he'd found something worse.

Fighting the shimmy of his sixteen-wheel, twenty-ton Roman candle, Wilder considered the things that might go wrong. The bolts holding the jet engine to the flatbed could shear, sending the engine-and-metal-plate unit slicing through the cab. And him. One of the axles could break, locking a set of wheels, flipping the whole rig end over end. And even though the cab and flatbed trailer were one solid unit and the tires and transmission were modified for the extreme conditions of the grueling outback, the whole machine would soon rattle apart at such high speeds . . . unless the tires exploded first. He forced the image of the dead Australians' bright young faces out of his mind and glanced at his watch. A minute had gone by and he estimated the Infiltrator's car to be about six miles—or another minute—away.

Boom! A tire blew, sending a shudder through the semi. Wilder clutched the wheel, reorienting the rig again toward the ever-larger cloud of dust in front of him. Then a burnt-oil smell and dark blue smoke began to fill the cab as the transmission, even in neutral, grew white hot from the bands spinning at a few hundred thousand RPM. The Infiltrator's getaway car grew close enough for him to see it—a green Land Rover. Wilder couldn't tell at his great speed, but it was traveling at 165 miles per hour, thanks to its own modified engine, drivetrain, and oversized tires. He counted on being on top of it before the Infiltrator realized he had someone chasing him. Wilder didn't want him quickly veering off—any attempt to turn the semi more than a few degrees in either direction would send it tumbling.

He checked his watch again: two minutes, twenty-five seconds into the burn. He slowly pulled the emergency brake lever up. Against the still-burning jet engine it meant almost nothing, but he did feel a slight dampening of his speed. The brakes howled like they were being tortured, adding a new burning smell to that of the frying transmission.

Over the roar of his own engine, the Infiltrator heard the approaching jet engine and the screeching of the brakes. He glanced in his rearview mirror, stunned at the sight of the huge truck approaching at an impossible speed. Before he could react, the front bumper of the semi hit the center of the Land Rover's rear hatch, crumpling it like a soda can and blowing its back tires out. Its shattered back end burrowed into the grille of the semi like a big hood ornament, and slowed the big rig down a bit more.

"Gotcha," Wilder muttered to himself. The front of the Rover's passenger compartment appeared intact, so its passenger was probably still alive, although he'd surely have a nasty whiplash. Sue me, he thought, and checked his watch again—the three minutes had passed and the engine should be winding down now.

It kept running. "Big surprise," Wilder grumbled. It'd been that kind of morning.

The foothills loomed larger by the second. He unholstered his Sig, covered his face with his jacket, and shot out the windshield. The safety glass exploded into thousands of green nuggets. Driven by the wind, they peppered the inside of the cab, cutting his jacket and upraised arm. He unbuckled his seat belt and pulled himself toward the opening in the windshield. He swung his leg over the edge of the windshield frame. His eyes watered so badly from the wind he could barely see. He crouched, then jumped out onto the hood, scrambling furiously to grab the bulldog hood ornament at the top of the grille before he got blown away.

He squinted ahead at the approaching foothills, figuring he had about fifty seconds before impact. The back window of the Land Rover had been buried inside the front of the truck, so Wilder shot the Rover's glass sunroof several times until he made a big enough hole to fit through. He clambered down the grille, grabbed a twisted hinge on the Rover's hatchback, and pulled himself onto the top of it.

A burst of machine-gun fire tore a row of holes through the roof of the Land Rover next to Wilder's head. Oh, yeah, he thought, there's a sadistic killer inside. Funny how the little details can slip your mind.

Wilder dove headfirst into the sunroof. The man tried to swing his machine pistol up again, but Wilder shot him through the back of the hand, blasting the weapon from his grasp. The Infiltrator turned and with his good hand pushed the passenger's seat sideways, bending its frame and shearing the bolts holding it to the floor. Wilder stared at him, dumbstruck. It became instantly clear how he'd overpowered the two Commandos back at the building. His demeanor was even more unsettling—despite the fact he'd just been shot, he had a small smile on his face.

The man grabbed Wilder's forearm and shoved it up toward the roof. Dropping his Sig, Wilder caught it with his free hand. He wanted the Infiltrator alive, if possible, so he smashed him across the face with the barrel of the weapon. The blow broke the man's nose. Although this did nothing to change his calm expression, it did lessen the power of his grasp. Wilder pulled loose, swung his feet up and kicked repeatedly at him, knocking his head against the door frame. The man caught hold of Wilder's foot and twisted; Wilder cried out. Just before his bone snapped he shot the Infiltrator, taking a piece out of his left shoulder. He kicked him in the face with his other leg, again and again, until finally the man became groggy.

Wilder climbed over him, grabbed the steering wheel, and jerked it back and forth, trying to jockey the Land Rover loose from the grille of the semi. The metal groaned and creaked but would not separate. Then, finally, the jet engine stopped shrieking as its fuel ran out. Wilder frantically shook the steering wheel as the foothills continued to loom larger. With a snap a sliver of daylight appeared between the two vehicles. He jerked the steering wheel one more time and the Land Rover broke free, its blown-out back wheels digging into the dry flats. The semi slammed back into it, sending it into a spin on the slippery salt. Wilder wrestled the wheel and pumped the brakes, trying to keep the Land Rover from rolling over.

The semi tore past and plowed into the rugged foothills. It crumpled into itself like an accordion, before twisting into a mass of sharp, spectacular angles, then exploding in a boiling, black-and-orange fireball.

Spinning out of control, the Land Rover also headed for the foothills. Wilder pushed the brake pedal all the way to the floor and jammed the transmission into first. The pedal under his foot fluttered with the antilock braking system and the bare metal rear rims sliced into the hard, salty ground.

The Land Rover came to a stop ten feet from an outcropping of rocks.

Wilder kicked the door open and rolled out. He wobbled to his feet, Sig in his right hand, and used his left to drag the bloodied, dazed Infiltrator out of the car and shove him to the ground. He patted him down for weapons; finding a knife, he tossed it into the rocks. The Infiltrator turned, looked back the way they'd come as if hearing something. Amazingly, despite his gunshot wounds, he pushed himself into a sitting position and tried to stand.

"Don't move!"

The Infiltrator ignored him. He still had that goddamn smile on his face.

"Won't matter to my bosses whether you can walk or not. You're five seconds from losing your kneecaps."

The Infiltrator put his hands at his sides as ordered, but continued to glance over his shoulder. Wilder peered across the flats. He saw no one, and could hear nothing through the ringing in his ears beyond the semi burning in the distance and his own heart pounding. He limped over and sat on a rock, twenty feet away, and leaned his forearm on his knee. The Sig felt like it weighed a hundred pounds. Also, he didn't want the Infiltrator to see his hand shaking. He felt this way every time he came down from one of his fury-and-adrenaline-stoked episodes—moments when nothing mattered but accomplishing his goal. They left him scared and exhausted, and he often thought this must be how the Wolfman must feel waking up the morning after a full moon.

His first good look at his enemy confirmed Wilder's guess regarding his nationality. The man, dressed in a cotton shirt and American jeans, appeared to be a hybrid of Asian, Arab, and European. Meaning, almost certainly, a citizen of the Trans-Altaic Alliance. And, Wilder presumed, one of Batu Khan's handpicked Khaldun Elite.

Wilder caught him shooting another quick glance back across the flats.

"Eyes front, shithead." Wilder wished he'd finished that cup of coffee.

Then he heard something, low and rhythmic, far in the distance—an approaching helicopter. Farm Boy must've found a working phone and called the Defence Support Centre. He looked at the Infiltrator. How in the fuck had he heard the copter so much earlier?

His captive suddenly swung his hands up, grabbing a thin chain hanging around his neck. Snapping it taut, he pulled a small, pewter-colored medallion from beneath his shirt. The medallion was shaped like the inside of the Mercedes logo—a three-pointed star. Each point consisted of a cylinder, two inches long and a half-inch thick, covered with an engraved design. He put one point of the star between his teeth and held the other two in his hands, then snapped them apart into three pieces.

Wilder shouted, but by the time it emerged no one remained to hear it. The separate pieces of the star—held in mouth, left hand, and right hand—exploded the instant they broke apart, creating three tight, modulated blasts. Wilder reeled back, scalded by the bursts of vaporized flesh, bone, and brains.

The Infiltrator's headless, handless body rolled slowly onto its back.

Two

Wilder woke up as something leaned into his ribs: the coffin-sized refrigerated unit containing the Infiltrator's body, shifting in its restraints as the C-17 banked into its landing approach. He'd spent much of the last leg of the flight from Sydney to Andrews Air Force Base on the metal floor of the cargo plane, sitting beside the Infiltrator, as if somehow by proximity he could gain a familiarity with the man, become privy to his secrets. He could understand biting a cyanide ampoule upon capture—he'd almost done it himself once—but vaporizing your head and hands is a mighty extreme way of avoiding identification and interrogation.

Wilder jumped down onto the runway and the humidity and hot, hazy sunlight reflecting off the tarmac came as instant proof he was home. Early June in Washington. The founding fathers were so smart about everything else, he thought; why the hell did they put the nation's capital in a swamp?

"Trash any part of yourself you'd actually miss?"

Wilder recognized the southern-gentleman drawl at once: Brent Spaulding, his commanding officer and closest friend. Brent, New Orleans–born, knew from heat and humidity. Like all OSI agents, he wore civilian clothes; unlike everyone else, however, he never seemed to sweat. Waiting in front of the hangar he looked Wilder over, never dropping his usual expression of someone enjoying a small private joke.

"I'm trying to think of some part of my carcass I *would* miss," Wilder replied.

"Tell me," Brent said. "Two, three parts, tops, worth anything."

Wilder knew *that* tune. An airman tossed him his duffel bag and to his surprise Brent said nothing more about his dangerous escapades in Australia. Instead, he talked about what had been happening at the OSI Washington Field Office. They'd first met through a mutual friend in Wilder's physical rehab program when he'd returned from the Gulf in 1991. They served together at Andrews Detachment 331 after Wilder graduated the Special Investigations Academy; later, they transferred together to the Washington Field Office—Brent as Special Agent in Charge, Wilder as a senior counterintelligence agent in the WFO's Tactical Operations Cell.

They watched an airman in a forklift lower the refrigerated coffin from the transport plane.

"Hey, quickest way to lose ten pounds of ugly fat," Brent said. "Blow your head off."

"Hands, too," Wilder said. "No fingerprints, no dental records."

"Little metal dingie, wore it around his neck, right?"

Wilder nodded.

"They're called Tritons," Brent said. "Never mind you can't be identified, using it also freaks the shit out of your captors. Another fine innovation brought to you by the Eastern European intelligence community. Former Commie-bloc countries can't build a goddamn toaster, but they're a buncha Edisons when it comes to gizmos that maim and mutilate."

Wilder smiled. He knew Brent's rants were mostly about getting a reaction, breaking up the monotony of his day.

"I sure missed those little insights of yours," Wilder said. "I'd better clean up before I pick Kate up at school." With his arm and leg wrapped up and his cheek bandaged he worried he might frighten her. "You told her I got a little . . . banged up?"

"Yeah. Cindy talked to her about it and she's okay. Look, I'll drop you home later. Tom's waiting for you—with rubber gloves on."

"Can't it wait?"

"Nope."

Dr. Tom Herrold's office was cold. His petite nurse and assistant, Gail Sealy, wore a white sweater over her nurse's uniform. Despite having recently celebrated her fiftieth birthday, her ebony skin didn't have a single wrinkle.

"Hey, beautiful," Wilder said, grinning at Gail.

"Hey yourself." Grinning back, she stood up and gave him a hug, then shook her head at his injuries. "Just *look* at you . . ."

"You should see the other guy."

"Knowing you, I can just imagine. You see Kate yet?"

"No; right after this."

"You tell her I say hi, 'kay?"

"Hell with that—tell her yourself. Come by for dinner. She's cooking now, you know."

Gail laughed. "Six and cooking?! Well, someone has to be the adult at your house."

"Cheap shot," Wilder replied, laughing.

Brent sat on Gail's desk and eyed her over. "Wouldn't have another sweater, would you?"

"I did, I'd be wearing it."

Thumbing through an old *Air Force Times*, Brent turned as Dr. Herrold came out of the examining room.

"Christ, Tom, climate inside this office oughta make a big bear like you want to hibernate." Brent shivered.

"There's a reason the brass gave you a desk job, Spaulding. To keep you sitting at it."

Herrold shook Wilder's hand. "Aussies take care of you okay?"

Wilder nodded. "Yeah, patched me up pretty good."

The doctor held the door of the examining room open. "Come on in." He turned to Brent. "And you, get your fanny off Gail's paperwork, before I tell your wife you're harassing the female personnel."

Indignant, Brent turned to Gail. "Is this harassment?"

"If it is, you got my pity."

Inside the examining room, Wilder sat on the examining table and unbuttoned his shirt. Dr. Herrold listened to his heart with a stethoscope, then took his blood pressure. Sighing, Herrold leaned back on the instrument table.

"No poking or prodding?" Wilder asked.

"Nope. Docs from Sydney faxed me your report." He glanced at the papers in his hand. "Lacerations, bruises, first-degree burns, glass cuts, a sprain or two. Typical day out for you. Prognosis: You'll live. This time."

He tossed Wilder's chart onto the examining table next to him. "You ever stop to consider that I, this facility's chief medical officer, am in the worst physical condition of anyone on base? OSI told me you got pretty banged up in Australia. Brent was all worried your new injuries might compound your old ones. Shit. I'd *love* to be in your condition."

"It has its downsides."

"Yeah. You can't fly. B.F.D. Try not being able to climb two flights of stairs without needing a week's vacation."

"Interesting treatment, Tom. Tell the patient how good he's got it compared to you."

"So, what really happened down there?"

"Thought you read the report," Wilder replied, annoyed at the question.

"C'mon, Matt . . . One man did all that? He must've had accomplices who got away before you got there."

"One guy, Tom. I fought him."

"Okay, maybe so. I've heard stories about how physically imposing the Khaldun Elite are. You got a firsthand taste. Mongolians, Central Asians, they're tough."

"This wasn't just *tough*. It took two gunshot wounds and a beating that would've killed a rhino to even get his attention. I've never seen anything like it. It was beyond adrenaline, beyond even angel dust. All the while he had this creepy little smile on his face, totally calm. And he heard the goddamn chopper approaching a full minute before I did."

"Well, let's see what the lab guys say when they get his chemistries."

Irritated by Herrold's skepticism, Wilder unwrapped the gauze from his arm, and showed the doctor an intense purple bruise on his forearm in the perfect shape of a hand grasp. Herrold's eyebrows shot up in surprise.

"Whoa! Talk about your viselike grip! Let me get a picture of that."

"Help yourself."

"I'll send it to Chang. Might get his mind off the image of you shooting across the desert with a jet engine strapped to your ass."

Chang, as in the OSI regional commander, Colonel Charles Chang. Wilder sighed. He respected the hell out of the Colonel; if anything made him regret his occasional extreme tactics, it was the regional commander's disapproval.

Herrold snapped some photos of Wilder's bruised arm.

"Lemme reread your report," he said.

Outside, Wilder paused to watch an F-22 Raptor take off from the flight line.

"Think the Infiltrator saw anything of value?" Brent asked.

"Absolutely. I found a digital camera and a smart-media reader connected to a satellite phone in the Land Rover. He'd melted the media card with a cigarette lighter. Something you wouldn't do unless you'd already uploaded the data from it."

"Fuck. Anything out of place in the buildings?"

"Not a thing. So there's no telling what he did or didn't see."

Brent shook his head. "I'll pass your report upstairs. Looks like case closed."

"Let's wait until we get the lab work. I want to know what made that guy act like he did. I'll tell you right now, Brent: If Batu Khan has any more like him at home, we got a way bigger problem than some stolen tech secrets."

Three

Burton Marsh smiled as he imagined how Theodore Roosevelt would've handled someone like Batu Khan. Standing in the hallway in the West Wing, tying his necktie and looking at Teddy's portrait, Marsh thought back on a world in which someone like TR could serve as president. He'd been the most intelligent man ever to occupy the White House, Jefferson included, but also the most brazen. In his day, he would've sent a half-dozen battleships to the other fella's capital city, and softened them up with a battery of sixteen-inch guns. If he were in office now and pulled that kind of stunt without first consulting the United Nations, his allies, the Congress, and the opinion polls, he'd be impeached on the spot. Marsh looked up at TR with envy. He longed for a game with simpler rules.

"Mr. President?" Marsh's chief of staff, Curt Levinson, handed him a red, legal-sized manila folder.

Marsh thumbed through it and frowned. Foreign affairs. Never good news.

"How current is this data?" Marsh asked.

"Six A.M., Eastern time."

Marsh checked his watch. Six forty-five.

"Everyone here?"

"Yes, sir."

Marsh stopped at one of the secretary's desks just outside the Oval Office. It had become a ritual: Every morning Mrs. Alhambra let the President check his Windsor knot while looking in a small mirror she kept in her drawer. Marsh had been president for two years. Handing back the mirror, it occurred to him just how damn pleased he was to still have his hair at fifty-one. Easily worth four to five points in the polls, according to his campaign manager. Marsh was a man of substance—even his enemies would agree to that—but also a pragmatic politician in an image-driven society. He had another important asset: a charming, great-looking wife. When a mutual friend in college set them up on a blind date, she said Amy was a dead ringer for Scarlett O'Hara . . . but likable. They were married after five dates. Thirty years next September 10.

Thoughts of Amy were an emotional bracer for Marsh as he headed for the Oval Office. The people waiting inside stood as he entered. Everyone looked glum, concerned.

"Morning, folks," he said.

Levinson poured Marsh and himself a cup of coffee and hit each one with a shot of half-and-half. Marsh surveyed the tired faces sitting in the room. Most of those gathered had been up all night. They seemed especially somber, even the usually deadpan director of Central Intelligence, Ted Jameson. Sixteen people were there, including key members of the National Security Council, the Joint Chiefs of Staff, the U.S. representative to the United Nations, Diane Drake, and several senior intelligence officers.

Founded in 1947, the NSC was part of the Executive Office of the President. Statutory members were Vice President Adam Taylor, Secretary of State Harry Burroughs, and Secretary of Defense Stan Woodruff. The Chairman of the Joint Chiefs of Staff, Army general Don Mancini, served as military adviser to the council, and CIA Director Jameson was intelligence adviser. Defense Secretary Woodruff, a former gentleman farmer from Vermont, called the meeting to order.

"Mr. President, as you know, we've been closely monitoring the situation in the former Soviet state of Georgia. As feared, a coup has taken place, effected with violent means. Ted Jameson has the details."

"What about President Gorovich?" Marsh asked.

Jameson answered: "Dead, along with his family and cabinet members."

"Goddamn it, we had good relations with him." Marsh's voice became softer. "His *family*?"

Jameson nodded sadly. President Marsh grabbed his red folder.

Inside were enhanced satellite photos and several intelligence digests—a tidy summary of a tragedy far worse than he had believed when Levinson woke him up forty-five minutes ago.

The Joint Chiefs had ordered the J-2 Directorate for Intelligence to prepare a presentation. Senior J-2 officer Major Robert Deems glanced at General Mancini for approval to begin. The General nodded and Deems stood up.

Vice President Taylor fidgeted nervously with his pen. He'd been warned of the ugliness in Georgia and dreaded hearing the details. Taylor, at forty-three, looked a lot like Sidney Poitier did at the same age. He was his own man politically, known to be much more of a conciliator than the President. Despite almost unanimous opposition from his campaign managers and his party, Marsh had chosen Taylor as his running mate because he liked the idea of someone more cautious and introspective than himself as his number-two man and chief adviser. When they won, Taylor became the first African-American vice president.

Major Deems displayed an enhanced satellite surveillance photo on a twenty-one-inch computer monitor. "Several small incursionary groups were airdropped into the capital city of Tbilisi, oh three hundred hours local time."

"How small, how many?" Marsh asked.

"Twenty men per unit, we believe there were twenty-five units." Deems continued, "By sunrise, they had the city under their control."

"Five hundred men took over a major city in three hours?!"

"Yes, sir. New leadership has already been installed, under a Field Marshal Stavros Kirminian."

"Who the hell is he?"

CIA chief Jameson interjected. "Their minister of agriculture. All we have is a one-page file on him."

Marsh shook his head. "Inspect enough fields, all of a sudden you're a field marshal."

Everyone laughed, lightening the mood in the room somewhat.

"Who are the troops?" Marsh asked.

"They're dressed as Georgian regulars," Deems replied.

"Dressed as?"

"We're fairly certain they're Khaldun Commandos from the Trans-Altaic Alliance," Deems said. "As you can see by these satellite images, their mode of approach and attack is very similar to other TAA operations. We have some other visuals that further confirm this. At the outside, these men were trained by Batu Khan's forces."

Marsh frowned. This came as no surprise, but it infuriated him nonetheless.

Deems cycled through several detailed pictures taken from above: dark silhouettes against the artificial green glow of infrared light enhancement, groups of men moving in a pattern into a building. Jameson continued the briefing. The tweedy, bookish type, he would've looked at home reading Emily Dickinson to a group of adoring English-lit students. But he'd made his bones in the intelligence trade, assassinating Russian spies from East Berlin in the mid-Sixties.

"There's more," he said.

General Mancini and Deems looked at each other, then at U.N. Ambassador Diane Drake, the only woman in the room.

"The images are quite graphic," Mancini told her.

She nodded thanks for the warning.

The tape showed nighttime video footage, low-light enhanced, of the river-port city of Tbilisi, the capital of Georgia. A group of dark-clad Commandos moved quickly and silently through the narrow streets and faded nineteenth-century buildings of the sleeping city. They approached a two-story, marble building. It sat behind a tall metal fence, topped with Moorish minarets with a cobblestone public square in front of it.

Deems narrated: "The president's residence."

Six half-dozing Georgian security officers at the stone-framed gateway to the grounds sat unaware of their approach. The Commandos spread out, positioning themselves in a semicircle across the square. In one synchronized move, each one got down on one knee, reached over their shoulders and drew something three feet long and slender from behind their backs. The video footage was grainy and unclear.

"Show me that again," Marsh asked.

The aide rewound the tape a few seconds and Marsh leaned forward in his chair. As he watched the action replay, he realized his eyes were not playing tricks on him: The men had *longbows*. As one, they drew back and let their arrows fly. The arrows struck the security men simultaneously—one arrow per man—and skewered them neatly, silently through the center of the chest. The bows had extraordinary power: Four of the security men slammed back into the metal fence as if they'd been hit by a fifty-caliber machine gun. The arrows hitting the other two actually embedded into the stone of the gate, pinning the dead men to it like butterflies.

"Jesus," Marsh gasped.

The Commandos moved onto the residence grounds in seconds, and went inside unopposed. From within the building, staccato sounds of gunfire, muzzle flashes visible through some of the second-story windows. The cameraman took the opportunity to move to a closer vantage, behind a parked van. The Commandos emerged from the front door of the residence, dragging with them four people dressed in nightclothes. A man, his wife, and two small children.

A clammy wave of dread hit Marsh's stomach. He glanced over at Ambassador Drake. She sat tight-lipped, hands clutching the arms of her chair. She felt the same dread as Marsh and almost couldn't bear to watch. Even the professional soldiers sat stone-faced—they knew if this tape had rattled Mancini and Jameson, it would be rough going.

"That's President Gorovich?" Marsh couldn't make out the faces.

"Yes, sir," Mancini replied.

The Commandos took the family to the center of the square and separated them, six feet apart. The kids—they appeared to be between five and eight—were crying, hysterical, unable to stand. Their captors held them up by their arms with chilling indifference. Mrs. Gorovich struggled against the men holding her, trying to get to her children. She repeatedly screeched a phrase in Russian, but no translation was necessary to understand her dread.

President Gorovich stood handcuffed, hands behind his back. A streak of dark blood stained one side of his light-colored pajama top. He barked orders, then questions, then pleas at the Commandos, until one of them hit him across the mouth with a pistol and he fell to the ground. Suddenly, the two Commandos holding the children pressed the barrels of their pistols against the base of the children's skulls and pulled the triggers. The back half of their heads were blasted apart. The Commandos let them drop to the cobblestones.

Aghast, Marsh pressed his hand against his mouth. He felt droplets of sweat rolling down his sides, and he had trouble focusing on the TV screen. No one in the Oval Office spoke.

On the tape, President Gorovich and his wife made a sound that grew in intensity like an emergency siren. A howl of anguish, deep and elemental. It connected with the people in the Oval Office below the centers of thought and reason, in the deepest, most ancient part of the brain. Marsh had never heard anything so horrific.

Mrs. Gorovich stopped struggling and crumpled to her knees. As she did, the Commando holding her drew a bayonet across her throat. Clutching at her neck, she pitched forward. Her head hit the ground next to her husband, still on his hands and knees. One of the Commandos tossed a rope over the top of a tall, steel streetlight. Sobbing, President Gorovich offered no resistance as the Commandos slipped a noose over his head and hoisted him up the streetlight. He kicked a few times, then was still.

Their work finished, the Commandos walked back into the president's residence, leaving behind a grotesque tableau: the dead president hanging from the streetlight with his butchered family below him.

The young navy aide, face flushed crimson with the struggle to contain his emotions, reached over and quietly turned off the TV. President Marsh looked at the others. Drake cried quietly, beyond caring what the others thought. Vice President Taylor and several of the others in the room came close to doing the same. Anger and disgust kept the President from speaking for a moment. The unusual intensity of his emotions frightened him.

"This footage . . . How did we get it?" Marsh turned to CIA director Jameson. "Central Intelligence?"

Jameson shifted uncomfortably in his seat. "Actually, Mr. President, we taped it off a CNN broadcast a half hour ago."

"They're showing this on the *air*?!"

Jameson nodded. "Already have some animated intro graphics and music to go with it."

"Goddamn ghouls."

Not that Marsh blamed any particular news organization, CNN just got it first. By tonight it'd be on all the networks. Marsh immediately went into what Amy called action mode. Grab it, understand it, fix it. He turned to Ambassador Drake.

"Call to convene the U.N. General Council, soon as possible," Marsh told her. "See if you can get them to do something more than threaten to think about maybe drafting one of their lame resolutions."

He then looked at General Mancini.

"Can we prove the men on the tape acted under the orders of Batu Khan?"

Mancini nodded. "We'll nail something down. It's nearly an open secret, as if Batu wants us to know. The only thing notable about Field Marshal Kirminian is his friendship with Batu. They served together in Chechnya."

"This is the first clear case of aggression for the TAA," Marsh said. "Maybe the other countries were absorbed of their own accord, maybe not. But this is an act of war."

"I agree, Mr. President," General Mancini said. "It's a safe bet that Batu will only be emboldened by this little adventure. We strongly recommend moving to DEFCON 3."

Marsh sighed. This wasn't the first time the Joint Chiefs asked for an increased alert. They'd been concerned about Batu Khan and his ever-expanding Trans-Altaic Alliance for months now.

"The media will salivate over an alert increase, call it saber-rattling. I hate like hell to see you make them so happy," Vice President Taylor said.

"I'm not about to make policy to suit the needs of the media, Adam," the President said. "Take us to Level Three. Let's hope, for all their promises and verifications, the Russians actually got all their nukes out of Georgia." He turned to Secretary of State Burroughs.

"Harry, use the Greek ambassador, let it be known I want to talk to Batu one-on-one. He may live in a damn felt tent, but he's got Virtual Summit technology."

"Ted," he said to the CIA director, "I want to know more about the man. Personal stuff, not statistics. A full briefing by tomorrow A.M. That's it for now, everyone. Thank you."

As the others left the Oval Office, Marsh stared silently out the window. The image of President Gorovich and his family being killed gnawed at him. He needed to make smart, thoughtful decisions, unclouded by the deep, profound hatred he felt for Batu Khan.

Four

A nervous artisan, a painter of pottery by trade, squinted at the map as he outlined with a small pointed brush, in deep magenta, the borders of the Republic of Georgia. He sat uncomfortably on a low, three-legged stool, facing the detailed, handmade, four-foot-long map. Painted on a crude sheepskin stretched on a frame of birch branches, it depicted an enormous swatch of the world, from the Mediterranean on the west, the Sea of Japan to the east, India to the south, and Siberia to the north. In its center were two magenta clusters of countries in the shape of the infinity symbol ∞—the Trans-Altaic Alliance.

The artisan sat inside a *ger*, a round, felt-covered tent fifteen feet in diameter, used by the nomadic peoples of the central Asian steppes. Its wall sections were constructed of wooden poles joined together with leather lacing at the crossings. The *ger* was furnished with a cot covered with sheepskins, an ornately carved folding desk, and some stools. A large wooden armoire stood across from the cot. Inside it, quite out of place, a thirty-five-inch television monitor and an audio receiver. A two-stringed instrument with decorated sculptured horse head at top, a *morin khuur*, leaned against the cot. A portable metal stove, unlit in the summer heat, sat in the center of the *ger*, and a blackened, grapefruit-sized meteorite sat on display atop a tripod made of branches.

It was stifling inside the *ger*—sunlight barely filtered through the walls and the air tasted stale. Sweat ran from the artisan's forehead and stung his eyes as he colored Georgia with a translucent purple wash to make it match the other states of the TAA. The western side included Armenia, Azerbaijan, Turkmenistan, Uzbekistan, Tajikistan, Kazakhstan, Kyrgyzstan, and Afghanistan; the eastern side consisted of the huge territory of Mongolia. Most were countries about whom the outside world had little knowledge or interest. Some had been politically irrelevant, others had been part of the Soviet Union for so long that they'd lost their national identity. With their consolidation into the Trans-Altaic Alliance, however, their anonymity had ended. The TAA motto, taken from an Uzbek proverb and written at the top of the map, stated it best: UNITY IS STRENGTH.

A man of thirty-four stood behind the artisan, hands on his hips, watching him work. He wore a *shalwar qamiz*, a long, loose, colorful garment favored by both men and women, and a sheepskin belt. An entirely traditional costume, except for a gold Patek Philippe watch and a pair of black Air Jordans. He wasn't tall—only five-foot-seven—but he was broad across the face, arms, chest, and legs, with a powerful body that no amount of gym exercise could have produced. It came from a combination of genes, a harsh environment, and a rock-hard will. Even the few soft years he'd had after the Army did little to weaken his natural strength. He'd been born of mixed Slavic and Mongolian blood, the product of an intermarriage common in Siberia, the place of his birth. Asian features dominated his handsome face—a flatness in the nose and cheeks, sepia skin, almond eyelids—but he also had striking blond hair and pale blue eyes.

The artisan breathed a sigh of enormous relief as he finished. It terrified him to give his back to the man supervising him, even though the man had never been anything but kind to him.

"Anything else, Batu?" the artisan asked.

"Thank you, no. But I'll need your services again soon. Have Yela get you something to eat."

Gathering his brushes and paints the artisan bowed, mumbled his thanks, and hurried out of the *ger*. Batu Khan squatted in front of the map and took in the sight of his newly expanded Alliance. It pleased him greatly—the addition of Georgia brought access to the Black Sea. Through it, his ships could sail to the Mermera Sea and then on to the Mediterranean. From there to the Atlantic or, via the Suez Canal, to the Red Sea, the Indian Ocean, and the Pacific. Prior to the inclusion of Georgia, his three-thousand-mile-long, three-hundred-million-person empire had no seaport open to the oceans of the world. Now, thanks to a handful of very special commandos and the will to deploy them, he'd made a key step toward the Trans-Altaic Alliance becoming a naval power.

Batu walked through the door of the *ger*, where two members of his special forces military unit, the Khaldun Elite, stood at rigid attention. They wore colorful robes similar to his *shalwar qamiz*, and long, low, leather holsters with a scabbard under the silk sashes around their waists. One held a Kalashnikov 5.45×.39mm AK-74U machine gun with a ten-inch barrel and a fifty-shot banana clip; the other held a razor-sharp, eighteen-inch scimitar. His *ger* sat in the middle of a mobile military encampment on a hillside, camouflaged by trees, in the foothills of the Caucasus Mountains overlooking the Georgian capital city of Tbilisi. The camp, like the interior of the *ger*, consisted of a curious mix of the ancient and the futuristic. Batu knew many things in warfare, as in life, had not improved with mechanization. For instance, nothing matched the mobility and simplicity of horse-mounted soldiers. So, camped beside a row of streamlined, French-made tanks bristling with fifty-caliber machine guns were three battalions of his beloved Khaldun Horsemen, without contest the finest riders in the world. Under their silks, decorated with vivid patterns of sun, stars, flowers, animal horns, and the shooting star from the TAA flag, the warriors and their highly trained Arabian stallions were cloaked in bulletproof Kevlar. They and the Elite Guard were the only units in the TAA military carrying the honored title of Khaldun. According to Mongolian ancestral myth, Mount Burkhan Khaldun stretched all the way to the heavens. It is the place where the first offspring of the blue-gray wolf and the fallow deer was born: Batachikan, father of all the warrior peoples of the steppes. To be associated with the sacred mountain is to be destined for great achievements.

Near the *ger*, Batu's two wives oversaw the preparation of his midday meal. Smiling, he quietly watched them for a moment, enjoying their grace and beauty. He kissed Panya, tall, serene, in her mid-thirties; then Kuri, seventeen, petite, spirited. He tasted the lamb stew boiling in the large iron pot, and promised he'd make time for them in the afternoon. As he walked through the bustling camp, everyone bowed. He possessed a rare and potent combination: iron-fisted leadership and a superstar's charisma.

He stopped to look at his newest acquisition, the city nestled in the broad valley below. Given its location on both the Kura River and the Transcaucasian Railroad, Tbilisi would serve as a key support center for battles yet to be fought, territories yet to be taken. The Republic of Georgia had been under the control of Batu's puppet commanders for two days now. They'd ordered its citizens to return to their regular jobs, and a quiet if uneasy sense of normalcy began to take hold. Indeed, the only sign of a change in rulers had been workmen erecting immense photos of Batu, and fifty-foot-wide TV screens on which he lectured in endless tape loops about the cornerstones of TAA life: Pride, Power, and Purpose.

He turned his gaze to the north. Tomorrow they would move their camp to the mountains on the other side of the city. He lived that way, always moving, and no one knew where he would turn up next—for security reasons and to further his mystique. The first Khan, Genghis, had said, "The Mongol does not count any spot of Earth his own, because everything is the property of Heaven." Using state-of-the-art communications equipment, Batu conducted all affairs of state from the wilderness in which he lived. Officially, the Trans-Altaic Alliance had no capital city. His camp, consisting of his servants, advisers, and a hundred Khaldun, served as the empire's permanently transient capital.

Batu had modeled his command structure on the Internet, in which all elements are connected laterally, not hierarchically. This ensured that in the event of nuclear war or some other catastrophe its partial destruction wouldn't cause a break in communications between the unharmed sections of the Net. So worked the government of the TAA: Its various branches and departments were scattered throughout the empire, in big cities and small, connected via landlines, radio, satellite, and microwave. All were ultimately controlled from Batu's mobile encampment.

He walked a few yards to the second-largest *ger* in the camp and pushed through the felt flaps. Inside, his shaman and chief adviser, Chu'tsai, sat at an electronic communications console. He was a short, plump man of mixed blood, like Batu, but his features were more Asian. He wore blue jeans, a pink Banana Republic shirt, and black cowboy boots. Although only thirty-one, he had crow's-feet from a lifetime lived outdoors. As they hadn't seen each other since the incursion into Georgia, they had much to discuss.

"Any word from Australia?" Batu asked.

Chu'tsai shook his head. "Our Khaldun is still missing, presumed dead. But he managed to upload his photographs, and our engineers are very pleased. It removes the last impediment to testing the prototype engines."

Like Batu, he spoke English—a habit they'd developed when together in an effort to perfect their mastery of the language.

Batu smiled at his friend. "Good. I want them mounted on airframes within the month."

He noticed a faxed report from the A.C. Nielsen service on the desk and picked it up.

"Came in last night," Chu'tsai explained. "For two days, none of the American television networks would show the unedited clip from Georgia. Then, finally, CBS aired it during *Face the Nation*. Look what it did to their ratings and share compared to the prior week."

Batu looked at the numbers and nodded, impressed.

"Did the others use it?"

"They all ran it on the national news that night!"

"And CNN . . . Do they still claim they shot the footage themselves?"

Chu'tsai laughed. "Of course."

That part annoyed Batu. He'd leaked the supposedly clandestine videotape in order to graphically demonstrate the ruthlessness of his men. Having the Americans *suspect* he leaked it made it all the more effective. He hadn't counted on the media taking credit for it themselves.

"So, this is the news you wished to discuss with me?"

Excited, Chu'tsai handed him another piece of paper. "An e-mail from our ambassador to Greece. Marsh wants to arrange a VS meeting with you!"

Batu Khan read it excitedly and his chest swelled with pride. The American President asking to have a Virtual Summit meeting with him, speaking as equals, face-to-face in the center of the world stage! During the last four years the United States had paid him only the smallest of courtesies. Even as the TAA grew from the merging of Mongolia and Kazakhstan. Even as, one by one, it absorbed the other member states, becoming stronger and richer. All this time the United States behaved as if by ignoring the TAA it would fade back into obscurity as quickly as it had come into prominence. Batu liked to say he awakened a sleeping giant by forging many weak countries into one powerful alliance. Apparently, America finally heard its great, thundering footsteps.

Looking out over his newly acquired territory, his smile faded. Chu'tsai couldn't believe his friend's sudden change in attitude.

"This is wonderful news! It's about time they pay attention to us."

"No, I welcome their indifference. If the Americans remain that way, warring with them need not be inevitable. After each move we make, I want you to study their polls, sense their mood."

Other countries didn't concern Batu—Russia's internal problems paralyzed her; the Chinese ignored Batu because he allowed them to believe he feared them. And as much as the Arabs hated having him as their neighbor, they viewed him as crazier than the most wild-eyed fanatic among their fold. Only America worried him.

"Our goal with the United States is simple," he said, "come as close to our ultimate objectives as we can, as quickly as possible, without invoking their wrath. So far Georgia has barely registered with them, meaning we've gotten tremendous gain with inconsequential cost. My biggest worry is Marsh uniting them in some righteous fervor against us."

Chu'tsai shook his head. "I don't see that happening, Batu."

"Don't underestimate the man. Think about it: Would you feel the same trepidation about war with the United States if their Vice President Taylor were the commander in chief?"

"True. Taylor would try to negotiate us to death. So what about the VS meeting?"

As much as Batu wanted the gratification of enhancing his position as leader of an emerging superpower, his every instinct told him not to rush into a dialogue with the American President just yet.

"Say nothing in response to Marsh's invitation. That will be our reply."

Batu turned to go.

"One other thing, Batu," Chu'tsai said, sitting in front of a computer monitor. "You know how we watch the Internet for anything pertaining to the Trans-Altaic Alliance . . ."

Batu nodded. He remembered when, not so long ago, the task consisted of Chu'tsai himself doing an occasional Yahoo.com search. Now, he employed a staff of ten for the job.

"One of my people came across a web site, originating within the United States, containing pro-Alliance rhetoric. It says we're a positive force in this hemisphere, a balance to American superpower status."

"It's either a fringe political group or an American intelligence ploy."

"I thought so, too. But I checked into it personally. Look whose site it is."

Seeing the web site Chu'tsai brought up on the screen, Batu became infuriated.

"I thought you'd told him never to reveal any connection to us!"

"He hasn't, beyond these essays. He's certainly said nothing of my work with him."

"I'd kill him myself if he did." Batu fell silent for a moment. "See if your arts indicate any ulterior motive to his actions."

As spiritual adviser, shaman, healer, herbalist, astrologer, and diviner to His Serene Excellency Batu Khan, Chu'tsai consulted the stars, the elements, the bones of sheep, and all other indicators known to him. This assured Batu that decisions about his person and his empire were made in sync with the immutable rhythms of nature, information he believed to be profoundly significant. He made no move, great or small, without following it.

"I will, although I've already expressed my anger to him," Chu'tsai said. "He claims to have some information of extreme value to the Empire, but will only impart it you personally."

"Tell him I will not speak to him until he has learned discretion. And humility."

Chu'tsai nodded. Putting the American out of his mind, he glanced at the e-mail from their ambassador. "It will certainly be interesting to see what kind of man Marsh really is."

"I'm more interested in showing him the kind of man I am."

Five

Laura Bishop turned from Allentown Road into the Main Gate of Andrews Air Force Base. It felt cooler out here in suburban Maryland than in Georgetown, where she rented a town house. The base's verdant landscaping surprised her. She'd never been on a military installation before and expected Gomer Pyle rows of Quonset huts and a treeless expanse of blacktop. She placed her hand on the black leather bag lying on the passenger's seat next to her, reassuring herself the notes she'd done in preparation for the interview were still there.

A guard waved her over to the Visitors' Center, where she signed in and showed her driver's license to get a drive-on pass. She followed the directions to the OSI headquarters building, driving along Arnold Avenue, parallel to the hangars and the flight line. At the end of the line she saw the special five-sided hangar housing Air Force One. She wondered whether President Marsh was in town. If so, the big 747 would be in its hangar.

The OSI had recently moved their headquarters and computer forensics lab here from Bolling Air Force Base, twelve miles away. With the Air Force Special Investigations Academy and the Third Field Investigative Region offices already at Andrews, they now had all HQ operations on one base. A trim young man in a blue uniform waited outside the main building for her. As she pulled closer, he pointed to a reserved parking place right by the front door. A sign, neatly computer-printed, read RESERVED FOR LAURA BISHOP.

She thanked the young man, Major Murray Stevens, director of public affairs for the OSI, for arranging the interviews. He led Laura upstairs through the main entrance. There were murals of airplanes of all eras in the stairwell, and the carpet matched the blue of Stevens's hat. Laura followed Stevens to a small conference room.

At the table, Wilder looked up from his notebook computer then stood as they came into the room. He'd seen Laura's pictures on her book jackets but they didn't do her justice, and he was surprised by her height—almost five-foot-ten—as well as how much less bookish she appeared in person. It also amazed him that someone her age, thirty-one, had already written three well-respected history books. He wanted to experience this interview about as much as gum surgery with a band saw—in fact, he'd purposely scheduled another meeting a half hour later to have a good excuse to leave—but at least it'd be with a good-looking, accomplished woman.

Laura smiled as he stood up and shook her hand. Major Stevens made the introductions: "Laura Bishop, Special Agent Matt Wilder."

"Thanks for taking the time to talk to me, Agent Wilder. I'm sure you've been volunteered for this assignment utterly against your wishes."

"Public Affairs asked me to be candid with you. So, yeah, 'utterly against' just about nails it."

Wilder regretted the comment the moment he made it. His anger at being there was toward the OSI brass, who insisted he do the interview, not Laura.

"But, hey, we'll make the best of it," he added.

Laura sat down at the conference table across from him.

"I'll try to get through everything as quickly as possible." She paused. "Also, I'll understand if you're uncomfortable talking about certain . . . events. Please let me know if I go anywhere I shouldn't."

"Fair enough."

"So," Stevens said, "I'll leave you two at it. Anyone needs anything, I'm in my office."

He exchanged a smile with Wilder as he left. Laura seemed nice. Real nice. He'd love to see the look on her face if Wilder actually started speaking his mind. Not that he would say anything rude or offensive—he was an officer and a gentleman, but also a man of conviction. A man who saw no benefit in muting his convictions to suit the circumstance. Laura, he accurately surmised, had a midwesterner's soft-spoken politeness and dislike for controversy.

Anxious to begin, Laura pulled a notebook computer from her leather briefcase. Wilder noticed it was the same model as his.

"Bet you thought we had nothing in common," he said.

"Except you probably *like* your computer. Guys can always warm up to the little beasts. It's just a necessary evil in my line of work."

Sitting with him, she felt as if she'd hit the jackpot. She'd planned on including him and his experiences in the part of her new book that covered the Gulf War, but never expected she'd be able to speak with Wilder himself. He'd never agreed to an interview before this. She'd been prepared to get whatever she could, secondhand, from the Air Force Public Affairs people, and try to flesh the rest out herself. Now that she had him alone in a room she felt desperate not to come away empty-handed.

"Is it all right if I record the conversation?"

"Sure. I'll try to say a few things worth taping."

She smiled, clicked the record button on a Lanier tape recorder, and put it in the table between them. She had read a bit about Wilder, and he wasn't what she expected. In person, he seemed surprisingly . . . regular. Tall and solidly built, but not muscle-bound or overbearing. And although he exuded strength, with a no-nonsense manner, he didn't seem stern or aloof. Laura found the overall package quite attractive. Distilling her initial impressions of the man seated across from her, she typed *like an eagle at rest* into her computer.

"They were a little vague about the subject of your book," Wilder said. "Tell me about it."

"Okay, but it's confidential. I'm one of those superstitious writers who hate discussing a work in progress."

"We're pretty good at keeping secrets around here."

"The working title is *Bloodlines*, and it traces the history of U.S.–Arab relations. The irony that the people whose way of life we probably least understand control the oil, the commodity most important to our way of life."

"A way of life they don't understand."

"Exactly. I usually write only about the past. This book is a departure for me. In the last few chapters I'm going to take a crack at predicting the future."

"Dangerous work."

He knew that coming from him, a comment about dangerous work could have sounded condescending. But he hadn't meant it that way.

"True," Laura said, "it's all there, in print, then time gets around to proving you right or wrong."

"Try some of your fortune-telling on me. I'll let you know if it agrees with anything in my crystal ball."

"My main premise is we're heading back into a bipolar world of two superpowers like during the Cold War—U.S. versus the USSR back then, U.S. versus the TAA now. However, this time around, the Arabs will stop squabbling among themselves and form their own alliance. They won't be ignored like before."

"Meaning a *tri*-polar world. Three superpowers. Sounds complicated."

"Like you wouldn't believe. The Cold War would seem downright quaint if, in addition to Batu Khan, we had a truly united Arab world to share power with."

"What are we supposed to do about it?"

"Simple. Make sure the United States stays the only superpower."

"Neat trick. How?"

"You'll have to read the book."

He smiled at her. A personal smile this time, not the professional-courtesy smile she'd gotten before. The warmth it revealed surprised Laura and the moment felt intimate, perhaps because she'd glimpsed something normally far from view.

"Guess it's my turn to talk," Wilder said.

"Yes."

"How do I fit in to the big story about the battle for world dominance?"

"Obviously, you've got a pretty unique and dramatic perspective on the Gulf War."

"Nothing to say that hasn't been all over the press already."

"Except your personal feelings. I respect your desire for privacy, but anything you might share with me . . ."

A tall order. Wilder didn't know where to begin. "Maybe if you could be a little more specific."

Laura scrolled through the document on her computer—pages of notes from her research about Wilder. She'd highlighted the ones that formed the basis of her questions. Looking them over, she frowned. No particularly pleasant topics.

"I'd like to talk a little bit about your experiences from January nineteenth through twenty-fifth, 1991."

"That's a lot of ground to cover, Ms. Bishop."

"Laura."

"You came all the way out here to hear some war stories?"

"If you're willing."

"Well, let's give it a try."

"To begin with, how do you think your experiences in Iraq changed you?"

Wilder laughed. "So, we're starting off with the easy stuff."

"You must've given it some thought."

"I can't remember how I was before the war. So I can't really say how I'm different."

A perfect piece of evasion, Laura thought. Clearly these topics made him uncomfortable, so she tried moving back to the professional perspective for a moment.

"How did you feel about the U.S. mission in Iraq? You know, liberating Kuwait, a country most Americans hadn't even heard of—"

"I didn't really have any feelings about it. I was deployed along with a half-million other Coalition personnel; I went where they sent me, I bombed what they told me to bomb. The concept that folks in the military are sitting around making judgment calls on our jobs just ain't realistic."

"The old do-or-die?"

"Yeah, pretty much. Do honor and duty seem so worthy of contempt?"

"No, not at all. I'm only trying to reconcile the classic image of the warrior imbued with righteousness, fighting for a cause worth dying for, with the reality that this was ultimately a war about protecting America's access to cheap oil."

Wilder knew she wanted to be provocative, get a rise out of him. The very subject of her book, as she described it, told him she was way too smart to dismiss the Gulf conflict in such simplistic terms.

"If we needed a cause worth dying for to do our jobs, no one I know would get their ass out of bed in the morning. Everything you're talking about, that's the politicians' job: convince the public whatever scrap we're getting into is worth the body bags on the evening news. Folks who actually do the fighting and the dying, all we need is the order to go."

"So that's what you were thinking all those days out in the desert, or when you were chained to that chair in Iraqi intelligence headquarters: It's only a job?"

"All I thought was I'm gonna get through it, come home, and forget all about it. 'Cause if I could do that, I'd win and they'd lose."

Wilder's mouth had gone dry and he wanted a sip of coffee, but the subject matter made his hands shake, so he kept them in his lap.

Laura was nervous, too. She questioned far more aggressively than planned, trying desperately to make Wilder reveal his mind to her. Or better, his soul. She wanted to know how it felt to be him, to live through his experiences. Her eagerness to grasp this knowledge reminded her of being a contestant on that awful TV game show where people get one minute to race through the grocery store, keeping everything they manage to pile into their carts. She had to get as much as she could right now. Certainly he'd never agree to meet with her again, now that he knew she wanted to get personal about the war. So she piqued him because it formed a connection. Kept him too angry to be glib and evasive. She found a highlighted passage on her computer.

"There's an interesting quote about you, from a doctor who treated your injuries after you returned to Dhahran . . . I'd like to know what you think it means." She read from the computer screen: " 'Last guy to wander the desert that long was Jesus, and look what happened to Him' . . ."

Wilder shrugged; he'd heard the line before. It didn't annoy him as Laura had hoped.

"He was upset because I broke three of his fingers."

"What prompted that?"

"He'd been stingy with the pain medication for a burn victim in the ward, so I gave him a quick refresher in the subject of discomfort."

"His comment implies you came back from your ordeal a changed man. You must've. The Jesus allusion—that's pretty strong stuff."

"Maybe those fingers were still smarting at the time."

Laura sensed she was losing him. He was getting cute with her again. Indeed, Wilder began to relax and he dared a sip of his now-cold coffee.

"You endured incredible abuse because of your refusal to cooperate with the Iraqis. After evading capture, critically injured, for five days. Once they saw you wouldn't tell them anything substantive, they would've been satisfied putting you on TV like the other downed pilots. No one ever held that against those guys; we all knew their statements were coerced. Why put yourself through all that when it would've meant nothing to placate your captors?"

"For you to even ask means we see life from two radically different places."

"Educate me. I'm only a book-writing gal from Michigan."

She said it as if she were flirting. It was worth a try.

"I like you better when you're trying to piss me off."

"I'm serious, Agent Wilder—"

"Matt."

"Matt. I honestly don't understand and I truly want to. I never made history. All I've ever done is write about it."

It surprised Wilder to find himself wanting her to understand. But how could he express feelings so long and so expertly hidden?

"Wasn't bravery. Wasn't fortitude. Wasn't even pigheadedness—even though that's what most people think. By the time they caught me, after five days eluding the bastards, I was already way past hurting. Only one thing could've made me feel any worse than I already did."

Laura looked at him. Then she got it.

"Giving in?"

"Even an inch."

She'd always imagined Wilder's jet crash, his avoiding the enemy in the harsh, cold desert, and the torments of his captors had systematically robbed him of his humanity. But instead he was saying the suffering actually gave him one small piece of humanity to call his own—his resistance.

Laura felt too excited to type anything into her computer, overrun with questions prompted by this intimate glimpse into his experience.

Her beeper went off.

"God*damn* it. I'm really sorry. No one beeps unless it's important."

She checked the number on the display. Area code 202—the District. The rest of the number seemed vaguely familiar, but she couldn't place it. She took a cell phone out of her purse and dialed the number.

Wilder watched as she made the call. Whatever the party on the other side said when they answered really surprised her.

"This is Laura Bishop. Someone beeped me?"

The reply made her look even more surprised.

"Yes, I'll hold . . . Yes, this is she . . . You're kidding; I mean, when?"

She quickly yanked her day planner out of her leather bag, spilling its other contents as she did. She wrote a notation in the column for the following Monday.

"No, I'll be there . . . Thank *you* . . ."

She clicked off the phone and put it back in her bag. She still looked amazed. "The *president* wants to talk to me."

Wilder smiled. "He consult with you a lot?"

"Hardly!" She reminded Wilder of a college kid; her excitement and befuddlement were natural and charming.

"Didn't say what it was about?"

"Nope, just be there at eleven-thirty—if I wasn't busy. What could he possibly want? I've never even met the President."

Wilder helped her put her things back into her bag. She turned to her computer and shook her head, forcing herself to put the call out of her mind for now.

"Anyway, I'm sorry . . . back to you—"

"Listen, I've got another meeting coming up . . ."

Shit, Laura thought, there he goes. The connection broken and she'd barely scratched the surface.

"But there's so much . . ." Her voice trailed off. "Guess that's it, huh? If I were you, I wouldn't want to dredge all this up either. You can tell your people you met with me, did your bit for God and Country."

Laura had it right—Wilder fulfilled his requirement. He had no intention of doing anything more. He would not revisit Iraq any more than he absolutely had to. They closed up their identical computers in silence, and Wilder shook Laura's hand.

"Good luck with your book."

"Thanks. Good luck to you."

Just as she turned to go, Wilder decided to slip his card into a pocket on her leather bag. Although he would do just about anything to avoid discussing the very things she came to see him about, he nonetheless felt a pang of guilt over cutting her off.

"In case you need any . . . clarification about anything, feel free to call."

Laura's smile lit up the room.

Six

ilder sat on a small wooden chair next to Kate's bed, smiling as she finished reading *Go Dog, Go!* Wasn't it just yesterday he'd read it to her, stopping to let her linger over the pictures she liked best? Now, at six, they'd switched roles—the bedtime ritual would from this point forward be her reading him the story. One of those profound changes in life that all but slipped by with little of the fanfare it warranted, just like Kate's move, almost four years ago, to her "big-girl bed." A few months after she came to live with him, her pediatrician said Kate should stop sleeping in her crib. So Wilder bought her a white bed with peach-colored wooden hearts affixed to it, with a matching quilt and sheets. Brent's half-Korean, half-Italian wife, Cindy, helped him pick it out. The first night Wilder tucked Kate in she'd seemed so tiny inside her new bed—the white mesh guard placed to keep her from rolling onto the floor completely obscured her. Now, the guard was long gone and the two little triangles her feet made under the same peach quilt came two-thirds of the way to the foot of the bed.

One part of their bedtime ritual had remained the same since Kate's first night in the house. After the book Wilder told a story, preferably with Kate in the starring role. Often, it was the happiest moment of her day. Kate wasn't particularly moody or difficult, she just had that tendency toward solitude common to children who'd lost their parents. And although she and Wilder had a fond and loving relationship, her emotional distance and his frequent absences prevented them from becoming as close as Wilder would've liked.

Tonight, she requested a story about visiting her mommy. Wilder wanted to mention Suzanne more often, but even after four years he could not reconcile himself to her senseless death, caused by a drunken loser driving with a revoked license.

The drunk was Kate's father. He, of course, had the nerve to live. Had his back not been broken, Wilder would've done it for him. Part of Wilder's bitterness could never go away because of Roy. Wheelchair-bound, institutionalized, consumed by the darkest bile imaginable, he disowned his two-year-old daughter after the accident and Wilder hated him intensely for it. Still, when Wilder could make himself stop and savor a special moment, like tonight, he took solace in knowing his sister's passing gave him the extraordinary gift of having Kate in his life.

"Do you want to hear a dream I had about your mommy?"

"Oh, yes!"

"Well, she wanted to show you a special place from when she was a little girl, so we all went to the lake where she and I grew up. That's all it was—a picnic by the water, a ride in our old aluminum rowboat, exploring the little islands and catching a turtle like we did when we were kids."

Ever since the war and the time in the desert, he'd dreamt of the lake often, especially during times of stress or depression. Wilder didn't tell Kate of his crushing sadness upon waking, when it struck him that it had only been a dream.

Kate looked over at her mother's picture, envisioning with all her might her uncle's words.

"What else happened?"

"Nothing much. We sat together in that way where no one needs to talk."

"But I would have so much to tell her!"

"I know, sweetheart, but in the dream she never went away."

Wilder took Kate's hand in his, remembering when it was so small she could only grasp one of his fingers when he walked with her.

"Sure wish *I* had your dream. Promise you'll take me to the lake someday?" Kate said, falling asleep.

"Promise."

Wilder came downstairs and got himself a beer. He'd always laughed along when Brent or Cindy teased him about the women he should've married, but his inability to make a more conventional home for his niece had been weighing ever more heavily upon him. He sometimes wondered how Kate would've fared with Roy's mother, who'd petitioned the court for custody after the accident. But the old woman's age, maladies, and modest income worked against her as much as the pleas Wilder's lawyer had made on his behalf. As Kate's only other living relative, he'd been granted sole custody.

Wilder's mother, who'd worked all her life as a part-time nurse, succumbed to a heart attack a few weeks after Suzanne's accident. His father, killed in the line of duty fifteen years ago, had been the kind of small-town cop who put on the uniform the way a priest put on the collar. As a boy, Wilder adored his father. He'd dreamt of taking public service and the good fight to a literal higher level—the cockpit of an Air Force jet. But when his travails in Iraq cost him his ability to fly and he returned home earthbound and heartbroken, the AFOSI seemed the most logical place to go.

Stepping outside into the warm night air, he looked around at the other houses tucked away in the residential corner of the base: clean, safe, orderly, as much like a TV neighborhood from the 1950s as one could possibly find in the United States at the start of the twenty-first century. He kept his small, two-story house as tidy as the rest of the base. Except for Kate's room, often mistaken for a Barbie museum, the furniture was mid-priced, Ethan Allen pine. Guy stuff. He'd bought a large-screen TV, his one extravagance, for movies and sports. The only items in the house betraying his life in the Air Force were found in the third bedroom, Wilder's office-slash-study. On the wall hung an eight-by-ten photograph of an F-117A Stealth fighter-bomber, with Wilder, twenty-one years old, in a flight suit, standing next to it.

Aside from being with Kate, reading was Wilder's favorite pastime. The bookshelves were overflowing with current and classic fiction, history, biographies, westerns, and especially aircraft-related information—white papers, spec sheets, and tech manuals. Although his career as a pilot had been long over, he stayed as current on all aspects of the Air Force inventory as any active flier.

With Kate in bed, Mrs. Lindstrom, their nanny-housekeeper, gathered up her things to head home. Suddenly, they heard an insistent, high-pitched tone. Wilder checked the beeper on his belt—Brent's cell phone. He went inside and returned the call.

"What's up?"

"I'm at the Officers' Club; there's a situation here, pard. We need you right away."

Given the urgent tone in Brent's voice he wasn't at the OC having a beer, and Wilder knew "situation" to mean a crime in progress. But he didn't understand what they'd need him for—he was a Tactical Operations agent. Andrews had its own Security Forces officers and OSI detachment responsible for criminal activity on the base. Before Wilder could ask, however, Brent hung up.

Wilder drove his government-issue Pontiac three-quarters of a mile to the Officers' Club. Three blue-and-white Security Forces cars with emergency lights revolving were parked in front of the one-story brick-and-glass building, and about fifty people were milling around outside. Everyone looked dazed and spoke in hushed tones, and several women were red-eyed from crying. Wilder got out of his car and looked around, concerned, then a young Security Forces officer escorted him toward the club.

"Sir, Agent Spaulding thought you'd have some luck talking to her."

"Talking to who?"

The officer didn't reply, being too busy pushing the onlookers aside so they could get into the building. Wilder noticed he moved with that overly officious urgency common to rookies when they're dealing with something far beyond the norm. The air-conditioned chill inside the big, fluorescent-lit banquet room reminded Wilder of Tom Herrold's office. The room was empty, except for a cluster of Security Forces officers standing together near the buffet.

"There's been an injury?" Wilder asked.

"Uh, yes, sir," the officer said.

"Anyone notify Dr. Herrold?"

Arriving at the scene negated the need for an answer. Wilder's friend Gail, Dr. Herrold's sweet-faced nurse, was sitting at a table for two, calmly eating a plate of chicken-fried steak, mashed potatoes, and peas. Oblivious to the half-dozen officers standing fifteen feet away with their hands resting lightly on their holstered pistols, she thumbed through a *Marie Claire*. She also appeared oblivious to Dr. Herrold. The big man sat across from her, head leaned slightly back, arms draped downward, mouth half-open in an *O* of surprise.

A serrated steak knife was buried up to its handle in his right eye. It had entered through the iris just below the pupil and broke through the orbital plate, the thin section of the skull behind the eyeball, and a good three inches of the blade was lodged in the tissue of his brain. He probably had just enough time to see the knife coming and register the pain of the puncture before he died, hence the look of great astonishment on his pink, round face. The wound was so neat that only a small trickle of blood ran down his cheek. It fell a drop at a time like tears onto his starched white doctor's jacket.

It took Wilder a moment to take it all in.

"Gail?"

She looked up from her magazine, smiling. "Hey, Matt. You have dinner yet?"

Before he could reply, he saw Brent flip his cell phone closed and step quietly into the banquet room from the kitchen. Brent shot him a look and slowly approached the table.

"Actually, no. Mind if I sit down?"

"Great. Oh, hey, Brent. Sorry I yelled at you before. My sister's always tellin' me to leave work when I leave work, if you know what I mean."

"Yeah, Cindy tells me the same thing."

"Bad day today, Gail?" Wilder asked.

"Nah, same old." She looked around the banquet room and frowned. "Don't know *where* my waitress went to."

Brent pulled up a chair and sat at the end of the table, not too close to Gail. Wilder sat across from her, next to Dr. Herrold's body. They didn't want her to feel threatened, so they gave her lots of space. Wilder glanced over at Herrold's dinner. Same as Gail's, but with gravy covering his meat and potatoes. He'd barely gotten to touch it. Gail noticed Wilder looking at Herrold's plate.

"Gravy. The man eats it on everything, I swear. Stuff'll kill you."

Wilder almost said "It'll have to stand in line."

"You feel like telling us what happened here?"

Gail shrugged, never losing her small, calm smile. She cut a small piece of her steak, wiped up a smudge of potatoes with it, and put it into her mouth. Wilder, Brent, and the security officers couldn't help but stare at the knife in her hand. She must've borrowed Herrold's since hers, presumably, was the one lodged in his eye. She answered Wilder's question while still chewing:

"No big thing. We got it all straightened out."

Wilder quietly unsnapped his holster under the table.

Gail looked at Brent. "Pass me the Sweet'n Low, will ya?"

Her voice gave no indication whatsoever of stress. Wilder guessed her heart rate to be seventy, max. Hands steady, breathing normal. Her mood bordered on jovial. Trying to match Gail's nonchalance, Brent reached for the little stainless-steel rectangle that held the sweeteners and handed it to her. She grabbed him by the wrist and pulled him up onto the table with such incredible strength his shoulder dislocated. Dinner plates, iced tea, and her magazine went flying. She stood up, pinning him down by the back of his neck. Clutching the steak knife in her fist, she lightly rested its tip just inside his ear canal. The tiniest thrust would make Brent just as dead as Dr. Herrold.

Wilder leaped to his feet and drew his Sig. The security officers, startled, stepped back and unholstered their weapons in unison. Wilder held up his hand, indicating that they chill. He hoped none of them was the nervous type—or worse, the heroic type.

Gail looked at Wilder. Only the slightest impatience and disappointment ruffled her calm demeanor.

"Why did you unsnap your holster, Matt? I thought we were friends."

"We *are* friends, Gail. Brent's your friend, too, but I think you're hurting him."

"You're my friend, how come you smell so scared?"

"I'm scared this isn't going to turn out too well. Help me out, give me the knife."

"Can't do it, Matt. Me and Brent are going to my car."

Wilder slowly crouched down and put his Sig on the floor.

"I'll come, too. Everything will be okay."

"Everything *is* okay." Gail smiled. She looked around the big empty banquet room.

"Tell the girl to bring the check, 'kay?" Her concerns and behavior didn't track with reality in an absurd and eerie way.

"Dinner's on me, kiddo," Wilder said.

"Actually," Brent said, "dinner's on *me.*"

Sprawled on top of the table, he was coated with food.

"You guys crack me up." Gail giggled, but she maintained her iron grip on the back of his neck. Suddenly, she turned toward the group of security officers.

"*Dumb* idea, bullethead!"

From twenty feet away she had heard their whispered plans to jump her, and instantly grew agitated.

"Oh, no . . . no way . . . Make 'em put their guns away. I don't need this aggravation, Matt."

"Holster 'em!" Wilder shouted.

He used Gail's momentary distraction to grab the edge of the table and topple it over, pulling Brent from her grasp. Several security officers piled onto her like a defensive line swarming a quarterback, all trying to grasp her right hand, in which she still clutched the knife. She slammed a couple of six-footers with her left forearm, sending them sprawling onto tables ten feet away. Four more came at her and she slashed at them with the knife, making bone-deep gashes whenever she connected. Then, with an animal-like scream, she flung herself at the remaining officers. One of them lunged at her from behind, but she turned and kicked him so hard in the groin that his feet left the ground. She grabbed him by the hair, snapped his head back, and swung the knife down to stab him in the chest.

A single gunshot rang out, severing her spinal cord at the base of her neck. She pitched forward, dead, on top of the security officer. Wilder, who'd made the shot left-handed, still balanced over Brent, sagged to the floor and let his Sig drop from his grasp.

"Shit." His voice cracked as he said it.

Clutching his dislocated shoulder, Brent nodded, grimly agreeing. A security officer rolled Gail onto her back. Death froze the strange, disconnected smile on her pretty face.

Seven

The emergency closed-door session of the United Nations, called in response to the Trans-Altaic Alliance's invasion of Georgia, ended thirteen hours after it began. In a late-night phone call, Ambassador Drake informed the President of the results. As Marsh hung up, his expression told Amy what had happened—or, more precisely, what hadn't happened.

"You *expected* inaction, Burt," the First Lady said.

"But not complete capitulation." Marsh sat on the bed, disgusted. "The best we could get was a nonbinding resolution encouraging Batu Khan to allow a U.N.-monitored election so Georgians can vote on joining the Trans-Altaic Alliance."

"I hope Diane vetoed the resolution."

"Damn right she did. That sort of limp-dick response is worse than none at all."

"They've made it more difficult, but they haven't stopped you from taking a stand if need be," Amy said. "You'll have to make your case directly to the people."

"I'm afraid the American public won't care any more than—"

The ringing phone interrupted him. He picked it up and listened for a moment.

"When? That's good news; get right on it." He hung up. "That was Levinson," he said to Amy. "Batu Khan has agreed to a Virtual Summit."

Three days had gone by since inviting Batu to direct talks, and he'd taken Batu's silence as a refusal—a direct insult to himself and the United States.

"The results at the U.N. must've influenced him," Amy said.

"No, the Greeks got word from the TAA before the General Assembly came out of closed session. I don't get it. If a man like Batu Khan wanted to talk he would've agreed at once, so he wouldn't appear weak or indecisive. He had no intention of opening the lines of communication, but something made him change his mind. What the hell could it be?"

Wilder, face haggard and eyes red-rimmed after a sleepless night, leaned against the arm of the sofa in Commander Charles Chang's office at OSI HQ. Beside him, Brent shifted uncomfortably in his chair, arm suspended in a sling because of his dislocated shoulder.

"I appreciate your time, Colonel, so I'll keep it brief," Wilder said. "I want the Herrold case."

Chang said nothing for a long moment. Born to a fifteen-year-old garment worker in south Chicago, he'd worked himself up from a series of foster homes to college, the Air Force Academy, and being the odds-on favorite of one day becoming Inspector General of the Air Force. Temperamentally he and Wilder couldn't be more different, but they had always enjoyed a cordial relationship because each man admired the other's abilities.

"Matt," the Colonel finally replied, "you haven't done any criminal investigative work since you joined the WFO three years ago."

"I'm not viewing the case as a criminal investigation, sir. I believe it may also have national security implications." Wilder handed him two sheaves of paper. "Here's a copy of my report about the incident in Woomera, and Brent's report covering the events in the Officers' Club. I've highlighted certain . . . similarities."

Chang laid the reports side by side and compared the highlighted passages, almost identical phrases in both reports: "*Extreme physical strength . . . inappropriate, disconnected emotional state . . . constant smile . . . acute sensory ability . . .*"

The regional commander looked up from the papers. "That's uncanny."

"Especially since there's no conceivable reason a nurse from Maryland would have *anything* in common with a Khaldun from the Trans-Altaic Alliance, let alone something this bizarre," Wilder said.

"When are you getting the John Doe's lab results?" Chang asked.

"Couple of days."

"And Ms. Sealy's autopsy?"

"Dr. Dharwadkar is performing it this afternoon."

Chang looked again at the two reports. "I don't know," he said. "An objective third party might be the wiser choice for the Herrold case. You're one of our best agents, Matt. But I'm concerned about bringing undue attention to the bizarre details in your Woomera report. I fear they'll be viewed in some quarters as embellishment, justification for your risky tactics in pursuing the perpetrator. Especially since, not long thereafter, you shot a fifty-year-old nurse—ostensibly to protect a half-dozen security officers—then attributed to her the same strange abilities and behavior. Put together, it's bound to raise questions I'd rather not be asked until we have some answers."

"The best chance of getting those answers is to work both cases as parallel, coordinated investigations," Wilder said. Then his voice grew softer. "Look, there's something else: Gail was my friend. I have to know what happened to her." He hesitated, uncomfortable with saying the words. "Why I had to kill her."

Immediately after Colonel Chang agreed to give him the Herrold case, Wilder drove down to Alexandria to speak with the doctor's widow and two college-aged sons. Such interviews were perhaps the most difficult part of a murder investigation—the anguish of people who have lost someone to sudden, deliberate violence is unparalleled in its intensity. As expected, the Herrold family told him nothing that would shed any light on the situation.

The next afternoon, he sat alone in the conference room at the Washington Field Office building and watched the videotape Brent had made that morning of the Sealy family interview, taken at their apartment on D Street in Washington. On the tape, Ruth, Gail's younger sister, glared at Brent throughout the discussion. Her sister was dead, shot by a white officer, end of story. Wilder being a friend of Gail's meant nothing to her. Ruth's seventeen-year-old daughter, L'Tasha, sat on the sofa and crossed her arms, mimicking her mother's hard, suspicious glare. Marion, Gail's mother, hadn't slept in two days despite the sedatives the doctor had given her.

"There is no way my sister done what you're saying she done," Ruth said.

"I'll be honest with you. If I hadn't been there I wouldn't believe it either," Brent replied.

"Stuff happens on that base, you all could say whatever you damn please about how it went down."

"You want to understand this thing. So do I. But if you close your mind, jump to conclusions, you're no help in solving it. You in or out?"

Ruth's silence indicated she was in.

"Tell me about Gail's behavior lately, state of mind. Anything unusual, or anything that might've indicated a change in feelings toward Dr. Herrold."

"Nothing to tell that I know of," Ruth said.

L'Tasha looked at her mother and grandmother, and then at Brent.

"Last week Aunt Gail said, 'I'm thinking Tom's got an eye toward retiring.' It was weird. I mean, she don't normally talk like that: 'eye toward retiring.' . . ."

"How did she feel about Dr. Herrold leaving?"

"I ain't sure. She didn't seem pissed or nothing about it. She was real calm. But then she said something like 'change ain't easy at my age.' "

While watching the tape in the conference room, Wilder jotted the phrases down in a notebook.

"Look," Brent began, "were Gail and Tom—"

"Not even once." Ruth frowned. "She liked the man, truly did. But not like that."

Marion sat on a dining room chair, hands in her lap, twisting a piece of Kleenex. She stared out the window onto the busy street as she spoke.

"My daughter was an educated woman. A registered nurse. A *fine* one. People loved her. Now folks are only gonna think of her as this crazy killer, and the rest of her life won't matter. I can't describe how much that hurts." She turned to Brent. "Taking Tom from his family . . . the *way* she . . ."

Marion began to weep again, somehow finding a few more tears. Ruth knelt in front of her mother, held her around the waist, head in her lap, rocking together, soothing her in rhythmic whispers.

The sight tore at Wilder. He had seen his own mother cry like that at his sister's funeral. Keening—desperate, helpless grieving, as if the mourner herself might die from the weight of her sorrow. Which, in his mother's case, had happened less than two months later.

Brent quietly stopped the camcorder. Interview over.

Wilder snapped off the VCR and sat in the darkened conference room with his eyes closed. It wasn't until this moment that he allowed himself to think about losing Herrold and Gail, to grieve for his dead friends, and a great, heavy sadness descended upon him.

Eight

As Laura got out of her car in the driveway leading to the West Wing of the White House, she finally decided what her undercurrent of nervousness felt like: being called to the principal's office. She still had no idea why the President of the United States would want to meet with her. An expressionless usher led her to the Reception Room, where White House chief of staff Curt Levinson came in at eleven twenty-eight to greet her.

"Thank you for coming on such short notice," he said as he enthusiastically shook her hand. Laura wondered whether everyone in politics went to hand-pumping classes.

"Well, it's not like anything else on my calendar would've taken precedent, Mr. Levinson."

"Curt, please. I'm trying to downplay the sad fact I'm five years older than the President of the United States."

I should look so good in my mid-fifties, Laura thought. Levinson had barely a wrinkle, and the gray at his temples blended in with his full head of sandy blond hair. He made knowledgeable small-talk about the various artwork and the perpetual White House restoration projects, then he opened the door into the Roosevelt Conference Room.

The Roosevelt Room, just adjacent to the Oval Office, was used for staff meetings or small press conferences. It had a long table in the center, with sixteen tall-backed leather chairs around it. The grandfather clock next to the portrait of FDR chimed eleven-thirty as Laura and Levinson entered. Laura saw several other familiar faces around the table: Vice President Adam Taylor; Secretary of State Harry Burroughs; Secretary of Defense Stan Woodruff; Chairman of the Joint Chiefs of Staff, General Don Mancini; the director of Central Intelligence, Ted Jameson; the other Joint Chiefs, wearing among them enough medals and ribbons to decorate the side of a battleship. Laura realized Levinson had brought her to a meeting of the National Security Council. She looked at Levinson—this can't be where *I'm* supposed to be.

Before Levinson could say anything, the door in between the Roosevelt Room and the Oval Office opened. Everyone at the table rose when President Marsh came in. He muttered hellos and crossed to Laura. He took her hand in his and greeted her with genuine sincerity.

"You must think we're either rude or utterly incompetent for asking you here without an explanation."

"I'm certainly curious."

"Sit down, you'll see there's madness to my method." He smiled. "And I mean it just the way it came out."

Laura sat in a chair just to the right of the President, who took his seat at the center of the table. She glanced around the room. The furnishings were Chippendale and Queen Anne, and her mouth practically watered as she noticed the bound volumes on the bookshelf—a series of presidential papers. Her fascination delighted the President. He wished he could take the afternoon off, so he and Amy could show the place to someone who would truly appreciate it.

"I think you know who everyone is," Marsh said, "so please forgive me if I skip the introductions. All I will say is they're all not the sour old grumps they look to be."

The Vice President of the United States, the Joint Chiefs of Staff, and the other members of the National Security Council shifted self-consciously in their chairs, trying to appear relaxed. Laura smiled, almost forgetting her own discomfort.

"I'd like to hear your thoughts on Batu Khan," Marsh said. "As far as we know, you're just about the only American who's met the man, let alone spent a substantial amount of time with him."

Now Laura understood why the President himself wanted to speak to her. Three years ago she'd written a book, *The Silk Trail*, about the ninth-century Mongol Empire. Her research had taken her to the Altai Mountains in western Asia. Word of her presence soon reached Batu Khan—then still a supporting player on the world stage—and he sent a team of Khaldun Horsemen to invite her to his camp. When she excitedly agreed, the Khaldun took her, blindfolded, to Batu's always-moving wilderness headquarters. She spent five days and nights speaking to His Excellency, filling dozens of legal pads while he expounded on the Mongols, himself, and a multitude of other topics. She devoted two of *The Silk Trail's* chapters to her experiences with him.

"I don't want facts and figures, or a rehash of what's in your book," Marsh said. "That's why we didn't want you to prepare. I'm interested in your *feelings* about Batu."

That sense of being in the principal's office returned.

"My God, I don't know. . . . Ask me a few questions to get me going. Once I do, I can be counted on not to shut up; it's the getting started I have a problem with." She looked around the room at the impassive faces.

"Fair enough," Marsh said. "Let's begin with your personal impression of the man."

"He pretty much lives up to the hype. Intelligent, charismatic, attractive, driven, intuitive . . . ruthless—although in our time together I certainly never saw that side of him."

"If you don't mind me asking," Marsh said, "how did Batu Khan react to the presence of an attractive woman in his camp?"

"He was always charming and occasionally flirtatious—when it suited his purposes, such as when trying to convince me of one of his dubious worldviews. He clearly wanted me to write favorably of him and the Mongol leaders of the past. However, he never made any amorous advances. From what I could see, he is passionately devoted to his two wives."

"Was his shaman, Chu'tsai, there during your visit?" Stan Woodruff asked. "We know practically nothing about the man."

"His real name is Edward Moy," Laura said. "He's got a degree in Eastern religions from the University of Southern California."

The President smiled at the look of utter surprise on the secretary of defense's face.

"Chu'tsai agreed to tell me his life story," Laura continued, "after he'd drunk a liter of *koumiss* and smoked about an ounce of marijuana, but only if I promised not to publish it. His mother washed linens in their tiny village in Mongolia. At four he'd taught himself to read; by nine, tutored by the village shaman, he could divine wisdom from the elements. A South African doctor who visited the village twice a year took an interest in him and convinced her alma mater, USC, to grant him a scholarship. He read about the new prime minister of Kazakhstan, Vladimir Baikalev, and his belief in shamanistic practices, so he wrote a letter to the future Batu Khan offering his services as shaman. Apparently he really impressed Batu with his skills at understanding the supernatural— and it didn't hurt that he divined unparalleled greatness in Batu's destiny. He took the name Chu'tsai from Genghis Khan's spiritual adviser, and within five years he'd risen to Batu's second in command."

Frowning, Ted Jameson wrote *Ed. Moy—USC—E Religions* on a slip of paper and stuck it in his pocket. "How much credence does Batu give this 'wisdom' Chu'tsai divines?" he asked.

"Quite a bit. Before making any major decision, he has him consult the elements several times."

"Can those readings be replicated by our people?" Marsh asked. "FDR ordered up Hitler's chart when they found out he used an astrologer while making battle plans."

"No, Chu'tsai's interpretations are too subjective," Laura replied. "The OSS could do an astrological chart because they're based on universally observable conditions like dates, the stars, and the planets. Not sheep bones or moonlight on the river currents . . ."

Marsh shook his head, amazed that such things had true relevance to the supreme leader of one of the largest standing armies in the world.

"Most Americans view Batu Khan as a stock villain," he said. "Can you take us past all that?"

Laura nodded, but she didn't feel particularly up to the task.

"In many ways, the Trans-Altaic Alliance is as amazing a phenomenon as the first Mongol Empire. Ever since the end of the Cold War, we'd had a worldwide trend of decolonization, the splintering of old unities, then Batu Khan came out of nowhere and reversed that trend. He convinced a group of floundering Central Asian countries that 'Unity Is Strength'—the TAA motto. Suddenly their political clout increased a hundredfold, and it happened right in the backyards of Russia and China, too busy with their own problems to notice."

"Not just busy, they didn't take him seriously. Neither did we," Marsh said.

"Still, if we started taking every kook in the world seriously . . . His own Russian army unit called him Mad Vlad when they were flying in Chechnya," Jameson said.

"Back in the Thirties, no one took the thugs in the Munich beer halls very seriously either," Marsh responded.

"Actually, Mr. President," Laura said, "Batu managed to do something even Hitler couldn't do. Until the recent violence in Georgia, he'd peacefully unified eight countries of three hundred million people without a common theology. The Soviets had to get around that one by banning religion altogether. The last person to create a multicultural, pantheistic empire in that part of the world was Genghis Khan, seven hundred years ago.

"That's why the core concept of a Trans-Altaic Alliance is so brilliant. Batu melded fairly diverse societies into one by convincing them they shared an overriding commonality. He said a proud culture of artisans and warriors exists in every nation that speaks one of the Altaic languages. It worked because disenfranchised people are always looking for something, however tenuous, to bring them together. He gave it to them in the guise of an 'Altaic' identity—whatever that might be—and in setting himself up as their khan."

" 'Khan'—that means king?"

"More or less, but with no royal connotation as we know it, in the Western sense of nobility. The word originates in the Mongolian: *qä'än*, meaning ruler."

"The psychology amazes me," Marsh said. "There's this ambitious Siberian-Mongolian named Vladimir Baikalev. He reinvents himself—Russian army pilot, television newscaster in Kazakhstan, politician, empire-builder. He takes the name Batu Khan as some sort of homage to Genghis?"

"Not quite. There's a fascinating twist. The original Batu Khan was Genghis's grandson, the third Great Khan in the Mongol Empire, which actually reached its zenith under Batu's rule, not Genghis's. The original Batu is most famous—or notorious—for leading the fiercest army ever assembled, the Golden Horde, through the heart of Russia and on into eastern Europe in the years 1238 through 1242.

"Hungary, Poland, and Bavaria were decimated. Ninety thousand killed in Hungary alone. Entire cities were put to the sword. Had he not been forced to return to the capital, Karakorum, to become Great Khan when his uncle died, Batu almost certainly would've kept marching until the Golden Horde reached the Atlantic."

General Mancini shook his head skeptically. "You don't think the Europeans could've stopped them? There were some pretty fierce tribes on the Continent in the Middle Ages."

"The Mongols had several advantages: very intelligent leadership; initiative, always taking the high ground, using the enemy's weakness against him; and amazing mobility—in extreme cases they could move a hundred twenty miles a day on horses. Think about it. How many miles a day can a modern mechanized army move?"

"Thirty, maybe."

"They also had superior weaponry. They were the first to use firearms. Even their bows were extraordinary. Modern competition bows have a thirty- to forty-pound draw weight. Hunting bows, about fifty pounds. The Mongol bow had a draw weight of one hundred sixty pounds."

A murmur went around the room as everyone remembered the powerful bows used by the TAA Commandos in the CNN videotape.

"Okay, say Batu is modeling the TAA on the old Mongol Empire," Marsh asked. "What can you extrapolate from that?"

"Past Mongol glory is certainly a part of his inspiration. Batu was born in the same area as Genghis, the Lake Baikal region of southern Siberia. To many people in central Asia, even today, Genghis is a combination of Jesus and George Washington. It's commonly believed he will be reincarnated and lead them again to world dominance. And if you have to model your goals after someone's, you might as well pick a winner. Mongol territory under the original Batu Khan was the largest land empire in history."

"So you think he's trying to replicate it?"

Laura hesitated.

"Be frank, please," Marsh said. "The beauty of giving an opinion is there're no wrong answers."

"Yes. I do think he is trying to replicate the old empire, and probably more. Which means, like Georgia, all future gains will happen with brute force. If he's strategizing like the first Batu Khan, he'll continue to gobble up as much territory as he can—perhaps even trying for a nuclear power like Pakistan or India—then move into Europe, using up the time it takes for the U.S. to be willing and able to do something about it."

Woodruff and Jameson exchanged a skeptical look.

"Official military and political doctrine since the fall of the Berlin Wall would tell us otherwise, Miss Bishop," Woodruff said. "Wars will occur, of course, but we expect them, by and large, to be regional affairs. U.S. policy and preparedness are geared accordingly, and there is a high level of satisfaction with this position in the Pentagon as well as in the halls of Congress."

Marsh gave Woodruff a look that said shut up and listen.

"Please, Laura, continue," the President said. "You're making a lot of sense."

"The major powers persist in dealing with Batu as if it were three years ago. That's like feeding a tiger cub. You keep giving him Little Friskies and milk without noticing how big he's gotten, one day you're going to lose your arm."

For someone who looked like she'd pass out from fright when she first walked into the room, Laura was certainly on a roll.

"Stop underestimating him," Marsh said. "I absolutely agree."

"But at the same time, I also wouldn't underestimate his awe of America's position and might. During the time I spent in his camp, he questioned me incessantly about, for lack of a better term, the American psyche. He desperately wants to understand us. Although he still respects us and fears the U.S., I believe that respect is yours to either retain and enhance, or to lose.

"If there is any one lesson I've taken from history, it's that again and again, the course of monumental events was determined mainly by the personalities of the people at their center. Usually one or two men. Coming to that understanding frightened me, because it made me appreciate the fragility of world order. I think it's especially germane when considering the consequences of dealing with Batu Khan."

"You're saying that in order for Batu Khan to fear America, he must fear me."

"Mr. President, if everyone were as quick a study as you, I'd consider a teaching job."

Marsh smiled, then returned to Batu's questions about America. Something about the way Laura spoke of them made him believe there had been more to the conversation than curiosity about an alien culture.

"What was he really looking for?" Marsh asked.

Again, Laura hesitated before answering. Anything beyond a direct quote or specific historical example would be interpretation, a foreign-relations policy call—a task for which she felt monumentally unqualified.

"Batu knows his expansionism will place him, sooner or later, on a collision course with the United States. He's searching for an insight into us that will give him the wisdom to defeat us."

Now even Marsh thought Laura ventured into the fanciful.

"I know it sounds absurd," she said. "We're a nuclear superpower, the TAA isn't . . . yet."

"Nor will they be in the foreseeable future, Ms. Bishop," Woodruff scoffed. "Iraq is farther along in their nuclear program than the Trans-Altaic Alliance, and they're nowhere, thanks to our monitoring."

"Weapons of mass destruction aren't the only issue, Secretary Woodruff." She turned to President Marsh. "You have to view warfare from the philosophy of the Mongol. To Batu Khan, like Genghis and the first Batu, a strategy based upon understanding one's enemy is just as important as military might. Should conflict ever erupt between the United States and the Trans-Altaic Alliance, the critical fight won't be on the field or in the air. It will be a very personal battle of will and intellect between you and him."

Nine

Wilder lay on his sofa in front of the TV, trying to unwind enough to go to bed. That afternoon, he'd watched Gail Sealy's autopsy, conducted by the chief pathologist at the Malcolm Grow Medical Center. He hadn't attended a postmortem in several years. That the deceased had been a friend he'd been forced to shoot made it an excruciating experience. Although there were still chemistries yet to be analyzed, the pathologist had so far discovered no abnormalities whatsoever to explain Gail's actions or condition.

Flipping through the channels, a brief report on the late news caught Wilder's attention. In Santa Rosa, California, a fifty-one-year-old pharmaceutical-company executive had been arrested for killing his next-door neighbor. Not so strange an occurrence, except he'd stabbed him with hedge clippers, then *dropped* a ride-on power mower, while it was still running, on top of the dying man. The executive had no prior history of violence. He and the victim had been friends until the executive had complained to the victim that he could hear, from inside his house, the victim and his wife having intercourse in theirs. The Santa Rosa police detective handling the case called it "the most striking case of sudden personality change" he'd ever witnessed. The detective's description of the perpetrator's behavior sounded eerily familiar—the lack of recognition of his crime, calmness turning to sudden rage, physical and sensory abilities far beyond the normal range. Wilder made note of the phrase "sudden personality change," the name of the detective, and crossed to his computer.

The next morning, Wilder stopped in front of the Francis T. Evans Elementary School just inside the Virginia Gate of Andrews AFB. He unbuckled Kate from the back of his Grand Prix and helped her put her pink Barbie backpack on. Then he kissed her and handed her off to the car-line monitor. He liked to linger for a moment to watch her run onto the playground and greet her friends as if she hadn't seen them for a month. Making a U-turn out of the school driveway he drove north through the base, past the base's East and West Golf Courses, and pulled up to the OSI's Washington Field Office building.

Brent liked to hold monthly meetings with small groups of Tactical Operations agents so they could brainstorm their cases. Although Wilder always made an effort to be one of the team and tried not to let his tendency to keep to himself be mistaken for snobbery, he didn't often participate. Today, however, he needed some outside opinions.

As he came in, Brent took him aside. "We need to chat in private, after the meeting."

Senior agent Bob Hyler relieved Wilder of the white bag of doughnuts and bagels in his hand and put them on a folding table in the briefing room next to the Mr. Coffee. Hyler, a tough, dogged, nuts-and-bolts investigator, viewed any open case file as a sharp pebble in his shoe. J. Nelson Franz, bearded, intense, thoughtful, with a doctorate in criminal investigations, got in line for the food. The other agents called Franz "Joey H"—H as in Hollywood—because he once worked in Detachment 110 at the Los Angeles Air Force Base and had a few friends in the entertainment business. More important, he allegedly dated a working actress. Wilder nodded to the director of the OSI's Computer Crime Lab, Dennis Shirlaw. He and his team were acknowledged the finest computer forensics experts in the Department of Defense. Brent, his arm still in the sling, balanced a plastic plate of three doughnuts, a bagel slathered in cream cheese, and a cup of coffee in one hand.

"I'd like to get this powwow started," he said, sitting at the conference table. "Since Matt brought the noshes, he gets to go first."

"That way he doesn't even have to pretend to be interested in our shit," Shirlaw said.

"When have I bothered to pretend?"

Shirlaw shrugged—good point.

"Okay, hoss, what's up?" Brent said, his mouth full of doughnut.

Wilder opened his notebook computer and told the others about the killing in Santa Rosa.

"I talked to the detective in charge. There are identical pathologies to

Gail's behavior, as well as the guy in Woomera. Then I checked the NCAVC and VICAP databases for any others that might fit the pattern."

Wilder's mouthful of acronyms referred to the top sources for the sharing of law enforcement data, administered by the FBI—NCAVC, the National Center for the Analysis of Violent Crime and VICAP, the Violent Criminal Apprehension Program.

"You're looking real pleased with yourself," Brent said. "What'd you find?"

"Aside from the occasional asshole on angel dust, here in the U.S. in the last three months there have been fifteen documented cases of murder or serious, unprovoked assault involving a perpetrator who exhibited unusual physical or sensory ability."

"Really . . ." Brent said, genuinely surprised.

"In the entire year prior to that—" Wilder began.

"Lemme guess: Zip."

"You got it. Prior year, nada. None the prior *five* years, except a couple of aging Hell's Angels who went wacko on homemade amphetamines. And get this: All fifteen perps are between the ages of forty-seven and fifty-two."

"How come it hasn't hit the papers yet?" Brent asked.

"Usually the more bizarre details are not made public, in deference to the families of the perps. Santa Rosa was an exception. But in all cases they were solid citizens, professional people. Spookier shit was also underreported in some of the police reports; sometimes I had to read between the lines on the summaries to pick up the similarities. I think some of the small-town PD chiefs simply didn't believe what the arresting officers were telling them."

"Stuff about smaller jurisdictions editing the case files makes sense," Franz said. "Working-stiff cop doesn't want anything on paper he might have to explain. So it won't do you much good to get copies of their reports if they're not complete and accurate."

"That's what I'm thinking," Wilder replied. He looked at Brent. "I'd like to check out a few of these situations firsthand. Talk to the arresting officers, families, eyewitnesses. Seven of the perps are still alive. I want to look in on a few. Maybe I can find a common link beyond age and social status. And I'd *really* like to know why they share the same pathologies with a thirtyish Khaldun Elite from the other side of the planet."

"I'll ask Chang, but I don't know if he'll okay it. Now's a bad time to be leaving base, all this shit going on with the TAA. We'll need our best CI agents here, especially in the Washington Field Office. And as far as any possible Woomera connection goes . . . that's another reason we need to talk later."

After the meeting, Wilder followed Brent to his office. As soon as his friend closed the door, Wilder knew it would be bad news.

"The Aussies are taking over the Woomera case," Brent said. "I got the order this morning to ship the John Doe remains back to the Australian Defence Force."

Wilder looked at him, angry and confused.

"What's going on?"

"Look, I know what you're thinking. But it isn't because anyone's pissed about you playing cowboy down there. It's beyond that. They're tabling the whole investigation."

"Why?"

"No explanation given."

"You got this from Chang?"

"Yeah. He thought maybe the Australians made such a stink about their boys getting slaughtered the State Department decided to throw 'em the case."

"Come on," Wilder said. "This wouldn't be the first time politics got in the way of somebody doing their job, but don't tell me the U.S. government would let a case of high-level espionage go without a fight."

"I happen to agree," Brent said. "So I called a friend in the Australian Defence Force, off the record, and he's as confused as we are. The ADF's taking the case file, but they're putting the investigation on hold, too. That's 'need to know,' and you really didn't."

"There's no fucking reason for *two* governments to close such an important investigation unless they don't want it solved."

"Not closed. Tabled. Chang was very specific about the language."

A distinction not lost on either man. It indicated that Colonel Chang, and probably whoever above him actually issued the order, didn't like it either. Nor were they able to discern the reasons through the informal channels normally available to them. Conclusion: Orders to cease an investigation into the infiltration of a top-secret propulsion-testing facility came from the very highest level of government.

"This stinks."

"Right out loud."

"What are we gonna do about it?"

"Not a damn thing."

Brent took a manila folder out of his desk drawer and tossed it to Wilder.

"We were ordered to send these along with the remains," Brent said, "*without* making copies for our records."

Inside, Wilder found a stapled stack of paper with long tables of medical data. The lab work he'd been waiting for. He flipped to the bottom of the last page, where the Malcolm Grow pathologist Dr. Kumar Dharwadkar certified that the Infiltrator's body chemistries were one hundred percent normal—disease-free and no detectable trace of drugs.

"Is this accurate, or another goddamn cover-up?" Wilder asked.

"Absolutely accurate. Kumar said he finished just before we were told to drop the investigation."

Wilder tossed the records back to Brent.

"We still have the Herrold investigation. Far as everyone knows, I'm not even *thinking* about Australia. But there's a connection there— somehow. Maybe with the other case I can backdoor my way into a few answers about Woomera."

On his way home, Wilder sat in his car near the edge of Runway Four as two orderlies moved the Infiltrator's body from an ambulance to a small Gulfstream jet with no military markings. An aircraft, Wilder noticed, in neither the USAF or ADF inventory. An aircraft with far less than the necessary range to fly to Australia.

Whoever wanted the investigation killed, he realized, had enough juice to get *two* governments to go along with his or her wishes.

After dinner, Brent called Wilder to say Colonel Chang had okayed the trip to Santa Rosa. Cindy got on the phone to make arrangements for Kate to stay with them in Wilder's absence. When Wilder told Kate he would be gone for a few days she did her best to act like it was all right with her. In truth, Wilder would've preferred she be angry or cry. Her inability or unwillingness to express her emotions tore at him, and accentuated all the negatives in his head: his awkwardness in his role as parent, his inability to truly connect with her, his guilt over leaving. He secretly felt relieved she'd be spending more time with Brent and Cindy— although they had no children of their own yet, theirs was a far more stable home than his ever hoped to be. He banished those thoughts so as not to ruin the evening for himself, and sat on the front porch with Kate. Neither of them spoke as they ate Dove Bars and watched the sunset together.

Ten

At a little before one P.M., Chief of Staff Curt Levinson walked into the Virtual Summit Room on the first floor of the West Wing and faced the wall-sized video screen. The fifteen-by-twenty-foot room had been furnished to resemble a nineteenth-century study with a fireplace, forest-green wood shutters over the windows, leather club chairs, and a crystal bowl full of hard candies on a credenza. The ceiling had been raised five feet to make room for lighting equipment. Hidden behind the wall-sized screen was a high-definition television camera, and microphones were placed behind various objects in the room, allowing the President to roam freely while speaking in a normal tone of voice. When connected to one of the other world leaders or to key U.S. embassies using the same technology, VS created the amazing illusion of a face-to-face conversation.

The United States had never established diplomatic relations with the Trans-Altaic Alliance—no ambassadors, embassies, or direct channels of communication. The Greek ambassadors to Washington and the TAA handled what little intercourse existed between the two powers. Through them, diplomatic attachés from both sides worked the arduous task of organizing a Virtual Summit transmission between President Marsh and Batu Khan. All the usual concerns for protocol were amplified because there existed no modern precedent for Batu's rapid ascendancy to prominence. Three years ago he would've rated no more than a meeting with the American assistant undersecretary for Central Asian affairs. Now, the Alliance's political weight matched that of China and Russia.

Unlike normal Virtual Summits between Marsh and other world leaders, the TAA would not agree to a direct downlink. The TAA engineers gave their American counterparts a transponder code for a satellite feed mirrored in at least two sites before reaching Washington in order to make its originating location impossible to trace. One point of agreement on both sides: The conversation between the two leaders would be completely private. No audio- or videotaping and Batu would speak English to avoid the use of translators. All in all, much protocol-driven wrangling for what everyone expected to be a short, insubstantial meet-and-greet.

The video wall filled with electronic snow then color bars. At exactly one o'clock, an image of the Trans-Altaic Alliance flag appeared. The green band on the bottom symbolized the pristine grasslands of central Asia. The rest was blue, for the sky; and the yellow arc across the sky represented Batu Khan's shooting star.

Seeing it, Levinson recalled the significance of the meteor from his intelligence digests: TAA legend said a magnificent meteor fell to earth on the night of Vladimir Baikalev's birth. His parents were a Siberian civil servant father of Kazakh descent and a Mongolian mother. As a boy, Baikalev had been a loner with no love for Russia, but neither did he feel Kazakh or Mongolian. His father enlisted him in the Russian military at seventeen. He became a pilot, and found he had a talent for leading men. Ruthless and charismatic, he rose quickly to squadron commander during the rebel uprising in Chechnya. After the army, Baikalev felt depressed and aimless. A girlfriend found him a job as a news announcer on Kazakhstan state television. His unique appearance and intense manner fascinated viewers, and his popularity helped him win a seat on the Supreme Kenges, the country's 177-member legislature.

A year later, someone mutilated and murdered the prime minister in his bed. No one ever knew Baikalev had been the killer . . . except the Kazakhstan president. In a private meeting, Baikalev placed a Styrofoam cup containing the PM's testicles on the president's desk. When the president finished vomiting into his wastepaper basket, Baikalev handed him a handkerchief, asked him to be his friend, then left. News that the president of Kazakhstan had appointed twenty-seven-year-old Vladimir Baikalev as the new prime minister stunned the country and the international community. From his new position of prominence Baikalev began preaching the power of unity. He spoke of an "Altaic" identity, using the Altaic family of languages as a common cultural bond shared by all the disenfranchised countries of Central Asia. He linked this identity to the past glories of the twelfth-century Mongol Empire, and it was the perfect confluence of a man, his message, and people eager to embrace it. Eighteen months later, the moment he took the oath of office as the president of Kazakhstan, he dissolved the Supreme Kenges and signed an agreement to merge Kazakhstan and Mongolia under his rule, forming the Trans-Altaic Alliance. He combined the two identities of his blood and soul into one country, and on that day he became Batu Khan. Within nine months, all the other member states of the TAA voluntarily surrendered their national identity to become part of his new empire.

Believing the shooting star had foretold his ascension to power, Batu offered a ten-kilogram brick of gold bullion to anyone who'd bring him the meteorite. An elderly shepherd found it in a field in central Mongolia, and it has remained in Batu's *ger* ever since.

On the VS Room video wall the image of the flag dissolved to that of the interior of Batu's *ger*. Because of the Alliance's refusal to use a direct fiber-optic link, the picture was blurrier than usual, but it still seemed as if only a large if somewhat dirty window separated the room from Batu's tent. His hand-painted map showing the Trans-Altaic Alliance in royal purple hung on the back wall of the *ger*, next to the wooden stand holding his prized meteorite. Levinson noticed that Georgia had been added to the map.

"General Chu'tsai?"

Batu's shaman, Chu'tsai, walked into frame and bowed.

"Welcome, and peace to all who visit here."

Dressed in L.L. Bean clothes and a pair of hand-tooled cowboy boots, Chu'tsai appeared to Levinson like a smug grad student.

"I bring greetings from Burton Marsh, President of the United States, to his Excellency, Batu Khan. I speak for the President and all people of the United States when I wish Batu Khan and his subjects good health, prosperity, and peace." Levinson felt like adding "so wipe the grin off your face, you Jiminy Cricket little prick."

"His Most Serene Excellency Batu Khan—the Good, the Wise, the Discoverer of Hidden Things—thanks you for your kind words and wishes, and asks me to express his solemn prayers for the happiness and fulfillment of your president, his wife, and the citizens who entrusted him to lead your mighty nation into this new and exciting era of true kinship and understanding with our humble people."

"President Marsh awaits with great anticipation the pleasure of speaking to His Excellency. As statesmen, as leaders of great powers, and soon, he hopes, as friends," Levinson replied.

"It would be His Excellency's highest honor and privilege to please the President."

At this point, the screen faded to blue. As had been carefully arranged, Batu Khan would take his position, the image would go back on line, and President Marsh would enter the VS Room. The diplomatic subtleties to this arrangement were that Batu would greet Marsh, the senior world leader. In the hallway, the President nodded his approval of Levinson's performance, then smiled conspiratorially.

"Remember when we were kids they kept telling us that you could grow up and be anything you wanted to be? I sure wish they hadn't told *those* guys that."

Levinson laughed, then glanced into the VS Room. The image of the interior of Batu's tent had returned, meaning Batu must've taken his position.

"You're on, sir. Good luck."

Marsh walked into the VS Room and closed the door behind him. Everything said from this point forward would be entirely private. He glanced over at the video screen.

No Batu.

The image had shifted somewhat, so that it now included the wood-burning stove in the center of the *ger*. One of Batu's wives, seventeen-year-old Kuri, stood at the stove. Wearing sandals and traditional Mongolian dress, she ladled a thick stew into a wooden bowl. The President of the United States stood speechless as she continued, seemingly unaware of him, and filled another bowl with stew. Then she cut two red slabs of rare roasted mutton and put them on top of the bowls. When she finished, Batu Khan walked into frame and took one of the bowls. He whispered something, kissed her, and ran his hand sensuously along her ass. She giggled, dipped in a quick curtsy, and left. Then Batu looked over at the President.

"Mr. President, you do me and my people the highest honor by appearing here this momentous day."

Dressed as usual in his brightly colored *shalwar qamiz*, he spoke in a calm, friendly voice and had a warm smile. Unwilling to give Batu the satisfaction of knowing how much the business with the girl annoyed him, Marsh did not reply.

Batu carried both bowls to a low table in front of his video camera. He sat on a three-legged stool and put one bowl on the table across from where he sat and the other one in front of himself.

"It would be unthinkable for any visitor to happen upon one of our tents in the grasslands without sharing our humble food. It is tradition, so it is law. As tradition offers no guidelines for how to behave if our guest is only a shadow on the wall, I shall eat both our portions in order not to contradict our ancient ways."

Marsh expected Batu Khan to be full of shit. He just didn't expect him to be *this* full of shit. "Traditions exist to help people behave with civility," the President said. "It insults tradition to use it as a pretense for rudeness."

Batu picked up the mutton with his hands and chewed loudly. That is fine, he thought, Marsh called him out on veering from protocol. What would he do about it?

"We'll talk when you're not quite so hungry. Good morning." Marsh turned away from the screen and headed for the door.

Batu tossed the mutton back into his bowl and dipped his fingers in a tureen of warm water and flower petals. "Forgive me; you're right. Better to share meat when we are actually in one another's company."

Indeed, he wished Marsh was right there, sweating in the *ger* with him, near enough to smell. He'd finally corresponded personally with their ally in the United States, and received from the man a stunning piece of information with absolute proof of its veracity. This newfound knowledge immediately changed Batu's belief that any dialogue with Marsh would be of greater benefit to the President. Now, every shred of understanding he could gather would serve *his* goals.

He watched Marsh stop at the door, pause, then slowly turn back to the VS screen. How genuine are his feelings? Batu wondered. Is he really angry, or merely pretending because it's the necessary response? Is he a man of the heart or of the mind?

Their eyes met and a cold wave of revulsion went through the President; the sound of Mrs. Gorovich's cries as she watched her children being murdered still haunted him. This may be a game to Batu, but not to him. Sitting in the VS Room easy chair, he saw no reason to exchange pleasantries.

"I want you to explain something," Marsh said. "You made no attempt to hide your role in the Georgian coup. Your methods were deliberately inhumane and vicious. Your men killed the president's family—his *children*—unnecessarily and with cold premeditation. Why, when there are so many other ways to achieve your objectives?"

Batu stood up and started pacing. "Everything I know about how to influence the internal affairs of another sovereign nation I learned from your country. Chile, El Salvador, Iran, a dozen more. America *takes* from other people. I *gave* to Georgia. I gave her pride, power, and purpose, a chance to share my destiny. Her citizens are now a part of a great adventure—they will have a place in history, along with me."

"You forced your will upon them with violence and terror. The most important skill of world leadership is using power responsibly. Any coward with an army can throw his weight around, killing innocent people."

Batu scowled. "It is my belief that the future will judge our actions as righteous."

"History will record suffering and cruelty . . . all for nothing."

A perfect challenge, made only more ominous by its vagueness. Batu had hoped Marsh would make a specific threat they would both know to be empty and unenforceable, meaning the Georgia issue had been resolved between them. Instead, Marsh cleverly kept it a matter still to be reckoned with.

"You view further growth of the Trans-Altaic Alliance as undesirable, threatening. That is selfish. Why should the people of my hemisphere be denied the benefits of unity you have enjoyed for so long?"

"No reason, as long as they become a part of the Alliance of their own accord, without fear."

"I banish fear from their lives. They are no longer subject to the whims of other nations."

"No, they're subject to *your* whims."

"The citizens of the Alliance are not my subjects, they are my brothers—"

"Why haven't you joined the international community? There are buyers for your riches—oil, iron, sheep, grain. You would get hard currency, high technology, maybe even tourism in return."

Batu put his hands on his hips. "So, you want to civilize us! Who would the newspeople talk about if the TAA got fat and lazy like Europe or China? Or like your country. Besides, I've not been waiting to join the international community, but for the international community to join us."

"The rest of the world has reached out to you several times before—"

"Yes, as a parent chastising an errant child."

Marsh tried not to smile. Batu, for all his bravado, clearly wanted his due as a major player. He wanted to sit at the big folks' table.

"As I said," Marsh replied, "you are in a position now to exhibit strength not by what you do but by what you are wise enough not to do. No one disputes your power. But a vicious spectacle like the one in Georgia tells me you're not a responsible custodian of that power."

Batu resumed pacing without taking his eyes from the President, and Marsh stared back. As much as Batu wanted to keep his new relationship cordial—it was too early in the game to see how Marsh would react if angered, challenged, or defied—Marsh's contemptuous attitude infuriated him.

"No man tells me how to govern—" he began.

"This isn't about governing, and you know it. It's about the kind of savage behavior the civilized world simply will not tolerate."

"There it is . . . what it has always been! We're nothing but barbarians to you in the West!"

"I'm talking about *your* actions, not disparaging your race or culture. Are you not man enough to take responsibility for what you've done?"

Batu looked away for a moment. He'd expected the language of diplomacy from Marsh, some deference to his being the leader of three hundred million people. He didn't expect a scolding. He pressed his palms together as if performing a yoga exercise, then looked back at the VS screen.

"You want something from me, President Marsh. Tell me what it is. If it is within my ability to grant it to you, and if it does not compromise the Trans-Altaic Alliance in any way, it shall be yours."

Marsh walked closer to the VS screen. "It *is* within your power, and yours alone. I want a simple guarantee, right now, that you will not attempt to expand your empire another square foot by violent means. We cannot extend a hand if you mistake our friendship for weakness. You're right to think we don't want a fight; you're wrong to think we'd ever back down from one."

"I will relate this discussion to my counselors. I depend on their wisdom, and must not make any definitive statements without consulting them."

"That's not good enough. You're the Supreme Leader of the TAA. Surely you can make such an assurance on your own. It's simple: either you plan more actions like that in Georgia, or you don't. Which is it?"

"You ask much for a man who could not get a single resolution through the U.N. condemning my so-called illegal actions."

"I don't care what the U.N. did or did not do. Nor do I care about NATO, our international allies, or even public opinion. This is between you and me, and I hope I make myself clear: I will not stand for any further aggression."

"This has been a very informative discussion," Batu said, barely containing his anger and indignation. "I will respond—but in my own time. Now, there is something you can do for me."

"Yes?"

"Please express to Mrs. Marsh the great admiration I have for her. My wives and I have seen her on television and she appears to be an extraordinary person."

Marsh nodded. As a master politician, he appreciated Batu's smooth exit from the conversation.

"I'll tell her you said so."

After the meeting, Batu and Chu'tsai sat on sheepskin mats in front of a small campfire outside the *ger*. Twilight was fast fading into darkness and the air became chilly. Chu'tsai poured two bowls of *koumiss*, a pungent, bitter, alcoholic beverage made from fermented mare's milk. Sullen, Batu stared into the fire.

"Marsh is worse than expected—arrogant and condescending! He spent the entire conversation intent upon angering and insulting me!"

"I am not surprised, given what we know about him. He can threaten all he wants, but his allies won't back him up, and in his own country the public doesn't care. His hostility is irrelevant, because he cannot act upon it."

"I am not so sure about that," Batu replied.

"Do you think we should slow our plans?"

"No! Marsh does not dictate my schedule! The elements instruct us to continue quickly, as do my instincts. Nothing will change that."

"I don't know, Batu. You always said not to push the Americans. Given what we've learned, maybe patience is the wiser course."

Batu drained his bowl of *koumiss* in one gulp.

"You let me worry about how to handle Marsh."

On the other side of the planet, President Marsh powered off the VS screen, then opened the credenza below the control panel and tapped the Stop button on one of a pair of mini-DV—digital video—VCRs inside it. Despite the agreement prohibiting the use of videotape during the VS meetings, he believed in the historical significance of his conversations with Batu and would not let a soon-forgotten arrangement prevent him from documenting them for future generations. After locking the credenza and pocketing the key, he opened the VS Room door. Levinson, Vice President Taylor, and Secretary of Defense Woodruff came in, and Marsh grinned at them.

"I'm getting the impression it went well," Taylor said, smiling back. He'd been nervous about the VS meeting—even for someone as politically skilled as Marsh, opening a constructive dialogue with the unpredictable Batu Khan would be challenging.

"Yes, quite well," Marsh replied. "I think we understand each other."

"That's terrific! When can we get our liaison teams started?" One of the key goals of the VS meeting had been getting Batu to agree to an open-ended series of meetings between their respective diplomats.

"We'll deal with that next time, Adam. Batu needs to get back to me on something else first."

"I don't understand."

"He thought the U.N.'s lack of resolve cut me off at the knees, so I set him straight. I demanded his personal assurance, man to man, of no further aggression. You should've seen him backpedaling. Goddamn dictator acting like he couldn't make a decision without a committee of advisers."

Taylor, Woodruff, and Levinson looked at one another. They hadn't expected the President to go beyond a cordial exchange, a noncombative expression of U.S. displeasure with the Georgian coup, and its intention to resolve the issue by diplomatic means.

"Did you get any assurances from him?" Woodruff asked.

"No, he wouldn't be pinned down."

"It must've been a strange conversation for him. I doubt he gets many direct challenges since becoming Khan," Taylor said.

"I'm optimistic," Levinson said. "Maybe the hard line headed off any other plans he may have."

"It won't be that easy," Marsh replied. "I think he has every intention of more aggression. But at least he knows there'll be consequences next time."

Marsh crossed into the private residence area of the White House and went into his bedroom. Amy lay propped up in bed, a book resting on her chest, waiting up for him, and he told her how far he'd taken the conversation in the VS meeting.

"It's still short of where I wanted to be. No matter how much I threaten against further action, Georgia's still a done deal for him. I don't know who I'm more angry at: Batu Khan, for killing the Gorovich family and overrunning their country, or the folks on our side for not caring."

Amy nodded. "You're absolutely right to draw the line, but chances are you'll be out there entirely on your own."

Marsh sat on the edge of the bed to pull his shoes off. Catching a glimpse of his reflection in the mirror across the room, he suddenly hurled his shoe at it, shattering the glass. Amy stared at him, startled and very surprised, and two Secret Service agents burst into the room.

"Everything's fine!" the President said, his voice sharp with anger.

The agents glanced at the broken glass on the carpet, at one another, then retreated. Marsh composed himself and looked over at his wife, instantly embarrassed.

"Christ, I'm sorry. I've been a raw nerve lately."

"Look, Burt, you can handle *ten* petty tyrants like Batu. If it comes to challenging the TAA militarily, you'll just have to remind people of what it means not to stop someone like him before it's too late. There are plenty of past examples, that's for sure. In the meantime, you can't let him distract you from all the good things still to accomplish in this presidency."

Eleven

A shaman's acolyte, barely out of his teens, robed in white silks, head shaved, placed a satin mat in front of Batu Khan. Batu knelt on it, bowed his head, and closed his eyes. Chu'tsai knelt on another mat facing Batu, and tossed several bleached sheep's bones from a woven basket onto the floodlit macadam between them. The young acolyte and five others stood in a tight circle around the two kneeling men, a strange sight indeed in the middle of a military airfield, outside the Georgian city of Sokhumi on the coast of the Black Sea. As the six acolytes and Batu softly chanted in unison, Chu'tsai intently studied the positions of the bones, particularly how the smaller ones had fallen in relation to the largest.

Whenever embarking on a great adventure, Batu sought assurance from his shaman that his actions would be in harmony with the Koeke Moengke Tengri—the Eternal Blue Heaven. His faith had no father figure or personal God endowed with human characteristics as did monotheistic religions. Batu believed in destiny, in a Universe governed by an omnipresent, all-pervading reality. Countless lesser and greater spirits filled the Universe, each with its own area of jurisdiction, but all connected and interdependent. All things living and dead—a man, an animal, a lake, a forest, a river, a mountain, Earth herself—had energy and were ruled by spirits. The All, or the Ultimate Cosmos of the Koeke Moengke Tengri, had a ruling spirit, too. The interconnection between the smallest and the mightiest forces was the key to the shaman's power. By understanding the state of harmony of the smallest spirit, such as a slain sheep's, as discerned through the study of its bones, Chu'tsai could determine Batu's state of harmony in relation to the whole Universe. The

Shaman's art derived limitless understanding from careful observation of the smallest phenomenon because every tiny facet of information invested him, simultaneously, with all knowledge.

Batu felt humbled and privileged to have such intimate contact with the essence of life itself, and he gave its guidance great import. Chu'tsai sat up and the acolytes stopped chanting. Batu opened his eyes and looked at his friend expectantly. Chu'tsai grinned.

"Let's rock!"

Batu's command craft, a modified Chinese-built IL-7 the size of a Boeing 707, took off from the Sokhumi airfield at one twenty-five A.M. ETA to optimal position: ninety minutes. Following it, dozens of other aircraft took wing from commercial airports, military bases, and small airfields across the western part of the Trans-Altaic Alliance.

Another solemn ceremony took place on each aircraft. Chu'tsai's acolytes walked along the ranks of Batu's Khaldun Elite. As the Khaldun kneeled before them, they placed on each warrior's tongue a postage-stamp-sized piece of rice paper treated with a colorless drop of liquid. The Khaldun then sat cross-legged, quiet and contemplative, finding peace with the Eternal Blue Heaven. Within twenty minutes, and for the next twelve hours, their heightened physical and spiritual state would make them the most formidable fighters who'd ever lived.

Batu had ordered all commercial flights quietly suspended for the night in order to allow his aircraft to take off without an undue increase in air traffic emanating from the TAA. Batu knew of the American surveillance satellites monitoring his empire, and he'd become quite adept at finding ways to accomplish his goals right under their unblinking eyes.

His precautions bought about an hour of anonymity, then a routine download of infrared-photographic surveillance from a U.S. satellite revealed to the National Security Agency an unusual number of aircraft converging onto parallel headings over the Black Sea. Over the next thirty minutes the raw data worked its way through various channels as it was analyzed and interpreted, distilled into usable intelligence, and then acted upon in a command decision to warn the Ukrainian military, via their NATO counterparts, of the approaching aircraft. By then, however, long-range radar technicians in a tower above a huge Russian/Ukrainian naval base in Sevastopol at the tip of the Crimean peninsula spotted the intruders. Moments later, air traffic controllers for the Borispil International Airport in Kiev saw them, as did the over-the-horizon backscatter radars in Komsomolsk and in the Carpathian Mountains near Mukachevo. Unlike the orbiting U.S. satellite, however, the ground-based stations picked up only forty percent of the incoming aircraft. Fifteen groups of attack helicopter teams—each team consisting of six helicopters—were following on the same vectors as the fixed-wing craft, but below the sight of local radar. The copters had been modified by removing heavy armoring and installing additional fuel tanks to extend their range from 400 to 650 miles, and Batu had timed their approach so all aircraft would reach their targets simultaneously.

The aircraft were part of Batu's air force, which he inherited from the former Soviet Republics now part of the TAA. His scientists and engineers were working feverishly to replace it—in secret facilities all over the empire they were constructing a whole new generation of aircraft and weaponry. Gaining the knowledge to build such things, thanks to operations such as the one in Woomera, were Batu's greatest tactical success to date.

When Batu's command craft entered Ukrainian airspace he emerged from his private compartment, an exact duplicate of the interior of his *ger* and holding all its contents. Because everything seemed to be falling into place, he felt energized, imbued with the confidence that destiny guided him. The world belonged to the clever and the daring. The twentieth century had been the American century; the twenty-first would be his. He walked aft, where fourteen of his best battle-command and radar-surveillance techs manned the high-resolution Tactical Information Terminals displaying data gathered by interconnected technologies similar to the American AWACS and J-STARS tactical radar systems. One terminal took in the entire country, showing the position and velocity of all aircraft, friend or foe. Another identified the positions of all TAA ground-based vehicles, as well as unfriendly ground equipment, such as tanks, light armor, and mobile missile launchers. Other terminals were city-specific. Every target had been carefully chosen, color-coded in red, and would turn green when secured. Other locations, coded yellow, were determined to be off-limits. Not because of any concern for civilian casualties. Rather, Batu forbade his attack team to destroy any place he determined to be of historical or cultural significance. He took great pains to show the world he was not a barbarian. He would not lay cities to whole-sale waste, as the first Batu had done. He came as a liberator, to free the populace from the shortsightedness of their petty rulers, not as a destroyer of civilizations and the artistic expressions that define and celebrate them.

Batu saw himself as unique among world leaders. Unlike Burton Marsh, he commanded his military personally, intimately, from the front of his forces, not thousands of miles away. To him the other leaders, smug in the belief of their own invulnerability, were contemptuous cowards. Batu also had practical reasons for flying in the command craft himself. It eliminated the need for a ground-to-air communication link—the one, in his words, from the brain to the eyes. The only links were to his attack forces: the brain to the hands. He also wanted to own the high ground, literally and figuratively. He loved to tell the story about Genghis, who never entered a battle without being able to assess the battlefield from a hill or other high position. When unexpectedly engaging an enemy army on a vast, flat plain, he ordered a division of his men to lie atop one another to make a human mound. Five thousand men suffocated to fulfill this command; then Genghis rode his horse atop their bodies and from there directed his army to a glorious victory.

As the alarm went out to the Ukraine's air defense systems, Batu ordered his penetrators to fire their laser-guided air-to-surface missiles at the radar installations. Separate bombers hit each target twice, to ensure a one hundred percent kill. In less than ten minutes, radar coverage went dark at the perimeter of the country and then in its interior. Batu timed everything so the penetrators responsible for the southerly cities—Balakleya, Feodosiya, and Mykolayiv—reached their targets simultaneously with their counterparts assigned to the northern cities of Irsha and the capital, Kiev. Excited, Batu rushed from terminal to terminal, conducting the attack like a chess master playing a dozen games at once. The hard targets flashed red on the screens: command buildings and officers' quarters on military bases; police and militia headquarters in the cities; branch offices of the Ministry of Justice; and antiaircraft installations protecting the Black Sea Fleet in Sevastopol.

The sleeping population awoke to the scream of jets and missiles finding their marks. Explosions shattered all windows within a quarter mile of the impact points, and their deep rumblings shook the ground for miles beyond. Some people huddled in their homes and apartments, terrified and confused. Others, trying to escape the deafening concussions and flying glass and debris, ran haphazardly into the streets. Ukrainian Army personnel sleeping in their ratty, uncomfortable barracks were deafened by missiles destroying the command and control buildings around them. Above, in his command craft, Batu Khan raised a clenched fist or clapped his hands as on the various screens red targets flashed green, indicating success.

Precision bombing had come a long way since the Coalition bombing of Baghdad. In the hilly, architecturally beautiful capital city of Kiev, the M-shaped Council of Ministers building on Kirova Vulytsya sat just southeast of the Museum of Ukrainian Art. Batu spoke into a headset, urging his pilots to be careful, to approach from the northwest, so the angle and momentum of their missiles would not cause any residual damage to the museum. Five missiles, precision placed at each corner of the M, left nothing of the building but its steel skeleton. The pilots responsible for destroying the huge, square Central Committee building on Ordzhonikidze Vulytsya attacked from the south, to spare the Great Patriotic War Museum and the Komsomol Children's Theatre. Several missiles fired through the Committee building's roof obliterated its interior, leaving nothing but fragments of its redbrick exterior still standing. As they flew off, Batu effusively congratulated his pilots on their skill.

He turned his attention to the next target: the Mariinsky Palace in Kiev, home to the president. Grass and tree-lined walkways surrounded it in the Central Recreation Park next to the river. Inside, President Tsikora frantically dialed the phone, trying to reach his defense minister. Above, in a whisper, Batu gave the order to destroy the palace. From three penetrators came a salvo of high-explosive bombs, obliterating it, leaving in its place a crater thirty feet deep. In that instance, Batu rationalized that the necessity of a preemptive strike on its occupants outweighed the palace's historical significance.

Batu ordered the bombing stopped, and paused for a moment to thank the Eternal Blue Heaven for his success thus far. He knelt in supplication, eyes closed, hands clasped together and held against his forehead. Then, with Phase One complete, the TAA penetrators banked sharply away and disappeared into the night. For a moment, an eerie silence fell over the Ukraine. Surviving members of the military, national militia, and municipal police forces rushed to their respective headquarters.

Most had been damaged heavily or destroyed completely. Communications were completely severed. No one knew how to reach any of the 450-member Supreme Council, so it fell to the individual soldier, airman, or policeman to try to restore order and equip himself to resist any further aggression.

Batu, intoxicated with the thrill of battle, ordered the commencement of Phase Two. It came in low, from the south, felt in the gut before it was heard, heard before it was seen. Six black attack helicopters per city or military base, flying in teams of two, shoulder to shoulder, thirty feet off the ground. Air-to-ground missiles flamed off the sides of the copters and sizzled through the air like huge fireworks. They slammed into the rows of tanks and other armored vehicles at the Army base just east of the Dnieper River, blasting them apart in a succession of bright yellow fireballs and deafening explosions. The copters then crossed the river to the western part of Kiev and cruised slowly up the main thoroughfares—the wide Tarasa Shevchenka Bul'var, the Lenina Vulytsya. Bursts of machine-gun fire herded civilians inside the buildings and contained soldiers at their bases.

With Kiev falling to his forces exactly as planned, Batu turned his attention to Sevastopol in the south. Here he anticipated resistance from the Russian Black Sea Fleet and the Ukrainian Navy, both stationed at Sevastopolska Bay and its miles of military facilities. The Russians alone had 25,000 personnel and 100 combat and support ships in Sevastopol, their continued occupancy after the breakup of the USSR the result of a long and contentious negotiation with the Ukrainians.

The ports across from the Russians housed about half of the Ukrainian Navy—70 of the 150 ships in their Navy, along with a 2,000-man Marine brigade, 50 tanks, 200 armored vehicles, and 70 artillery pieces. The remainder of their forces were in Kerch, also on the Crimean Peninsula, and in Odessa and Ochakov, farther north. Batu, however, let his generals direct his attacks there, while he focused his personal attention on the key locations, Sevastopol and Kiev.

The surprised Russian night crew manning the Black Sea Fleet in Sevastopol could mount only a semblance of a defense—some antiaircraft fire from a few of the battleships, cruisers, and submarines lying at port. Batu reminded his pilots not to fire on the ships. They were to become the foundation of the Trans-Altaic Alliance's Navy. Bad enough the Russians and Ukrainians had let their nearly obsolete ships go to rust for lack of maintenance; Batu wasn't about to make it worse by blasting holes in them. The TAA copters agilely dodged antiaircraft fire and moved into position over the Russian and Ukrainian Marine barracks.

Then Batu ordered Phase Three to begin. Immense, propeller-driven cargo aircraft appeared over the cities and the ports, their engines droning ominously in the warm night air. Their tail hatches yawned open. Falling from each plane, at precise intervals, dozens of streamlined, boxcar-sized objects floated to earth suspended from rectangular parachutes. The objects were Batu's Incursion Tubes (ITs). They had four oversized, five-foot wheels on either side, heavily shock absorbed. A pilot sat in a windowed compartment in the front of each Tube, using levers to angle the chutes and guide it to a precise landing. The ITs came to rest all over Kiev's central city: on the grounds of the Fomin Botanical Garden; in the center of the Bike Track; within the circular landmark of the Ploshcha Kalinina, and in the middle of the business district along the Khreshchatyk Vulytsya. Terrified citizens watched the ITs as if they'd come from another planet. Tailgates opened on the ITs and from each burst six Khaldun Horsemen, who hit the ground at a full gallop. They wore brightly colored decorated silks and armored headgear. Their horses—perfectly trained Arabians—were also cloaked from shoulder to feet. Four layers of bulletproof Kevlar lined the coverings on men and horses.

Batu himself had come up with the idea of armored horsemen and Incursion Tubes and insisted they be deployed, despite their impracticality and over the protests of Chu'tsai and his generals. To him they were the very symbol of his culture. He believed a modern, well-trained warfighter on horseback, armed with automatic weaponry and a broadsword, to be a potent force, especially against civilians. Of course, it didn't hurt that his beloved Khaldun could now be imbued with extra powers. They were more mobile than motorized infantry in urban assaults or on rough terrain and much more formidable in terms of psychological impact—didn't everyone in the Eastern Hemisphere have a deep, elemental fear of the mounted Mongol warrior? Also, he'd told Chu'tsai, laughing, when stranded in the wilderness or in hostile territory, men cannot eat their jeeps.

The Khaldun Horsemen spread out to their predetermined assignments. They took control of the offices of television and radio stations, utility and telephone companies, the post office, newspapers, police stations, the highways coming into the cities, the train station, the three main transfer stations for the metro line: Zoloti Vorota, Palats Sportu/Ploscha L'va Tolstoho, and Maidan Nezalezhnosti. Anyone who tried to stop them, like a few brave officers at police headquarters, were either shot with an AK-74U machine gun or cut clean in half with a scimitar.

The TAA invasion did not come wholly unexpected by the citizens of Kiev. Their city had once before been attacked by a Batu Khan—Genghis's grandson, leader of the Golden Horde, in 1240. He'd burned it to the ground. Everyone who could not escape the advancing Horde had been killed on the spot. That violation remained vivid in their cultural memory, ranking with the years of Russian domination, Stalin's forced collectivization in the 1930s, and the Nazi occupation. The new Batu's arrival struck such fear into the populace that the TAA invaders had to control a hysterical exodus rather than fight any manner of organized opposition.

More ITs landed, each with thirty Khaldun Commandos aboard. Like their mounted counterparts, the Commandos wore brightly decorated silks over Kevlar. Batu ordered them to seal off the Russian barracks in Sevastopol and storm the ships. They could kill the small crews aboard the ships if necessary, but those in the barracks were only to be detained. Batu planned to return the 25,000 Russian soldiers unharmed. Unlike his ancient namesake, whose Golden Horde won with a combination of brutality and sheer numbers, Batu believed to kill a snake one need only cut off its head with a swift blow. Indeed, his forces' strength and fury simply overwhelmed their horrified adversaries. Before the night ended, a few dozen Khaldun had killed hundreds of Russians and Ukrainians and taken thousands prisoner.

Dawn approached when Batu's command craft landed at the Borispil International Airport. His Khaldun Elite set up his *ger* within a grove of trees on the grounds of Kiev's most celebrated historic site, the Kiev-Pechers'kyy, or Monastery of the Caves. Founded in 1051, it covered seventy-five acres, comprised of numerous churches, cathedrals, bell towers, and monastic cells. Batu's *ger*, his personal staff, and his wives had been flown in, along with his Arabian, Mika. Batu rode to the

Golden Gate, a medieval church built on the original city wall, and, exactly as he'd planned, sat alone watching the sun rise on the city. Afterward, he took a satellite call from Chu'tsai in Sevastopol. So excited he could barely talk, Chu'tsai confirmed the entire port had been secured. Batu ordered him to personally oversee the loading of all Russian military personnel onto two of the most dilapidated ships, for transport to the Russian port of Novorossiysk on the eastern coast of the Black Sea. Returning to the monastery grounds, Batu made love to his wives. Surely after such a great victory we'll produce a strong and worthy heir, he told them.

Taking Sevastopol, Batu made military history. During the Crimean War, Russian forces in that city had withstood an eleven-month siege by the combined armies of Great Britain, France, Turkey, and Sardinia. In World War II, it fell to the mighty German war machine only after an offensive of 250 days. The invading forces of the Trans-Altaic Alliance, under Batu's command, took it in two hours and thirty minutes.

Twelve

"**T**he President of the United States."

Curt Levinson signaled the start cue to President Marsh, who sat at his desk in the Oval Office, facing a television camera and a battery of lights. Amy Marsh sat behind the camera in his direct line of vision, as she always did when he addressed the nation, so he could pretend he was speaking only to her. She smiled and mouthed "I love you."

"Good evening. A few hours ago, armed forces of the Trans-Altaic Alliance staged an illegal, brutal, and unprovoked attack on the free Republic of the Ukraine. The invaders took total control of the country's civilian authority, its military, and communications infrastructure. Although preliminary intelligence suggests there were minimal casualties, Batu's bombers killed President Tsikora when destroying his residence, and the whereabouts of the other top members of the government are unknown. No American citizens appear to have been harmed, and our ambassador and his staff were permitted to leave the country.

"Since the end of the Cold War, there have been numerous acts of aggression, cruelty, territorial squabbles, ethnic cleansing, and outright wars. Iraq, Central Africa, Kosovo—the list goes on. Just days ago TAA forces staged a brutal and illegal takeover in the Republic of Georgia. We Americans read of these atrocities; we see them on the news. They have become so commonplace that the human suffering they cause barely registers with us. Still, at times, when our national interests or concern for human rights has warranted it, we've sent American forces beyond the safety of our own borders. There is never unanimous agreement among the policymakers or the people as to whether we should take such action. Its cost is always measured, ultimately, in blood. The dearest currency of all.

"For this reason, it is my duty to explain why the events of the last few hours may compel us to answer those events. Why I might soon have to ask you, or your son or daughter, to risk and perhaps even sacrifice your life for a nation and a people most of you know little about.

"At the height of the Cold War, many of the intercontinental ballistic missiles pointed at this country and our allies were located in the Ukraine. Then, in 1991, the Soviet Empire collapsed and the Ukraine became a free and independent country. But with all those weapons still based within her, she also became the third-largest nuclear power in the world.

"The men elected to run the new, free Ukraine were wiser than most. They understood history. They did not want the responsibility of nuclear weapons on their soil. They knew how easy it would be for them to fall into the wrong hands. Representatives of the United States and Russia offered to exchange the missiles and warheads for power generator fuel, and for hard currency. The missiles would be removed and destroyed under international supervision.

"To this end, the Ukraine, Russia, and the United States signed the Tripartite Agreement in January 1994. Soon after, the Ukrainians began removing their weapons of mass destruction: 1,300 warheads for intercontinental ballistic missiles; over 600 cruise missile warheads; 176 silos for strategic nuclear weapons. By 1998, all had verifiably been destroyed and the world became a safer place.

"In order for this unprecedented disarmament to occur, we guaranteed something beyond fuel and money: the Ukrainians' security. They held up their part of the bargain and destroyed their nuclear weapons. Had they not, Batu Khan would currently be in possession of a terrifying power. Now it is time to hold up ours.

"Batu Khan and I spoke for the first time, face-to-face, via Virtual Summit only three days ago. I believed then we had laid the groundwork for a constructive dialogue. I can only presume he mistook America's willingness to engage in conversation as weakness. He seems to have forgotten those many times in which, in the words of Theodore Roosevelt, this country had its national character tried with conflict and found worthy. America will always pass the acid test of its commitment to freedom.

"Therefore, all presence, military or otherwise, of the Trans-Altaic

Alliance within the sovereign territory of the Ukraine must be removed by one minute after twelve A.M., Greenwich Mean time, Tuesday, August twelfth—exactly eight weeks from today. In addition, the TAA-controlled dictator in Georgia, Field Marshal Stavros Kirminian, must resign. Free elections, under international supervision, will then be held to choose a new leader for that country, and to decide whether the people of Georgia actually wish to remain part of the TAA. If these conditions are not met on or before the deadline, I shall direct the United States military to effect these demands with the full force at their command.

"Thank you, God bless you, and good night."

After the red light atop the television camera went off, Marsh removed his jacket. He'd been broiling under the hot lights, and his TV makeup was sticky and uncomfortable. Levinson shook his hand and the two old friends looked at each other, the momentousness of the speech weighing upon them.

"Are you available for phone calls, sir?" Levinson asked. "There'll be a bunch of them."

"They can wait until tomorrow morning. Goodnight, Curt."

Amy gave Marsh a moistened towel, and he wiped his makeup off as they walked back to the residential wing. Since he'd been with his staff the entire time since news of Batu's invasion reached them, Marsh had barely a chance to discuss the crisis with Amy.

"Phone calls?" she asked.

"From our allies. I set down the demand for TAA withdrawal without consulting them."

The First Lady was shocked. Not only by the unprecedented nature of such a unilateral move, but also because he hadn't first told her, his closest adviser.

"You didn't tell the U.N. or NATO?"

"Ambassador Drake informed Secretary General Ibrahim of my intentions ten minutes before the speech." Marsh smiled at his wife's consternation. "The cabinet didn't like it either. They thought I should let the U.N. vote a few resolutions before I set a hard date, and they really wanted me to issue the ultimatum in the name of the United Nations or NATO as opposed to the United States."

By the time they got to their bedroom, the TV talking heads were in a frenzy of commentary and debate: first the invasion, then President Marsh's immediate and unexpected response to it. The pundits were particularly skeptical that the military could mount an offensive in only eight weeks, less than half the time it took to prepare for the war against Iraq or even the airstrikes against the Serbs. Many questioned Marsh's wisdom in committing U.S. forces without a clear-cut national security or humanitarian purpose to liberate a couple of countries most Americans couldn't locate on a map. Others, however, believed that Batu ultimately intended to expand into Europe and perhaps beyond. The consequences of such violence would trigger what had seemed all but impossible anymore: at best, a devastating disruption of the global economy; at worst, another world war.

"I have several reasons for proceeding like this," Marsh said to Amy. "I think Batu Khan got the balls for this latest attack because of the U.N.'s inaction after Georgia. By taking them and NATO out of the equation, it tells him it's just between the two of us. He knew the U.N. limited my options and NATO would decide everything by committee, so he rushed into the Ukraine to take advantage of those weaknesses. But he's not the only one in a hurry: The more time the American public has to think about it, the greater chance their support will wither to nothing. There's also a strong possibility he could overrun other countries in the meantime, creating a multifront offensive beyond our capabilities."

"You don't feel waiting a day or two, a week, would've been more prudent?"

"No. I wanted my response to be immediate and definitive, in part to throw him off balance."

Marsh sat on the bed next to Amy, and she rested her head on her husband's shoulder. He wanted to tell her how much he personally disliked Batu Khan, how nightmares of Batu's men killing the Georgian president's children still haunted him. But he couldn't admit to anyone, even his wife, that his decision was personal as well as geopolitical.

"What's the back-channel reaction from Congress?" Amy asked.

"Muted, unlike all their chest-pounding for the cameras. They know I'll proceed without them. They'll make the usual noise about the War Powers Act, and I'll remind them that every president since Gerald Ford has ignored it. My biggest danger is losing public sentiment, especially when they realize this will be a ground war and not just air strikes. Without public support to protect me, Congress could cut off funds to the military to stop the deployment, even impeach me. But if I had to back down from my threat to Batu I'd be worthless in office anyway."

Amy nodded. "I'll tell you what maddens me: prevailing won't win any prizes. It only reinstates the status quo. Reining in that jerk will only make people think he posed no threat to begin with."

"There'll be a thousand reasons not to stay the course, Amy. It could cost us everything we've been trying to accomplish."

"You didn't want this job 'cause it's easy, Burt. Every president who ever mattered had a defining moment, when he chose to do what's right, almost always in the face of powerful opposition and public disapproval. The poll-takers weren't elected to lead this nation, you were."

Marsh put his arms around his wife. Although he sorely wanted the support of the people and the Congress, ultimately, the approval of only one person mattered, and he'd just received it.

"There's one other issue," he told her. "Apparently, it took only a handful of Batu's Khaldun to conduct the attack. Same as in Georgia: A few hundred men seized control of an entire country. We have reports of individual Khaldun killing dozens of Ukrainians at a time."

"Do you think it's true?"

"It isn't the first time we've heard such rumors. The Pentagon's telling the media the stories are grossly exaggerated, but in private they're extremely concerned."

One hundred and fifty Khaldun Elite and Horsemen stood on the beautiful Kiev-Pechers'kyy monastery grounds. None showed the least indication of fatigue after the prior night's battle and all had a small smile on their faces. Accompanied by two of his generals and several of his shaman's acolytes, Batu Khan walked along their ranks, his long blond hair and yellow *shalwar qamiz* radiant in the midday sun. He personally pinned a Service to Khan and Empire medal on each of the Khaldun's chests.

Chu'tsai sat watching beneath a nearby shade tree, then crossed to Batu when the ceremony came to a close. The others dispersed and Batu's poised demeanor fell away. He unbuckled his ceremonial sword scabbard and threw it to the ground.

"I'd like to see Marsh threatening us if we had a few hundred warheads pointing at him, like the Chinese and Russians do!"

"I just don't see it happening, Batu. Even if he deploys troops over here, his people won't let him start a war."

"I can't count on that. He's smart—that's why he laid out such a short deadline. He wants to move while he can. The public and Congress will barely have a chance to react."

Batu sat on a rock and ran his fingers through his hair. "Pull our forces from the Pakistan border. That offensive is now on hold until we rid ourselves of the American problem. Move the men to the new territories in case we need them."

" 'In case'? You've been saying war was inevitable."

"In Marsh's mind it is. That is why it's up to us to prevent it from happening."

Before Chu'tsai could reply, Batu stood up, his heart filled with pride, as a magnificent column of Khaldun Horsemen galloped by, their right arms swinging low alongside their saddles in deference to their khan.

Wilder was on a commercial flight to Santa Rosa, reading Laura's book about the Mongols, when the President made his speech. He knew what Marsh's hard deadline meant. War. A radical change in the climate and posture of every American military base on the planet, with a million details to attend to. The OSI, especially the Washington Field Office, would take primary lead in protecting the safety and security of the Air Force bases, identifying and assessing threats to commanders and personnel, and managing offensive and defensive activities to detect, counter, and destroy any hostile intelligence services or terrorist groups that might target them.

A message awaited him when he arrived at his hotel room. Cursing Batu's timing, Wilder returned Brent's call.

"Sorry Bucko," Brent said, "you gotta book a return flight for tomorrow morning. It's pretty intense around here. Colonel Chang is moving us to Threatcon Alpha."

"I just need a couple of days—"

"Can't do it. We got a new set of priorities all of a sudden."

"Look, it'll take the base and OSI brass at least twenty-hour hours to coordinate a duty roster. I'm ten hours away from talking to the perp. Give me one day."

Brent was silent for a moment.

"All right, but that's the best I can do. You heard the man tonight. The clock's ticking down to a major offensive."

Wilder had major doubts about the President's timing. The kind of force needed to pry Batu Khan out of Georgia and the Ukraine would take several months to muster, if at all, given the U.S. military's downsizing.

"Not in eight weeks," he said.

"Absolutely in eight weeks. We'll talk about it when you get back."

Brent obviously knew something. Something they couldn't discuss over an unsecured line; something pretty amazing if the military indeed expected to prevail over Batu's massive war machine in so short a time. The Pentagon, Wilder thought, must have one hell of an ace up its sleeve.

Thirteen

Wilder woke from a fitful sleep at four A.M. and turned on the light, surprised for a moment to find himself in the La Rose Hotel. No sense trying to go back to sleep, he was still on Washington time, so he showered and drank a cup of coffee from the small machine on the bathroom counter. While dressing, he turned on the TV. Normally, he didn't watch much television, and he had stopped taking the paper years ago. He subscribed instead to the theory that if anything really important happened, he'd hear about it. Case in point: President Marsh's speech, which had found him at 37,000 feet. Surfing the early-morning news shows, he spotted a familiar face on the Fox News Channel: Laura Bishop.

During a press briefing after the President's speech, Curt Levinson had mentioned her visit to the White House, so overnight she became a must-have guest. After a long night of her answering machine picking up call after call, Laura had finally decided to contact Levinson to ask if it were okay to talk about her conversation with the President. She only wanted to relate the broad details so everyone would leave her alone. Levinson told her to speak freely, but to do so as if Batu was listening to her every word. When Wilder caught her appearance, she was sitting on a discussion panel. It seemed as though the moderator judged which guest won an argument by who spoke the loudest.

"Laura, give us your impression of the President's state of mind. For instance, do you think he'd been contemplating action against Batu Khan before the invasion of the Ukraine?"

The other guests grew uncharacteristically quiet.

"I have no idea," she began. "The President knows Batu is a student of history, which cannot help but shape one's character and beliefs. Mr. Marsh simply wanted to discuss history with me the way Batu sees it, because it's certain to be a different perspective than an American would have. Now that I hear they'd had a VS meeting soon after that, I believe he wanted to get a sense of the man underneath all the myth and hyperbole."

"What did you tell him about how Batu sees history, and how it might affect what he'd do?"

There were a lot of people who would've loved to say that in a private discussion with the President of the United States they predicted Batu's continued aggression before it happened. Not Laura.

"That's beyond what I'm comfortable discussing. I'm sorry."

Good for you, Wilder thought. The other guests on the panel all jumped in at once, pontificating as if they'd been the ones at the White House instead of her. Wilder decided to call her when he got back to Washington. He told himself it would be an offer to talk further about her new book, to make up for being such a pain in the ass about it when they'd first met. But he stuck the little mental card noting "call Laura" in the Personal file in his brain, not the Business file.

At eight A.M. Wilder drove a rented Toyota to the Santa Rosa Police Department. Santa Rosa, a small town grown up, had the typical California city-sprawl—outward as opposed to upward growth. Wilder appreciated the perfect weather—warm, dry, with a gentle breeze. Through no accident did Mediterranean grapes flourish in Napa and Sonoma Counties.

The SRPD detective who'd been handling the case, Nathan Chianta, definitely had that Italian-cop-macho thing going, but nothing had prepared him for dealing with "Lawnmower Man," as the local press dubbed the killer. Chianta had been the first detective to arrive at the crime scene. He tried to be glib about it now, but Wilder could tell it really spooked him.

". . . So there's the fuckin' perp, trimming his goddamn hedges," Chianta said. "Totally oblivious to the fact half the victim's body is gettin' turned into Cobb salad under his ride-on mower. I never saw so much fuckin' blood. Soaking through the canvas trimming bag, running down the slope of the lawn. Puddles collecting on the sidewalk and road. Man, I called for backup before I even got outta my cruiser.

"We walk up—five of us. Perp looks up from his yard work, no fuckin' idea why we're there. Chatting us up . . . I swear, offers us some iced tea. Thank God he put the clippers down. I tell him, look, you gotta come with us, and he turns on a dime. Lets out this fuckin' animal howl and rushes us. I try to get him in a choke hold with my baton; perp snaps it in half. Then he shoves a piece of it through my buddy's gut, clean through, out his back. Rest of us, we pile on. Beating he got shoulda killed him. Next day, we're all in the fuckin' hospital, he's barely got a bruise. We finally get him down, cuff him, and he tears the chain on the cuffs in two. Had to use two pairs of cuffs, Taser, and a whole damn can of Mace to restrain him. We got two officers still in intensive care. One with a broken back."

It amazed Wilder how many of the details reminded him of Gail.

"We got the twisted fuck warehoused at a county drug and alcohol hospital. Rubber room, all that. Family's gonna plead insanity—big surprise—and they want to move him to a private loony bin. But the judge won't okay nothin' till after the hearing."

"Any chance of me talking to him?"

"I figured you'd want to. His wife's been amazing during all this. I told her why you were here and she called the center, gave her permission for you to go over. She's hoping you might figure something out, since you already had some experience with this wacky shit."

"Not much. Our perp was killed before we could talk to her."

"Lucky you."

Wilder let the comment slide. He rode with Chianta to a high-security hospital facility, the Orenda Center on Bennett Valley Road. Jonas McKee, or Lawnmower Man—funny how nicknames like that stick so quickly—was quiet, intelligent, polite, just the kind of guy you'd like for a neighbor. Until that pesky, deranged-killer problem kicked in.

"Look, Chianta, I'd appreciate it if you'd let me go in alone. I don't want McKee associating me with cops or doctors." As Wilder left his gun and OSI shield at the desk, Chianta got a priority call on his two-way. Wilder told him he'd catch a cab back to the station.

McKee's fully isolated, suicide-watch cell, deep within the facility, had nothing movable inside it. Just a cot welded to the wall; a stainless-steel head with no seat; table and chair bolted to the floor; and a large, thick, sealed Plexiglas window on one wall with an observation room on the other side. Communication was electronic, so the sound from the observation room could be turned off. McKee wore an orange, one-piece hospital jumper and blue paper slippers. He was balding, with a neat comb-over and high, arched eyebrows that made him look perpetually surprised. McKee sat quietly at his desk, hands folded, facing the Plexiglas window, smiling. Wilder used the dimmer switch in the observation room to turn up the lights so McKee could see him.

"Mr. McKee, my name's Matt Wilder. I'm a special investigator for the U.S. Air Force."

McKee stood up and approached the Plexiglas. He stared at Wilder, then began to sniff the air. Wilder pulled up a chair, tried to act offhand and unaware, but the hair on the back of his neck stood up. Something about McKee made him feel like a mouse being stalked by a cat. McKee moved to one side of the Plexiglas and sniffed at the joint where it was cemented to the wall. Finally, he stood back and regarded Wilder again.

"Did you fly here just to see me?"

"How do you know I flew here?"

"I can smell the jet fuel and exhaust on your clothing."

"Or you made a lucky guess."

"Whatever you're comfortable with believing, Mr. Wilder."

McKee grinned at Wilder's incredulous expression. The residual odor Wilder's clothes might've picked up in the plane or airport would be way beyond the range of human perception, especially since he and McKee were separated by three-quarters-of-an-inch-thick Plexiglas.

"Fact is, I'm still not quite used to it myself. There's something uniquely elemental about the olfactory sense. It's the only one of the five known senses where the information being perceived—odor molecules— actually come into contact with the brain. It's very intimate."

"How long have you been able to do this?"

McKee shrugged.

"I don't recall when it began. Recently. They medicate me; I believe it's affected my short-term memory. I was dozing until I sensed you coming. I'm happy for the company, however. When it's only one, it usually means a visitor, as opposed to the doctors."

"How did you know it was just me?"

"Footsteps. I could feel them through the floor as you approached."

A concrete floor, Wilder noticed. Not a substance known for transmitting the footfalls of a two-hundred-pound man.

"It also serves as my timepiece. I have no wristwatch, you see, and there are no clocks within view. Nor an outside window. So I am able to roughly estimate the time by the sensation of the traffic flow on the street outside. Seven A.M. begins the morning rush hour, four P.M. or there-abouts the afternoon."

It pleased Wilder that McKee wanted to talk. He glanced at the doctors' and psychiatrist's report he'd brought with him. They stated that in the absence of a perceived threat, McKee appeared absolutely normal, physically and mentally. Wilder looked up and realized that McKee was standing on his toes, looking through the Plexiglas at some medical reports spread out on the desk in front of Wilder.

"I could've told them all that."

"All what?"

"Brain chemistry, CBC, SMA-twenty-four. No surprises there."

McKee spoke as if he could read the medical reports' tiny print, upside down, from ten feet away.

"Okay, what are the levels on the blood panel?" Wilder asked.

"Potassium, 4.1; calcium, 6.8; magnesium, 1.1; sodium 143 . . . Shall I continue?"

"No, that's fine."

Wilder wondered if McKee's routine was an act. Maybe he'd seen the numbers before, and memorized them. He was a chemical engineer, after all.

"How else have you changed?"

"I am content."

"Why?"

"I've reached my potential."

"In what way?"

McKee suddenly turned his back, and didn't speak for a long moment. "If we continue, I need your assurance our conversation is personal. I've developed an intense dislike for my keepers. I refuse to allow them knowledge of my thoughts."

"Fair enough."

"Why do you wish to see me?"

"There was recently a murder on our base—"

"Friend of yours."

"I didn't say that."

"Yes, you did. With your voice. A small catch, or quiver. Repressed emotion. Why would a professional like you have an emotional stake in a case if not for a personal reason?"

"Well, it was two friends, actually. Victim and the killer."

"I'm sorry to hear that."

"Thank you. Tell me more about what you were saying. About your potential. What does that mean?"

McKee smiled. "I feel terrific. I've been sleeping well, appetite's hearty, regular bowel movements. Despite the poison they force me to ingest, I've been alert, focused, creative. I miss the wife and children, of course. Especially the wife; I've been extraordinarily aroused lately. Tell me, how long have you suffered that vision deficiency?"

"What?"

"You're favoring your right eye. Can't be congenital, or you'd not have the prior reference to make the compensation. Partial or total loss?"

Wilder was stunned. No one had ever noticed that he'd lost the vision in his left eye during his travails in Iraq. There were no outward scars or indications, and his behavior, he'd always thought, was completely normal.

"Total."

"Trauma? Disease?"

"Trauma."

"That's unfortunate. I hope it doesn't interfere with your lifestyle in any way."

Only keeps me from fuckin' flying, Wilder thought.

"I get by."

"Is that sufficient for you?"

Wilder didn't answer. McKee smiled at him and sprawled out on his cot.

"You seem relaxed," Wilder said.

"I am. The doctors understand I won't be trifled with."

"You don't view me as a threat?"

"You are here to understand what happened to your friends. I interest you only to that extent."

"How do you feel about what you did?"

"Sheldon should've known better."

"Better than what?"

"Let me rephrase. Sheldon should've known his betters."

"I don't understand."

McKee suddenly shot to his feet.

"You see? That's my very problem! I've always had to explain so much to everyone. Talking down. It's so boring! People come to me, approach with caution, touch me for an instant then retreat—screeching their incomprehension like the pack of dim-witted simians in that psychedelic space movie . . ."

"*2001.*"

"Yes, that's the one! It's an unspeakable violation, their poking and prodding and questions. They wish to vivisect me. Not on the table, but on the couch. Psychiatrists . . . they're the villains! They desperately yearn to feel what it's like inside my mind, the way you or I would crave feeling our manhood inside the body of a beautiful woman. It's an apt analogy, my friend, which is why I so intensely resist them. Consider the purpose of penetration: It is not to take something out; rather, it is to leave something within."

McKee stopped talking and studied Wilder. A big grin spread across his face.

"By God, you agree!"

"You're way over the top with your imagery, but the premise has some merit."

"Bravo, Mr. Wilder!"

"So why did you kill Mr. Sheldon?"

"Yuh Honor, ah claims the Texas dee-fense: 'the sumbitch *needed* killin'!" McKee laughed at his own bad southern accent.

"I've known a few folks needed killing. What was his particular reason?"

"The effrontery of the man! Ask anyone who knew him. Ask my dear wife, she knows . . ."

Then his smile disappeared as something agitated him. He started pacing, squeezing his hands together. Wilder tried to move the discussion away from the victim.

"All right, let's talk about your job—you're with a pharmaceutical—"

"No more until you tell Tweedle-Dum and Tweedle-Dumber to leave me alone!"

A moment later, the director of the center and the chief of psychiatry came into the observation room. As he'd claimed earlier, McKee must've felt them approaching. Wilder met them when he and Detective Chianta first arrived. If anyone could get close to McKee it was these two northern Californians. They were young, competent, about as nonthreatening and unobtrusive as it got. They were not used to dealing with a case like McKee, but were making the best of it until the judge could determine what to do with him. The director, Dr. Rabin, smiled at McKee.

"Jonas, if you'll excuse us, we'd like to speak to our guest in private for a moment."

He turned off the power to the microphone in the observation room and subtly indicated to Wilder to turn his back in case McKee knew how to read lips.

"Sorry to interrupt, but you have to leave."

"What's wrong?"

"McKee's lawyer caught wind you were here. He said Chianta had no right to go to the wife on your behalf without clearing it with him first."

"Shit. Think there's any chance she'll talk to me?"

"You could try, but the attorney's got her pretty spooked about saying anything."

"McKee claims his wife knows why he killed the neighbor," Wilder said. "But there's nothing from her in the record."

The chief of psychiatry, Dr. Jacks, shot a look over at McKee, who sat scowling at them through the Plexiglas.

"Look, these are churchgoing people, this is still a small town in a lot of ways. The crime is grotesque enough, nobody wants to add any further embarrassment for the family. Mr. McKee is sexually dysfunctional; his wife felt that perhaps the neighbors engaging in frequent intercourse had been very threatening to—"

A tremendous thud shook the whole room, interrupting Dr. Jacks. McKee flung himself against the Plexiglas, his face crimson with rage. Through the microphone in his cell Wilder and the others could hear him growling through clenched teeth, spitting invectives at them.

"Cocksuckers! Dickless, cocksucking cunts!"

He rammed his shoulder against the Plexiglas again. Tiny, spiderweb stress marks appeared in the clear plastic. The two doctors instinctively backed away; Wilder didn't know quite what to do.

"You gonna get someone in there to chill him out?"

"Last time he was like this, he put an orderly in the hospital. The rage will pass in a moment."

McKee kicked the window with powerful, flat-footed blows, then punched it with his fists, hard and rapid, like a prizefighter. After a few times his knuckles started bleeding, so each blow left a red, splattered stain on the window. He was oblivious to the pain. Frustrated at his inability to break through, McKee looked around his cell. He grabbed the metal-and-molded-plastic chair by its legs and tore it loose from the bolts holding it to the floor. He slammed it into the window, but it did less damage than his fists had done. Next he tried the table, easily wrenching its legs from the thick chrome bolts in the concrete. Wilder and the doctors just watched—the doctors with helplessness, Wilder with horrified fascination.

"You guys sure he can't get through that window?"

"No way."

They didn't convince Wilder. He glanced around the room, wondering what he could use as a weapon against McKee if he did manage to make it through the Plexiglas. McKee bashed the table against the window. The cracks in the Plexiglas widened. Another blow from the table made a crack in the window much deeper than the thin, surface fissures. Rabin reached for the telephone. McKee tossed the table aside and flung himself with amazing force against the crack.

It gave way. McKee and some jagged slivers of plastic burst into the observation room. Bleeding from the nose, mouth, hands, and deep gouges from the sharp edges of the broken Plexiglas, he looked at Dr. Jacks, smiled, then pounced on him like a cheetah. Jacks held his arms up to protect his face. McKee pulled them away and got his hands around the doctor's throat. Wilder and Rabin tried to pull him off of Dr. Jacks. McKee effortlessly threw Wilder aside and turned his attention to Dr. Rabin. He grasped Rabin's crotch and squeezed. Rabin let out a pained, terrified scream.

"Now who's dysfunctional, you cunt!"

Wilder took off his belt and looped it through the buckle. He got behind McKee and slipped it over his head, around his neck. Putting his foot in between McKee's shoulder blades, Wilder pulled as hard as he could, cinching the leather belt tight. McKee stood upright, clawing his fingers in between the belt and his throat. He tried to remove Wilder from his back by shaking him off, then by slamming him against the walls and furniture. Wilder hung on, avoiding McKee's attempts to twist around and grab him. Finally, unable to breathe, McKee slowly crumpled to his knees. Wilder pulled the belt tighter, wanting McKee to pass out completely before he let him loose. Suddenly, a foot connected with

McKee's face, knocking him and Wilder over, rendering McKee unconscious. The foot belonged to Dr. Rabin. He was limping painfully, but Wilder had gotten McKee off him before any permanent damage could be done. Dr. Jacks wasn't so lucky. He lay in a heap, dead, his throat grotesquely caved in. Wilder kept one eye on McKee and dialed the phone for help. Dr. Rabin sat down on the floor next to his friend and began to cry.

Wilder spent the next several hours making a statement for the Santa Rosa PD. Nathan Chianta's boss, the chief of detectives, was furious there'd been more trouble in his town and accused Wilder of getting McKee all worked up. But Dr. Rabin confirmed Wilder's claim McKee had been calm until he and Dr. Jacks came in and carelessly spoke of McKee's impotence.

Wilder's theory about news finding him proved true once again. Back in Santa Rosa, he and Nathan Chianta finished dinner in the hotel coffee shop; on the way out, Chianta unwrapped an Avo cigar and tossed the cellophane in a garbage can. He turned to say something to Wilder, who bent down to pull something out of the garbage. The *Enquirer.* A banner above the headline read MAD YUPPIE DISEASE???

There were two color photos on page five. One was a résumé head shot showing a sharp, thirtyish woman in a gray Liz Claiborne business suit. The other photo had been taken outside at night, illuminated by a strobe flash. It showed the same woman being dragged in handcuffs by three policemen, her hair askance, dressed in a bloodstained T-shirt and sweat pants, a small, calm smile on her face.

Wilder read the accompanying text, which described the murder of a young lawyer at the City Attorney's Office in Santa Monica, California. He and his fiancée, Julie Nelson—the woman in the picture—had been working on new gun-control legislation when she shot him and the two police officers who tried to arrest her. The article also referenced two other recent stories about cases of sudden, extreme violence from upper-middle-class people, one being Jonas McKee.

Wilder grew ever more convinced these events were somehow related. Aside from the similar pathologies, he'd recognize that strange, disconnected smile on McKee's and Julie Nelson's faces anywhere. Gail and the Infiltrator in Woomera had the same expression through-out their violent outbursts. However, before he could call Brent to cajole another twenty-hour hours and a trip to Los Angeles, the OSI dis-patcher paged him with orders to fly immediately to Nellis Air Force Base in southern Nevada. Top priority, top secret; he'll be briefed at the base.

Fourteen

t Nellis, Wilder found himself among a group of twenty-five senior OSI agents from bases around the country, including his OSI regional commander, Colonel Charles Chang. In a secure conference room at five-thirty A.M., Chang addressed Wilder and the others, telling them they were there to attend a briefing for President Marsh and senior members of the Air Combat Command.

"The unfortunate reality of facing a well-armed foe such as the Trans-Altaic Alliance is thus: Due to U.S. military downsizing during the last decade, our victory will depend in great part on the emergency deployment of several highly classified weapons systems still in development. Upon the President's order, the Air Force and our systems contractors will accelerate the delivery of the prototype weapons you are about to see. As each piece of equipment is combat-certified, we will secretly move it to one of several bases on the East Coast, where it'll be housed under absolute security until being shipped to the theater of operations. Your attendance today is due to the OSI's principal responsibility for on-base security. If anyone has a question during the briefing, put it in writing and pass it to me."

As they walked to the runway for their flight to the secret base where the briefing would actually take place, Chang told Wilder that President Marsh wanted to see the weapons and aircraft in person, not on a videotaped presentation, nor in an artist's rendering on the cover of a report. Since it would be impractical for the Chief Executive to fly around to a dozen Air Force bases and testing facilities across the country, all the full-scale prototypes and X-vehicles in development that had any potential for deployment before the deadline were brought to one site.

The President's desire to personally inspect new weaponry had precedent. During the Civil War, Lincoln asked for a demonstration of a newly developed, multibarreled cannon that could rapidly shoot multiple rounds without being reloaded. A team of Army cannoneers and the contraption's inventor, Dr. Richard Jordan Gatling, set up a prototype on the north lawn of the White House. The Great Emancipator sat behind it, turned its firing crank and gleefully shot the bejesus out of a dozen Johnny Reb dummies hanging in front of a stack of sandbags. Duly impressed with the Gatling gun, Lincoln immediately ordered its deployment into the Union ranks.

For Wilder, the military's game of catch-up put the prior days' media frenzy in an interesting light. The newspapers were full of hand-wringing editorials, most saying Marsh's ultimatum to Batu Khan was nothing more than presidential hubris. Congressmen of both parties were climbing over one another to get in front of a camera in order to call the President reckless and Georgia and the Ukraine less than crucial to American national interests. Oh, they'd be happy to support Marsh if the timing were only a little better, if Batu Khan had the decency to wait another five or ten years before overrunning other nations. By then, America would have had the chance to gear up its twenty-first-century military machine in order to fight a relatively painless war. Wilder had been hearing lots of bitter grumbling from his colleagues in the Air Force; stories were circulating about the difficulty General Mancini and the other Joint Chiefs were having trying to plan a major offensive with a fraction of the forces they had a decade ago. And in the most frustrating irony of all, many of those same people who'd pushed for military cutbacks were citing an underprepared fighting force as a reason for not taking action.

At seven A.M., a UH-1N helicopter ferried Wilder, Colonel Chang, and the Andrews AFB commander, Brig. General Hank Dryden, to the base in the desert, unmarked on any map, where the "black projects" presentation would take place. Ten minutes after they arrived, another copter—this one carrying the President, White House Chief of Staff Curt Levinson, Secretary of State Harry Burroughs, and Secretary of Defense Stan Woodruff—landed. Chang waited with General Dryden and the Nellis commander, Brig. General McClure, on the runway to greet the President. Vice President Taylor, Chairman of the Joint Chiefs General Don Mancini, and the other guests were already in Hangar N, along with the team from the Air Force Materiel Command (AFMC) that would make the presentation. A car waited to take the President and the others two-tenths of a mile to the entrance to Hangar N, but Marsh wanted to walk. He'd had cabin fever in the White House the past few days and it felt good to be out in the hot desert sun. As they walked, General Dryden introduced Chang and Wilder to the President. Wilder had a fleeting urge to say "love your work" when they shook hands. Meeting the President felt like meeting a movie star or any other celebrity. After all, their most notable feature was their fame; these days, why they were famous became practically irrelevant.

Two security officers stood guard outside a small door leading into the enormous, sealed hangar. General McClure returned their salute, slid an ID card through a reader, and punched in a security code. This last step seemed a bit overdone to Wilder—they were expecting maybe a stranger to sneak into the place with the President of the United States and the Secretaries of State and Defense in tow?

Inside, Vice President Taylor and General Mancini stood talking with the Four-Star Commander of Air Force Logistics, the AFMC, and representatives from the defense contractors building the various weapons systems. Wilder had been to several of these presentations over the years, but never saw so many big shots in one place at one time. The senior program manager, General Jeffrey Callum from AFMC HQ at Wright-Patterson AFB in Ohio, would personally make the presentation. With him were high-ranking people from the Aeronautics Systems Center at Wright-Patterson; the Armaments Systems Center at Eglin AFB in Florida; the Electronics Systems Center at Hanscom AFB in Massachusetts; the Space and Missile Systems Center at Los Angeles AFB; the Air Combat Command (ACC); and the Hypersonic Vehicles Office from Langley AFB in Virginia.

A large carpet had been rolled out at one end of the hangar. On it were a row of upholstered chairs and a long conference table. The chairs faced a podium, over which hung a white projection screen. Computerized PowerPoint slides were projected onto the screen along with the presentation. Each frame was bordered in red, with TOP SECRET at the top and bottom of each border in chunky white letters. Beyond the podium, several huge, hulking mechanical forms sat shrouded in darkness, awaiting inspection. Big, rolling platforms were lined up in front of them and each held an example of the prototype hardware to be discussed. At least, Wilder thought, they hadn't covered them with silk sheets to be whisked away after a drumroll.

Marsh sat down, eager to begin. The other executive branch VIPs joined him. Wilder, Chang, Dryden, and the military men sat behind them. Wilder heard someone whisper "This oughta be called Operation Candy Store."

"Good morning, Mr. President . . . gentlemen."

The DoD made a good choice in Callum to make the presentation, Wilder thought. He had Jimmy Stewart's all-American sincerity without any of the aw, shucks.

"We've organized the presentation in two parts, new weapons systems and munitions, and then new aircraft. I'll begin with speed-of-light weapons. After years of portrayal in science fiction, some are actually ready to deploy: High Power Microwave—HPM—devices with the full-spectrum capability to deny, disrupt, degrade, and/or destroy their targets." He smiled. "As a kid, you called them ray guns. Large HPM cannons will be mounted on fighters, bombers, and helicopters; miniaturized versions are 'man-portable'—as small as a shoulder-fired bazooka. HPM technology moved way up our list of priorities after intelligence reports indicated the TAA has tested such weapons."

Secretary of Defense Woodruff shared a look with President Marsh. They were quite aware of this and other TAA advances in technology. Even without the pending offensive against the TAA, such concerns gave great urgency to the development of new American weapons.

Callum offered the President and the others a chance to inspect the equipment more closely, then his assistant spoke into a walkie-talkie and one of the hangar doors rumbled open. Everyone followed the President onto the tarmac where some scrapped tanks were lined up, two hundred feet away. A row of a bazookalike, man-portable HPM cannons sat on several tables. Marsh hoisted one of the HPM cannons to his shoulder. Its light weight surprised him.

"All the weight's in the belt-hanging power packs. Want to give it a try, sir?"

"Sure . . ." Marsh said. Callum helped him don a helmet with a sight-ing monocle that flips down in front of one eye when the prefire power-up trigger is activated on the cannon. The helmet and the weapon connected wirelessly, via jam-proof radio waves.

"Just look at what you want to hit through the monocle, sir, the equipment does the rest. For armored vehicles, I'd set it to five. Aim for the rear quarter-panel, that's where the fuel tank is. There'll be no recoil, obviously."

Marsh sighted in on the tank and squeezed the trigger. The yellow bead superimposed on the tank through the monocle turned red. After a split-second electronic whine came a sharp pop. The sound reminded Wilder, standing behind Marsh, of an electronic flash unit on a camera. As the cannon sprayed an intense, concentrated stream of high-powered microwaves at the tank, Wilder could smell the acrid, metallic odor of the air ionizing in the energy flow. The tank ripped apart in a bright, diesel-fuel explosion.

"Christ," the President muttered as he handed the cannon back to Callum. He turned to the Vice President. "Adam, you want a shot?"

Taylor shook his head. "I think I get how it works."

General Mancini and Secretary of Defense Woodruff, however, each indulged their privilege of rank and blew up a tank. Callum's assistant offered an HPM cannon to anyone else interested in trying and Wilder leapt at the opportunity. Shouldering the cannon, he fiddled with the controls to get a feel for them. Then he narrowed the beam, set it to intensity seven, and aimed it just in front of his target—a scrapped tank—so the energy would reflect off the macadam and up into the underslung fuel containers. The tank exploded so violently that it flipped over and crushed the one behind it. Everyone turned to see who'd made such an effective shot.

"Seems we've got a man with aptitude for this stuff," Marsh said, smiling.

Wilder smiled back and handed the HPM cannon to the officer behind him. Everyone went back inside the hangar for part two of the presentation. General Callum took his place at the podium.

"The Air Force decided some time ago to develop small, uninhabited aircraft to augment our fleet of traditional, inhabited warplanes. These Uninhabited Combat Aerial Vehicles—UCAVs—will be piloted from an Execution Control Center, located in the U.S., over high-speed, massively redundant satellite communication routes. They'll give us enormous advantage in high-risk situations for both surveillance and offensive missions.

"Acceleration limits for inhabited aircraft are, typically, plus-nine or -ten g's—the outside of human endurance. UCAVs do not have those constraints. They were built without concern for a cockpit or life support and, as you'll see, they've been shaped symmetrically to accelerate immediately in any direction. Also, antiaircraft missiles are designed with a factor of three margin in lateral acceleration over that of their target aircraft. The UCAVs have an acceleration capability of beyond twenty g's, meaning they can outfly most antiaircraft weapons."

A bank of lights came up on a small, stealth-gray aircraft in the shape of a smooth, triangular saucer, fifteen feet across. It most resembled a stingray with three heads.

"Each triangle point has rows of sensors enclosed in small circles of flush-mounted, heatproof quartz, like smoked-glass portals. Its weapons— HPM cannons and small conventional missiles—are recessed to reduce drag and radar signature."

While Callum spoke, a large screen rolled down from the ceiling and a high-definition video projector showed top-secret footage of the UCAVs in flight over the Nevada desert. They could fly, change direction, and hover with speed and agility far beyond any inhabited aircraft.

"The decision of where and when to use UCAVs will depend on variables in the theatre environment, such as the density of enemy jammers. In most situations, both inhabited and uninhabited warplanes will be deployed. Like all the aircraft we discuss today, the UCAVs are hypersonic. Their cruising speed is between mach sixteen and eighteen."

Callum paused for a moment to let the numbers sink in. "The speed of sound in air is about 660 miles per hour, so mach sixteen is 9,240 miles per hour, or 2.5 miles *per second*. Their function ceiling is 150,000 feet."

"In other words, they can go into space," Marsh said.

"Yes, sir. In fact, they are designed to be deployed from low earth orbit."

Even men like General Mancini, who'd been living with the development of these craft over the years, were struck by the fact such extraordinary capabilities would soon be at their command.

"Fabulous stuff, General, but what are we gonna do when the bad guys develop this technology?" Secretary of State Burroughs asked.

Secretary of Defense Woodruff looked again at the President before saying, "We're working on that one."

A pilot stepped out from the darkness behind Callum's podium. He wore an ultralight, Air Force blue space suit, not much bulkier than an atmospheric flight suit, and a clear, goldfish-bowl helmet.

"I know few of you have actually worn zero-pressure space suits," Callum said, "so I think you'll appreciate our simple demonstration of the amazing improvements made in the new ultralight model."

Callum placed a dime on the concrete floor. The pilot in the ultra-light space suit crouched down and picked up the dime. A murmur of amazement spread through the spectators.

"Such freedom of movement in a zero-pressure suit had been thought impossible. Also, note the lack of a bulky life-support pack. Clusters of inch-thick, seven-inch-long oxygen-processing cylinders are sewn into the upper arms and legs of the suit. A man can survive two hours in the vacuum of space without any external air source, should the aircraft's life-support fail. Plenty of time for a hypersonic aircraft to return from orbit and land. Theoretically, the suit could be used for an emergency space walk, although it hasn't been fully tested for such use."

After a few technical questions about the suit from the former pilots in the audience, Callum continued his presentation.

"I've been leading up to the centerpiece of this new generation of weapons: the F-77 Centurion. It's an inhabited fighter developed out of the research conducted with NASA for the X-33 program. We combined everything we learned about radical new designs in solid-fuel rocket propulsion; a new generation of booster fuel; a secondary, air-breathing scramjet engine; and an airframe built entirely of composite materials. What we have is an aircraft smaller than an F-22 that can perform a short, horizontal takeoff, fly in low orbit in order to reach a target any-where on earth, and then return to its home base within two hours—all on one tank of fuel."

The lights came up on the aircraft sitting just behind the UCAV. It had a low, SST-like nose, indented cockpit, and small, swept-back wings on the rear third of the fuselage. Below the wings were squared, chan-neled ports for the engine intakes, neatly integrated into the sweep of the design. All its weapons were retractable for reduced drag, increasing its streamlined look. Wilder stared, instantly in love. He would've loved to take her for a spin. If the Centurion were a car, it'd be a 1961 V-12 Jaguar XKE. A red one.

"Note the delta-shaped fanwings," Callum said. "They extend almost perpendicular to the fuselage for takeoff and subsonic flight; this jet aircraft is actually capable of flying slower than 150 miles per hour at low altitudes. Depending on velocity and altitude, its wings retract, right up to its maximum speed of mach twelve."

A murmur of amazement went through the crowd.

"How many Centurions do we have?" Marsh asked.

"This and two others have been built so far."

President Marsh could see at once how the accuracy and performance latitude of such new weapons would drastically decrease the number of ground troops necessary to pry TAA forces out of the occupied territories.

"Are they deployable now?" Marsh asked.

"They're airworthy, but only at speeds up to mach three. We haven't brought the flight-control computer on line. At hypersonic speeds, conditions change so rapidly that it's too dangerous to fly with unassisted human control. The Centurion's flight-assist system uses a whole new generation of processor architecture, patterned on the neural pathways of the brain, continuously learning and adjusting its response as it flies. In fact, the neural net is so fast its frame of reference for position has to be self-contained, independent of even the speediest data transmission."

"How can a plane carry position reference for the whole planet?" Marsh asked.

"We call it the *onboard world*. It's a computerized map of the entire surface of the earth, accurate to one meter."

"I'm no computer whiz, but that sounds like a hell of a big database."

"Yes, sir. Twenty terabytes."

"Tera?"

"Trillion. Ten to the twelfth power."

"Has the neural net been flight-tested?"

"Only with prototype miniatures. Our first manned test is scheduled in ten days."

"That's cutting it close, General. We need this equipment deployed to forward position before August twelfth."

"Sir, I guarantee it will be."

Marsh glanced over at General Mancini, who nodded. Callum's assurance was good enough for him.

"I can't stress enough the importance of meeting our deadline," Marsh said. "Batu Khan is not the only one who concerns me. Even though President Karzhov swore he'll only pursue diplomatic remedies after Russia's loss of the Black Sea Fleet and Sevastopol Harbor, I don't believe him. He'll be desperate to save face."

"Yes, sir; in light of that situation we've doubled the frequency of our Shell Game Reports," Woodruff said.

"Good. Is there anyone here not receiving that information who should be?"

"General Mancini and I will review the distribution list." Woodruff turned to the civilians at the table. "The Shell Game Report tracks the locations of all Russian mobile nuclear weapons. As you know, under the START agreements they retired many of their silo-based, multiple-warhead ICBMs and replaced them with medium- and long-range thermonuclear strategic missiles—SS-twenty-fives. They're mounted on multiaxle tractor-trailers called Transporter-Erector-Launchers, or TELs, and to keep their whereabouts secret the Russian military periodically moves them, usually under cover of darkness or weather. They hide them in airport hangars, special railroad boxcars, even within urban warehouses. But despite this semimonthly shuffling by our friends in Moscow, we—as well as Britain, France, China, and the TAA—are always aware of the weapons' locations."

Vice President Taylor frowned. "Surely Batu Khan is expecting a response from the Russians; I think we should rethink our strategy and warn them about the breach in their security measures. It's a miracle the world's nuclear nations' club has managed to keep control of all extant weapons so far."

"No miracle, sir," General Mancini interjected. "A lot of people have worked real hard to keep Iraq, Iran, North Korea, Libya, and other outlaw nations from getting nuclear warheads and the capability for delivering them."

"Batu's made no secret of his desire to be a true superpower, but he can't do it without an intercontinental nuclear arsenal," Taylor replied. "The TAA and Russia share a thousand-mile-long border. It must be extraordinarily tempting for him to penetrate a couple hundred miles into Russia, hijack the finished product, and achieve instant superpower status."

"Anything's possible with Batu, Adam, but we're closely monitoring the situation," Marsh said. "We constantly weigh the risks and benefits of warning the Russians to change their methods for handling their mobile assets. So far, given their internal instability, we've decided it's best for our national security to keep track of the missile locations ourselves, even if the TAA knows them as well."

The briefing over, Marsh stood up. "Gentlemen, based on what we've seen here today, I'm very encouraged. I want an outline of our offensive strategy within forty-eight hours."

Wilder shot a look at Colonel Chang. It promised to be a hell of an eight weeks.

Fifteen

ith Colonel Chang's permission, Wilder flew to Los Angeles for the afternoon to interview the woman pictured in the *Enquirer*, Julie Nelson. He was again struck by the amazing transformation, her incredible strength and sensitivity, but came away no closer to understanding its origins. Like the others, her body chemistries were perfectly normal.

Wilder returned home to Andrews on Sunday morning. He'd missed Kate's last-day-of-school party the prior Friday, so to make it up to her they went for brunch at the House of Pancakes and then for a swim at the base-housing community pool. In truth, he'd made the swimming suggestion as much for his own sake as hers—the creepy feeling in his gut from the Herrold case had only grown stronger after his meetings with Jonas McKee and Julie Nelson. Something about water soothed him—maybe that was why he dreamt so often of the lake near which he'd grown up in northern New Jersey. While Kate splashed around with some other kids under the lifeguard's watchful eye, Wilder sat under an umbrella with his notebook computer. He glanced up as an attractive young woman in a thong bikini applied sunscreen to her even-more-attractive friend's back and legs, and it took him a moment to return his attention to his computer. Using his wireless modem, he checked his e-mail and logged on to LEO (Law Enforcement Online) to check for responses to the queries he'd posted and found files from Chicago and San Francisco awaiting him. Chicago PD enclosed a note with theirs—they weren't sure if it fit all his criteria for perpetrator behavior, but they were forwarding a police report anyway. Wilder read eagerly through the materials, noting the key points:

Suspect Ralph Bonner, fifty-one, actuarial analyst for Illinois Whole Life and Casualty Insurance Co, Chicago, killed two people: his department supervisor, stabbed multiple times, and a claims adjustor, neck broken, head turned 180 degrees. Bonner killed resisting arrest, Glenwood Springs, Colorado.

The head-twisting caught Wilder's interest. Movies and TV shows often portrayed killing in such fashion, but in reality it took enormous strength to snap a person's neck. He next read a transcript of a local TV news report about the San Francisco case:

Liz Evanston, a forty-nine-year-old housewife with no prior record, became the chief suspect in an arson case when an exclusive private school was destroyed with a timed incendiary device. There hadn't been sufficient evidence to file charges until, at a Nob Hill barbecue, she doused the headmistress of the school with charcoal-starter fluid and ignited it. Apparent motive: her daughter had not been accepted to the school.

Wilder added the cases' details to a "link-analysis" database program custom-designed for the OSI. Normally, police reports do not include detailed background information, which meant he would need to follow up by talking to the arresting department, families, doctors, coworkers, and friends. Somewhere within the mountains of unrelated phone tolls, tips, trash inventories, biographical backgrounds, and such he might possibly glean some common characteristic among the perpetrators. So far he'd discovered twenty-one cases fitting the profile. Sixteen uncovered through his preliminary research on the law enforcement databases, plus Gail Sealy, Jonas McKee, Julie Nelson, Ralph Bonner, and Liz Evanston. All were in their early fifties except for Julie and the Infiltrator in Woomera, a maddening inconsistency.

A fascinating behavioral pattern began to emerge. The perpetrators' actions were always aimed at someone perceived to be a threat. Their outbursts of uncontrollable violence didn't occur until they were discovered, cornered, or in a situation where they could no longer mask their guilt. Until then, they were capable of calm calculation. Even in their madness, they structured elaborate scenarios to feign indifference to the threat, lead their victims to a trap, and then cover their actions.

Wilder interrupted his analysis to attend an OPSEC (Operational Security) meeting with Brent and General Dryden later in the day. The FBI had reason to believe TAA computer hackers were targeting U.S. air bases in an attempt to disrupt the flow of men and matériel overseas. A direct physical attack on Andrews such as a truck bomb was also deemed possible, given its visibility as home to Air Force One and its importance as the debarkation point for troops on their way to Aviano Air Base, Italy, and Incirlik, Turkey, the main centers of overseas operations.

Later that evening, after putting Kate to bed, Wilder sat in his upstairs office and stared at the blank row of fields in his database program. He hated this part of the work. Raw data by itself is worthless; it only has value when, by its organization, reduction, and classification, it becomes information. He began with Gail, for whom he had the most complete file. First, all the no-brainer stuff from her birth certificate. Then he worked his way through her early life, siblings, blood type, childhood illnesses, schools attended, marital status, background on spouse, children, home life. Composition of her dwelling, its age and location, type of furnishings and appliances. What kind of clothes she wore, where she got them. The car she drove; where she bought her groceries; what she ate. Religion, hobbies, political affiliation, vacations taken; sexual orientation, practices, frequency. What TV shows she watched, books she read, whom she called on the phone. Et cetera.

An hour later, he started on Julie Nelson. He'd gathered some information about her from the Santa Monica PD, the City Attorney's Office where she had worked, a couple friends of hers and her late fiancé's. She had nothing in common with Gail Sealy. Except, perhaps, for the ordinary nature of their lives, right up until the moment they became profoundly *un*ordinary. Finishing with Julie, exhausted, he glanced up at the clock, but decided to put in some preliminary information about Jonas McKee to get it out of the way.

He skipped through the fields to input the info he had when a word jumped out at him. He'd seen it before. In the field called Education. Rexford University. McKee was Class of '74. Gail had been a Rexford grad as well, in 1973. She'd majored in biology, McKee in organic chemistry. Wilder dug through Ralph Bonner's and Liz Evanston's files, but couldn't find mention of their educational histories. And all he had about the sixteen other cases were the bare details of their crimes and behavior. Going on-line, he drafted an e-mail to the various law enforcement organizations who'd supplied him with the cases, asking which college their perps attended, and when.

He looked at the clock again. Ten-fifteen. Eight-fifteen in Chicago. He called area code 312 directory assistance for the number of the Illinois Whole Life and Casualty Company. Someone at the twenty-four-hour claims line agreed to call the human resources director at home, and after some cajoling she accessed the employment records through the company's Intranet. As she named Bonner's alma mater, Wilder typed it into the database.

Rexford.

Wilder stared at the word on the computer screen. He refused to get excited. Even if a few of the others attended Rexford, what could it possibly mean? He dialed the police department contact number in Liz Evanston's file. It was a beeper, so he punched in his number. While waiting for a callback, he ran the other perps' names through an Internet search engine. Perhaps some of them posted their résumé or some other vital statistics on the web.

Two hits came up. The first was J. Barry Holland, Attorney at Law. Wilder read through Holland's résumé: JD, 1976, Harvard School of Law; BA, 1973, Rexford University. Wilder saved the résumé on his hard drive and clicked on the next link. It took him to a photo of a Mutual Fund adviser named Eileen Svaco on the broker's home page. He called their 800 number in Seattle, and asked to be connected to Svaco's division. The other advisers were still in shock over Mrs. Svaco killing her mother and brother for no apparent reason. Wilder explained his investigation of similar cases to the supervisor and asked if anyone knew where Svaco had gone to college. The guy in the next cubicle remembered. Rexford University.

Fuck a duck.

His call-waiting beeped; a detective from the San Francisco PD answering his page. He asked how he could find out where Liz Evanston got her college degree. The cop put him on hold and called Liz's husband. Wilder held his breath until the cop came back on the line:

"Negative. Evanston don't have a degree." Somebody yelled for him; he was at a crime scene and anxious to get off the phone. "Sorry, guy—"

"You ask if she ever *attended* college?"

"Shit . . ." The cop didn't feel like calling Liz's husband back, but knew he should've asked in the first place. He put Wilder on hold again. Two minutes later, he clicked back.

"Yeah, she went for a couple years, then dropped out."

"Where?"

"Down in the Bay Area. Rexford University."

Laura returned to her town house from a late-afternoon bike ride and turned on the shower. She hadn't gotten much done on her new book lately. Current events, in her life and in the world, were far more interesting than her work. Each day the polls showed further erosion of public support for President Marsh's offensive against TAA, now called Operation Swift Sword. The House of Representatives, smelling a trend, began a debate on the floor in preparation to vote on a nonbinding resolution on whether to support the operation. Many congressmen questioned the President's wisdom in laying down a hard deadline and in planning action without international participation. Laura briefly considered making a statement supporting the President's position on the TAA, but quickly dismissed the idea. There's a reason it's called the political fray. Enter and it's not politics that get frayed, it's you.

Just before she stepped into the shower the doorbell rang. She grumbled and pulled on her robe. The man at the door, a Department of Defense messenger, handed her a large envelope from Andrews Air Force Base. Surprised, Laura signed for it and tore it open. Inside she found an inch-thick bound report. A black DECLASSIFIED stamp, dated two days ago, had been placed over the original red CLASSIFIED stamp. The title identified it as the full text of USAF Captain Matthew James Wilder's debriefing after his return from captivity in Iraq, February 26, 1991. A note tucked inside the top of the pages read:

Laura:

I pulled this out of mothballs and Public Affairs cleared it for use in your book. I think it'll answer many of your questions.

Best, Matt.

Laura grinned—it felt like Christmas. Forgetting all about the still-running shower, she found Wilder's card in her leather bag and dialed his office at the Washington Field Office. While it rang she had a fleeting urge to brush her hair and glance at herself in the mirror, then she laughed at herself—it wasn't a VS meeting, after all.

Wilder, waiting for yet another status meeting with base Security Forces to begin, sat at his desk, trying to determine where the remaining Mad Yuppies went to college. So far, he discovered three more in their late forties or early fifties had attended Rexford, meaning everyone whose educational history he knew, except Julie Nelson, went to that one university. The Woomera Infiltrator remained the only other wild card.

When his secretary announced Laura Bishop on line two, Wilder had a fleeting, pleasant recollection of Laura's scent when they'd met. He couldn't put a description to it. Not artificial like perfume, just . . . appealing. He remembered buying a paperback of hers at the airport and reflexively holding it to his nose, perhaps hoping it would smell as terrific as its creator—no such luck. He settled for looking at her picture on the back cover.

"Hi," Laura said. "I got your report, and don't know how to thank you. It'll be extremely helpful."

Wilder left his true motivations unsaid. He sent it mostly because he felt bad about being uncooperative when they'd met—and also because it kept him from having to relive those experiences himself.

"No problem; glad it'll help. How's the book coming along?"

"Lousy. I've been working on this one section for weeks. I'm at that stage where I've researched the subject enough to be bored with it, but won't get my enthusiasm back until I've actually started writing."

"So, you're looking for inspiration."

"Always. Aren't we all?"

"I could sure use a little."

"Personally or professionally?" Laura asked.

The almost subliminal note of flirtation in her voice intrigued Wilder.

"Both. Although professional has priority at the moment."

"Anything you're allowed to talk about?"

"Yeah, in this instance I can. You read the tabloids?"

"Beg pardon?"

"Mad Yuppie Disease."

"Oh, yes, I've heard something about that. Upstanding citizens suddenly turning homicidal."

"That's them."

"It's not really true, is it?"

"Next part stays between us."

"Of course."

"Not only is it true, but there are far more cases than reported. Over twenty. And it gets better. Almost all of the perpetrators went to the same university, at the same time." He didn't mention the Infiltrator in Woomera—the events that occurred there were not public knowledge.

"Really? That's an incredible coincidence. But aren't the people middle-aged?"

"That's right, late forties, early fifties. It makes no damn sense. Most haven't been to college in thirty years."

"What do you mean by most?"

"There's one in particular who fits the pathology profile perfectly, except for her age and school background. When the others were in college, she hadn't even been born yet—"

As soon as it came out of his mouth, Wilder felt like the biggest fool in three counties.

"Hang on . . ."

He tossed the phone aside, grabbed his notebook computer, and pulled up Julie Nelson's records. Born in 1974, she'd been *conceived* when the others were in college.

He picked up the phone. "Sorry."

"What happened?"

"I got a little jolt of that inspiration we were talking about. Should've hit me days ago. I have to call you back."

He knew he would, too, the instant he found anything out, because he had a strong desire to share the moment with her, whether it ended up a dead end or major breakthrough.

Wilder had Julie's parents' names from her birth certificate—Mike and Cheryl Nelson, née Packard. Like the vast majority of people in the world, they lived and passed on quietly, leaving nothing tangible behind but their progeny. As he dialed the Santa Monica City Attorney's Office, his secretary buzzed again.

"The security chief is here; they're ready for you."

Wilder groaned. Another goddamn procedural meeting held less than no interest to him. He needed to know if either of Julie's parents went to Rexford.

"Ask them to give me five minutes."

He got Julie Nelson's office-mate in Santa Monica on the phone and asked about the Nelsons. She said Julie never spoke of them, nor could she recommend a friend or family member who might know more. Frustrated, Wilder thanked her and hung up.

He grabbed his OPSEC papers for the meeting with the security chief, but he felt lucky and didn't want to interrupt a streak. Tossing the papers aside, he returned to his case files. Julie, an only child, grew up in Cherry Hill, New Jersey. He slid a CD-ROM Street Atlas program into his notebook and input the Nelsons' old address. Zooming in on the map of Cherry Hill, down to their individual block, he noted the addresses for the houses surrounding the Nelsons'.

He then called the Verizon business office. A supervisor called him right back to confirm his claim of being a law enforcement officer, and looked up the phone numbers he wanted in her reverse directory, indexed by street addresses. Wilder glanced up at the clock—his five minutes had passed. Okay, he'd just try a couple of the numbers . . . it would only take another minute or two . . .

First two numbers, no one home. Third, the people moved in after the Nelsons died. Fourth, an old lady who knew the Nelsons, but only to say hello. Then, just before she hung up her husband chimed in, said the Nelsons sold their car to a kid who worked at Hirsch's, the hardware store. He didn't know whether there'd been a relationship beforehand. Kid's name was Jimmy, Joey, something like that. Car was a blue, 1969 Pontiac Firebird. Wilder called the hardware store. The kid, Jerry, worked there a couple of summers, ten years ago. He now worked, the owner thought, as a loan officer in a bank in Merchantville, just down the road. Wilder called the bank and found Jerry. No, he hadn't known the Nelsons. He'd only met them to buy the car, having seen an ad for it in the *Pennysaver*.

Shit, thought Wilder. Dead end.

"Tell me," Jerry asked, "how come a guy from the Air Force wants to know about the people who sold me a car ten years ago?"

"I'm trying to figure out if either of them went to Rexford University."

Jerry started laughing and said "Ask my wife." His experience with higher education totaled two years at the County College of Morris, the most his family could afford. He met his future wife in the parking lot of a movie theater. Seeing him unlocking his car, she'd said hello. She thought he was Joe Rich-Boy College—because of the REXFORD U sticker on the back window of his cherry '69 Firebird.

After his OPSEC meeting, Wilder phoned Laura back. His excitement delighted her, and also flattered her that he wanted to share it.

"The kid totaled the Firebird a couple years later. Fortunately, his insurance company had the Firebird's VIN on record. Guy named Karl Packard bought it new in 1969, cosigning for his minor daughter, Cheryl Packard. Julie Nelson's mother. The Rexford student."

"Pretty good detective work."

"I got lucky. Now I've got a bunch of new mysteries, like what in the hell *within* the Rexford experience Julie's mother and the others have in common and how it could have affected her unborn daughter."

And, although he said nothing to Laura about it, he found it maddening that discovering this link among the Mad Yuppies made them seem even more disconnected from the Khaldun infiltrator at Woomera.

In Sevastopol, Chu'tsai suggested to Batu Khan that he might have better luck producing an heir if he heeded his wives' desire to return to their homeland. At once, Batu packed up his mobile encampment in a half dozen helicopters, and like a modern-day caravan moved from the Ukraine to the TAA interior. He'd also been tense and irritable, so he decided to spend a few days at the remote hot springs near Olgiy in the Altai Mountains of eastern Mongolia.

Once there, he rode, exercised, slept, ate, and made love like an eighteen-year-old in the cold mountain air. Arising each day at sunup, he sparred for an hour with a Khaldun swordsman in a field—both men shirtless, sweat streaming from their bodies like stallions, their bare feet crunching in the white dew-frost on the grass. Chu'tsai sat naked, submerged in a natural rock pool of hot spring water just yards away. He had a notebook computer hooked up to a satellite phone. The computer sat perched precariously on a rock, while he smoked a joint and surfed the Internet news services.

"Here's an interesting one . . ." he said, and read aloud from a Reuters article:

During a televised speech to his people yesterday, Batu Khan made an offhand remark about not repeating Saddam Hussein's and Slobodan Milosevic's mistake of sitting idly by while the United States amasses a war machine against him. U.S. military commanders took the comment very seriously—already over sixty thousand of an expected hundred thousand armed services personnel have arrived at the Aviano and Incirlik Air Bases, and a Navy carrier group is harbored at Istanbul, Turkey. Chairman of the Joint Chiefs General Don Mancini immediately raised the 'Threatcon' alert level for every U.S. military base in the world. . . .

Batu did not break his stride while sparring. "I would've preferred that they packed up and gone home."

Chu'tsai's e-mail program chimed as a PGP-encrypted message arrived. He typed in his password to decode the e-mail and read it.

Batu stopped sparring and looked over his friend's shoulder at the notebook screen. Seeing the return address on the e-mail didn't particularly surprise him; Chu'tsai and their American friend had been corresponding regularly in the last few weeks.

"What does he want now?" Batu asked.

"Bringing some new names to our attention," Chu'tsai explained. "Also, to be honest, Batu, I asked again for assurances the compound we're giving our men is safe."

"And?"

"He promises it's ten generations of development past the original."

"Of course it is," Batu said, annoyed. "Stop worrying. Just remember how well it's served us in Georgia and the Ukraine."

Chu'tsai looked at the names on the screen: *Liz Evanston, Julie Nelson, Jonas McKee.*

"He expects it to be no more than a few weeks before the rest of them are affected," Chu'tsai said.

"I hope so. I'm becoming very impatient."

Sixteen

ncreased security at Andrews meant the Washington Field Office would have to attend to dozens of predetermined details, such as altering all the flight plans in and out of Andrews, Bolling, and Fort Meade to avoid any consistencies in air travel times, especially with troop and equipment transports. The WFO also became involved in aiding the FBI's surveillance of two foreign nationals who worked for a civilian contractor at Andrews. And security at all gates went to a one-hundred-percent check of identification, which slowed traffic to a crawl, creating backups during rush hour all the way to Interstate 95.

Two days after the Threatcon increase, Wilder got a call from the main gate. A civilian messenger service had a parcel to be delivered only to him. He drove over to retrieve it, a small engraved envelope originally addressed to Laura Bishop. Inside, to his great surprise, he found an invitation and one of two entry tickets to the International Freedom of Expression Dinner at the White House put on by PEN, the writer's organization. He read the handwritten note accompanying the invite, a note Laura had labored over for an hour, trying to strike just the right tone of nonchalance:

Dear Matt:

Most writers' dinners are pretty dull. But this one's at the White House so it shouldn't be half bad. May I impose terribly upon you to be my escort?

Laura.

Wilder looked up from the note. All the security officers were staring at him, undoubtedly because of the huge, out-of-character grin on his face.

Wilder took Laura's invitation to be a thank-you for the files he'd sent her, so he didn't view the PEN dinner as a date, per se, and he felt none of the inescapable first-date awkwardness as they drove together from Georgetown to Pennsylvania Avenue. He'd never had difficulty meeting and dating women, but Laura was not the type of woman he'd normally pursue. Not for lack of confidence and certainly not for lack of interest; rather, it would never occur to him that someone of her caliber would be unattached. It seemed a given that one so beautiful and accomplished would have a significant other. Indeed, this was the very reason why Laura was rarely asked out—mankind, collectively, could not imagine she'd be available. And Laura, with a complete lack of egotism, simply presumed no one was interested enough to ask, so she grew accustomed to life on her own.

Wilder's relaxed attitude was contagious; whatever misgivings she'd had about asking him to accompany her to the dinner were gone by the time they arrived at the White House gate. Liveried doormen opened the car doors for them and they stood silent for a moment, both struck by the magic and grandeur of the place.

"Something just occurred to me," she said as they walked along the red carpet leading to the glass-enclosed colonnade. "This dress cost more than I made from my first book."

"Whatever it cost, it looks like a million."

Laura smiled. "You clean up pretty nice yourself."

Indeed, they both looked dazzling: Laura in a sapphire-blue Ralph Lauren gown, Wilder in a tuxedo. They fell in line with the other guests heading toward a metal detector at the entrance and Wilder looked around, recognizing a few of the faces in the crowd—congressmen, media people, a famous writer or two. A Secret Service agent glanced at the tickets in Wilder's hand. Noting they were tan as opposed to white, he gestured him and Laura around the metal detector along with the congressmen and other VIPs.

"Friends in high places?" Wilder asked Laura.

"I guess so. After my TV appearance—and remind me never to do *that* again—Curt Levinson called. He said the President saw me on the show and appreciated my discretion. A few days later this personal invitation from him and Mrs. Marsh arrived."

Wilder nodded, impressed. He presumed she'd come because of her PEN membership, not at the behest of the President of the United States. Smiling, Laura gestured toward a large-busted, tanned blonde in her sixties wearing a diamond and platinum necklace that easily contained a hundred carats of jewels.

"Good thing she didn't have to go through the metal detector with all that jewelry," Wilder said. "Isn't she Senator Ballard's wife?"

He answered his own question when catching a glimpse of the short, gray-haired, African-American senator all but eclipsed behind his massive wife.

"Everyone says they're the oddest couple on the Hill," Laura said. "He's a former Civil Rights lawyer and federal judge. Used to sleep in his office to save rent money when he got to Washington. Then he married Ms. Winters; she's from one of those families rich from having money. I saw her on TV once, talking about how the evening she brought Jonathan home to meet her parents played out exactly like *Guess Who's Coming to Dinner*. Although I doubt anyone predicted he'd become president pro tem of the U.S. Senate and the President's tennis partner."

Wilder and Laura followed the line along the ground-floor corridor, then up the stairs to the State floor. They heard Marsh's favorite band, The Chieftains, playing a cheerful Irish folk tune up ahead. Then Laura spotted Chief of Staff Curt Levinson and his wife, Naomi, a striking brunette born in Israel, at the entrance to the State Dining Room. Levinson waved to her and everyone looked around to see who rated the personal acknowledgment. Levinson introduced his wife and Laura introduced Wilder.

"Terrific to meet you," Levinson said to Wilder, then grinned when a hostess handed Wilder a small card with their table number. "I think you'll like your seat assignment."

"As long as you didn't seat us with any other historians," Laura said. "I seem to be the only one who has an inkling how dull we are."

"Mr. Wilder certainly doesn't look bored."

"Not likely," Wilder agreed.

Laura looked at Wilder and her smile, he thought, outshone Mrs. Ballard's gem collection by a magnitude of ten. Several people behind them jockeyed for the chief of staff's attention, so Laura mouthed "see you later" and they went into the dining room. Inside were twenty round dining tables, each set for eight, covered with a green tablecloth and a vermeil flower bowl overflowing with wildflowers. The President hadn't arrived yet, so the guests stood grouped around the two bars. Wilder returned with a glass of white wine for Laura and found her looking at the large, intimate portrait of Lincoln above the mantel.

"It's easy to forget they were just men," Wilder said. "Until you see a portrait like this."

"Yes. How sad he seems," Laura replied. "Oh, look!" she said excitedly, referring to the inscription carved in the mantel below the portrait. "It's from a letter written by John Adams on his first night in the White House."

I Pray Heaven to Bestow the Best of Blessings on THIS HOUSE and on All that shall hereafter Inhabit it. May none but Honest and Wise Men ever rule under this Roof.

They turned as the band switched to "Hail to the Chief." President and Mrs. Marsh arrived and Laura put her clutch purse under her arm to join in the applause. The Marshes, Wilder and Laura agreed, were the most glamorous first couple in quite some time. President Marsh had the uncanny skill of appearing comfortable in a tuxedo. Amy Marsh, dressed in a knockout Chanel gown, looked radiant. Following the President, everyone made their way to their seats. Wilder glanced at the card the hostess had given them.

"Table twenty," he told Laura.

"Oh, well," Laura said. "Must be Siberia."

Wilder shrugged. It wasn't that he didn't understand the nuances of power seating, he just didn't care. They circled the perimeter of the now-crowded room, looking for their table. Much to their surprise, the low-numbered tables were on the outside. Table twenty sat in the center of the room. A man at the table stood up as Wilder pulled out a chair for Laura. President Marsh.

"Laura, great to see you. I presume you're a member of PEN?"

"Oh, yes. For years."

"They're making me an honorary member tonight. I'm delighted, of course, but I wish I'd had the guts to make it in on my own."

"Guts?"

"If I ever wrote a book and it got bad reviews I'd be bedridden for a week."

"Nature's way of keeping you from embarrassing yourself, my dear," Amy said.

"Amy Marsh, Laura Bishop."

"Mrs. Marsh, Mr. President, this is my friend, Special Agent Matt Wilder, Air Force Office of Special Investigations."

The men shook hands. Wilder could tell the President recognized him from the prototype weapons demonstration in the desert, but chose not to reveal that connection.

"OSI. Washington Field Office?" Marsh asked.

"Yes, sir."

"Glad you could join us tonight. I'm an old Navy man, but I'll spare you the war stories. Which is easy because I spent my two years at the Presidio pushing papers, wishing I was a flier like you guys."

Wilder nodded. "Yes, sir, it does have its moments." He wondered if the President had connected his name with the war in Iraq—not many OSI agents are former pilots—or whether he simply meant the Air Force in general.

Laura sat between the First Lady and Wilder, and Marsh returned to his seat on the opposite side of the table. Also with them was the president of the PEN Center USA, Geoffrey Sabine, a white-haired New England writer of short fiction, and a pair of novelists married to one another who'd abandoned prose to write screenplays. Or, more accurately, rewrites of other people's screenplays. While Sabine enthusiastically told Marsh and Wilder stories about his own Navy days during World War II, Amy leaned over to Laura.

"So, after the meeting where Burt picked your brain about Batu Khan, he comes upstairs all excited. Says there's this fabulous woman he wants me to meet. Goes on about how much I'll like her because she's a history buff. Then he tells me it's Laura Bishop and I say 'really, a history buff? No kiddin'?' "

Laura laughed. "I could barely get past sitting in the Roosevelt Room. Until that day I'd never been in the West Wing."

"Tell you what. This shindig will break up by eleven. Stick around. Burt and I are night owls, we'll show you two the place at the best time to see it—when there's no one around but the ghosts."

Laura, giddy with excitement, whispered the news to Wilder. Even he, one not easily impressed, realized this would be a rather unique evening.

Dinner was a succession of small, rustic Italian dishes, each course complemented by a glass of just the right wine, prepared by a Tuscan chef the First Lady knew from New York.

"I saw you on television last week," Sabine said to Amy. "That interview show with what's-her-name . . . the Oscar-night woman."

She nodded. "Lord, she went on for*ever* about what great shape Burt's in. I'll tell you, when she asked if he had some sort of workout program, I came *this close* to leanin' back and sayin' 'You're lookin' at it, darlin.'"

Everyone laughed, Marsh beamed at his wife, and Wilder marveled at how at ease the First Lady made them all feel. While they ate, the President asked Laura to tell him some stories about his predecessors—how they dealt with the day-to-day demands of the office, as well as the crises. Laura understood his hunger for such information; he only had forty or so prior examples of how to do his job. In bringing the other presidents to life, her knowledge and enthusiasm captivated everyone at the table. Wilder smiled to himself. To say he'd never met anyone like her would be the understatement of the century.

After dessert, Geoffrey Sabine presented Marsh with his honorary membership in recognition of his administration's strong support of PEN's free-speech efforts. He read a letter from a Chinese author of children's books who'd been jailed and tortured by the Chinese government for his "subversive" literature. PEN brought the case to the State Department's attention, finally embarrassing the Chinese into releasing him. Sabine added a postscript: The author emigrated to the United States after receiving a job offer from a firm in the Silicon Valley to coauthor computer games for $300,000 a year.

Marsh rose, holding his framed PEN membership certificate.

"First, thank you, Geoffrey, for the wonderful honor of adding my name as a friend and supporter of the PEN organization. Since we're celebrating the artist-citizen's participation in world affairs, I believe it's appropriate to speak for a moment of things political. I'd like to reflect on the nature of two words inexorably linked by an old saying: the pen and the sword. Your tool, your weapon, is the pen.

History is rife with examples of its might. There will never be an armament created that is more powerful than an idea. A pen, like a sword, may be wielded in the service of righteousness, or it can be used destructively.

"For those of us who lead nations, our will must sometimes be exerted, as an option of last resort, by the sword. It will be true as long as there is even one member of the world community unwilling to match the civility of her sister nations, as long as the sword speaks the only language rogue nations understand. So why am I mixing my metaphors in front of a room full of expert phrase-makers? To ask you, who wield the pen, to lend your support should it come to pass that we must wield that righteous sword.

"In these crucial weeks before the deadline, the lack of a unified voice from the American people, especially from opinion-makers like yourselves, can only make the aggressors doubt our determination. Should hostilities be unavoidable, skepticism or negativity at home will only prolong them. Now, I'm not implying that people haven't the right to disagree with my policies. I seek only your free and honest support. I feel confident in asking, for who among us could possibly find acceptable the brutal, unprovoked attacks and merciless oppression of any country and its people? Americans united in their resolve are capable of surmounting any challenge put before them. I hope I can count upon *your* resolve."

Marsh sat down. Wilder and Laura applauded at once, but it took a moment for it to spread through the room. The President had hardly ignited a burst of patriotic fervor. Apparently, no one had expected more than "gosh, thanks" for the honorary membership, certainly not a direct appeal for support of war against the TAA.

The applause died down and Marsh stood up again.

"One last thing. Thinking forward to a time when I no longer occupy this office, I'd like to know just exactly how one gets a job in the Silicon Valley for three hundred grand a year."

After the waiters served port and sherry, the guests walked across to the East Room, where the band reassembled around the Steinway grand piano.

"I'm not much of a dancer," Wilder said to Laura, holding his hand out to her, "but if the occasion calls for it . . ."

He led her out onto the floor, slipped his arm around her waist and they fell into step together. The music was a slow Irish ballad, but neither of them noticed. For a moment they forgot the place, the company, the time; Laura didn't even care that Thomas Jefferson himself had danced in this very room. It felt too exciting to be so close to each other. Finally, to remove the embarrassingly dreamy look from his face, Wilder tried to make conversation.

"I always thought writers led fairly quiet lives."

"This one sure does. Evenings, I'm usually home with a book or a rented video."

"That's about my speed, too."

"You mean you're not out saving the world every night?"

"It's pretty much beyond saving, and I'm beyond trying."

"You're just being modest."

Wilder smiled. If it were only that simple.

As the party wound down a protocol officer escorted them to a private sitting room. A half-hour later, President and Mrs. Marsh joined them. Marsh poured Amy a sherry; he, Wilder, and Laura had port, and the First Couple showed the White House to their appreciative visitors. Amy led the tour. Like most First Ladies, she had detailed knowledge of each room and its furnishings. Also, like her predecessors, she planned to leave a legacy of their occupancy of the house. Hers would be a permanent VS Room. Although it began as a temporary set inside a large reception room, it had become one of the most important places in the West Wing, and she intended to make it as elegant as the rest of the house.

As they entered the room, the big VS screen that took up one entire wall glowed standby blue. Metal mounting racks, on which the electronic controls would be located, hung half-installed in an area of exposed Sheetrock above the credenza, perpendicular to the screen. Marsh sprawled on the sofa, listening while his wife told Wilder and Laura how the over-head lighting units would be hidden inside glass recesses in the ceiling and high up the walls, and how the images of several cameras would be electronically linked, seamlessly, to create a more natural view of the room. She said everything had to be simple and automatic because there were times, like the meetings with Batu Khan, when no one but the President would be in the room.

"My wife's attempt at discretion. What she means is simple and automatic because *I'll* be working it."

"Hard to wow the other big shots with American technological superiority when you've got twelve o'clock flashing on your VCRs, darlin'."

"Hey, those VCRs were my one presidential prerogative." He turned to Wilder. "The designers wanted to put a broadcast-quality recording console in the wall. I said forget it, give me the same machines I use to record Red Sox games off the satellite dish."

"Speaking of videotaping," Laura said, "I was disappointed when I read both sides agreed not to record your meetings with Batu. It's a great loss to posterity."

"Probably so, but Batu wanted it that way and I'm sure we got a little something in return."

Marsh suddenly rose and crossed to the credenza housing the DV video recorders. The doors were open, the two machines and a stack of cassettes visible inside. With his back to the others he closed the doors, carefully locked them, pulled them several times to confirm they were locked, then pocketed the small key. Wilder and Laura exchanged a glance at his odd behavior.

"Relax, Burt, they're not gonna run off on you," Amy said, just as perplexed by his actions as Wilder and Laura.

Frowning, Marsh turned around. He knew his anger at Amy's comment was unreasonable so he said nothing for a long moment. He stared at the video wall, thinking back on his conversation with Batu.

"We created Virtual Summit technology to allow world leaders to meet face-to-face whenever we want. Like the red phone connecting the Oval Office to the Kremlin, it's supposed to foster instant communication, and therefore understanding and camaraderie. I'm not so sure getting that close to one's adversary is such a good idea. Personally, when we spoke, I wanted to reach through that video wall and ring Batu's neck."

Amy laughed. "So now the truth comes out—*that's* what you were trying to do!"

She rubbed her hand across a six-inch-wide plaster patch in the area of bare drywall. Marsh looked sheepish for a moment, then laughed along with his wife.

"Go on, tell them if you want," Marsh said. "I'm not *too* ashamed of my Irish temper."

"My hubby, our president, put his fist through the wall the other day."

"Let me state for the record, however, not because of Batu Khan. I'm not about to let a jerk like him get me mad."

"He sure manages to tick me off," Wilder offered.

Laura laughed along, but felt slightly uncomfortable talking about Marsh losing his temper and his all-too-human reaction to Batu. Marsh poured everyone another drink and smiled at Wilder.

"Right after Batu did exactly what Laura said he would I gave my national security advisers some homework—read all her books."

"It wasn't so hard to predict, really," Laura said.

"Not for you, perhaps. I had a dozen top experts telling me no one would have the brass to make the move he did."

"I believe human nature is a constant, at its best and its worst. Nothing I've learned about psychology contradicts what you see in a twenty-five-hundred-year-old Greek tragedy."

"Or on the playground in kindergarten," Wilder said.

"Exactly!" Marsh said. "I wanted to make a playground-bully analogy in my speech, but cooler heads among my advisers prevailed."

"Too bad, sir. It's a lesson people still need to learn."

"Well, my friend, you're one of the few in the country who feel that way. It's pretty obvious how the vote on Operation Swift Sword in the House will go."

"Nothing new, Mr. President," Laura said. "In 1939, 1940, there wasn't much enthusiasm in the U.S. for taking action against the Axis powers. Even though they were at war with our closest ally and there were *three* despicable tyrants to dislike."

"Ah, but FDR got lucky," Marsh said.

Laura nodded. "Sure did. Pearl Harbor."

Wilder and the First Lady laughed. "There's a headline that'll win friends," Amy said. " 'President Marsh says Pearl Harbor a lucky break' . . ."

Marsh raised his port snifter.

"Here's to luck."

Wilder's cell phone rang, startling everyone. Grumbling, he unclipped it from his belt and said, "Excuse me." This better be real god-damn important, he thought, otherwise, hey, I'll just tell them I'm having drinks with the President and First Lady and I'll call back later.

"Wilder." Listening for a moment, he frowned. "On my way." He stood up. "Sorry, sir. We've been surveilling some foreign nationals employed at Andrews. One of them just tried to bolt; our men have him cornered on base but he claims to have an explosive device."

Seventeen

As if the emergency lockdown because of the bomb threat weren't enough, the Andrews air traffic controllers got word an HH-53 presidential helicopter had departed from the White House lawn ten minutes earlier and wanted landing clearance at the base. The controllers switched to a secure frequency to warn them of the situation. In the copter, Wilder took the headset from the pilot.

"Control, it's Matt Wilder."

"*Wilder?!* Go ahead, sir . . ."

"Don't worry, the President's not aboard, he just loaned me the chopper. Have a car waiting for me on the runway."

The controllers shot each other an amazed look but did as Wilder ordered. Conspicuous in his tuxedo, he arrived moments later at the scene—the parking lot of the dry cleaner's building adjacent to the NCO dorms. Floodlights mounted on the Security Forces jeeps and a searchlight on a hovering helicopter illuminated the area with intense blue-white light. Behind the nearby dorms, security officers quietly led half-asleep airmen out the back door. Wilder spotted Brent crouching near the commander of the Bomb Disposal Unit at the edge of the parking lot.

"How the hell you get here so fast?" Brent asked.

"Got a lift. What happened?"

"FBI asked us to bring a mark in for questioning."

"Which one?"

Brent glanced at a piece of paper. "Tavo Joval. Knocked Shirlaw upside the head with the butt of a nine mil, but we got him pinned over there." He pointed to a low cinder-block enclosure for garbage bins by the rear entrance of the building.

"What about the bomb?"

"Taking his word he's got one, either on his person or hidden at the cleaner's beforehand."

Wilder had a strong hunch which one it was. "What's the plan?" he asked.

"We want him alive, meaning no shooters. I'm afraid we just gotta wait him out."

"Yeah, with most of base operations locked down in the meantime."

"Open for suggestions, pard."

Wilder turned to a nearby security officer. "Lemme borrow your piece." He snapped off the safety and stuck it in his cummerbund elastic, behind his back. "Walk with me," he said to Brent. "I got a thought, but it's gonna take teamwork." As they approached the building, he explained his plan. Despite some misgivings, Brent agreed. Otherwise, a standoff like this could go on for hours—not an option at one of the most important Air Force bases in the world.

"You do the talking," Brent said. "He'll believe it coming from you."

They slowly moved forward toward the building. About fifty feet from its side door the man came partially into view, sitting in between two large plastic trash bins, bathed in sweat.

"Joval? My name's Wilder, I'm with the OSI." No reply. "Hey, shithead, answer me!"

The security officers at the scene looked at one another—*shithead??*

"Stop right there, I got a bomb!"

Wilder and Brent kept walking. "Yeah, so I heard," Wilder said. "Look, you can either give yourself up or blow the goddamn thing and get it over with. Bomb can't be very big, or you never would've gotten it on base, and no one gives a crap if you muss up the fuckin' dry cleaner's. We can all get some sleep, hose away your guts in the morning."

"I'll do it! I swear!"

"I hear you talkin'. But I doubt you got the balls."

Joval took several deep breaths, and, as Wilder anticipated, reached for the explosive Triton hanging underneath his shirt. Wilder and Brent quickly drew their pistols, aimed and shot him in both forearms, preventing him from pulling the Triton apart. He went down screaming and the security officers were on top of him in seconds.

———

Early the next morning Wilder drove over to the Malcolm Grow Medical Center, where he'd left Joval in a guarded hospital room. The bullets had gone right through the man's arms and only one had fractured a bone, so it took only minor surgery to patch him up. By now his head would be clear of the sedatives and anesthesia, and Wilder was anxious to question him. Turning the corner of the fourth-floor hallway, he saw no guards at the entrance of the room as were expected. He pulled his Sig, broke into a run, and slammed through the doorway to the room. The bed was empty.

"Shit!"

He grabbed the phone at a nurses' station and dialed Security Forces Dispatch.

"It's Wilder. Where's my prisoner?"

The dispatcher asked Wilder to hold for Chief Kaylen.

"Matt?" Kaylen said. "You better talk to General Dryden. Orders came from him."

Wilder slammed down the phone and drove to the base commander's office. General Dryden was expecting him.

"Close the door."

"All due respect, sir, what the *fuck* is—"

"Calm down, Wilder, I don't like this any more than you do. I got a call at oh five hundred with orders to personally escort the prisoner to the flight line in fifteen minutes. An aircraft picked him up twenty minutes later. His destination was not shared with us."

"Orders from who?"

"My superiors; that's all I know. Off the record: They were as confused as the rest of us."

Wilder, feeling frustrated and betrayed, took some comfort in Dryden's belief this business originated outside the Air Force. If that were true, at least their own people weren't fucking with them.

"Does Colonel Chang know about this?"

"I had instructions not to inform the OSI prior to the transfer."

"Was the aircraft a small Gulfstream, no military markings?"

"Yes, how did you know?"

"The same one picked up the body of my Woomera infiltrator."

Just as they'd done when Wilder had lost the Woomera case, both Chang and Brent told him to move on. Thanks to the looming deadline for the commencement of Operation Swift Sword, now only six and a half weeks away, the OSI had too many other responsibilities to deal with. But instead of channeling his frustrations into his duties at the Washington Field Office, Wilder asked Brent to allow him a quick trip to Rexford University in California.

After a long tirade about losing his position, his pension, and his peace of mind, Brent gave him Friday through Monday.

Wilder flew from Andrews to Oakland, California, on an Air Force transport, then drove down through San Francisco to the university. The Rexford campus was a sprawling collection of beige brick buildings with red-tile roofs, located on the south end of the San Francisco peninsula, its beauty a marked contrast to the run-down neighborhood surrounding it. Wilder arrived at the University Relations Office at eight-fifteen. A very pregnant receptionist with a pierced nose asked him to have a seat in the small waiting area. At eight forty-five a University Relations Liaison appeared. Wilder explained why he needed the university's cooperation and the liaison's polite smile melted like warm ice cream. He escorted Wilder to the office of the university's general counsel, Ethan Nichols. Nichols, sixties, trim, with white hair in a TV evangelist cut, smiled at Wilder.

"Special Agent Matt Wilder, United States Air Force. My word. An honor to have you visit our campus, sir." Nichols had that transparent, soft-spoken humility common in old-school trial lawyers. They were trained to look smart, but not too smart. Sitting, Wilder glanced at the framed degrees, certifications, and awards on the walls.

"May we get you a beverage?"

"I'm fine, thanks."

"So, it's your contention that Rexford is implicated in some horrible murders—"

"I didn't say implicated. Only that in the twenty-one cases I've been investigating, there is one common factor in the perpetrators' lives: they, or a parent, all attended Rexford at the same time." Wilder did not mention the Infiltrator in Woomera; he wanted to keep his story focused on the already-established Rexford connection.

"If you don't mind me asking, who else is aware of this alleged commonality?"

"It's not alleged, it's a fact. I'm happy to print a copy of my notes for your records. As far as I know, I'm the only one currently aware of it. The FBI would only be interested if all the crimes were the work of a killer still at large. Same with local cops. They're only concerned about closing their files. If they have the perp, they've done their job."

"That's quite true. It is up to the courts to determine the whys and wherefores. What about the media?"

"Tabloids picked up on a few cases—Mad Yuppie Disease, all that crap. They talked about the possibility of a connection, hence the catchy name, but they haven't actually found one. Their reporters don't have the skill or patience for real investigative work if something isn't fairly obvious; it's easier and more amusing to embellish with fiction. Mainstream media covered a couple of the more outrageous cases but never went anywhere with the idea they may be related. Remember, these incidents are spread out all over the country. Also, many of the more bizarre details were never made public or widely reported. The cops, families, whatever, were able to play down the weird stuff, witnesses were not believed—"

"Rather far afield from your normal jurisdiction, is it not? I seem to recall reading somewhere that the OSI, like any other military law enforcement entity, is proscribed in its authority to military bases, personnel, and dependents."

Wilder tried not to smile at Nichols's attempt to portray himself as possessor of only modest knowledge regarding legal issues.

"I'm working with the appropriate civilian authorities."

"Indeed. And you truly believe Rexford holds some further clue to this mystery."

"That's what I'm here to find out . . . with your help. I respect the university's desire to avoid negative publicity. All I want to do is examine the enrollment records to learn how these people might've intersected during their time here."

"I would have to discuss your request with the university's president, Dr. Idelman. There are profound issues to be considered, not the least of which is our students' privacy. May I telephone you tomorrow afternoon?"

"How 'bout we call Dr. Idelman's office now?"

"I don't actually know whether he's currently on campus . . ."

Pick up the fucking phone and find out, Wilder thought. Rather than push Nichols, though, he decided to give him some breathing room. He stood up.

"I need to check into my hotel. Okay if I call you in an hour or so?"

"That would be just fine. Anything Rexford can do to help."

When Wilder got to his hotel room he hooked his computer up to the phone to check all his research sources for any new cases. There were none. He called Nichols's office at nine forty-five. The secretary said the general counsel had left the campus. Wilder replied he had Nichols's home address—he'd looked him up in *Who's Who,* just in case—and that he'd head over there to look for him. The secretary put Wilder on hold. A moment later she patched Nichols through from his cell phone.

"Mr. Wilder, my apologies. The time for an important appointment changed unexpectedly."

"Did you discuss my looking at the enrollment records with Dr. Idelman?"

"Yes. Access is a courtesy we would like to extend. However, it requires the express permission of the full board of trustees. You may petition them when they convene next Tuesday."

Wilder thanked Nichols for his assistance and hung up. The university had obviously shifted into cover-your-ass mode. He called the WFO at Andrews and asked Bob Hyler to e-mail him a sample Request for Forthwith Subpoena. OSI agents had the power to seek subpoenas through the U.S. Attorney's Office, who would present it to a federal judge for issuance. If granted, such a subpoena would empower him to go to the university registrar's office and require them to produce the records he needed. After getting the document from Hyler, he worked into it the specifics of his case.

Finishing in forty-five minutes, he called the U.S. Attorney's Office in the San Francisco federal building to request an attorney to assist him. Leah Marcus, the office's eager beaver, got the task of bringing the Request before a judge. She called him after receiving the document via fax.

"I am not going into a courtroom with *this,*" she said indignantly. "E-mail me the file so I can clean it up."

"I need it presented before lunch."

Marcus laughed. "You don't ask for much, do you?"

"Just the moon and the stars. Your boss said that's why he put you on the case."

The compliment softened Marcus's normally combative attitude a bit.

"Meet me on the steps of the Federal Court for the Northern District of California, 450 Golden Gate Avenue, at eleven-thirty. I'll be the pissed-off brunette in the tan pants suit. They break for lunch at noon, so I'm not promising anything."

"Fair enough."

Wilder fought the traffic into the city and tossed his keys to the public-lot parking attendant at eleven twenty-five. A short, stocky woman with wavy black hair arrived ten minutes later. Marcus grumbled hello and marched inside, getting in the line to the court clerk's desk. Finally, her turn came up.

"I have a Request for Subpoena that needs to be considered immediately."

The clerk examined his roster for what seemed like an hour, then shook his head. "Impossible."

Marcus stood on her tiptoes, leaned across the desk and got in his face. "Unacceptable."

"All righty," the clerk said with a sadistic smile, "the Honorable Raoul de Cordoba will hear your motion in Division Fifteen."

Marcus took it like an invitation to tea with Jack the Ripper.

"Problem?" Wilder asked.

"No." She said it with too much conviction.

As they approached the courtroom for Division Fifteen, a thunderous voice could be heard from within, echoing through the wide hallways. Marcus slipped timidly into the courtroom and found a seat. Wilder followed. Judge Raoul de Cordoba was scolding a long-haired attorney from the Public Defenders Legal Collective. The attorney, dressed in a flannel shirt and a mismatched tie, stood before the bench, literally wincing under de Cordoba's tirade. Several thick veins stood out in the judge's bald head as he shouted, and he threw a blue-paper-backed brief at the attorney.

"Amicus curiae, or friend of the court, Counselor, does not mean 'casual acquaintance'! You wear a jacket in my courtroom! That you work pro bono, noble in your poverty, does not grant you the privilege of appearing slovenly and disrespectful! If your revolutionary aversion to dirty lucre precludes the purchase of appropriate attire, borrow something from whatever Che Guevara thrift shop your firm no doubt shares its storefront with.

"And as your overwrought brief demonstrates a near-simian inability to grasp the nuances of the mother tongue, I will supplement my words with action. I'm holding you in contempt of this court and ordering either a fine of three hundred dollars or three days in jail."

The attorney skulked away and the bailiff stepped forward to inform de Cordoba of Marcus's need for an immediate hearing. The judge gave her a long, contemptuous once-over.

"Mizz Marcus. I'm bursting with curiosity as to what profound predicament would put such a hurry-up feather in the hindquarters of the U.S. Attorney's Office. Please elucidate."

"Your honor, I've distilled the salient issues in the introduction . . ."

Judge de Cordoba skimmed the top page of the brief. Marcus braced herself for a volley of tough questions. Or worse.

"Very well, Mizz Marcus. You'll have my ruling tomorrow."

"Uh, Your Honor, with all due respect . . . today would be considerably more . . . *helpful*."

Judge de Cordoba scowled at her for what seemed like a week. "Be here when we reconvene after lunch." He brought down his gavel.

At one-thirty P.M. court reconvened and Leah Marcus appeared before Judge de Cordoba.

"Mizz Marcus, I'm going to grant this request . . ."

In the spectator seats, Wilder clenched his fists in a silent exclamation of victory.

". . . with the following limitation: Access is limited to one set of attendance records, those belonging to the individual named Gail Sealy."

Furious, Marcus slammed through the courthouse doors and lit up a Virginia Slims. "This stinks of Ethan Nichols!"

Wilder looked at her, perplexed.

"He and de Cordoba are asshole buddies, golf partners!" she explained. "The judge even bought some fabulous yacht from him last year. At a fraction of its true value, you can count on that." Thinking about it really set her off. "Big jerk is out on the Bay every weekend, never even raises her sails . . . fucking old-boys'-club dilettante!"

"I don't care about the judge's goddamn boat trips! What's our next option?"

"Nothing encouraging. You could try to improve your case, refine the link among the perpetrators, add a substantial new ingredient to your argument. Then we could go back to court with a new request for a subpoena. But without a clincher, de Cordoba will never reverse himself. All we'd do is piss him off."

"What else?"

"Appeal to the Ninth Circuit. But it could take months for a ruling."

Wilder got the picture. In Technicolor.

"Redraft the subpoena request so it looks like it has some additional evidence. Be ready to present it first thing Monday."

Marcus laughed. "Judge de Cordoba would bounce my ass in prison for contempt if I showed up in his courtroom with a warmed-over request."

"I'll handle de Cordoba," Wilder said.

Eighteen

Burton Marsh had trouble breathing. He became aware of a smell—sharp, sour, medicinal. Rubbing alcohol, disinfectant, rubber tubing, linens laundered in strong bleach. He felt like he had a sandbag on top of his chest, and his limbs were numb. In the darkness he couldn't see his surroundings, but the odors and the incessant beeping of machinery were familiar to him. He sat propped up in bed, unable to turn his head. The room grew lighter, and Marsh began to make out shapes. Chairs, sofa, windows, TV . . . a dresser? No, it had small rows of lights along its front. With a gasp, Marsh recognized it—a respiratory therapy apparatus, and beside it a Heuser Lift for moving paralyzed patients in and out of bed. He was in his late father's sickroom, now *his* room, lying paralyzed in bed the same way his father had been after his stroke. He started to panic. He couldn't speak, although he had something urgent to say.

He shifted his gaze to the open windows, illuminated faintly by artificial lights outside; through the sheer, gauzelike curtains he could see the White House grounds below. Then, movement: two small children, a boy and a girl, laughing and playing. The children looked up as several dark shapes passed overhead. Helicopters—big, dark-green Hueys. Troop carriers. The children returned to their play, unconcerned. A sickening sense of dread seized Marsh as he watched. The copters landed nearby, their doors opened and dozens of armed Khaldun Commandos poured out. One group saw the kids and crossed toward them. Now Marsh recognized the kids—the murdered children of Georgian president Gorovich. He desperately tried to warn them, and tears stung his eyes. Two loud gunshots startled him and his sobbing became uncontrollable. A moment later the door opened. On the other side he saw the inside of Batu Khan's *ger*, as if he were in the VS Room. He heard more gunfire outside, the frightened shouting of men, and the heavy concussions of grenades, rockets, and large-caliber weapons. The TAA forces attacking the White House cut through the Marine Guards and Secret Service, killing everyone.

Then, silence. Two Khaldun Commandos walked through the door. Each carried something in his arms—the dead children, with the backs of their heads blown away. The Khaldun tossed the children's bodies onto Marsh's bed. He felt their weight across his legs and their blood soaked into his pristine white sheets. He struggled against his immobility in a futile effort to push the bodies away.

The Khaldun stood aside as Batu Khan entered. He held a glistening sharp scimitar in his hand, and his brightly colored *shalwar qamiz* flowed in the gentle breeze from the open windows. Batu stared at Marsh contemptuously, then spoke in a foreign tongue. Coming closer, he kicked the children's bodies off the bed and Marsh could only stare, helpless. Still talking, Batu used the tip of the sword to pull the sheet slowly off Marsh's legs.

Whack! With a single blow, Batu chopped Marsh's right foot off at the ankle with his sword. Searing pain shot through the President's body. Batu brought the sword down again, cutting off his other foot. The Commandos picked up the severed appendages and tossed them onto the floor next to the children's bodies. Down came his sword, slicing through Marsh's leg just above the knee. And again, severing the other leg. As Batu raised his sword over his head yet again, Marsh felt a scream building in his throat. Out it came, resonating suppressed terror and pain.

He awoke to find two Secret Service agents, backlit by light from the hallway, standing over his bed. Amy, clutching his head to her chest, waved the agents away. They left, closing the bedroom door behind them.

"My God, what was it, darlin'?"

"Nothing. It's okay . . ."

Soaked in sweat, Marsh lay back on the pillow. His legs ached where he dreamt Batu Khan had hacked them. The lingering terror from his dream roiled through his mind, amplifying his already deep hatred of Batu. He'd never felt such a strong desire to punish—no, *obliterate*—his enemies. At the same time, contrary to his helplessness in the dream, he never felt more powerful. Not because of being president, but personally. The strange changes in his mental and physical capabilities he noticed lately were accelerating, amplifying. Except for a corresponding increase in emotional volatility, the change was wonderful.

He tried to quiet his racing mind and doze off, but the new intensity of his senses distracted him: an acute awareness of the sweet, musky smell of Amy's body next to his, the closed-up mustiness of the antiques in the White House family quarters, and the metallic dryness of the central air-conditioning. He could hear the Secret Service men whispering among themselves in the hall; a fax machine receiving a transmission in the study at the far side of the wing. Just as he fell asleep, the President thought Curt Levinson had come in awfully early: It's not even five A.M., yet he could distinctly smell Levinson's Aramis cologne and the cup of French vanilla coffee the chief of staff drank every morning.

President Marsh got to the Oval Office a little before eight A.M. His thoughts were fuzzy and he felt irritable. Even though he'd spent the past thirty minutes reading his daily briefing digests, his nightmare still lingered vividly in his mind. Levinson came in to remind him of the upcoming meeting to discuss the shocking new atrocities in the TAA-occupied territories.

"Oh, Curt, what time did you get to the office today?"

"A little before five."

"Did you come to the family quarters at all this morning?"

"No," Levinson said, puzzled. "I was in my office in the West Wing, as usual."

Marsh didn't explain his reason for asking. Secretary of Defense Woodruff knocked on the Oval Office door. "Stan, come in." Marsh turned to Levinson. "Tell everyone we'll be along in a moment."

Levinson nodded. It annoyed him that the President spoke in private with Woodruff so often—several times a week, the only conference he, as chief of staff, did not attend. Woodruff closed the door to the Oval Office when Levinson left.

"I see the ExOps reported an infiltration last night," Marsh said, holding a secret briefing file.

"Yes, sir. Definitely some rattled nerves up in Seattle." Woodruff smiled. "But our visitors took the intended information, and as my grandmother would say, may it bring six horse-loads of graveyard clay on top of 'em."

"Tell the boys good work."

Marsh thought back on how, nine months ago, the Department of Defense became aware of TAA infiltrations into several facilities developing new weapons systems. He'd ordered Woodruff to create a top-secret counterintelligence team directly under presidential command. Woodruff recruited a dozen ExOps, short for Executive Operatives, from the best agents at the National Security Agency, which had the most sophisticated intelligence-gathering and antiespionage skills in the world. The arrangement was similar to the one between Nixon and his famous Plumbers, so named because their job—at first, anyway—had been plugging news leaks coming from within the White House. No one knew the ExOps team existed except he and Woodruff, and their particular method of counterintelligence seemed to be working. He'd gradually found other uses for the ExOps—handling assignments unknown even to Woodruff—under his direct personal command.

"Anything new on the prototype weapons systems?" Marsh asked.

"We're still on schedule. Main concern for the manned aircraft is the hypersonic flight-control computers. Contractors are reluctant to sign off on the neural net without more in-flight testing."

"Fine. I don't want to lose a pilot or a half-billion-dollar plane on account of a computer glitch either. Make sure they have whatever they need."

Marsh and Woodruff crossed into the Roosevelt Room, where the Joint Chiefs, Vice President Taylor, and the rest of the National Security Council waited for them. The prior day the CIA had received a videotape, smuggled out of the Ukraine, that showed in vivid detail some TAA forces, including Batu Khan himself, committing atrocities against civilians. President Marsh planned to hold a press conference later in the day to reveal what had happened; he and his advisers first needed to write the President's statements, and decide how much of the graphic video to show on national television.

Batu and his command company were camped inside a dense forest on the Crimean peninsula near Yalta. With the camp spread out below the trees, he felt safely hidden from the American spy satellites. Nine P.M. eastern, the time for Marsh's press conference, was five A.M. in Yalta. A few minutes beforehand, Chu'tsai came into the *ger*. An oil lamp turned down low on the table cast the tent in a pale yellow glow. Batu, it appeared, lay on his sleeping roll on the floor. As Chu'tsai's eyes adjusted to the darkness, however, he saw Batu making love, lying on his back, and he could hear soft moaning. Batu's wife Kuri, the beautiful seventeen-year-old who'd made the mutton during the VS meeting with President Marsh, straddled him, facing his feet, slowly gliding him in and out of her. His other wife, Panya, knelt behind his head. She bent over him, massaging his chest, letting her bare breasts brush across his face.

"Batu, it's almost time," Chu'tsai said softly.

Batu took Panya's face in his hands and kissed her while arching his back and coming inside Kuri. After a moment, the women climbed off of him and, heads bowed, backed away from the bed. Batu rolled over, picked up a remote, and turned on the TV in the wooden credenza. He flipped through the channels on the satellite box, paused for a moment on VH-1, then continued until he found the image of reporters in the White House press room awaiting the President's arrival. He grinned at Chu'tsai.

"I'm starving."

"I'm not surprised. I'll have Yela bring you something."

Chu'tsai opened the flap on the *ger* and said something in Mongolian to one of the Khaldun. He returned to find Batu still stretched out on the floor, his hands held behind his head.

"I made love to Kuri six times last night. It's her fertile time. Tell me what you sense. Will we finally have a son?"

Chu'tsai hesitated before replying. His gifts predicting the future were good but not perfect, and he knew how deeply Batu wanted a true answer. After a moment, he smiled.

"I think you can get some rest."

Ecstatic, Batu sighed, closed his eyes and offered a prayer of thankfulness to the Eternal Blue Heaven.

On the TV, the networks filled in the time before the President's arrival in the pressroom by showing footage of the massive U.S. deployment to the Mediterranean: troops, ships, aircraft, support personnel, equipment, missile batteries. An animated map showed the routes of the two carrier groups and various other ships and submarines approaching the theatre of operations for Operation Swift Sword. Batu sat up and scowled, his happy mood ruined. He shot a look at Chu'tsai.

"Putting these images on the television is part of Marsh's game. He thinks he'll frighten me into submission. Instead, my blood quickens at the thought of battle."

Chu'tsai gestured at the TV. "There he is."

The reporters stood up as President Marsh came into the press room. Batu turned up the sound on the TV, and Chu'tsai sat cross-legged on the floor next to him.

"Evening, everyone. Let me start with a short statement, then you can fire away with your questions. We have stated from the beginning that the Trans-Altaic Alliance occupation of Georgia and the Ukraine are acts of wanton aggression, illegal by any measure of international law. Despite claims by the TAA that the citizens of those countries willingly chose to join in the Alliance, we've maintained the vast majority of the people of those countries opposed being overrun and subjugated and have resisted their oppressors whenever possible. We now have proof of such opposition, as well as of the horrific punishment Batu Khan has exacted on those civilians who bravely stood against him."

Batu Khan shot an angry look at Chu'tsai. "Who writes this propaganda for him? 'Subjugated!'" Scowling, he turned back to the TV.

"We have in our possession a videotape smuggled out of the Ukraine yesterday afternoon—"

Batu looked at Chu'tsai again.

"What's he talking about?"

"I have no idea."

"It took extraordinary bravery to bring you this footage," Marsh continued. "I must stress in the strongest terms that these images are very graphic."

Agitated, Batu jumped from his sleeping roll and draped a sheepskin over his shoulders. A small, wrinkled woman, Yela, came in with two wooden bowls of food.

"Get out of here!" Batu shoved her out of the tent.

The TV showed an extreme telephoto shot, taken from the top of a four-story building, of a soccer field at the edge of a Ukrainian town. Rows of people, at least 150 of them, were kneeling, hands tied behind their backs. Men, women, children, in no particular order, guarded by Khaldun Commandos carrying machine guns and Khaldun Horsemen. Three men got out of a jeep and walked into the scene—Batu Khan, recognizable in his *shalwar qamiz*, and two of his generals. He addressed the captors but could not be heard—the sound was garbled by distance and the noise of wind against the open microphone.

In the *ger*, Batu stopped pacing and turned to Chu'tsai.

"Did you know about this video?"

"Absolutely not."

On the TV, Batu walked along the rows of captives. He stopped at the tenth person, a woman in her sixties, and unbuttoned the front of his *shalwar qamiz*. He held his arms out and back behind him and one of the generals slid the garment off Batu's shoulders. He was naked underneath. The other general handed Batu a five-foot-long, bright steel scimitar. A Khaldun stood behind the woman and pushed his boot against her back to bend her over. Batu stood alongside her, raised the scimitar high above his head and brought it down with all his strength, cutting the woman's head off. Her body slumped against the person kneeling next to her and a wave of horrified cries arose from the captives. Blood splattered everywhere, making Batu's reason for removing his *shalwar qamiz* quite evident.

Batu walked quickly along, stopping again at the tenth person. A teenaged boy. Down came the sword. By the fifth victim, blood soaked Batu's entire body. He still tried to be heard over the captives' cries, his tone sounding as if he were imploring, reasoning with them. He paused to wipe his face with a cloth. The camera zoomed closer. The focus went in and out, then a clear view of him could be seen.

He was crying.

It went on for another three victims, every tenth one of the captives. Then there were angry voices and gunshots close to the camera. It fell to the ground and the image went black.

In his *ger*, Batu shouted indignantly: "Marsh is a hypocrite! He would've bombed the whole village into oblivion from the air! He'd kill them with a phone call, as if that makes his hands less bloody. My punishment showed mercy! One in ten! I didn't exterminate them, not like the Americans would've done! I taught the village to respect me, yet spared ninety percent of them! For my kindness Marsh makes me out to be an animal!"

President Marsh returned to the TV screen. Reporters called out questions. He pointed at a National Public Radio correspondent in the center row.

"Will this cause you to reassess your deadline for the TAA withdrawal from the occupied territories?"

"We haven't made any determination about that yet." He pointed to a woman from the *Washington Post.*

"Will the United States ask the U.N. for a war-crimes investigation into this event?"

"Ambassador Drake has already done so."

Marsh looked to the back of the pressroom to take a question from there. A man in a blue blazer caught his attention.

"Bobby, good to see you back on the beat."

"Good to be back, Mr. President. Please thank Mrs. Marsh for the flowers and kind note."

Marsh smiled. "I will. At least we know security hasn't forgotten you—letting you in with an expired press pass."

The reporter twisted the plastic White House security pass clipped to his jacket so he could read it. He registered surprise to see that, indeed, it had expired at the end of the prior month.

"Do you think this latest atrocity, at the hands of Batu Khan himself, will increase support here and abroad for military action against the TAA?" he asked.

Marsh paused for a moment before answering. "If anyone can view this tape without being horrified, I . . . I wouldn't know what to say to them. Politics, moment by moment, is a fickle business. But the moral compass of the American people, in the long run, is not. One challenge of leadership is knowing the difference, staying the course through moments of dissent and doubt."

The questions came faster now, mostly about the President's specific military plans for Operation Swift Sword, and how he expected to remove the TAA from the territory they held without becoming mired in a costly ground war. He could not reply with any specifics, as such information was classified. The reporter with the expired pass raised his hand again and Marsh pointed to him.

"Returning to the discussion a moment ago, Mr. President, about trusting the moral compass of the American people. Even now your policies toward the TAA do not hold majority approval. Should that support wane further—not transiently, but decisively, like during the Vietnam war—would you rethink your position?"

Marsh paused as a flash of rage seized him for a moment, a deep-in-the-gut fury far stronger than the question warranted. He tried not to let his anger show.

"I don't mean to be evasive, Bob, I really don't. However, it is simply not within our national character, when the need is real, to turn a blind eye to cruelty and injustice."

Marsh made a prearranged signal to Curt Levinson, who stepped forward.

"That's it, everyone, thanks for coming . . ."

The reporters murmured with disappointment as Marsh left the podium.

In his *ger*, Batu threw the remote control at the TV.

"He *is* insane!"

"I still say he's bluffing," Chu'tsai said. "The polls and the media will scare him into backing down. Even his own Congress doesn't support him."

"He's the commander in chief; he can make war if he desires."

"Okay, maybe so . . . provided the Vice President hasn't replaced him before then. If that happens our concerns are over. Taylor has no stomach for a fight."

"Forget about all that. I cannot wait any longer, hoping Marsh's condition will manifest itself and force him from office."

"But it will happen any time now—remember the people in California?"

"Or it might take weeks, maybe months. Don't forget the others, aside from Marsh, who haven't snapped yet."

"Yes, but they're ready to. All it takes is an intense enough experience to trigger them."

The moment Chu'tsai made the comment a great excitement flooded Batu. He felt the Eternal Blue Heaven speaking with perfect clarity: A man must forge his destiny, just as destiny forges him.

"There *is* a way to know exactly when Marsh will cross the line," Batu said, his eyes ablaze. "By pushing him over it ourselves."

President Marsh came into the small anteroom behind the press room where Amy waited for him and threw his jacket on the sofa. Levinson saw by Marsh's mood he should give the President time to calm down, so he herded everyone out, leaving the first couple alone. Amy stared quizzically at her husband. The wild look in his eyes concerned her.

"Burt?"

"You *hear* that fucking guy? They won't be happy till people are rioting in the streets."

"You're overreacting."

For an instant, the thought that she was on their side crossed Marsh's mind. With it came a surge of intense fury. It scared him, so he took a deep breath.

"I'm being an asshole."

"Well put."

"I don't understand why I'm so *angry* about everything lately."

Amy put her arms around him. Instantly, Marsh could feel his rage mutate into a powerful lust. His interest in Amy had never lessened over three decades of marriage, but this went way beyond his usual urges. He pulled her close and kissed her, mouth open, his tongue pushing hard against hers.

"Now?!" she whispered.

"Door's locked . . ."

Marsh ripped Amy's panties from under her skirt and tossed them aside. They fell onto the sofa together, fumbling to get Marsh's belt and pants undone. She gasped as he plunged inside her. He pinned her arms over her head with one hand and covered her mouth with the other to stifle her cries. Normally, he made love to her slowly and sensuously. Now he pounded against her with the urgency of a teenager in the backseat of a car. Riding toward a climax, Marsh pressed his lips against Amy's, slammed into her and held himself fully inside as he ejaculated. Amy could feel it, unusually hot and deep, and she came, sharp and sudden. They lay across the sofa, gasping for breath, then Marsh rolled onto the floor. A moment later, he started to laugh.

"Please share the joke," she said.

Pants around his ankles, Marsh shuffled over to her on his knees and grinned. Amy looked down and stared incredulously. He had a brand-spanking-new hard-on. He climbed back on top, put his hands under her ass and pushed inside her, just as energetically as before.

"Mr. President, you are a force of nature. . . ."

Nineteen

fter he'd asked U.S. Attorney Leah Marcus to rewrite his subpoena request, Wilder gathered some details about Judge de Cordoba's weekend fishing trips. His itinerary, according to a friend of Marcus's who'd once gone with him, never altered. He zigzagged north on the Bay twenty-four miles to Midshipman's Point on Saturday night, spent all day Sunday anchored off the point fishing, then motored back late that night.

At six-thirty Saturday evening, when de Cordoba's seventy-foot teakwood sloop, the *Kathleen Rose*, puttered out of the Yacht Harbor on the north shore of the San Francisco peninsula under power of her inboard motors, Wilder watched through binoculars and shook his head. Taking that beauty out without raising her sails was like driving a Ferrari with the parking brake on.

Standing on shore at the Marina Green, he could make out His Honor standing at the sloop's wheel while his wife, twenty-five years his junior, served their four guests from a tray of drinks. He recognized one of them—Ethan Nichols, Rexford University's general counsel. Wilder checked a small black-and-silver electronic unit clipped to his belt. Low, steady beeps came from its speaker at one per second, and a bright green pinpoint of light flashed in unison on its round screen. He drove past the East Harbor to the touristy Fisherman's Wharf, parking near a small Portuguese place with a spectacular view of the water and the USS *Pampanito*, then walked to a shack office with motorboats for rent. He'd arranged to rent a motorboat earlier that day, right after attaching the homing device to de Cordoba's sloop. Darkness fell as he set out across the water; he followed the homing beacon until spotting the cabin lights of the *Kath-leen Rose* then throttled back, staying three hundred yards behind her.

The judge reached the Point at ten-thirty P.M. and anchored for the night. Wilder watched Mrs. de Cordoba make the rounds with her bottomless margarita pitcher, until, after much loud talk and laughter, everyone went below at midnight. Wilder beached his motorboat on an uninhabited stretch of shore below the Island Land Club and waited until an hour after the last light went out on the *Kathleen Rose*. He pulled on a wet suit. Swimming the two-tenths of a mile to the sloop, the cold salt water of the Bay stung his eyes and windburned face. He pulled himself quietly aboard on the aft ladder near the engines, retrieved the homing beacon and put it into a waterproof container on his belt.

He took off his wetsuit cap so his ears wouldn't be covered, and heard no sound except the sloop's rhythmic creaking and the lapping of waves against the hull. He opened the hatch leading to the engines and found the air inlet. He unscrewed a wing nut and removed a round cover to expose the air cleaner, a foam and corrugated fiberboard doughnut eight inches in diameter, then cut a two-by-three-inch hole in the inner surface of the air cleaner and tucked a plastic-wrapped package inside it. Replacing the cover and the engine hatch, he moved quietly to the wheelhouse, well-equipped with navigational aides, depth indicators, and a sonar fish locator. Wilder pulled the microphone plug out of the two-way radio and compared the five-pin connector against the diagram of one he'd drawn in ballpoint pen on the inside of his forearm. He took a tiny glass bottle of clear nail polish out of his belt pack and carefully coated pins one, four, and five on the microphone connector, then blew on them to dry the polish before replacing the plug. Next he rummaged through the cabinets until finding an emergency flare gun. One sharp twist with a pair of needle-nosed pliers snapped the firing pin off the gun's hammer.

Now for the fun part, he thought. There were six people aboard, with easily as many cellular phones among them. He pushed open the aft cabin door. A notion struck him—perhaps this operation had crossed the line into overkill. Then again, the extreme always worked for him. In this case, its very outrageousness would aid its deniability. Inside the cabin Nichols and his wife snored in unison, and the air around them smelled boozy enough for Wilder to feel confident they slept soundly. He found Nichols's phone in the pocket of a windbreaker and held a flexible strip of metal against its battery terminals, completely discharging it. He then went through all the luggage; Mrs. Nichols appeared not to have a phone, nor did Nichols carry a spare battery.

Next door, another guest tossed restlessly in his too-small bunk next to his chubby wife. Wilder went through their belongings, finding two phones and two beepers. Digging for spare batteries, Wilder found something unexpected: a nine-millimeter Beretta. Next to it, an ID and a shield. Shit. The man was the goddamn chief of police of Daly City. Just then, the chief sat up in bed. Wilder, crouched at the foot of the bunk, shoved his penlight into the sleeve of his wet suit and froze. The chief stumbled half asleep to the head to take a leak. Wilder looked around, saw no place to hide. He would surely be spotted if he tried to slip out of the cabin, so he stayed put.

The chief finished pissing, coughed and spat a few times, then shuffled back to his bunk, almost brushing against Wilder as he went by. Wilder waited fifteen minutes before he dared try to leave.

In the forward cabin, lying in bed with his hands clasped on his chest, de Cordoba looked like an angry Mayan deity. Even in sleep he scowled. Wilder rifled through the bags and tiny closets, coming up with one more cell phone. Just as he finished running down its battery, he heard a louder-than-usual creak behind him. He pressed himself into the shallow closet and saw the chief, Beretta in hand, peer through the half-open doorway into the cabin. The wily old cop must've sensed something earlier, even with four margaritas in him. After a long moment, the chief went topside. Wilder spent thirty minutes jammed in de Cordoba's closet. As he did during the stakeout at Woomera, he willed himself into a trance of perfect stillness, waiting for the son-of-a-bitching chief to go back to bed. Finally, he tired of waiting and ventured slowly up the ladder. The chief sat on a deck chair, wrapped in a robe and a blanket, content as a fat old tomcat, smoking a cigar. Another hour went by until Wilder felt confident the chief had dozed off, and he slipped back into the icy water of the Bay.

By Sunday night at six-thirty, when de Cordoba finally pulled anchor, Wilder had discovered something more boring than fishing: watching people fish. The *Kathleen Rose*'s inboards chugged to life, and she headed south for home. Wilder followed in his motorboat. He'd calculated the point on de Cordoba's route where the sloop would be farthest from shore, two and seven-tenths of a mile, to be about five and a half miles south of Midshipman Point. When the sloop reached that spot, he pressed a button on a model airplane control box.

The plastic package he'd put inside the air cleaner contained a matchbox-sized, radio-controlled model-airplane control servo, with the tip of an X-acto razor knife soldered to its tiny arm. Surrounding it in the plastic package were rice-sized metal shavings, which Wilder had taken from the trash behind a machine shop. As the servo spun around, the razor cut the plastic and the engine air intake sucked up the metal pieces. In seconds, the *Kathleen Rose*'s engines ground to a stop.

Leaving the hot springs after three days, Batu moved his encampment a few hundred miles to the shore of the Dörgön Nuur lake, west of the Altai Mountains. A remote, dramatic landscape in the Mongolian plains, it consisted of rugged ridges, vast plateaus, and sweeping steppes. As always, it gave Batu immense pleasure to be in such pristine surroundings and still command his empire. At sunrise he was riding his stallion, Mika, along the lakefront when the roar of a TAA helicopter destroyed his solitude. Batu calmed Mika while the copter landed and Chu'tsai opened the door.

"We have a problem!"

A Khaldun Horseman jumped from the copter to walk Mika to the command camp and Chu'tsai briefed Batu during the short flight back:

"There's a fire in Mountain Five. They're trying to get it under control, but it's bad."

"Have they secured the aircraft components?"

"They're moving everything into the tunnels."

This was terrible news—damage to one of Batu's seven underground aircraft storage facilities could mean a serious setback in the development of his new air force. Everything so far had gone brilliantly. Thanks to a wildly successful program of stealing American design secrets, the TAA had made enormous advances in its hypersonics program. And by duplicating American technology Batu's engineers were able to build their aircraft with minimal flight testing because factors such as fatigue analysis and engine behavior had already been tested by their original builders.

Batu had struck upon a twofold solution to hide his progress from his enemies. Occasionally, he'd allow the United States, the Russians, or the Chinese to think they'd seen something they shouldn't, like a testing mishap. He'd leak small shreds of false intelligence, detailing his frustrations and setbacks, easily convincing the Americans and others that they were years away from upgrading their aging aircraft. Masking his real success had proven more difficult. His people could fabricate pieces of aircraft in the old Soviet factories now under his control, but where could they assemble, test, or store them? The solution came to Batu while watching *The Great Escape*, where the prisoners hid the dirt excavated from their escape tunnel in their pants legs and deposited it a bit at a time around the prison camp. This had gotten him thinking about the Trans-Mongolian Railroad. Built in Bolshevik times, it followed ancient trade routes for thirteen hundred miles, crossing the Mongolian mountains, the highland steppes, and the Gobi Desert. Traversing the Hentiyn Nuruu range, north of the capital city of Ulan Bator, it went through dozens of brick-and-concrete tunnels blasted through the rugged mountains.

So, in the desolate Hentiyn Nuruu, hour after hour, day after day, long, slow, freight trains began carrying men and matériel to the tunnels inside the mountains and hauling away millions of tons of rock and dirt. In eighteen months the Trans-Altaic Alliance had built seven enormous underground storage and final-fitting facilities.

The copter touched down at his encampment. Batu ran into his *ger* and used the VS equipment to video link with the Mountain Five control center. On screen, the chief engineer stood coughing in the thick, toxic smoke. Behind him an electrical fire spread throughout the huge underground area while terrified workers lay on the floor in search of breathable air. Batu now understood why Chu'tsai had come for him: much more stood at risk than the loss of this one facility.

"I need permission to open the ventilation system!" the engineer said to Batu. "We need fresh air. We must allow the smoke to escape outside—"

"I know you must, but we both know why you must not," Batu replied. "Spectrographic analysis, temperature sensors . . . our enemies' satellites will see your smoke so far from civilization and know it comes from flames of man's making, technology afire. If this becomes known, all is known."

The engineer nodded, accepting the death sentence without argument. Fighting back tears, Batu watched as the flames grew inside the mountain. Hundreds of his finest aircraft builders were suffocated and burned alive before his eyes, then the video transmission ceased.

Batu bowed his head for a long moment in meditation and prayer, then looked up at Chu'tsai, standing next to him.

"You foretold a great sacrifice. Is this it?"

Chu'tsai shook his head. "I'm not sure if it is . . ."

He'd been struck with an unsettling premonition that Batu would suffer a profound loss in the near future, but the tragedy in the mountain did not mesh with that vision. Whatever terrible event he'd been sensing would be more intimate and personal—although he would not reveal that belief to Batu until he could discern some specific details beyond a vague sense of dread.

"This didn't happen without purpose," Batu said. "It's another sign we must move quickly! Our new planes are worthless if our enemies discover them on the ground and destroy them before they've taken wing. . . ." His voice trailed off. "How many aircraft are deployable now or within the next two weeks?"

"Six or eight; I'll have to check."

"Have them ready. As many as possible. The command craft, too. Do whatever it takes."

Leah Marcus found Wilder waiting for her outside the Federal Courthouse in San Francisco at eight-thirty Monday morning.

"Is the OSI going to make my bail when de Cordoba throws me in the slammer for contempt?"

"No, but I will." Marcus wondered why Wilder seemed so . . . pleased with himself. When he held the door open for her, she dragged her feet like someone walking to the gallows. The court clerk confirmed Marcus's place on the calendar—first up. Good, Marcus thought, better to get the pain over with quickly. Precisely at nine A.M., the bailiff announced, "All rise."

At five-foot-nothing, Marcus couldn't see over the people standing in front of her as the judge came in and sat down. The bailiff continued: "Court is now in session, the Honorable Naomi Franklin presiding."

A murmur of surprise went around the room. Marcus stared at Judge Franklin, a pretty black woman in her forties, with utter disbelief— Franklin, new to the bench, still presided over procedural hearings and subbed for other judges while she learned the ropes. Judge de Cordoba's strictness and tantrums were well known, but the fact he'd never missed a day on the bench in thirty-seven years was legendary. Marcus looked at Wilder again and he replaced his smile with an expression of studied innocence. She briefly wondered if he'd knocked the old bastard off. She didn't have time to pursue the thought, because the bailiff called her forward.

She presented the revised request for a forthwith subpoena for the Rexford class transcripts. This time she'd added an affidavit from an insurance actuarial expert, who certified the chance of twenty-one perpetrators of violent crimes who theretofore had no history of criminal behavior all attending the same college at the same time had a statistical probability on the order of one billion to one.

"I see Judge de Cordoba reviewed this same motion just last week, Counselor, and granted access to only one set of transcripts."

"It's, uh, not the same, Your Honor. Some key information is newly presented herein."

Marcus would have a big problem if Judge Franklin asked *what* additional information. The statistical statement was not new, per se, only an opinion rendered upon the existing facts.

"Billion to one. Huh. Sounds like the lottery ticket I bought this morning."

Judge Franklin looked over Marcus's paperwork, then took the pen from de Cordoba's carved-wood trout desk set. "I'm inclined to grant this request, Ms. Marcus."

Marcus shot a quick victory smile at Wilder. He grinned back. Just as the judge began to sign the papers, a federal marshal entered from chambers and whispered something in her ear. She nodded, put down her pen, and announced to the courtroom:

"There'll be a moment's delay, ladies and gentlemen; the Honorable Judge de Cordoba has arrived. I'm going to turn the bench over to him, and he'll pick up where I left off."

Wilder watched with disbelief as Judge Franklin reached for the gavel.

"Uh, Your Honor . . ." One would never have known from the offhand tone in Marcus's voice how dearly she wanted to scream.

Judge Franklin looked at Marcus and remembered what she'd been doing. She signed the subpoena and the bailiff handed it to Marcus. As everyone rose for Judge Franklin's departure and Judge de Cordoba's arrival, Wilder and Marcus hurried out the rear doors. Wilder turned as he left, just in time to see de Cordoba sweep into the courtroom, surly and red-faced, and stomp over to the bench. His eyes narrowed as he saw Wilder slip out the door. Wilder couldn't swear to it, but it sure sounded like the judge's shoes were squishing wetly as he walked.

When Wilder arrived at the Rexford University registrar's office later that morning he found Ethan Nichols waiting for him. Although the lawyer's demeanor remained professional and cool, the time and necessity for pleasantries with Wilder had passed.

"If any of this information becomes public or is used outside of the scope of your subpoena, I'll see you're court-martialed as well as face civil penalties."

"Just doing my job." A phrase, Wilder knew, recognized worldwide to mean "fuck you, buckaroo." He slipped the stack of Xeroxed, letter-sized transcripts into a manila envelope.

Nichols looked him over. "Seems you got some sun over the weekend. Out on the water, I'd venture. You're burned under your chin. Reflection."

This, Wilder mused, is the great benefit of overkill. It would take more than an angry lawyer's unfounded suspicions to make anyone believe he did what he did. Annoyed at not getting a reaction, Nichols persisted. He told Wilder the story of how he'd been on de Cordoba's sloop. How the motor conked out, stranding them all night. How, mysteriously, none of their emergency equipment worked. And how His Honor had been so determined to get to court on time that at dawn he raised the sails for the first time since he owned her. She'd promptly capsized, tossing everyone into the Bay, and they'd spent an hour sitting atop the hull until a Coast Guard cruiser righted the sloop and towed her home.

"That's a real kick in the ass," Wilder offered.

"We'll see whose ass ultimately gets kicked."

"Keep me posted."

Wilder hurried back to his hotel room to comb through the transcripts, compare course schedules, and look for a common denominator. Most of the perps had been in the School of Humanities and Sciences, and had similar required courses in their freshman and sophomore years, such as English and physical education. Most of those, however, were not at the same time or with the same instructor. Before beginning to enter all the subject and session codes into his database he went to the bathroom and splashed some water on his face. The transcripts had been scanned from microfiche, so they were fuzzy and hard to read. Returning to his computer, he opened Ralph Bonner's transcript. The code CH 302 caught his attention; he'd seen it a few minutes ago. He paged back to Liz Evanston's records. CH 302, Cowling. She'd been in the same class, same time as Bonner. Winter quarter, 1972–73. As had Julie Nelson's mother, Cheryl Packard, and Gail. Jonas McKee had taken the CH 302 class in the fall quarter, 1972. CH, Wilder presumed, meant chemistry. Made sense—McKee had a degree in chemistry, and he was an exec at a pharmaceutical company. He soon determined that indeed, the name Cowling appeared in nineteen of the twenty-one transcripts, and the classes he'd taught were within a quarter or two of each other. Two transcripts, however, made no reference to Cowling. Wilder stared at those pages, sensing some difference in them, something physical, but he couldn't quite place it.

He looked up Cowling on the Rexford web site. Would the professor still be alive, still teaching? His luck remained with him: He soon located Professor Walt Cowling, Ph.D., chairman, Department of Organic Chemistry. Excited, Wilder glanced at his watch. Only ten hours remained before he had to catch a transport back to Andrews. He decided that rather than going back to the university administration he'd pay an unofficial visit to Professor Cowling himself. Surely he would be concerned about the possibility of additional outbreaks of violence.

Searching the Net, Wilder expected to find some obscure references to Cowling here and there, as would be the case with most academics. Instead, he found thousands of search hits, including a vanity web site dedicated entirely to the Professor and his works. Its design was very Sixties, in that splashy, psychedelic colors Peter-Max-flower-power way, a visual motif Wilder hadn't seen in years. He read Cowling's bio:

Walter Cowling, Ph.D., graduated with a B.S. from Berkeley in 1962, earned a Ph.D. in organic chemistry from Rexford in 1965. He remained as one of the university's most popular lecturers, authoring several chemistry texts, a half-dozen counterculture books, and a youngish-professor-and-coed-in-love novel. Professor Cowling's greatest fame came from his involvement in the Human Potential Movement in the Sixties. Encounter groups, meditation, yoga, drugs—all were acceptable as a way to enlightenment. Cowling stood among those true believers within the movement who envisioned using its techniques for a broader range of social and personal ills, and as a way to rid oneself of long-buried emotional traumas, inhibitions, and the culturally programmed roles of race, class, and gender. As did the movement, Cowling continuously reinvented himself to keep up with ever-changing tastes and attitudes. One year he was part of the scene surrounding the teachings of the Maharishi. Next it was est. Then Rolfing, bioenergetics, Silva Mind Control, Zen, transcendental meditation, Baba Ram Dass, and Timothy Leary.

Wilder read it all with amusement. In his world, one's personal beliefs were kept private. Professor Cowling, on the other hand, espoused and defended every position, great or small, with the fury of a holy jihad. He concluded either the Professor would pour all his formidable energies into helping him solve his mystery, or fight like hell to prevent him from doing so.

That afternoon, Wilder entered the Rexford campus through an unguarded pedestrian gate—he wouldn't put it past Nichols to have circulated his photo to the security guards with a standing order to evict him from the grounds. He followed the campus directory to Professor Cowling's classroom in the Organic Chemistry building. It and the adjacent Old Chem building, housing his lab and office, were near the Ellipse, just west of the central part of campus. The Org Chem hallways were cool and dimly lit. Wilder found a set of doors to Cowling's lecture hall, but they were locked. He peered through the small windows, made from the old-fashioned glass with crisscrossed wire reinforcement inside it, and saw the silhouette of someone standing behind a tall podium facing the deserted rows of seats. Wilder almost knocked on the door, then changed his mind. He continued along the hallway, finding another set of double doors leading to the back of the hall. Someone, apparently, had tried to lock them in a hurry, because the extended deadbolt on one door had missed its female counterpart on the other. Wilder went inside. All the lights were turned off; the only illumination came from slivers of daylight through the yellowed venetian blinds on a bank of high windows.

He instantly recognized Cowling, standing at the podium, from his web site photos—tall, reed-thin, with a craggy, tanned face, round wire glasses, and a full head of white hair cascading down his back in a long, neat ponytail. The Professor didn't see him enter. Head down, eyes closed, he was wearing headphones turned up so loud Wilder could hear a tinny rendition of a rock song. He almost laughed when he placed it—"In-A-Gadda-Da-Vida," the 1968 acid-rock hit by Iron Butterfly. Suddenly, Professor Cowling clutched the podium, turned his face heavenward, and moaned. After a moment he caught his breath, took off the headphones, and stepped back. Someone stood up from behind the podium. At first it looked to Wilder like a teenaged boy. Then he realized it was a girl, maybe eighteen years old, although her short auburn, pageboy hair and waiflike body made her seem twelve. She wore nothing but a pair of cut-off jeans, and glistening streaks of semen ran down her chin and onto the middle of her chest. Smiling at Cowling, she smeared it all over her tiny breasts. He held her face in his hands, kissed her deeply, then licked her wet chin. Wilder tried to slip quietly out of the room, but the Professor caught sight of him.

"Greetings. Do I know you?"

"No, Professor. My name's Wilder."

Neither Cowling nor the girl seemed remotely embarrassed. While he zipped up his trousers, she calmly pulled on a midriff-length T-shirt.

"Well, my friend, what can I do you out of?"

Wilder came down to the front of the hall. As he began to explain who he was, Professor Cowling interrupted him.

"Forgive me; Patti will be late for class." He used his fingers to arrange her hair, then carefully wiped a smudge of lipstick from her face. "Love you, baby. See you tonight."

"Love you, Walt." She waved cheerfully to Wilder as she left. "Bye!"

Professor Cowling turned to him with a pleased, I'm-fucking-her expression on his face.

"So, you're from the Air Force."

"Office of Special Investigations."

Grinning, Cowling stood ramrod straight and mock-saluted several times. "You can count on my full cooperation, Admiral. I can't have your boys napalming the student union . . ."

Wilder screwed up a smile and played along. "In that case, I'll call back the squadron."

Cowling guffawed, a little too enthusiastically. "Call back the squadron. That's rich." He gathered up the papers from his podium and headed for the door. "I've got office hours."

"Mind if I tag along? I'd like to ask you a couple questions."

"Absolutely. Anything. Secrets are a toxin to the soul."

As they walked across the patio to the Old Chem building, everyone they passed greeted the Professor in much the manner one would greet a rock star. He reveled in the adulation, and seemed remarkably fit and energetic for a man in his sixties.

Because of its many labs, a heavy, acrid smell hung in the air of the Old Chem building. Professor Cowling led Wilder to the suite of faculty offices, where his big corner office had a view of the tree-lined Ellipse in the center of campus. They went through the open door and Cowling tossed his papers onto one of the teetering piles already on the desk. The office looked like a museum exhibit of counterculture wall posters: Free Huey, Free the Chicago Seven, Free Love. A group photo of Andy Warhol's Superstars circa 1967, all nude, the men wearing women's makeup. There were newer vintages, too: Fur Is Dead, Meat Is Murder. One wall was devoted to pictures of Cowling himself—lecturing, appearing on TV, doing book promotions, out on the town with various actresses, conducting seminars. Cowling leaned against the arm of the ratty sofa and pulled his shoes and socks off, then dug around in a small refrigerator.

"Drink?"

"Whatever you've got."

Cowling tossed Wilder a kid-sized carton of apple juice, took one for himself, and sat behind his desk. "Sorry, Chief, need to make a quick call . . ."

"Go right ahead."

He brought up an electronic day planner on his computer—a dual-processor PC with a huge, twenty-five-inch monitor—to look up a phone number. He punched in a seven-digit number on the phone, paused, keyed another seven digits, then hung up. He paged someone, Wilder thought. Cowling leaned back in his chair, put his bare feet up on the desk, and sipped his apple juice. Wilder noticed he had a tattoo on his ankle, a very unusual subject for body adornment—one of those line-and-circle, color-coded diagrams of a molecule.

"Okay. I'm entirely yours, Generalissimo."

Wilder glanced at the open door. Several teaching assistants sat within earshot in the common area outside. "The nature of my questions is rather sensitive."

"No secrets here, soldier boy. We leave the cloak-and-dagger stuff to you military-industrial types."

Wilder ran the background: Gail Sealy's murder of Dr. Herrold, the similar cases of violent behavior from other people living all around the country. The discovery they, or, in one case, her mother, all attended Rexford during the 1973–74 school year. How, more specifically, they'd all had him as their instructor. As Wilder spoke, Professor Cowling dropped his condescending attitude and leaned forward, attentive and concerned.

"Good Lord, that's quite a troubling tale. Have you discovered anything else?"

"That's as far as I've gotten. I'm hoping you can take me to the next step. I'm worried there are others out there who could snap at any moment."

"How can I help?"

"Student transcripts from that far back aren't computerized, they're scanned images on microfiche. It'd take months to manually cross-reference them in any way. If you had your class rosters from that year—"

Professor Cowling laughed. "As you can see, I'm a hopeless pack rat. But even I don't keep class manifests from three decades ago!"

Wilder handed him a printout of the perp list. "Do you remember any of these students?"

Professor Cowling put his half-glasses on and examined the list carefully. "I believe I recall having your friend Ms. Sealy in one of my classes.

People of color were still something of a novelty at the university back then. . . . Ah, Jonas McKee. I wrote him a letter of recommendation a while back."

"Any of the others?"

"I don't believe so. It's been an age, and I've had thousands of students over my career." He looked at the list again, then smiled. "Well. Cheryl Packard. There was a brief personal thing, if you gather my meaning."

"Can you tell me anything about her?"

"Petite, slender, fetching little overbite. Smallish tits. Red hair . . . up-stairs and down."

Wilder ignored Cowling's lecherous leer and pressed on. "Are there departmental archives? Anywhere your class records might've been stored?"

"Nothing would go back that far. The files are purged every ten years."

"Do you have any idea what could be causing this outbreak? What these people had in common?"

Professor Cowling didn't answer. His attention turned to something behind Wilder's back and he grinned.

"Counselor, greetings!"

Wilder turned. Ethan Nichols and two beefy security guards stood in the doorway. They were ex-Marines or ex-cops and armed; one had a shaved head, the other had a face like a moose. Curly and Bullwinkle, thought Wilder. Christ, when he went to college the security guys looked like retired crosswalk guards. Then he remembered Rexford was a re-search university and had security in some areas as tight as any Air Force base.

Nichols handed Wilder an envelope. Wilder opened it, read the heading of the five-page legal document inside it, then flipped to the end. It had been signed in bold blue ink by Judge Raoul de Cordoba that morning.

"You're fuckin' kidding me."

"No, Mr. Wilder, we are not, in fact, fuckin' kiddin'. This restraining order prohibits you from coming within two hundred feet of university property without explicit written consent from me, and without escort even then. It prohibits you from coming within two hundred feet of any

Rexford employee off university grounds, and from contacting same by any form of written or electronic communication. Failure to adhere to these restrictions will result in immediate arrest. The order authorizes university security to fully enforce these restrictions in lieu of or in conjunction with any local, state, or federal law enforcement organizations."

"Look, you pin-striped piece of dog shit, you can't get a restraining order without due cause, or an incident of prior harassment."

"Which is why you should not have gotten so rough with Professor Cowling."

"Bullshit. We never met until ten minutes ago."

"You seem to be forgetting that ugly little fracas at the Professor's house over the weekend."

Wilder looked at Professor Cowling, who leaned back in his chair and wiggled his piggies.

"A case of unprovoked brutality to which the Professor has sworn in an affidavit," Nichols continued, "which has so far remained sealed to protect the United States Air Force from embarrassment. Judge de Cordoba was most inclined to believe the Professor, given your well-documented history of violent tactics as a Special Agent of the OSI. You should consider yourself lucky Professor Cowling and this university have not filed criminal charges. Yet. Of course, if you can attest to your whereabouts over the weekend and disprove Professor Cowling's claim, by all means take it up with His Honor. I'm certain he'd be happy to lift the order under those circumstances."

Wilder felt like he just stepped into an open manhole. As if on cue, his beeper vibrated on his belt and he glanced at the number. Colonel Chang's line. Shit, Wilder thought, Chang had to be mighty pissed to call himself as opposed to having Brent do it. He stood up; he hadn't felt such an intense bellyful of rage since Woomera. Curly and Bullwinkle crowded in on either side of him.

"We goin' steady?" Wilder asked.

"Till you're off this property we are."

They each grabbed one of his arms.

"Bad idea, monkey-boys. Move 'em or lose 'em."

The guards replied by trying to drag him out the door. Wilder stepped suddenly to one side, slamming Curly against the wall. He pulled his arm loose and shot his fist upward into Bullwinkle's nose. The big man howled and Wilder doubled him over with a powerful punch to the solar plexus. Curly lunged for Wilder, who shifted his weight and kicked him in the balls. Curly's legs buckled and Wilder smashed him in the face, sending him spinning into Cowling's filing cabinets.

Wilder picked up his apple juice, finished it off, and tossed the carton into a trash can with Jim Morrison's picture on it. Professor Cowling shot to his feet.

"How *dare* you come here with your suspicions and accusations! Look around, I have no locks on my office door!" He pulled open some cabinets and his credenza. "No locks here, either. We have nothing to hide!" He slapped his computer keyboard to turn off the R. Crumb–Mr. Natural screensaver. "See!? No password. We're the good guys!"

"Mr. Wilder was just leaving, Walt . . ." Nichols said.

"They told me all about you, flyboy. Don't think because you're some war hero you have the moral prerogative to question us," Cowling continued. "Quite the contrary. Killing from an airplane is bald cowardice. You should thank whatever pig god you pray to the Iraqis didn't tear your nuts off and shove 'em up your ass!"

Wilder stepped over the groaning guards on his way out. "Bummer about the restraining order, Walt, 'cause I can tell you and I would've been best buds."

President Marsh was in a foul mood. To no one's surprise, the House of Representatives voted 289 to 141 against a resolution of support for Operation Swift Sword. Although they did not go so far as to cut off funds to prevent the deployment, the vote was a massive run for cover by the lawmakers. Privately, many of them conceded to the President the importance of stopping Batu Khan before he moved into Europe, but they were quite happy to let blame for the inevitable casualties of war fall to Marsh.

The President ate lunch alone in the Family Dining Room then went back to the Oval Office for a private appointment. Each Monday afternoon for the past eight weeks an ExOp had met with him, without Secretary Woodruff's knowledge, to hand-deliver a special surveillance digest. Included among the people and institutions the ExOps now monitored for Marsh, such as his enemies in politics or the media, was the Colleges of Sciences at Rexford University. The President had a simple cover story for its inclusion: Rexford hosted several highly classified research projects, and after the Chinese spying scandal in the Nineties he said he wanted his best people watching for any signs of espionage. In actuality, Marsh had almost nothing in his past that could embarrass him except for one incident at Rexford in the early Seventies, and the ExOps gave him a good way to watch for any sign that this information might come to light.

Therefore, something immediately leapt out as he paged through the digest, and it terrified him: The Rexford general counsel had e-mailed the university president about an Air Force investigator alleging a link between the university, Professor Walt Cowling, and the so-called Mad Yuppie Killers written up in some of the tabloids. A sickening flash of self-realization hit the President. He'd heard talk about the Mad Yuppies on one of those cheap, "reality" TV shows one night and their symptoms sounded eerily familiar, but he'd dismissed such thoughts at once. Suddenly, however, his conscious mind could no longer deny what the unconscious had known for weeks.

Marsh looked up at the ExOp and waited a moment before speaking to make sure his voice betrayed no emotion. "Wait outside."

The ExOp left and Marsh leapt from his chair. He walked in circles around the office, clenching his fists and gasping for breath. "Goddamn it . . . God*damn* it . . . !"

He fell to his knees and pressed his hands against his face, wanting to howl with the terror and frustration of being trapped inside his damaged brain and body. He moaned while struggling to hold a scream inside, then fought to regain control of himself. He realized from now on he must constantly be on guard—protecting his privacy, limiting his public appearances, watching every word and gesture, and above all keeping control of his wildly volatile emotions. Not even Amy could know what was happening to him.

He opened his eyes and found himself kneeling on the Presidential Seal woven into the blue carpet. On his first day in office he'd told Amy the Seal seemed like the precise center of power for the human race—*top of the world, ma*. A sudden calmness befell him and he began to laugh. His childish fear of the changes overtaking him must not blind him to their benefits. His advanced physical and mental capabilities were profound and beautiful gifts, far outweighing any liabilities. The President got to his feet. This dizzying evolution may have destroyed lesser creatures, but it gave him clarity, power, and grand intentions to fulfill.

Calm now, and once again presidential, Marsh buzzed the ExOp back into the Oval Office. His little team would have much work to do.

Wilder stood in the doorway of his hotel room, staring at another nasty surprise: The lockbox in the back of the closet had been jimmied open and his computer and papers stolen. The computer was worthless to anyone but him; its postage-stamp-sized Fingerloc sensor made it inoperable without his fingerprint scan and he had on-the-fly encryption on the hard drive. The transcripts were the big loss: all the evidence supporting the information he'd keyed into his database. He hadn't yet made copies; he'd planned to fax them to the Washington Field Office that night, and the subpoena didn't cover going back for replacements. He knew this had been no case of petty burglary. But he'd have about as much luck proving Nichols's culpability as the lawyer would have pinning de Cordoba's engine trouble on him.

He sat on the bed and returned Colonel Chang's page.

"It's Wilder."

Chang came on the line, as angry as Wilder had ever heard him. "The university didn't only copy me on this restraining order, Matt. They copied the Air Force Inspector General, the Secretary of the Air Force, and the Secretary of Defense."

"Sir, the story about my harassing Cowling is complete bullshit! They set me up because they know I'm onto something."

Chang fell silent. As angry as he was, he believed the denial—Wilder had done a lot of wild things in his career at the OSI, things that had certainly caused some migraines, yet he'd never once lied about or minimized his tactics or deeds. Chang listened as Wilder told him of the Cowling connection among all the perps and the theft of the transcripts.

"If the OSI backs me I can fight the restraining order and get back to work."

Chang sighed. "If it were up to me, I'd let you."

"Sir?"

"I've been ordered to transfer the case to the FBI. It came from on high."

Wilder couldn't believe it. "What's going on here? Woomera, Joval—I never had a single case yanked away before, let alone three in a month!"

It worried Chang, too. By all rights the restraining order should've gotten the case transferred to another special agent in the OSI, not a different law enforcement agency altogether.

"Let it go, Matt, and be thankful Secretary Woodruff isn't asking for your ass on a platter with a side of fries."

Angry and hurt, Wilder hung up the phone. Shit rolls downhill, he thought, and someone had hit him with an avalanche.

Twenty

Major Dimitri Savchenko piloted his three-man assault sub through the warm waters of Yalta Bay toward shore. In the faint reddish light of the sub's interior he checked his bearings against the waterproof map of central Yalta, then looked at his watch: two-thirty A.M. He steered toward the western side of Primorsky Park, which ran for sixteen hundred meters along the water. If their intelligence proved correct, his quarry would be in the park. If not, he and his men would search several other locales, including the old palace complex on nearby Mount Mohabi. Unfortunately, his assignment smelled like a world-class waste of time. He feared the other team leaders in his Spetsnaz (Russian Special Forces) battalion would become national heroes, while he and the eight men under his command fruitlessly wandered this side of the peninsula. Still, Savchenko would not go home completely empty-handed. He'd brought a small waterproof camera and planned to take pictures for his wife and daughters of the sun-swept villas where Russian leaders—from czars to Soviet premiers to federation presidents— spent their vacations. It'd be the closest he'd ever get to such luxury, unless he happened to find what they came for. Then he'd *buy* himself a palace.

Fifty meters from the shore the hull of the sub scraped the sandy ocean floor. Savchenko clicked his radio twice, signaling the others to swim the rest of the way. He slung a double-layered rubber pouch the size of a mailbag around his shoulder and zipped it tight. More than for the glory, the fame, the service to country, he prayed for success for the sake of his three young girls. To see their faces glowing with pride. Someday, God willing, he'd have sons, too. And by fulfilling his mission he'd bequeath to them a father's greatest gift: a proud and famous name that would give them all the advantages he'd never had.

Thirty miles to the west of Yalta, twelve more subs and thirty-six other Spetsnaz approached the Sevastopol deepwater harbor. The Amphibious Leader and his men didn't need to consult their maps; they were among the twenty-five Russian servicemen Batu had expelled from the city with barely enough time to gather up their belongings. Ethnic Russians once comprised over two-thirds of the Crimean population, ninety percent in the city of Sevastopol. Then Batu offered safe passage to Russian soil to each family who wanted to leave, and over a hundred thousand people accepted his offer. A perpetual clog of traffic had moved east across the peninsula to the town of Krym. From there, on four lanes of roadway and two rail tracks, the Russians crossed the five-kilometer-wide Kertch Strait on the fabulous new Mikhail Gorbachev Bridge; in less than ten minutes they were in the Russian town of Kavkaz. Despite their financial troubles, the Russians had built the Gorbachev, one of the longest, most expensive bridges in the world, as a desperate effort to maintain connection with the Crimea, a place they viewed as theirs by right of title and blood.

At the same time Savchenko and his men hit the beach at Yalta and the Spetsnaz amphibious team neared Sevastopol, a swarm of black, silent, one-man ultralights carrying airborne Spetsnaz approached a darkened TAA garrison near the town of Bakhchisaray, thirty-two kilometers north of Sevastopol along the main north-south Crimean highway. The ultralights were motorized hang gliders, constructed from radar-absorbing materials. They had internal-combustion engines made of plastic composites, with a special recirculating muffler to mask their sound. They landed in the open fields behind the garrison and each member of the "Black Ghosts" team folded his ninety-pound ultralight like a pair of batwings and hid it in the tree line. While gunners quickly set up fifty miniaturized grad-II missile launchers—each launcher tube smaller and lighter than a bazooka—the Black Ghost Leader examined the troop barracks with a pair of infrared-detection binoculars. With them he could see "through" the wooded walls to the nebulous red outlines created by the body heat of the TAA soldiers asleep in their bunks.

He also located four guards positioned on the perimeter. Once ready, he spoke a single whispered word into his radio to indicate they were in position, and received a one-word acknowledgment from the Amphibious Leader approaching Sevastopol Harbor. Now they waited. All the pieces were in place, including two wings of MiGs fueled and ready on a runway in Krasnodar, three hundred miles away in southern Russia, should an aerial escort be necessary.

Among the many fishing vessels just beyond the twelve-mile limit beyond the mouth of Sevastopol Harbor were several large, creaky, factory ships. Three in particular, including the one from which the Black Ghosts were deployed, had been in Crimean waters for two weeks. After a while, the TAA harbor masters had stopped paying them any attention. Tonight, none of the radar operators noticed them slowly converging to exactly twelve miles from the harbor entrance. Nor did anyone notice thirty-six amphibious Spetsnaz as their heads broke the surface below the wooden pilings of the Sevastopol docks. They climbed the cross-bracing and, hidden from view, stripped off their wet suits. Some wore shipbuilders' overalls, others wore TAA army uniforms. They spread out and made their way to the area of the former Russian Naval Base. A million watts of floodlights lit the massive complex of docks, warehouses, machine shops, and bristling artillery stations like an NFL night game. Already, several huge portraits of Batu Khan had been erected. Expert technicians and shipbuilders worked around the clock to repair and upgrade the old Russian Black Sea Fleet—over a hundred vessels, mostly in abysmal condition. As the Spetsnaz approached the docks, they saw fewer TAA overseers than they'd planned on. Maybe Batu had gotten lazy and overconfident. The Amphibious Leader tried to banish the thought, but it kept coming back. Would this be *easy*?

Across the globe, President and Mrs. Marsh were hosting a private reception in the Blue Room: cocktails with Vice President Adam Taylor, Senator and Mrs. Jonathan Ballard, and several other senior congressmen and their wives. All part of Marsh's attempts to get those he called in private "the attention-span-challenged, bereft-of-conviction Capitol-Hill blowhards" to support Operation Swift Sword. Even after revealing Batu's atrocities in the Ukraine, the public's support for war against the TAA continued to drop. So he got naked and cut off a bunch of heads. In a world numbed by religious and cultural wars, killing fields and ethnic cleansing, such behavior seemed like no big deal.

Among these congressmen and their overdressed, big-haired wives only Marsh's friend Jon Ballard held his respect. But the president pro tem of the Senate had been cornered all evening by another senator trying to sway his vote on a highway bill. Vice President Taylor worked the room with enthusiasm. Privately, however, Marsh knew the VP would not have taken the same hard line with Batu Khan if he were President. A former labor law attorney, Taylor believed any situation could be negotiated, regardless of the adversary or his position on the issues.

Amy picked up on Marsh's I-hate-this mannerisms—shifting from foot to foot, twisting his wedding ring, clenching his jaw. He caught her eye and with a subtle nod directed her attention to a young representative from Arizona standing near the piano with the mid-fortyish wife of an influential committee chairman from Idaho. Amy shot back an equally subtle shrug. Their posture seemed entirely unprovocative. Amy, though, couldn't hear them. Marsh could, as clearly as if he'd been standing right between them. Mrs. Committee Chairman was whispering to Mr. Young Representative that after he'd left their hotel she'd remained in the room, thinking of him and masturbating, even though he'd already given her such a sore little fuzzy. Mr. Young Representative replied that his big throbbing cock was threatening to pop out over the top of his cummerbund. The conversation didn't surprise Marsh, because he'd smelled Mrs. Committee Chairman all over Mr. Young Representative when he'd greeted him earlier.

The representative laughed ever-so-innocently with Mrs. Chairman and wandered over to greet the First Lady. Marsh's face flushed as he watched the young man turn on the charm. As Amy spoke with him, he brazenly admired her firm breasts, toned arms, and long legs, visible through the slit up her gown. Marsh had rock-solid trust in his wife, beyond question, but he deeply resented the representative taking such flagrant pleasure in her beauty. He had an overwhelming urge to knock the representative's movie star teeth down his throat, and actually feared he couldn't keep himself from doing so. The President forced a smile onto his face, crossed the room to Amy, and slipped his arm around her waist.

"Excuse us," Marsh said, pointedly avoiding the obligatory small-talk. As he and Amy walked away, he turned back. Still smiling, he grabbed the representative's arm and squeezed, hard. The young man gasped with pain and surprise and Marsh reveled in the realization of how easy it would be to crush the bone.

"By the way," he whispered, "you left your little fuzzy by the Steinway, tiger."

Amy looked over her shoulder, curious about the representative's fist-to-the-solar-plexus reaction to his moment with her husband.

"What was *that* about?" she said to Marsh.

"Fuckin' jerk. You'd need a crowbar to pry his eyes off your tits."

If not for his barely hidden rage, Amy would've thought Marsh was joking. In almost thirty years of marriage he'd never exhibited any jealousy.

"Jesus, Burt; you're *way* overreacting—"

Marsh wasn't listening. Approaching a group of guests, he forced down his ire, grinned, and started shaking hands.

"Senator! How are you?"

Just then, Curt Levinson slipped into the room and crossed quickly to the President.

"Sorry, sir, I need to talk to you."

Marsh excused himself from Amy and the senators. On their way to the Oval Office, Levinson started his briefing. "One of our birds over the Crimea picked up an intense explosion about seven minutes ago."

"What kind, and where?"

"Near a town called Bakhchisaray, twenty miles up the main drag from Sevastopol. Batu had some troops there to guard the port's north flank. The explosion appears to be a cluster of smaller, concurrent ones, meaning they were Russian grads, or grad II's. They were popular in Chechnya: forty or more small missiles fired in concert completely destroys a quarter of a square mile."

"The fucking *Russians*?!"

The depth of Marsh's anger caught Levinson off guard. It's not like the Russkis were attacking Florida, for chrissake. Seeing the startled look on Levinson's face, Marsh took a breath and calmed himself. He had to be especially careful about letting his guard down, especially around an old friend and confidant like Levinson, who knew his every mood.

"Jesus, Curt, I just had the goddamnedest reaction. I felt jealous, furious someone else might be getting a piece of Batu before we could."

"I'm not too happy about it myself, sir. We don't need this thing escalating out of our control."

"Any other activity, other indicators?" Marsh asked.

"Nothing overt. We're repositioning the satellite for a closer look. Ted Jameson thinks the fireworks are a diversion for other action, probably in Sevastopol."

Marsh changed direction and went down the stairs, then stopped at a security desk and picked up the phone. "I'm going to the VS Room. Find Secretary of State Burroughs. Tell him I want a VS with President Karzhov. No, now. Put Burroughs through to the VS Room after he's arranged it with the Russians." He turned to Levinson. "Can NORAD patch us into the satellite data so I can see it on the VS screen?"

"I'll see if someone can route the feed from the Situation Center into the VS circuits."

In the VS Room, Marsh turned the lights up while Levinson instructed the Situation Room technical officer over the phone to transfer the satellite image. President Marsh took a key from his pocket and unlocked the credenza. He put a tape in one of the VCRs and set it to start taping when the VS connection began. Levinson found it strange that the President of the United States would carry the credenza key on his person and take such personal control of the videotaping process. Then Marsh further surprised him by pouring them each a couple fingers of Scotch. Even at meals or when relaxing, Marsh drank nothing more than wine or an occasional beer.

The phone rang and Levinson answered. "Roger that." Levinson hung up. "Karzhov will be on-line within five minutes."

The satellite image appeared across the VS screen. The bright, still-burning area where the TAA military installation once stood all but washed out its green-tinted night vision. Marsh and Levinson could see some small green glow-worms of movement in the field behind it—the Spetsnaz, moving their equipment into position to secure control of the road.

"What the hell are they thinking?" Levinson asked. "They don't have a prayer of hanging on to the Crimea."

"Curt, can you shrink the image, move it to one side? I want to see Karzhov's pretty face when he calls."

Levinson fiddled with the controls until the image became as the President requested. Video snow suddenly replaced the blue background.

The Russian three-color flag appeared, then the rumpled Russian president, Nicholi Karzhov. The image of the Kremlin, direct via satellite, was much clearer than the one from Batu Khan's *ger*. The Russian VS Room was an overdecorated rendition of czarist splendor: paneled walls, ermine-covered chairs, marble tables, copies of art treasures from the Hermitage, and, Marsh's personal favorite, two large, stuffed borzoi hounds sitting beside the fireplace. Karzhov's hair was matted and he wore a long, green velvet robe. The unfortunate descriptive modifier thick applied when thinking of the Russian leader. It described his fleshy face, his soft body, and, sadly, his mind.

"Christ almighty, Burt! It's the middle of the damn night! What's wrong?"

"Gosh, Nikki, did I wake you up?"

"Of course you did!"

"Bullshit. Even an old farmer like you couldn't sleep in those clodhoppers."

The Russian president frowned at an offscreen translator. He spoke excellent English but often missed the colloquialisms. After receiving the translation he glanced down at the pants and shoes visible below the bottom of his robe, and stepped behind a chair to hide them from view.

"I want to show you something, Nicholi . . ." Marsh turned to Levinson. "Turn off the output filter so the satellite feed is visible on the other side."

Levinson hesitated. Even this long past the end of the Cold War, he couldn't imagine sharing highly classified satellite surveillance with the Russians. He took a deep breath and flipped the switch. Karzhov's eyes grew wide under his bushy eyebrows. The Russians had some functioning surveillance satellites, but nothing remotely matching this resolution.

"So, busy night for the Spetsnaz." Marsh could practically hear the rusty wheels in Karzhov's head trying to spin out a plausible story. "Look, Nikki, I'm sure you want to get back to your situation room, so here's the deal. Tell me exactly what you're doing. If it's the truth, and it's not an incredibly awful plan, we'll provide full intelligence support for you to finish the job, including satellite data."

Karzhov pounced on the offer. "The Trans-Altaic Alliance illegally seized the Russian Black Sea Fleet. We're taking back what is rightfully ours!"

"How?"

"Russian Spetsnaz are about to secure the Sevastopol Harbor, off-load Russian personnel from nearby ships, and sail the Russian vessels away from the thieves who hold them."

Marsh almost laughed. The Russians knew they couldn't take the Crimea back from Batu Khan and keep it, but grabbing their rusty old fleet in a daring nighttime raid would be an enormous morale boost. The ploy also explained why Russia had stalled on joining the U.S. action against the TAA on Marsh's deadline. They didn't want to share the glory of tonight's raid. They wanted to kick ass unassisted, show the world they still had spunk.

"And what about when TAA fighters blow your ships out of the water?"

"My MiGs will prevent that. We have an agreement on the intelligence, Burton?"

Marsh nodded. Karzhov bowed slightly in thanks.

Lying motionless on the beach in Yalta, Major Savchenko monitored the activity of the other teams through his radio earpiece. The Black Ghosts had secured the northern highway, and soon, the Amphibious Team would control Sevastopol Harbor. Now came Savchenko's turn for action. He flipped up his night-vision goggles and scanned the trees above Primorsky Park. He spotted what looked like a campfire or a wood-burning stove and about a dozen people sleeping on the ground. Savchenko clicked the safety off his Dragunov 7.62×.54 semi-auto rifle, tightened the muzzle break, and signaled his men to encircle the target area. As they entered the stand of trees above the park, their night-vision goggles showed two small round tents and a larger one behind them. Savchenko, who had a grandmother from Siberia, recognized it as a *ger*, traditional home of nomadic peoples on the treeless Asian steppes. Seeing a *ger* hidden within a stand of date palms beside the ocean was like seeing an igloo in the Sahara.

The Spetsnaz team closed in. Someone stepped on a twig, alerting a Khaldun Elite Guard outside the *ger*. He shouted and fired his weapon into the darkness. Savchenko gave the order to return fire, but aim *only* at the smaller tents. All nine Spetsnaz swept the two smaller tents and the Khaldun's area with their automatic weapons. After thirty seconds Savchenko blew a whistle and the shooting stopped. The Spetsnaz quickly reloaded, and turned on pairs of bright floodlights mounted on either side of their helmets.

Moving slowly toward the *ger* Savchenko called out in Russian: "Come out of the tent! Vladimir Baikalev! Out with your hands up!"

All Russians, as a matter of stubborn indignation, refused to call Batu Khan by his chosen name. To them, he would always be Vladimir Baikalev, the Siberian half-breed traitor. Savchenko stepped carefully through the door of the *ger*. Some bullet holes had punctured the felt beside it, and he heard someone crying—a man, kneeling next to a young woman. She lay on the floor of the *ger*, naked, eyes staring skyward. A bullet had hit her in the back, blasting her sternum open with a hideous exit wound. Savchenko recognized her from his briefing: Kuri, Batu's younger wife. She must've panicked during the attack, he thought, tried to run instead of staying low for cover. Unfortunate, but he doubted his commanders would care about collateral casualties.

The man beside her wore a *shalwar qamiz* and sheepskin belt. He seethed hatred at Savchenko and the other Spetsnaz. The Russian briefing pictures were a few years old, but Batu Khan still seemed impossible to mistake: flat face, powerful body, blond hair, and blue eyes.

"Vladimir Baikalev?"

All Savchenko got from him was a halfhearted nod. Two of Savchenko's men frisked him for weapons and dragged him outside. The Spetsnaz rounded up the other survivors: five women in servant's clothing and a wounded Khaldun. Savchenko could barely contain his excitement. But before they celebrated, there were two things he had to do. First, he stood eye to eye with his prisoner and spit in his face. This seemed such a swell idea that the other Russians holding him also took a turn spitting in his face. The great Batu Khan didn't look like an emperor now, did he?

Savchenko took the rubber pouch from around his shoulder, unzipped it, and handed it to his lieutenant. He really wanted to savor this moment, but President Karzhov would be anxious to receive this excellent news. So without ceremony Savchenko pressed the muzzle of a machine gun against his prisoner's chest and fired a three-shot burst. The women servants cried out in anguish; the Russians shoved them back and threatened them with the same if they didn't shut up.

I did it, Savchenko thought. Vladimir Baikalev, Mad Vlad, Batu Khan, father and soul of the mighty Trans-Altaic Alliance, dead at my feet! Savchenko ripped the *shalwar qamiz* from him and fired his machine gun at the body's neck until his men could twist the head loose. He wrapped it in the *shalwar qamiz* and put it into his rubber pouch—Savchenko needed only Batu's head to collect the Russian government's million-dollar bounty. So, this is how it feels to be rich. Nice. He would buy his wife a white sable coat and fuck her while she wore it. Surely that'd bring them a son!

The Spetsnaz let out a cheer. One of them took a picture with Savchenko's camera while another produced a flask of vodka from inside his wet suit. As Savchenko's men passed it around and complimented each other, they gradually lost interest in the old ladies cowering near the *ger*. One of them, Yela, stepped quietly to the front of the others. With an underhand softball toss, she lobbed a hand grenade into the group of Russians. The explosion and shrapnel ripped apart six of the eight and seriously wounded the other two. Savchenko, standing apart from them, was knocked to the ground and peppered with small pieces of shrapnel.

Woozy, his ears ringing, he looked over at the servant women. One who'd remained hunchbacked behind the others now came forward, pushed back a cloth headdress, and opened a modest brown frock. A gray-haired wig fell to the ground, and under the frock Savchenko could see a *shalwar qamiz* identical to the one worn by his slain prisoner.

Standing before Savchenko, Batu Khan looked *exactly* like the briefing pictures. The four women surrounding him, including Panya, his number-one wife, pulled Browning Hi-Power nine-millimeter pistols from under their garments and Savchenko wondered if his terror would kill him before Batu did.

Without speaking, Batu walked past him and stepped into the *ger*. He choked back a cry as he spotted Kuri dead on the floor. He came outside with her in his arms and gently laid her down in front of Panya. Weeping, she covered the body with a blanket. Batu helped Savchenko sit up and slipped the rubber pouch from his shoulder. He took the head out, unwrapped it, and tried to wipe the blood from its face. Overcome with grief, Batu sat next to Savchenko with the head in his lap and cried.

"Mikey, look at you. I'm so sorry . . ."

Batu turned at Savchenko. "It took extraordinary bravery to be my double. Assassins lurk everywhere, yet he accepted the risk in order to keep our dream alive. He has two babies—Billy, after Buffalo Bill Cody, and little Nina." He wiped his eyes. "How did you find me?"

Too terrified to lie, Savchenko spoke at once. "Russian intelligence picked up a cellular phone call from one of your bodyguards and triangulated its signal."

"Listening, listening, listening, with great big ears . . . you're incapable of making history anymore, so you eavesdrop like schoolgirls on those who do."

One of the surviving Spetsnaz groaned in pain nearby, so Batu turned and shot him through the heart. He looked back at Savchenko.

"Please, Batu . . ." So, it was "Batu" all of a sudden. "It was our duty. I believe in Jesus."

"Do you believe my beautiful Kuri now sits at His right hand? Or my slain child, the one she carried inside her?"

Savchenko started weeping. "It was an accident."

"Shhhh, shhhh. You can help me, Spetsnaz. I must give something to Billy and Nina, to show them their papa did not go unavenged."

Savchenko's crying became racking sobs.

"Although nothing will help me explain this to my mother," Batu continued. "How can I tell her that in one night she lost a daughter-in-law, an unborn grandchild, and her eldest son?"

As the realization hit him, Savchenko let out an agonized howl. What kind of monster would allow his own brother to die in his stead?

"Shhhh. It's not your time to meet your Savior." Batu hugged Savchenko and patted his back. "I want you to go home. Tell them to stop listening, listening, listening . . . yes?"

Savchenko nodded vigorously. Batu smiled, then grabbed Savchenko's right ear and quickly sliced it off with a curved dagger he took from his belt. Savchenko screeched with surprise and pain. "That one I'll give to Billy"—Batu switched the dagger to his left hand and cut off Savchenko's other ear—"and one for Nina."

He motioned Panya and the old ladies over. The four of them, with surprisingly powerful hands, pinned Savchenko to the ground.

"Now, what is it *I* shall have for the murder of Keri and our child?"

Kneeling near the window in a small room, overlooking the brightly lit Russian shipyards in Sevastopol, the Spetsnaz Amphibious Leader gave the all-secure order over his radio. Twelve miles from the mouth of Sevastopol Bay, the three factory ships opened their immense rear doors.

From each ship twelve high-speed skiffs burst onto the water and raced toward the Inner Harbor at forty-five knots. The thirty-six skiffs each held half a hundred men, enough in all to take control of every seaworthy Russian ship.

Near the town Bakhchisaray, the intense heat from the grad-II missiles had dissipated enough for the Black Ghosts to assess the damage to the TAA garrison. Some movement in the blackened grass caught their eye—a man, severely burned, crawling toward the creek at the edge of the field. Moving closer, they heard him mumbling in a wheezy whisper in Ukrainian. This made no sense, there were no Ukrainian members of the Trans-Altaic Alliance armed forces. One of the Black Ghosts spoke the language, and asked the man his name and unit. His burns, outside and internally, made it almost impossible for him to speak loud enough to be heard.

"Why? We stayed, as you commanded . . . Everyone dead . . . you bastards." As he spoke, the Black Ghosts realized this was not a TAA military installation, as it had been designed to look. All the people inside were Ukrainian. The Black Ghost stood mute, horrified—they'd just killed several hundred innocent people instead of enemy troops. He radioed his counterpart in Sevastopol to warn him they'd been duped.

In Sevastopol, the Spetsnaz Amphibious Leader acknowledged the warning and ordered the Black Ghosts to stand by. He finished his transmission and handed the radio back to Chu'tsai, who patted him on the cheek. The other Amphibious Spetsnaz lay dead on the floor at the Leader's feet. Enormously pleased with himself, Chu'tsai pointed his MK-23 Heckler & Koch forty-five at him and leaned back in his chair.

"Batu said you would try to get your fleet back. I consulted my sheep bones, the constellations, and the midnight river currents to predict your methods, but they told me nothing. Then I read Russian military history. From it, I anticipated four attack possibilities; Batu had us prepare for all of them."

Chu'tsai grabbed a remote-control device the size of a carton of cigarettes and led the Spetsnaz Amphibious Leader outside onto the docks. Cigarette dangling from his lips, he climbed onto the railing around the outside deck of the tower, balancing precariously in the stiff breeze. A red LED lit up on the control unit. Party time. With an excited whoop, he flipped one of two switches next to the LED.

The thirty-six Russian speedboats running abreast, their speed across the black water almost sixty knots, didn't see the daisy chain of eight-foot-wide metal spheres, one every one hundred meters, gurgle up from below and pop to the surface in a line spanning across the entrance to the harbor.

Chu'tsai hit the second switch.

Major Savchenko, delirious with pain, blood pouring down either side of his neck and inside his pants legs from his groin, was limping to his tiny sub on the Yalta beach when the western sky became bright as day. The fireballs could also be seen four hundred miles away in the town of Batumi on the east side of the Black Sea, and in the coastal towns of Turkey, Bulgaria, and Romania. In the White House and the Kremlin, the Russian and American presidents shielded their eyes as the satellite image on the VS screen washed out with an intense white burst. Marsh turned to Levinson.

"Find out what kind of explosion that was!"

Frightened, Levinson nodded—it seemed powerful enough to have been a small nuke.

The metal spheres—stretched across the harbor mouth, filled with a mixture of aviation fuel and magnesium—turned several million gallons of seawater to steam and incinerated the Russian boats. The boats' flaming shells, carried by momentum of their great speed, skipped across the boiling, flaming water like the glowing remnants of spent fireworks.

Chu'tsai stretched his arms out on the tower railing to catch the intense, hot wash of air from the faraway blast.

"What a fuckin' *rush*!!"

He shot the Spetsnaz leader in the head, perfectly completing the moment.

For the next forty-eight hours, tens of thousands of ethnic Russians fled the Crimea, gridlocking every exit point. Batu Khan had given them only that long before the borders would close for good. After the deadline, the roads became empty, the trains stopped running, and people stayed in their homes. The magnificent Mikhail Gorbachev Bridge stood deserted for the first time since it had opened. Then, at dawn, a long, Russian passenger train approached the bridge from the Crimea side. It traveled at an impossible, breakneck speed with no conductor or brakeman to slow it down. No one was aboard except fifty dead Spetsnaz—Savchenko's men, the Black Ghosts, and the Amphibious Team. Barely holding the tracks, the train flew across the bridge, reaching 150 miles per hour by the time it got to the Russian side. The workers at the Kavkaz station had no time to run from their posts before the front of the runaway train slammed into a line of empty cars at the far side of the station. The heavy engine shoved them hundreds of feet forward without slowing. The cars behind it jackknifed and folded into one another, then the tail cars snapped loose and tumbled, end over end, bounding over the tangle of twisted metal in their path.

The moment the wrecked train came to a halt, five TAA fighters flying subsonic in a V formation came in low to the water from the south toward the bridge. Each fired two missiles in quick succession, then banked away. A line of explosions worked its way along the bridge, sending thousands of tons of concrete and steel raining into the strait. In moments, nothing remained of the beautiful structure except an occasional pylon or crosspiece. It looked like an instant Roman ruin.

Batu and his surviving wife, Panya, stood together on a windswept bluff overlooking the Kertch Strait with tears streaming down their faces, watching the bombing. The train is for the murder of my brother, Batu thought, and the bridge, you savage, peasant fucks, is for killing my Kuri, my love. And these things are nothing compared to how you will suffer for the death of my unborn son. Wiping his eyes, he turned to his wife and took her hand.

"Panya, look at me. We'll never be vulnerable again, I promise. Not us, our people, or the empire. Best of all, our safety will come at the expense of the same demons who attacked us . . . no matter how many of their loved ones it costs."

Twenty-one

Wilder had little time to obsess about losing the Herrold/Rexford case. After Batu's humiliation of the Russians, President Marsh raised the alert level to DEFCON 3. Also, two of the prototype weapons systems were due at Andrews for their final fitting and deployment. He also worried about spending enough time with Kate. She had plenty of kids to play with in the neighborhood and Mrs. Lindstrom took her to dance class and T-ball practice at school, but Wilder wanted to enjoy some of her summer-vacation hours himself.

"Brent and Cindy are having their Fourth of July party today," he told her at breakfast. "But I was thinking . . . we never see each other at parties—you hanging with the little kids, me with the big kids—"

Kate nodded. "Yeah . . ."

"Even though it's a holiday, I have to go to the city for a few minutes to sign some papers." He was referring to a wiretap request awaiting his signature at the Hoover FBI building—the OSI and FBI had detected some hackers breaking into the Bolling AFB computers and they needed a judge's okay to begin electronic surveillance at once.

"So, instead of you and me and my new friend Laura going to the barbecue, how about the three of us spend the day in the District, then watch the fireworks at the Mall?"

"Oh, yes! Can we go now?!"

Wilder smiled, delighted at her uncharacteristic enthusiasm. "Soon as you're dressed."

He'd already talked to Laura that morning to say he'd be running the change of plans past Kate; when he called back to report her enthusiastic acceptance Laura was equally excited. She'd been anxious to meet Kate and had only talked to Wilder a few times since the White House dinner, so a quiet threesome appealed to her much more than a noisy party.

Kate had never seen Georgetown, so she spent the morning dragging Wilder up and down Wisconsin Avenue, racing from shop to shop, amazed at the bustling, colorful disorderliness of it all—especially today, on the Fourth. For a kid used to the tidy confines of Andrews Air Force Base, Georgetown seemed like a huge, messy closet ripe to be explored. Wilder shared her fascination. Before he came to the Washington area, he'd always pictured the fashionable Georgetown district as a cluster of stately southern mansions, not tight rows of town houses and collegiate shops.

They met Laura in an Italian restaurant on M Street across from the Georgetown Park. Laura whispered "she's beautiful" to Wilder when he introduced her to Kate.

"Uncle Matt showed me your picture on the back of a book," Kate said. "He says you wrote it. Was it hard?"

"Yes, but fun, too. Would you like to write a book someday?"

"I already have. For school."

"What's it about?"

"My mom. She's in heaven."

"Yes, your uncle told me. May I read it sometime?"

"Sure. I made the pictures, too."

As they ate, their conversation stayed on topics of interest to Kate. Wilder hated to talk shop in front of her. Laura didn't want to talk about her work either. It felt great to have it out of her mind for a while. After lunch they walked along the Canal, browsed the boutiques, and played catch in the park. The nearby church clock chimed four, surprising both Wilder and Laura with how quickly the afternoon went by.

"Three more hours to fireworks time," Wilder said.

"Four o'clock is tea time in England," Laura told Kate. "A lovely tradition—tea and crumpets."

"What's crumpets?"

"Little pieces of sweet, toasted bread." This fascinated Kate. "Would you like to take tea at my house?" Laura asked. "It's only a block away."

While she filled the kettle at her town house, Wilder and Kate removed the tea service from the china closet. He cautioned her not to drop anything—even a guy with no knowledge of porcelain recognized its age and value.

Kate looked around the town house, keeping her hands behind her back to combat the temptation to touch. "You got lots of books," she said. "You read 'em all?"

"I believe so. Let me show you something." Laura opened the glass door on a book case and took out a thick, leather-bound volume with gold tool-work on its face and binding. "This is a book called *Robinson Crusoe*, by a man named Daniel Defoe. He wrote it in 1722, almost three hundred years ago. That's why books are so special. I can read someone's words, right here and now, as if all those centuries aren't between us." She pointed to the gilt-work. "See the edges of the pages? It's real gold." Kate fell silent, her brow knitted in concentration. "Now, watch . . ."

Laura carefully grasped the pages and bent them so their outside edges fanned out. As if by magic, an intricate watercolor painting appeared on the edge of the pages: Crusoe meeting Friday on the beach, with a blue sky, clouds, and rich green jungle foliage behind them. When Laura released the pages, the normal gilt edge once again concealed the painting.

"Cool!"

"It's called a fore-edge painting. Years ago, many fine books were adorned like this. Most people today don't even know about it because nobody's done fore-edging in over a hundred years."

Laura had a few other fore-edged books, and she let Kate look at the paintings through a magnifying glass. As Wilder watched them together— Kate's fascination, Laura's delight in her—he became aware of an unaccustomed sensation. Contentment. He wished he could put the moment in his wallet like one of Kate's school pictures so he could take it out and relive it whenever he wanted. After tea, he and Laura talked and Kate occupied herself with Laura's collection of antique illustrated storybooks. At six o'clock Laura went into the kitchen.

"Pasta and salad work for you guys?"

"Don't bother; we'll go out for something before the show."

"It's no bother. Besides, Kate and I already have our shoes off."

Wilder didn't quite follow what shoes had to do with anything, yet it surprised him how comfortable it seemed to stay for dinner. He followed her into the kitchen. Neither felt compelled to speak as she made the salad dressing and he set the table. Laura noticed he found everything as if he'd put it there himself. He stopped to look at her as she reached up to the wine rack above the refrigerator. She'd pulled her hair up while cooking, and the reddish light of sunset coming through the kitchen windows filled her ponytail with golden highlights. In profile, her fine features and graceful neck reminded him of those old-fashioned silhouettes made from black opal and white mother of pearl. She couldn't reach the Chianti, so he got it down for her. Her eyes caught his as he handed her the wine bottle, and their bodies brushed lightly. Neither one of them wanted to step back. Her fresh, sweet scent actually made him light-headed. A wisp of hair hung down her forehead, and Wilder brushed it away. Laura felt equally intoxicated by her proximity to Wilder. Even in the warm kitchen, she could feel heat radiating from his body. As he moved his hand away from her face she took it in between hers. It was large, with long fingers, strong without being rough or callused.

She'd sensed from the first time they met a core of vulnerability hidden far beneath his strength and bravado, and it made her feel privy to the greatest secret in the world. He was the most confident, focused man she'd ever met, yet she had an urge to say "everything's all right" to him. She brought his hand back up to her face, closed her eyes, and gently kissed his fingertips. The intimacy of her touch sent a shudder through Wilder. He put his hand around her waist and drew her closer, resting her head against his chest. He leaned his face into her hair and inhaled, drawing her in. They stood without moving, their eyes closed, losing themselves in the exquisite sensation of closeness, the first time in a long while he'd allowed any sentiment of warmth or real affection beyond his love for Kate enter his consciousness. His life felt removed from direct perception, as though experienced from within a soundproof glass enclosure. Laura hadn't smashed through it, but he could finally hear someone calling faintly to him.

After dinner, Kate accompanied Laura as she let herself into the town house next door to feed her vacationing neighbors' cat. When they returned, Wilder and Laura sat in the living room drinking a 1966 port. It impressed him that she drank the stuff, never mind that she had a set of Waterford port glasses and knew how to strain and decant it.

He told her what happened at Rexford, including how Nichols used his one weakness—his inability to give his whereabouts the weekend he crippled de Cordoba's sloop—to concoct the false claims against him.

"Orders or no, how can you stand letting the case go?"

"It ain't easy, especially since I'll probably be the only one to ever know about the Cowling connection."

"Do you think the university knows what he has to do with those people, or are they just trying to keep their name from being implicated in any way?"

"I don't know. It goes beyond the university. I also reexamined some of my research. Many of the web pages I'd seen—perp résumés, stuff like that—are no longer in existence. Then I called back some of my phone contacts. Several people told me some suits had come by, asking for any written records as part of an investigation."

"Suits?"

"Men claiming to be FBI. But the Bureau hasn't put a single agent on the case."

"Maybe the FBI is lying to you."

"No. I'm getting my information from a friend there, and I trust him completely. He also thinks someone ordered the Bureau to drop the case, but no one will confirm or deny it."

"Really . . ."

Laura knew, as did Wilder, that a guy like Ethan Nichols might influence his good buddy the judge, alter records within his own university, even have his goon security men break into a hotel room. He could not, however, influence senior people in the Department of Defense, the U.S. Air Force, or the Federal Bureau of Investigation. He couldn't coerce them into tabling an investigation, nor could he eradicate public information on the vast, decentralized, unregulated Internet.

"What are you going to do?" she asked.

"I don't know yet." He hesitated for a long moment. "Especially since there's another wrinkle I haven't mentioned." He told how the Infiltrator at Woomera had exhibited the same bizarre behavior and extraordinary powers as the people from Rexford.

Laura listened with great concern. When researching her book she'd heard rumors in the TAA about the amazing fighting prowess of the Khaldun Elite, but she'd given it no credence. After all, many Kurds in Iraq believed the Republican Guard to be manned by soldiers eight feet tall. After hearing Wilder's description of the Infiltrator's abilities, the unsubstantiated news reports of a couple hundred men on horses seizing control of modern Georgia and the Ukraine—vigorously dismissed by the Pentagon as TAA propaganda—suddenly seemed quite believable.

As they walked to the car Wilder tried to put it all out of his mind. But talking about it infuriated him. He *had* to get back to Rexford, orders or no.

"Where are we possibly going to park?" Laura asked, as they inched through the heavy traffic on Virginia Avenue.

"Wherever we want," Wilder said, tossing a special permit onto his dashboard. "Damn few perks in my line of work, so I got no problem using this one once in a while."

A harried traffic cop waved them around a barricade into the parking lot of the Federal Reserve building, then they walked across Constitution Avenue and spread a beach blanket on the grass among the huge crowd on the Mall. Thrilled by their excellent vantage point, Laura sat on the blanket and Wilder sat next to her. But just as he was putting his arm around her, Kate plopped in between them and covered her ears in anticipation of the fireworks.

They enjoyed the fireworks above the Washington Monument as much as Kate—maybe more. Aside from the noise and color and spectacle, they both loved the *meaning* of the holiday. As a historian, Laura appreciated the uniqueness of the American Experiment. And although it wasn't in his nature to discuss such feelings out loud, Independence Day had deep significance for Wilder, too, because it celebrated the ideals he'd sworn his life to defend. He glanced over his shoulder toward the White House, wondering how America would fare in the upcoming battle. She had never faced a foe like Batu Khan or his Khaldun Elite before.

After the show, Wilder drove Laura back to Georgetown and Kate insisted she walk Laura to the door along with him. At the top of the stairs she gave Laura a hug.

"Thanks for dinner, Laura."

"Thanks for spending the day with me, Kate. I sure had fun."

"Come to my T-ball game tomorrow?"

"Oh, I'd love to, but I have an interview to do. Can I come next week?"

Wilder jumped in before Kate could answer.

"You tell Laura it's a definite date."

Holding Kate's hand and an illustrated, first-edition *Wizard of Oz* that Laura had given her—despite Wilder's protestations about its value—Wilder took his turn to say goodnight.

"It's been a long time since . . . since I had such a great day."

"Me, too." That smile of hers got him every time.

He kissed her lightly on the lips, turned to go, stopped, leaned in, and kissed her again. Then he went down the steps—if he'd kissed her one more time he doubted he could stop. As they walked to the car together, Kate looked up at Wilder with a very serious expression.

"You coulda kissed her more, Uncle Matt. I wouldn't peek."

Wilder laughed. "Next time, that's what I'll do."

Laura, standing in the doorway, overhearing them, hoped that was a definite date, too.

Twenty-two

Everyone in the Washington Field Office returned to their desks early after the long holiday weekend. Wilder knocked on Brent's office door and Brent, dictating a memo into a handheld recorder while trying to balance a pencil by its point on the tip of his index finger, waved him in.

"Matty, me lad."

"I found another case. Middle-aged guy from Boston, never even had a speeding ticket. Killed a cop who pulled him over to warn him he'd forgotten to put his lights on after coming out of a gas station. Three dead hostages and two wounded cops later, Boston PD finally took him out. Officers at the scene claimed they'd collectively put fourteen nine-millimeter slugs and two loads of number-four shot in his chest, abdomen, and legs before a headshot from a sniper rifle dropped him. I did some checking. Perp went to Rexford."

He sat on the edge of the desk.

"Brent, listen, this has me so nuts I'm thinking about quitting the Air Force and pursuing the investigation on my own."

"I hear ya." Losing the case had been nagging at him as much as at Wilder, especially given its troubling connection with Woomera. And although he and Chang never specifically discussed it, he believed the regional commander felt the same way. Brent took from his desk Chang's written order transferring the case to the FBI and looked it over. The memo had that same, uncharacteristically vague wording as the order to cease the Woomera investigation. In fact, Chang had written to Brent in a distant, formal manner, as if his note were for the benefit of a third party.

"Last night someone tried to steal some classified propulsion components from a subcontractor working through Travis. The MO sounded a lot like the Infiltrator at Woomera."

Wilder sat up, suddenly very interested.

"Grab a flight out there, stick around until we take delivery of the prototypes," Brent continued. "If the West Coast boys don't need a hand, I'm sure you can find something to occupy your time for a few days."

Wilder grinned. Travis AFB was only seventy miles from Rexford University.

"On my fuckin' way!"

Brent looked decidedly queasy. "I'll fill in for you while you're gone, but remember, Chang might jerk you back in a heartbeat. If you don't give a crap about your own career, try to care about mine. This is as far as I'm gonna go, and as much as I want to know. Don't make me regret this more than I already do."

After the Russians' losses in the Crimea, President Marsh convened the National Security Council to consider the possibility of moving up his original, August 12 deadline, even though it was less than five weeks away.

"If the Russians dare to do anything else on their own, they know it'll have to be prior to the start of Operation Swift Sword," he said. "Once our forces are engaged they'll either have to ally with us, which they've once again refused to do, or stay on the sidelines."

"You're right, sir, another Russian offensive is a definite danger," CIA chief Jameson said. "Given the pressures Karzhov is facing from the ultranationalists and old-line Communists in the Duma, even a limited nuclear attack against the TAA has become a possibility."

Everyone in the room fell silent for a moment.

"Any unusual movements in the Russian arsenal?" Marsh asked.

"No. According to the current Shell Game report, all transfers occurred on schedule," Woodruff replied. "Nor have we seen any troop buildups."

"Make sure they're monitored twenty-four/seven," the President said. "I don't want any more surprises."

The conversation moved to the feasibility of deploying the prototype weapons ahead of schedule, but General Mancini stopped it before it went any further.

"Sir, everything is geared to the original deadline. We've already moved close to a hundred thousand personnel and untold tons of matériel to Aviano and Incirlik. We've got a dozen warships harbored in Istanbul, with two dozen more en route. But as you know, even with such a force assembled, our war plans are critically dependent on the unique capabilities of our prototype systems. They will barely be ready on twelve August. Earlier deployment would pose too great a risk to troop safety and system effectiveness."

His sobering assessment disappointed Marsh.

"Believe me, sir, I wish it weren't so," he continued. "The Russians not only failed in their attack on Sevastopol, they caused Batu Khan to augment his forces in the occupied territories far beyond our original projections. Each day that goes by makes it more difficult for us to remove him."

After the meeting, Secretary of Defense Woodruff stayed behind to speak to the President in private.

"With tensions between the Russians and the TAA as they are, perhaps we should expand the surveillance parameters at Svalbard."

Svalbard, a U.S.-owned, Cold War–era radar station, sat on a desolate island midway between Norway and the North Pole in the Arctic Sea. As part of their highly secret strategy of intercepting defense-contractor break-ins, Marsh and Woodruff had arranged for the ExOps, their secret counterintelligence team, to install a new satellite downlink there. Using standard data from one of the U.S. radar satellites perched in geosynchronous orbit above the Northern Hemisphere, its specially tuned equipment watched for one particular type of aircraft. An ExOp monitored the signal around the clock. As with the infiltration interceptions, only the President and the Secretary of Defense knew of the operation.

"Let me think about it, Stan," Marsh said.

Marsh knew the reply surprised Woodruff—ordering the ExOps to increase the scope of their surveillance would be an effortless addition to their duties at Svalbard. But despite that, the President, in a sudden flash of paranoia, didn't want the defense secretary talking to the ExOps, *his* ExOps, any more than absolutely necessary.

"Sir, perhaps we should—" Woodruff began.

"That's enough! I said I'll consider it!" It came out far more sharply than he'd meant it to, and he struggled to suppress an onslaught of unreasonable rage. For a long, uncomfortable moment he glared at Woodruff while clenching and unclenching his fists beneath the desk.

"Yes, sir; of course," Woodruff said, startled by the harsh response.

The President, instantly calmed by Woodruff's conciliatory tone, leaned back in his chair and shook his head.

"I'm sorry, Stan. Too much of Levinson's double-caf French Roast will be the death of me yet."

Woodruff nodded, much relieved, and returned the smile. Hell, he thought, if I were President these days I'd be pretty damn short-tempered, too.

Kate took it hard when Wilder told her he had to go away again. She'd expected he'd be around for a while. Also, to his surprise, it upset her that Laura wouldn't be coming to her soccer game. He promised to tell Laura the invitation still stood. He called Laura after Kate went to bed. It touched and flattered her that Kate wanted her at the game, and she promised she'd be there. Wilder told her the official version of his return to California, not of his secret understanding with Brent to quietly continue his investigation of Rexford.

"I'll miss you, you know." Laura felt a little uncomfortable saying it out loud. Was it too soon in their relationship, if she could even think in terms of such a loaded word, to be missing him?

"I'm taking a couple of your books with me. Think they'll keep me from missing you?"

"I sure hope not."

Wilder believed the answers he sought could be found in Cowling's office, tucked inside his big turbocharged PC. The machine sat on a desk return sideways to the rest of the office, so he'd seen the back of the CPU the day he was there and noticed something unusual: it had no ethernet connection. Why would Cowling, a guy so adamant about having nothing to hide, isolate his office computer from the university network? It would be mighty inconvenient for researching, e-mailing, and linking to the library catalogues, but staying off the network was the only foolproof way of protecting a computer from electronic intrusion. No, Professor Cowling had protested a little too loudly about not having any secrets.

After Kate went to bed, Wilder opened a password-protected PDF file he'd requested from the DoD Computer Crime Lab archives—a paper written in 1985 called "Electromagnetic Radiation from Video Display Units: An Eavesdropping Risk?" by a Dutch scientist named Wim van Eck. It demonstrated how computers emit electromagnetic radiation similar to radio waves, which can be intercepted, reconstructed, and viewed from a remote location.

The Dutch and American governments immediately classified the paper, hence its unavailability to anyone without a high-security clearance. Unknown to van Eck, the Western intelligence community had been using this very phenomenon for clandestine purposes since the 1960s, and the technology for monitoring CRT emissions remained top secret and officially unnamed for twenty-five years. But after details of van Eck's paper leaked out, electronic-privacy advocates named it Tempest, for Transient Electromagnetic Pulse Emanation Surveillance Technology. Aside from some classified know-how, only a handful of components were needed: a wide-band radio receiver, a horizontal-and-vertical sync generator, an active directional antenna, a monitor, and a VCR to record the images. By using the schematics in van Eck's paper, Wilder hoped to find his answers from far beyond his restriction of two hundred feet from campus.

He left at midnight on an Air Force transport for Travis AFB and arrived at six A.M. A couple of OSI agents he met for breakfast in the Officers' Club hit him with a stunning piece of news: a terse note from the OSI western regional commander had ordered the Travis detachment to cease its investigation of the break-in at the defense subcontractor plant and transfer the file to the FBI office in San Francisco.

Wilder could barely believe it: Someone had quashed the investigation in precisely the same way his Woomera and Rexford cases were pulled from him, and the same way Andrews spy Tavo Joval had been shipped to destinations unknown before being questioned. Whatever small doubts he had about these occurrences being related and sinister were now gone. But despite his anger he said nothing to Brent or the Travis OSI, as he didn't want the loss of the case to force his immediate return to Andrews.

He would only have two or three days at most to take advantage of the black hole the situation created for him between Andrews and Travis, so he rented a Chrysler minivan with tinted windows, put the Tempest equipment in the back, and drove to the university. During Cowling's morning office hours Wilder reconnoitered the campus perimeter, far enough away to avoid Nichols's gestapo, stopping wherever he could see the Old Chem building. He aimed the small dish antenna at the building and slowly clicked up and down the frequency spectrum on the wide-band receiver. Whenever he'd pick up a signal, he'd nudge the controls on the sync generator until a stable image appeared on his notebook screen—a perfect replication of the computer monitor whose impulses he received. A few possibilities for Cowling's machine appeared: some-one viewing chemistry formulas; someone else looking at molecule schematics; another reading an arcane research paper.

Then he hit upon a powerful signal—a hopeful sign, as Cowling's big twenty-five-inch monitor would create particularly strong emissions. He locked the sync and began to laugh. This *had* to be his man. The image was a web page—http://www.nudeteens.com—showing a picture of a thin young woman with bright red hair, naked apart from her sunglasses, glistening with suntan oil, reclining on a patio chair. She held her legs apart and her pubic hair, shaved into a narrow V, was the same vivid color as on her head. Wilder noted the exact frequency then searched for a place to park the van—no easy task in a crowded college town. He found an ideal overlook a few blocks from campus: a three-car parking lot behind a place called Mo's Pizza & Sandwich. Cowling's signal came in perfectly.

Wilder looked up, startled by a small, dark-skinned man in a white paper hat rapping angrily on the window.

"Employee only!"

The man gestured emphatically at the NO PARKING sign hand-painted on the back wall in ten-foot letters. Wilder rolled the window down.

"How about I rent this space, hundred bucks a day, for the next two days?"

The little man shook his head. "Employee only! You see how bad goddamn parking is! I need this spot; please move!"

"Two hundred a day?"

The man cast a suspicious eye on him.

"What, you deal drugs? Please, go away!"

Wilder sighed and pulled out of the spot. He didn't need the guy calling the cops on him. But when he drove past Mo's something in the window caught his eye and he made a U-turn.

Inside the narrow, now-deserted shop, Formica booths lined the walls, with small square tables between them. Rexford athletic posters and Eighties-vintage rock concert flyers were taped to the walls, the cellophane turned amber by the sun. The radio played an Arabic language talk station. The man, Mo Assefi, glared at Wilder.

"I goddamn hope you're here to eat, amigo."

Wilder tossed the cardboard sign he'd taken from the window onto the counter. It read: HELP WANTED—WAITER OR WAITRESS. Mo looked at it, at Wilder, and guffawed.

"I look for *student* to help. I pay five bucks an hour."

"I'll take it."

Mo's expression clouded.

"You got trouble with the goddamn law or something?"

"Nope."

Mo eyed Wilder over. He didn't look like a drug dealer or a fugitive, and the goddamn sign had been in the window for a week. Snot-nose kids at Rexford thought they were too good for a job waiting tables.

"Screw up the goddamn food orders, I fire you. Steal, I goddamn fire you. Come in goddamn late, I fire you."

"Deal."

Wilder moved the van back into the prized parking spot and shoved an eight-hour tape in the DC-powered VCR, then completed the requisite employment forms for Mo and began his new career. At lunchtime, a dozen tables filled with loud and impatient Rexford students. To Wilder, the most confounding counterintelligence case seemed easy compared to taking orders and getting the food to the right people at the right time. Four pretty sorority girls hung around for a long lunch, sipping Diet Cokes and flirting with him. One in particular, a brown-haired beauty from L.A., couldn't take her big green eyes off him. The girls' attentions flattered Wilder, but his interest lay with Laura.

During the lull before dinnertime, he went to the van and switched tapes in the Tempest video recorder. He used a second VCR to skim through what he'd recorded so far. Cowling had viewed more porn, then uploaded an essay to his web site about how the United States should give California back to Mexico. Wilder noticed the site also had a lengthy treatise about how the United States had no business threatening war with the Trans-Altaic Alliance; the whole affair was just another excuse for American imperialism. Wilder smiled—the expression seemed so dated and of its time, perfectly matching the web site's flower-power design motif. Then he saw bad news: Cowling used an on-line ticketing service to confirm a flight to Denver for the following evening. Given this new time limitation, Wilder desperately hoped Cowling would spend some quality time with his PC.

At dinnertime Mo's was packed, almost entirely by young women. Word about the new guy at Mo's had apparently swept the sorority circuit. The brown-haired beauty and her friends returned, and when Wilder came to their table with a tray of beers and salads, the whole place got quiet. Apparently, everyone except Wilder and Mo knew what would happen next.

"You're, uh, off at eleven-thirty?" the girl asked Wilder.

"Yep."

"Can I buy you a cup of coffee or something?"

Someone nearby said, encouragingly, "Go, girl!"

Wilder smiled. "Definitely the nicest offer I've gotten all week. But my wife worries that if I stay out too late I'll get mugged."

The whole room groaned in unison.

"Married or gay."

"Huh?"

"The good ones."

"That's what they say. Sorry."

"Not as sorry as I am."

Wilder excused himself as two male customers sat down in a booth. They did a classic double-take as he brought their menus over. Curly and Bullwinkle, the security guards he'd fought in Cowling's office. Bullwinkle sported a bandage across the broken nose Wilder had given him. Wilder, smiling, tried to hand them menus. They shoved them aside and stood up.

"The fuck *you* doing here?!"

"Brushing up my people skills. You should give it a try."

"You're in violation, prick."

"Get a tape measure. We're a thousand feet from university property. Now, you eating or leaving?"

"Fuck you; *eating*!"

"Knock off the language. There're ladies here. Eat or leave."

"C'mon, hotshot, I'm off duty," Bullwinkle said. "How 'bout we get personal?"

Wilder thumped Bullwinkle's broken nose with the tip of his finger. He bellowed and stepped back, holding his nose between his hands like an injured bear. Curly pulled a short steel bar from his back pocket and lunged. Wilder ducked under the swing. He laced his fingers together behind Curly's thick bald head and snapped his knee into Curly's face, holding him by the collar so he wouldn't stumble into the girls behind him. Curly shoved Wilder's hand away and balled up his fists. But with his eyes watering and his nose bleeding, he had trouble focusing on his adversary.

"You really want to catch a beating in front of all these pretty women?" Wilder asked.

Curly shoved Bullwinkle in front of him, sucked in his gut, and sauntered toward the exit. As they left, the brown-haired girl led her friends in a round of applause. Mo, however, glared angrily at Wilder. He didn't want trouble from anyone wearing a uniform, and Wilder didn't feel so jovial either. As the two security guards hurried past the pizzeria window Curly dialed his cell phone.

Later, in the van, Wilder scanned the videotape from that evening. Cowling got on his computer after lab hours to read his e-mail, the newswires, and . . . Wilder sat up. Cowling had stopped at an article about the perp in Boston, the one he'd mentioned to Brent. Cowling kept the article on the screen, brought up one of his nudie pictures in a small window, and clicked on an unlabeled program icon that looked like a ball-and-stick diagram of a molecule:

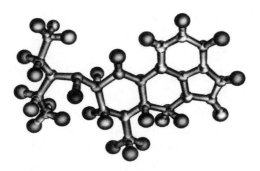

Wilder recognized it from somewhere . . . where the hell had he seen it? Then he remembered—Cowling had the same diagram tattooed on his ankle. A blank command line appeared on screen and Cowling typed:

STEGO /D HOTASS.JPG TSTGRP.FM5 *******

To the untrained eye, meaningless. To Wilder, a major breakthrough. The key word *stego*, short for steganography, referred to computer programs that invisibly mingle data of one file within that of another carrier, usually a picture or sound file. Even on close examination, the data looks unchanged. An innocent digital snapshot of Aunt Martha could contain a stolen formula, a secret love letter, or the plans for blowing up New York. Unlike conventional encryption, which creates lots of strange gibberish, no one could tell any secret data existed. Professor Cowling took this sleight-of-hand one step further. He'd hidden his real secrets within his pornographic pictures—themselves something most people would want to keep from view—then left them in plain sight as proof he had nothing to hide.

Wilder guessed HOTASS.JPG identified the carrier picture, so TSTGRP.FM5 would be the name of the file hidden within it, /D the command to decrypt, and the asterisks appeared when Cowling typed in his password. He recognized the file extension .FM5 from a popular database program called FileMaker Pro. Sure enough, Cowling started it next.

Wilder nearly burst with anticipation while he watched the tape. The main FileMaker screen opened on a small database with thirty records. Cowling opened record twenty-three, identified as 558497341. Nine digits—must be a social security number, Wilder thought. Cowling went to a blank field called Resolution. He typed in the details of the Boston perp's shoot-out with the cops, underlining the unique abilities he'd exhibited. Closing the field moved him for an instant to record twenty-four, then he exited FileMaker. Wilder rewound and advanced frame-by-frame until he reached the moment record twenty-four flew by. He noted its identifying number, 628942551, barely visible through the video noise on the VCR freeze-frame.

Thrilled, Wilder called Boston PD; although it was three A.M. there he talked the desk sergeant into waking up the detective in charge of the case so he could check the file for their perp's social security number. In a few moments the sleepy detective with a comically thick Boston accent got on the line and gave him the social: 234-88-5764. Not even close to the one in the database. Well, at least Wilder learned the Professor was tracking the perps. And that he'd gone to record twenty-three, the same number of perps Wilder knew about. More important, he hoped the thirty-record length of the database meant there were only seven more potential lunatics still out there, not seventy or seven hundred.

Walking to his hotel room to shower before returning to spend the night in the van, his thoughts returned to the perp's social security number and the number in the database. If Cowling's list dated back thirty years, before personal computers and the easy encryption they offered, surely he would've done something manually to obscure the identities on the list. Wilder examined the two numbers side by side on a piece of paper. He'd always been good at brain teasers as a kid, and he ran the numbers in his head, backward and forward. How did they relate?

Twenty minutes later, in the shower, he had a satisfying flash of realization. If 558497341 were reversed to 143-79-4855 and compared to 234-88-5764, the first, third, fifth, etcetera numerals were one digit *higher*, the second, fourth, sixth, etcetera were one *lower*. Using this formula, Wilder transfigured the number of Cowling's database record twenty-four and called the FBI VICAP hotline to ask for an ID on the social security number it gave him. The tech on duty read him a name and address: William Harlin, 99600 Lancaster Drive, Sun City, Arizona.

Twenty-three

Wilder continued his Tempest monitoring until Cowling left for Denver, but the Professor didn't open his database again. Quitting his waiter's job, he gave Mo his salary and tips and told him to buy some goddamn new posters for the walls, then he booked a commercial flight back to Washington, D.C.—with a stop-off in Phoenix.

The American Airlines flight landed at Sky Harbor Airport and the captain reported a temperature of 119 degrees. It took most of Wilder's forty-five-minute drive from the airport with the air-conditioning running full blast for the car to cool down.

Wilder increased the volume on the radio as the network news interrupted the music on the local jazz station for breaking news, and they went to a live Pentagon news briefing. A high-altitude TAA spy plane had just been shot down by American antiaircraft missiles as it overflew Incirlik Airbase in Adana, Turkey, the U.S. forces command center for Operation Swift Sword. Although the Pentagon spokesman downplayed the incident's significance, Wilder didn't like the sound of it. Batu Khan must've wanted detailed intelligence about Incirlik quite badly. Why else, given the high probability of his surveillance plane getting shot down, would he send it into the most heavily protected airspace in the world, risking military embarrassment and increased international tensions?

Wilder turned right off Grand Avenue onto North 103rd Street and entered Sun City, the world's largest retirement community. Twenty-eight thousand housing units and a population of over forty thousand.

Nothing moved—not clouds, not wind, not people—except an occasional large sedan or electric golf cart driving slowly by. Not that Wilder could blame the locals for staying out of the brutal heat.

He parked in front of a row of single-story condominiums on West Lancaster Drive, walked through a small gate into the grass common area, and rang the bell at unit 99600. No answer. He went back out the gate and around back to the alley to look for Harlin's car. He found Harlin in his garage, head under the hood of a Ford Ranger pickup with a Dolphin camper shell on the back, tinkering with the engine. According to his social security records Harlin was fifty-six, but he looked much older—short and gaunt, with thin, yellowish-white hair and dark circles under his eyes. He had an unfiltered Camel cigarette in his mouth and Wilder guessed from his rhythmic wheezing he had emphysema. Wilder approached as casually as possible in a place where nobody walked.

"Howdy."

"How ya doing." Harlin turned his attention back to the engine. After a few moments, he looked up again and didn't appear too pleased that Wilder still stood in the alleyway.

"My brothers and I are thinking about buying the folks a winter place. Saw your garage open, thought maybe I could get some thoughts other than the real estate agent's."

Harlin wiped his hands with a rag and closed the hood of the truck. He seemed normal enough, Wilder thought, not aggressive or angry, shy even. But that's what everyone had said about the other perps until they went postal.

"Where're your people livin' now?" Harlin asked.

"Michigan. Just outside Ann Arbor."

"Yeah? I'm from up Saginaw way."

Wilder already knew Harlin's hometown; he figured the same-state story would make him seem less of a stranger.

"What line a work you in, son?"

"I teach high school history, back in Virginia." After reading some of Laura's books, he was confident he could bluff his way through the subject if necessary. "You live in Sun City full time?"

"Yep. No more a them winters, shoveling the damn driveway. Health can't take it no more. Soon as I turned fifty-five, down I come." Harlin lit a new Camel off the old one. "There's sun tea in the fridge, if ya want a glass."

"I don't want to put you out . . ."

"Nah, no bother. Come on through to the kitchen."

The folding aluminum sun shades were drawn in all the windows, making the condo so dark that Harlin had to turn on some lights. A blue haze hung in the air from lingering cigarette smoke, and the walls had the same nicotine-yellow tint as Harlin's hair and fingers. Everything was nondescript and inexpensive like a furnished apartment, except for one personal touch: ducks. Paintings and framed prints of ducks on the walls, duck figurines in glass, wood, brass, and ceramic on shelves, and hunter's decoys under the coffee table. Harlin handed Wilder a glass of iced tea.

"Haven't missed duck season since six years of age, 'cept in 'Nam. Quail or pheasant, neither. 'Fore I moved, I made certain they had good hunting nearby. Skeet range, too. Found some great spots, up by Lake Pleasant. "

Wilder let Harlin do the talking. A lonely widower, old before his years, he seemed glad for the company. After a while, Wilder turned the subject to Harlin's job, and his education.

"I'm a Rexford man," Harlin said. "Went on the GI Bill after gettin' out of the Marines."

"Rexford. That's great. I dated a girl who went there. Chemistry major, always talking about this interesting professor she had, fella named Cowling."

Harlin nodded and laughed. "Yeah, I remember Cowling. Just a kid himself at the time, real character."

"You stay in touch with him, or any of your Rexford classmates?"

"Nah, Christ, that was years ago." Lighting another cigarette, Harlin got up from the kitchen table. "I gotta hit the head. Help yourself to more tea."

Wilder, sitting with his back to the hallway, heard Harlin close a door behind him. After a couple minutes the door opened; Wilder heard his footsteps coming back down the linoleum hallway, but there'd been no sound of a toilet flushing. He glanced up at a reflection of movement behind him, caught on the glass covering a duck picture on the wall. Harlin stood at the end of the hall, holding something long and metallic. Wilder rolled out of the chair and into the dining room milliseconds before a shotgun blast shredded the kitchen table and chair. He ran for the only cover available—behind the sofa, near the wet bar in the living room. Harlin stayed in the dining room, out of view.

"Never met no history teacher packin' a side arm before. Hidin' 'er don't fool me, not how she reeks a Hopp's Number Nine."

The son of a bitch smelled the gun-cleaning solution I used on my Sig . . . two weeks ago, Wilder thought.

"I ain't goin' nowhere with you people. No goddamn way. I got my rights."

He sounded indignant, scared. Wilder had no idea who Harlin thought he was. Be nice to take him alive so he could ask, but under the circumstances he'd settle for getting himself out alive. He pulled the Sig from the hip holster under his shirt and looked across the room to the front door. No way to make it without crossing Harlin's path.

"Look, Bill, it's all right. I just want to talk to you—"

Harlin stepped into the doorway and fired. Wilder hugged the floor and the load went just over his head, ripping a four-foot-wide hole in the wall. He popped up and squeezed off a quick shot, hitting Harlin dead center in the chest. Harlin flew back a foot from the force of the bullet's impact, then came forward again. Before he could reorient his aim, Wilder leapt through the hole in the wall, into the guest bedroom. On his way he caught a brief look at Harlin—the feeble retiree was wearing a threat-level-four, tactical-entry police vest: multiple layers of Kevlar from crotch to neck. He also had a military-style utility belt heavy with over-sized magazines strapped around his waist and his shotgun was a long-barrel, semiauto, magazine-fed twelve-gauge. Goddamn ducks, Wilder thought, never had a chance.

Wilder crawled knees and elbows through the wood-and-drywall de-bris on the guest-room carpet and slipped into the room across the hall—Harlin's office. It had a desk with stacks of bills, a cheap typewriter, two metal filing cabinets, and a tall, oak gun cabinet with reinforced-glass doors. Inside were a dozen shotguns. Pumps, over-unders, side-by-sides, and a large collection of the bizarre, quasi-legal, definitely lethal specialty shotgun shells available at gun shows and through mail-order catalogues. There were bolo rounds, two lead balls connected by a five-inch piece of steel wire; fléchette loads containing twenty razor-sharp metal darts; chain rounds holding a half foot of coiled iron chain; and highly accurate BRI slugs, shells holding a single, hourglass-shaped lead projectile encircled with a plastic sabot. Getting hit with any of this nasty medieval shit would make regular lead shot seem merciful.

Remembering the other perps' extraordinary sensory abilities, he crouched motionlessly beside the metal desk, Sig in hand, and held his breath. He heard Harlin's footsteps approach.

"Tick-tick-tick . . . I hear your watch, Mister."

Harlin seemed to be in no hurry to finish off his quarry. Wilder fired three rounds in a triangular pattern through the outside window and heavy metal sun shade, ran across the room and crashed through the window just as Harlin let loose with a fléchette load. Some darts sliced through his calves as he dove outside, then he hit the pavement in the al- leyway and scrambled to his feet. Fortunately, he saw no one outside. Looking around for cover, he spotted the six-foot-high concrete-block wall on the far end of the alley and he ran for it, legs bleeding.

Inside the condo, Harlin calmly swapped magazines and fired two BRI slugs into the wall under the window, blasting a wide hole through it. Seeing Wilder running down the alleyway, Harlin switched magazines to bolo rounds, took aim, and fired. The bolos sliced the air inches from him and lodged in the cinder-block wall. Harlin nuzzled the shotgun stock against his shoulder and prepared to fire again. Wilder spun around and shot twice. One round tore a piece out of Harlin's left thigh. Harlin barely flinched, but it bought Wilder enough time to scramble over the wall.

He fell into an unexpected swarm of activity in the parking lot of a Trader Joe's specialty food store—cars fighting for parking spaces, one line of people shuffling toward the entrance, and another exiting with overflowing shopping carts. Harlin paused in the alley, fifty feet away, and switched magazines again. Wilder crouched behind the wall prepar- ing to spring up and take his shot. But before he could move Harlin fired four shots in succession. His loads this time were contact grenades— pineapple-scored iron projectiles in the shape of stubby cigars, encased within plastic shotgun shells and stuffed with explosives. They hit the wall at three-yard intervals like giant sledgehammers, blasting Volkswagen- sized holes through it and panicking the people in the parking lot.

Wilder only had two rounds left, and he had to divert the madman from the crowd. Harlin moved faster now, laying down a cover pattern of wide-scattering buckshot. Wilder spotted a steel garbage Dumpster on wheels at the edge of the parking lot. He got behind and pushed until he got it going at a full run, smashing it through the shattered wall into the alley. Harlin shot at it, but two layers of half-inch steel shielded Wilder from his volley. Wilder let it continue on its own momentum, then stepped quickly from behind. He shot twice, hoping to hit Harlin some-where it mattered. One bullet smacked into Harlin's left shoulder just at the edge of the Kevlar vest; the other hit his right thigh, shattering the bone. The leg buckled, but Harlin balanced on the other and kept firing single-handed from the hip until exhausting his clip. Wilder rushed him and tried to wrest the slippery gun stock from his bloody grip.

Even with a useless arm and two wounded legs, Harlin easily matched Wilder's strength. They fought face-to-face on the scalding-hot pavement, Wilder on top, but he could not break Harlin's iron grip on the twelve-gauge. He butted his head against Harlin's nose. Blood spurted from his nostrils and he howled with pain. Harlin suddenly shoved the shotgun and Wilder to one side, rolled over, and piled on top of him. He jammed the end of the shotgun barrel into Wilder's windpipe and their hands struggled for control of the trigger. Wilder's strength began to ebb.

Harlin smiled in that strange, familiar way. His teeth were as small as a child's, crooked and yellow. Just as he got his thumb inside the shotgun trigger-guard and squeezed, Wilder put both hands under the barrel and shoved it up. The blast obliterated Harlin's face from his chin to the top of his skull. Among the bone, muscle, blood, and cartilage that splattered all over Wilder, one rock-hard object lodged under the skin beside his eyebrow.

Even the jaded emergency-room doctors were aghast when they cleaned Wilder up and pulled the thing out: one of Harlin's yellow little teeth.

Twenty-four

"**L**aura Bishop?"

Sitting in front of her computer at her desk, Laura didn't recognize the businesslike woman's voice on the phone.

"Speaking."

"Please hold for the First Lady."

Before she could register her surprise, Amy Marsh's familiar Georgia-accented voice came on the line. "Laura, honey, how are you?"

"Mrs. Marsh! Very well, thank you."

"Do you think your fabulous Mr. Wilder would mind if I borrowed you tomorrow evening?"

Laura, the word expert, fumbled for a reply. "Well, I'm sure he wouldn't . . . he's actually out of town . . . besides, we're really just friends."

Amy laughed—she'd seen how Wilder and Laura looked at each other.

"*Friends.* Uh-huh." Her bemused tone made Laura laugh, too.

"Here's the situation," she continued. "The Israeli prime minister arrives tomorrow and I just found out his wife can't come. The staff scheduled a movie screening—a bona fide chick-flick, chosen by yours truly—meaning Burt and Ari are guaranteed to yak through the whole thing. What do you think, want to share my box of Kleenex?"

After the movie, Amy took Laura to the White House galley to fix them a snack. She loved the informality of it—only during those all-too-infrequent visits from her family could she set aside the responsibilities

211

and decorum of being First Lady. Laura reminded Amy of her two younger sisters, and the association put her immediately at ease. Carrying plates of ham sandwiches and potato salad and bottles of beer, the two women went upstairs to see the progress of Amy's pet project, the renovation of the VS Room. They sat on the sofa with their plates in their laps because a partially completed jigsaw puzzle covered the coffee table.

"Burt gave it to me a few months ago, 'cause I kept saying I feel like the wife in *Citizen Kane*, locked up in a big house day and night."

"I remember. She did those big puzzles all the time."

"Funny thing is, those were the good ol' days, as far as getting out. Since the crisis with the TAA started we've barely left White House. Now, where the hell's the box gone to?"

Amy pulled open several drawers and cabinets, then came to the credenza Marsh always kept locked. Annoyed at not being able to open it, she gave the doors several good tugs.

"It's not in there—whatever it is you want." Marsh, standing in the doorway, startled the women. He had a dark scowl on his face. "What are you looking for?"

"The damn puzzle box. Jesus, Burt, sneak up on us, why don't you? Suppose we'd been talkin' some real down-and-dirty girl stuff?"

The President's hard expression disappeared. He took a swig of Amy's beer and grinned. "I would've stood in the hall and eavesdropped."

Amy laughed along with him and Laura, but increasingly, honest to God, she didn't recognize him sometimes. Over the years, she'd seen her husband irritated, annoyed, pissed, and really pissed. During his first campaign for public office he even took a swing at a political opponent's dirty-tricks operative when they flung some mud her way. But she'd never seen his eyes go cold with a seething rage as they had lately. The moments were so fleeting, and he seemed so much himself afterward, that she hadn't discussed it with him.

"Ari toddle off to bed?" she asked.

"Yes. He's promised me some limited air support against the TAA but not much else. The Israeli public is overwhelmingly against involvement, and the Knesset has warned him they've got enough enemies already."

Marsh flopped exhaustedly into one of the overstuffed chairs, then looked at Laura. "You know, our intelligence operatives have yet to find another American who's spent ten minutes with Batu Khan, let alone five days like you did."

"Yes, my dumb luck. The equivalent of interviewing Elvis before the Sun recordings."

"We've been trying since the Russian disaster in Sevastopol to arrange another VS with Batu. If we succeed, I'd like to bend the ground rules a bit, have you secretly observe the conversation. I'm pretty good at judging people, but I'll be damned if I know what's going on in the man's mind. Maybe you can pick up on a personal or historical reference he might make, or some body language. Could you do that for me?"

Stunned at the request and the monumental responsibility it placed upon her, Laura simply shook her head in acceptance. Amy squeezed Laura's hand and smiled, understanding how out of her league she felt. The President switched the conversation to lighter subjects, critiqued the movie they'd seen, then said goodnight. After he left, Amy's jovial mood deserted her.

"He'll be at his desk till who knows what hour. The worst is how alone he feels." She sipped her beer, but it suddenly tasted sour and unappealing. "When he won the election, we'd barely even heard of some two-bit dictator named Batu Khan. Burt has great ideas for improving people's lives in this country; he'll even make some of them happen. But none of it will matter. His whole presidency will be defined by one thing: how he handles the Trans-Altaic Alliance."

Laura didn't have long to enjoy her excitement about observing the VS meeting. Two days later she received a handwritten note from President Marsh with his regrets and a heartfelt apology. Considering the extreme delicacy of the situation with Batu Khan, the arrangement they'd discussed had been deemed inappropriate by his senior military and protocol advisers, and even a President must defer to his experts' opinions in such matters. She was crushed.

In the VS Room, the image of Batu's *ger* replaced the TAA flag on the video wall. Batu shuffled into view with his hands clasped together in a gesture of prayer and his eyes cast downward, exhibiting none of his revival-tent theatricality. Marsh entered and surreptitiously pointed a small remote control at the partially opened doors of the video credenza, setting one of the VCRs to record.

Batu spoke without raising his eyes. "When assassins murdered my wife she carried within her a masculine child. My heir. Those responsible for those deaths, and my brother's, will answer for their crimes."

Marsh had a momentary impulse to express his condolences to Batu about his loss. Then he remembered the Georgian president's slain children. Those were premeditated murders, not an errant shot. He also remembered Batu beheading every tenth citizen of the dissident Ukrainian town.

"Did the United States assist the Russians in their treachery?" Batu asked. He already knew the answer—his spies deep within the Russian government had informed him of the Americans' intelligence support— he just wanted to hear Marsh's cowardly denial.

Instead, Marsh shrugged. "We didn't do much. By the time we learned about the incursion it had already started. We contributed some real-time satellite data, that's about it."

Batu involuntarily stepped back from the VS screen. Marsh's unexpected honesty and offhand attitude enraged him.

"By helping to *any* degree you have Kuri's blood on your hands as surely as the Russians do!"

"Look, Karzhov didn't tell me about the ambush. We only knew about the attack on Sevastopol. But after your spectacle in the Ukrainian village, you're in no position to judge who's got blood on them."

Batu walked slowly back and forth, barely able to contain his emotions.

"I am not the barbarian you think I am. My patience today proves it. I've certainly remained more civilized than you would if men entered your home and shot *your* wife in the back."

Despite his efforts to remain impassive, the President's expression clouded. That Batu dared make even a rhetorical threat at Amy infuriated him. He vividly imagined holding Batu down, gouging his eyes out with his thumbs, and then slowly twisting his head until he felt that gratifying snap.

Noting the momentary crack in Marsh's calm facade, Batu swept the hem of his *shalwar qamiz* behind him and sat cross-legged on the floor, so close to his video screen he almost seemed to be in the VS Room. Although he longed to further berate the President for his part in the Russian ambush, he forced himself to move on. He had a specific agenda for this meeting and would vent his wrath with actions later, not with words now.

"Very well; I like speaking frankly. First, let us imagine that terrible day when our great nations are at war. You won't be fighting in a hostile country like Iraq or Bosnia. My forces are intermingled with the civilian population in what you call the occupied territories. Your bombs aren't *that* smart; every dead innocent will make you look bad, not me. Secure in your white palace, indiscriminately raining bombs; that's not waging war, it's terrorism."

Marsh came fully armed with responses for such statements. Rather than reply, however, he let the harangue continue. Batu's need to pontificate and intimidate could yield an intelligence bonanza about TAA war plans or capabilities. One careless word could tell more than the gigabytes of information American satellites, spies, and surveillance gather each day.

"Or maybe you have plans for bombing the TAA herself," Batu continued. "But without a worldwide coalition behind you, that's not very appealing either. Do you think I'll bend to your will if you carpet-bomb my helpless citizens? No, I invite you to make martyrs of them."

"I have no doubt you'd sacrifice your own people."

"They'd welcome it! Already thousands have volunteered to act as human shields. How many such offers have you gotten? Your own generals are reluctant to put their soldiers in harm's way. They prefer airpower—high tech, low risk. Until your jets and attack helicopters prove useless in the ancient cities which will be our battlefields, and you're fighting the dreaded ground war. I pity the man who battles an Altaic warrior one-on-one."

Batu would be right, Marsh thought, especially if the Khaldun had somehow found a way to increase their strength and stamina, if not for America's trump card—the prototype weapons systems. Their accuracy, speed, and maneuverability will give the U.S. forces enormous advantage, even under the conditions Batu described. The President smiled. Angry, Batu stopped talking.

"Am I amusing you?"

"I'm sure your men are highly trained and motivated, but I'd put one of our Special Forces against five of your Khaldun anytime."

Marsh hoped by the comment to elicit some boast—and clue—from Batu about the strength of his warriors. But none came.

"Interesting you phrase it that way, because that's just about the ratio by which we have you outnumbered," Batu responded. "I have a million and a half men in my armed forces. What does America have, maybe three hundred fifty thousand? What have you sent to the puppet countries of Italy and Turkey, a hundred thousand? That's the number according to the Pentagon news briefings I see on television every night. A million and a half versus a hundred thousand. You Americans were insane—disarming yourselves as if the Soviets were the last enemy you'd ever face!"

Marsh's temper flared. He hated to be reminded of something he already found so frustrating.

"Our forces became more efficient—"

Batu sneered. "We both know better than that. And even if you had ten times the men, I still hold the advantage. Americans call themselves believers. But how many really believe, as we do, how many *know* as they die in battle that their soul is destined for the Eternal Blue Heaven? Your society values the individual above all. It is your religion and your fatal flaw."

"You won't be the first to underestimate us," Marsh replied, his voice rising.

Batu nodded with satisfaction, excited to be gaining the upper hand, lecturing the American for a fucking change.

"Your threats and ultimatums are empty, Marsh. You stand impotent, hoping I'm an ignorant Mongol who sees America as she once was, not as she is. At my pleasure I can order a million and a half warriors into battle. You, on the other hand, must have permission to fight from a spoiled, disinterested populace who are repelled by the notion of sacrifice."

Marsh was losing his struggle to remain calm. Batu had struck at his most frustrating weakness: his nation's refusal to support him.

"Think of the images: horrific battles, the wounded and the dead, flag-draped caskets coming home," Batu said. "Your people could never stomach the carnage it'll take to fight us. Unlike me, you serve at their whim. If you refuse to end it, you'll simply be replaced with someone who will."

"Maybe so," Marsh said. "They might actually try. But by the time they succeed in removing me I'll have gotten my way. There's only one thing worse than fighting an unpopular war—and that's losing it. I won't let that happen, no matter what it takes."

"You'll never last that long," Batu said, smiling for the first time. "You know exactly why . . . and I do, too."

An intense wave of paranoia seized Marsh. He shot to his feet. His rational mind told him there could be no possible way for Batu to know his innermost secrets, but he still felt exposed and vulnerable.

Batu saw at once he'd gotten to the President, but he didn't expect such a chilling transformation in the man. Marsh's eyes narrowed, and the light went out of them. His face tightened with repressed fury.

"Don't *ever* forget who I am!" he said in a loud, hoarse voice. "I lead the greatest nation that ever existed, you tent-dwelling piece of shit! And I'll last long enough to bury you and the fuckin' animals you call an army!"

He crossed quickly to the VS control console. "We're all out of reasons to talk."

"You can't run away!" Batu shouted. "Look at me, coward! *Marsh!*"

The President slammed his hand against the VS control switch, ending the connection.

It took Marsh almost ten minutes to regain his composure before he dared leave the VS Room. Once he calmed himself, he was able to shake off his fears that Batu Khan somehow knew of his condition—surely he would be the last person in the world to learn such a thing.

He stood in the Oval Office with his hands in his pockets, smiling calmly at Levinson, Woodruff, and Vice President Taylor, lying about every detail of what had transpired between him and Batu. His staff left the briefing in a jubilant mood, confident the President of the United States had given the Supreme Leader of the Trans-Altaic Alliance a firm but reasonable lecture, and had instilled grave doubts about Batu's odds of prevailing in a war between their countries.

Batu, meanwhile, emerged from his *ger* and stared at the sun setting over Koso Lake at the northernmost border of Mongolia. He had come to this part of the remote, highland steppes to bury his brother and wife as close to their Siberian birthplace as possible. As usual, he and his command contingent were camped on the high ground hidden within some trees. In the open grasslands below an old shepherd and his wife had pitched their *ger* for the night. Chu'tsai stood by a campfire, watching Yela roast a flank of mutton. Seeing Batu, he hurried over to find out how the VS meeting had gone and why it ended so quickly. Chu'tsai had never seen his friend appear as he did now: face flushed; jaw clenched; fiery, Rasputin-like eyes.

"Marsh *admitted* helping the Russians in their treachery and murder!"

"Yeah, but you already knew—"

"That's not the point! He thinks we're subhuman, so incapable of love or pain that it means nothing to confess this to me!"

"What did you say?"

"Much less than I wanted. Why give him the satisfaction of knowing he tore the heart from my chest? As we planned, I told him why his country would fail in making war against us. Then I threatened and insulted, and the beast within him appeared, just as Cowling predicted!"

"You actually saw Marsh lose control?"

"Just for a moment, then he ended the transmission."

"Amazing!"

Batu didn't share Chu'tsai's enthusiasm. Although he'd succeeded in his goal of angering the President and shaking his confidence in Operation Swift Sword, Marsh ended the transmission before he became so enraged that he would permanently snap. It almost didn't matter to Batu; he couldn't get Marsh's confession about aiding the Russians in the Crimea out of his head.

"He claims he did not know about the ambush, but I don't believe him any more than I believe the Russians when they say Kuri's death was an accident. They conspired together, wanting to hurt me in the worst possible way. Which is what they'll get in return."

His gaze turned to the old shepherd in the field, then grabbed Chu'-

tsai's arm and led him to the flock. The shepherd, at first surprised to see strangers and then thunderstruck to see Batu Khan, fell to his knees and pressed his forehead against the ground. Batu stopped in front of him and he crawled forward to kiss the hem of Batu's *shalwar qamiz*. Batu helped him to his feet. Shaking, the shepherd kept his glance cast downward. Batu took the old man's face between his hands and kissed him gently, once on each eye, then pressed a gold coin in his hand. Batu pulled his Browning pistol from a holster on his sheepskin belt and shot a lamb standing near its mother. He handed Chu'tsai a knife.

"I need your wisdom."

Chu'tsai sliced open the lamb's underbelly. Its intestines spilled out onto the grass and he slipped his hands beneath the organs in order to study them. On his knees, watching him, Batu spoke in a whisper.

"Marsh leaving office is not enough. We'll soon have the capability to eliminate America's will and means for intervention, now and for always. We must *take* that opportunity, not just threaten with it."

Chu'tsai didn't like it. "There's no need! If Marsh backs down or gets replaced we get what we want—"

"Don't say what cannot be when I speak of what *must* be! Destiny has illuminated each step in its time. We've already committed ourselves to expanding our means for power and security. Now I believe we must act as aggressively as possible in that moment."

Chu'tsai shook his head. He and Batu had spent several long nights since the ambush drinking *koumiss* and discussing ways to punish the responsible parties, but Chu'tsai had dismissed Batu's excessive plans as grief-driven rantings.

"This is the right path, I am certain," Batu murmured. "It's where we've been heading all along. Tell me what your arts show of these matters."

Chu'tsai closed his eyes and concentrated so the animal's spirit could instruct him. After a long moment he spoke—slowly, as the images formed in his mind.

"I see ships among the stars. A great palace . . . and a powerful storm. I see a thief in the night, like a ghost, obscured by the storm, stealing the lightning itself from the sky. You are there, ablaze with glory."

He opened his eyes. Batu Khan stood with his arms stretched wide in exaltation, his face turned heavenward. One hand reached toward the low, blood-red sun, sinking behind the lake to the west. His other hand stretched toward an immense blue-white moon, hanging above the mountaintops in the east, as if he could gather in his arms all of the earth and sky. Chu'tsai, caught up in Batu's fervor, soared with pride to have pleased his Khan. In his vision he truly saw the future. Which is why it terrified him.

Twenty-five

ccording to the Rexford University class catalogue, Professor Cowling held lab for his advanced biophysical chemistry class in the Old Chem building on Thursday nights. Fifteen minutes after lab began, a gray-haired man in a tie, blue blazer, and jeans climbed the steps to the Old Chem building. A small group of students smoking on the patio barely noticed him—just another aging, hunch-shouldered prof with tenure, thick glasses, and a beat-up briefcase. Coming through the doorway, the gray-haired man passed a pair of hand-holding undergrads in the otherwise-deserted hallway, then made a quick U-turn and slipped into Cowling's darkened office. Inside, Wilder removed the Coke-bottle glasses and took from his briefcase a small white box with a cable attached to it. He connected it to the USB port on the back of Cowling's PC; the computer recognized it as an auxiliary disk drive and assigned it a logical drive letter, then he entered a command to copy all contents of the main drive to the auxiliary. A bar-graph showed the time remaining: five minutes, thirty seconds.

As with most endeavors, in covert activities the simplest solution usually yields the best results. Despite the billions of dollars spent on computer security, all it takes to duplicate someone's computer data is a few minutes alone with the machine and an off-the-shelf external disk drive. Simple; just as Wilder considered a hundred clever ways to sneak on campus but wound up using his very first idea: drugstore hair tint and secondhand clothing. Later, with the external drive hooked up to his own machine, he would try to learn Cowling's secrets by attacking their greatest vulnerability: his password. The Tempest monitor showed it to be seven characters long. Most likely these seven characters formed a word or number of significance to the Professor, such as a birthday, name, or anniversary.

Wilder checked the progress of the data transfer—ninety seconds left. Then he heard a small noise behind him. As he turned, someone literally flew across the office and smashed him across the base of the skull with an iron rod. Multicolored lights exploded behind his eyeballs and nausea plunged through him, his legs buckled, and he slid to the floor. Professor Cowling stood over him, his face contorted with rage. Wilder felt a stinging prick as Cowling jabbed a hypodermic into his neck, and then darkness enveloped him.

As Wilder slowly regained consciousness, he first noticed a strange orientation to his body—midway between horizontal and vertical. He tried to move but his arms, legs, and head were immobile. Inch-wide steel straps, the kind used to hold cargo pallets together, bound him tightly to an inclined metal workshop table. His hair felt wet and he wondered if it was blood. Above him hung a row of old-fashioned fluorescent lights, and beyond, a dirty concrete ceiling. The air felt damp and moldy. A blurry face suddenly loomed over him—Professor Cowling, humming "The Mighty Quinn" along with his Walkman headphones.

"Welcome back, sunshine! Sorry your 'do is all wet. Just had to rinse out that stock-company color. I kept looking at you and getting the giggles."

Wilder strained against his bonds.

"Save your strength. You're going to need it."

"My people know where I am. They'll miss me."

"They know where you *were*. Not where you *are*. And given all the trouble you've been, I doubt they'll miss you very much." Cowling picked up a stethoscope and listened to Wilder's heart. "*Muy macho!* You should be crapping in your khakis, yet you show almost no physiological distress. Let's see what we can do about that."

He rummaged through a bag of medical paraphernalia and Wilder took in the rest of his surroundings. It seemed to be a basement storage area for old chemistry equipment. There were a few other workbenches, stained and burned by countless experiments; rusty oxygen tanks; crates of lab glassware; and ancient, tube-type monitoring equipment. At the far side of the room, wooden steps led to a heavy steel door. Above it, he saw a dusty, yellow-and-black Civil Defense logo.

"Legacy of your profession," Cowling said. "A bomb shelter. Relic from an era when the military and the government told us not only could we survive a nuclear war, but that we could win one. Goddamn you insane military cocksuckers to hell. You gave us nightmares for forty years."

He injected Wilder in the arm with a hypodermic.

"There, a nice hundred milligrams of PHP—phenylcyclohexylpyrrolidine. It's a psychotropic, produces a sharp increase in glucose metabolism within the frontal cortex, the hippocampus, and other centers of emotion. Large doses induce anxiety, dread, marked paranoia—"

"I can get all that watching the evening news."

"Ah, Mister Glib." Cowling took a hammer from under the worktable and smashed him in the ribs with it. Wilder groaned. "Good thing about sore ribs is they only hurt when you breathe," the Professor said. "Oh, I forgot, legacy of your stay with the Iraqis—you've transcended pain."

"You don't know shit about me."

"I know lots of shit about you. I'm a researcher, I do my homework." He pulled up a stool and sat beside Wilder. His breath smelled sour and harsh. "Those boys in Iraq fucked you up, didn't they? Tell me about it."

"My war stories would bore you, Cowling. Let's talk about Jonas McKee. Gail Sealy. Bill Harlin. Or any of the thirty people on your hit parade."

Cowling dropped his smile at the mention of Harlin and the number thirty. Pending notification of next-of-kin, the press hadn't identified Harlin as the Sun City madman, so even Cowling didn't know he'd gone nuts. And how did Wilder know the exact total on the list?

"I've never felt anything more passionately than the desire to hurt you."

"Right back at ya, Wally."

Cowling peeled a flesh-colored bandage off Wilder's forehead, exposing the wound where the ER doctors had removed Harlin's tooth.

"Ow, nasty. Girlfriend cross her legs while you were yodeling up the canyon?"

Wilder began to have trouble breathing—the PHP had kicked in and his whole body went slick with sweat. He tried to choke the feeling down, show no outward reaction. He didn't want to give Cowling the satisfaction. Cowling noticed, though, and it brought back his smile.

"Getting a little green around the gills there, big fella. You know, those things I read about you—unbreakable, iron will—really piqued my curiosity. *Everyone* has a breaking point. I'm anxious to find yours." He took a penlight out of his pocket. "One transcript said you have twenty/four hundred in your injured eye. Legally blind. Thing is, it didn't say which eye."

He shined the light in one of Wilder's eyes and then the other. "Left's a little slow dilating." He looked it over and nodded. "Good cosmetic work, though. You'd never know. Don't tell me one of those meatball Air Force docs patched you up."

He pulled a surgical glove onto his left hand, then held up a small glass vial with an eyedropper top and a clear liquid inside it. "Few drops of hydrochloric acid in this-here good eye of yours, now *that's* a bit of pain you'd be hard-pressed to transcend."

Wilder threw his weight from side to side, but the table didn't budge. Cowling had bolted it to the floor.

"Cup of pencils, a pooch, snazzy pair of Foster Grants—it'll be a good look for you."

As Cowling slowly unscrewed the vial, Wilder became convinced that his intense panic and terror would overwhelm and perhaps kill him. He stiffened and tried to turn his head away, but the steel strap across his forehead dug into his skull and made movement impossible. He tried to focus his mind elsewhere.

"How'd you know I was in your office? You were supposed to be teaching."

"I was, then I heard something familiar. Never noticed it beforehand, not consciously, anyway. My computer's disk drive—that scratchy little noise it makes when it's working."

Cowling's reply confirmed what Wilder most feared: The Professor had the same acute sensory powers as the others. The same madness. He drew some of the liquid into the dropper, then put his gloved thumb and forefinger on Wilder's eyelids and yawned them open. He poised the dropper three inches above Wilder's right eye, teasing him, applying just enough pressure to bring an almost-formed drop to the tip of the glass dropper.

"Go ahead and scream. No one will hear, and I rather enjoy the drama of it. It's so, what's that expression . . . *Grand Guignol.*"

Still the drop hovered. Wilder willed himself to think of Kate and Laura, desperately trying to hold their sweet faces in his mind. He looked away, toward the old Civil Defense sign, so Cowling wouldn't be the last thing he ever saw.

"Fuck you. Do it and get your shit-breath out of my face."

"Well, like they say in your line of work, bombs away!"

Cowling squeezed the bulb and three drops of the liquid fell onto Wilder's eye. He clutched the sides of the table as the drops began to sting. The burning grew in intensity and a scream formed in his throat.

Twenty-six

The burning got no worse. It receded, then stopped. Wilder blinked. Except for some numbness and stickiness his eye was unharmed. Cowling looked at him with a goofy grin, as if he'd just used a hand buzzer on him at a New Year's party. "Don't get too cozy with that feeling of relief, Pilgrim. Soon you'll *wish* this was hydrochloric acid."

"What is it?"

"Way more interesting kind of acid. Lysergic acid diethylamide-25."

"*LSD?* Shit, Cowling, wake up and smell the decade."

"No thanks. I had hope for the world during the Sixties, but each of the following decades have increasingly disgusted me." He checked Wilder's pulse again, pleased to find it a heart-attack-inducing 220. "So, as Jimi asked, are you experienced?"

"Never held much appeal."

"Shame you never turned on under better circumstances. Acid cleanses the doors of perception. It can be so beautiful and profound, the ultimate spirit and soul amplification. Word of caution, however: Your underlying emotions guide that amplification. Bad frame of mind, bad trip."

Wilder welcomed his chattiness, it kept his mind off the panic tearing at him. Cowling spread open Wilder's other eyelid and put several more drops of the LSD solution into it.

"Ocular dosing is one of my contributions to the literature. The system absorbs the drug with far greater speed and intensity than ingestion or IV."

Strange sensations began to manifest in Wilder's mind. As he glanced up at the fluorescent fixtures, he could hear the light coming from them in a steady, melodic stream. Conversely, he saw the music pouring from Cowling's headphones like rainbow-colored honey, running in globs down his shirt. The concrete walls fluttered like curtains in the breeze and he winced as they appeared to fall in on him. He became aware of the blood rushing through his body, rasping against his insides like sandpaper, and he watched the words fall out of Cowling's mouth in fat little sausages. It reminded him of a horse shitting while it walked, and he was not too fucked up to appreciate the appropriateness of such an image.

"A psychedelic dose is about 500 micrograms. The intensity of the trip is proportional to the size of the dose . . . you're up to about 12,500 micrograms so far."

Wilder's sweat felt metallic, oozing like mercury. Everything assumed a twisted, threatening form—moving, scratching, murmuring. His senses vibrated with hypersensitivity. He squeezed his eyes shut against the rush of stimuli, but the chaos inside his head grew even more frenetic. Kaleidoscopic images surged in on him, opening and closing in circles and spirals, exploding in colored fountains. After an indeterminate time, Cowling's voice came back into focus. It sounded thin, canned, like an old radio broadcast, and he realized it came from a television set. Cowling, standing near the steps, was adjusting a video camera on a tripod attached to a thirteen-inch TV/VCR combination unit on a bench. Wilder tried to concentrate on the black-and-white film on the television: Cowling in 1973, narrating his lab journal, a young firebrand with a beard, a wild mop of blond hair, and a Janis Joplin T-shirt under his sports jacket. While talking he drew on a blackboard, explaining how he resynthesized the LSD-25 molecule—9,10-Didehydro-N,N-diethyl-6-methylergoline-8 beta-carboxamide; N,N-diethyl-D-lysergamide—into a compound he called LSD-69. He spoke of using volunteers recruited from his advanced chemistry classes to test his new substance in a secret study. He intended to show LSD-69 offered the same mind-expanding potential of regular LSD without its hallucinogenic properties.

Cowling fast-forwarded the tape. A stretch of hidden-camera footage showed several college-aged test subjects under the influence of the hallucinogen. In an observation area, he sat questioning them, hugging them, laughing, sometimes crying with them. Even through his LSD haze Wilder recognized most of the faces: the young Gail Sealy, Jonas McKee, Ralph Bonner, Liz Evanston, Bill Harlin. And, just for a moment, another person he thought he knew. Someone familiar. He grew agitated and concerned but couldn't focus on exactly why.

Cowling switched the TV to the video camera input and zoomed in on Wilder. It created a mirror-held-to-a-mirror effect in his mind and sent him spinning through waves of raging, brain-hammering hallucinations. Cowling smacked him across the face to get his attention.

"I'm looking forward to the autopsy. No one's ever done a post-mortem on a human brain still in the throes of a massive dose of LSD. Terrible tragedy you won't be around to take care of that little niece of yours." He tsk-tsked and shook his head. "Losing Mommy, then you. No child could ever recover from such pain. How often she must dream of her dead mother. Seeing the crash, her mom as she lay dying inside the wreckage."

An agonized moan escaped from Wilder and he closed his eyes.

"The husband, a weak, pathetic drunk. You hate weakness, don't you? Well, take it from a scientist, the little girl will end up her father's daughter. Loser genes, childhood trauma; she'll be trading gash for a suck at the crack pipe before she's twelve."

Wilder strained against the steel straps and sobbed with anger and hatred. Frustrated that Wilder hadn't cracked yet, Cowling gave him another 150 milligrams of PHP.

"I see why the Ay-rabs got so goddamn impatient with you. Your temporal lobe should be running out of your ears like melted butter. No matter, I understand you now. Snapping the doctor's fingers when he wouldn't medicate the burn victim gave it away: It's other people's pain that hurts you. That's why the roughhousing in Iraq only made you stronger."

Wilder, anxious to change the subject, managed to croak out a question:

"Those people . . . your test group . . . what happened?"

Cowling shrugged nonchalantly. "Seems my original compound had a few bugs. But I've remedied all that. Now I can isolate specific properties—the soporific, or the hallucinogenic. I can even trigger those reactions manifest as unexpected side effects—the heightened sensory and physical abilities."

Cowling grew serious, thoughtful.

"Whether it's fate, luck, God . . . I've been placed at the center of these events for a reason. I mean, that one of my group years later would become who he is, and that his counterpart across the globe would be wise enough to answer my letters and accept my assistance . . ."

Remembering the people he saw on Cowling's videotape filled Wilder with sudden dread. He isolated the image of the one face that had seemed so familiar, and the realization felt like a fist slamming into his gut.

"*Marsh!*" he cried out. No, he thought, not the President. Not *this* President; not a good man like Burton Marsh.

Cowling beamed like a proud papa. "My Lord, I can barely stand the suspense myself! How far will he go, *can* he go, before the system stops him? Oh, he can't very well order up the nukes—there are too many safeguards to prevent *Dr. Strangelove*—so how will it play out?"

"What's in it for you . . . letting him go nuts without warning anyone?"

"The *world* is in it for me. The world the way it should be. It's about *balance.* For years the remaining superpower has arrogantly spread its presence across an increasingly destabilized planet. Only with an equalizing power can harmony return. So, in the name of peace, I gave the Emperor two wonderful gifts: my drug, to empower his warriors, and something infinitely more valuable—information about the President. It is so *perfect!* The very chemical that makes one side stronger will soon weaken the other! East will gain parity with the West, and the Earth will be healed."

Before Wilder could process all this information, let alone reply, Cowling administered several drops of LSD in his eyes. The drug took hold immediately. He felt like someone terrified of speed and heights strapped to a roller coaster at the beginning of its downward plunge. His mind whipped around, twisting, battered, his roller coaster traveling at the speed of light.

Coming out of his nightmarish stupor hours later, Wilder heard the steel door open, some giggling and excited whispering. Cowling led his girlfriend, Patti, carefully down the steps, holding his hands over her eyes as if she were a child at a surprise party.

"Walt, you're so crazy . . . where are you taking me?"

"You'll see, sweetheart. Promise to keep your eyes closed until I say?"

"Promise."

She stood smiling, obediently keeping her eyes shut. Cowling went back up the steps and bolted the door.

"Okay, lover."

She opened her eyes and looked around. Her smile faded. This was not the secret little love nest Cowling told her he'd found on campus.

"Walt?"

Then she saw Wilder strapped to the workbench. She gasped and stepped back. He could barely whisper a warning.

"Get the hell out of here!"

Patti turned and looked at Cowling.

"Walt, what's going on?"

"All in the name of science, honey pie."

He punched her in the face, breaking her nose, and she tumbled over the boxes scattered on the floor. Wilder battered against his restraints with such fury that the bolted legs of his workbench rattled from the force. Cowling tossed Patti like a rag doll onto a workbench next to Wilder's, pinned her down, hand across her throat, and grinned while hitting her repeatedly. Wilder understood Cowling's game—hurting Patti was for his benefit—so he lay still. Maybe if he didn't give Cowling the reaction he wanted he'd leave her alone, try something else.

Patti went limp. Cowling used a cordless Makita drill with a socket-wrench head to bolt steel straps around her ankles, arms, and chest.

"Look at her, still a little girl really," Cowling said. "Someone's daughter, someone's sister. They love her like you love your little niece. The way you loved your sister."

The words filled Wilder with unbearable agony. Cowling put a strip of duct tape across Patti's mouth. Wilder tried to come up with something to say to make Cowling not do whatever he planned. It was the worst torture he had yet endured, and Cowling knew it.

"I did my postgrad work in behavioral studies. Rats in mazes, Pavlov's dog stuff: a controlled set of circumstances to elicit a desired reaction. With you, it's a matter of creating a scenario where there's an innocent in distress and you have the possibility of effecting a remedy."

Cowling didn't finish the rest of his premise out loud: If he made Wilder believe he could help Patti, the frustration of failing to do so would accomplish what the drugs, the fear, and the pain had not. It would destroy him.

He took a twenty-four-hour electrical-appliance timer from a hardware-store bag and turned the dial to set the time. "Half-hour seems sporting, don'tcha think?"

"I think you're a cowardly piece of fuck."

Cowling plugged the timer into a hanging electrical socket next to the fluorescent lights. Black dust from the brittle cloth insulation inside the socket box fell onto his hands. He wiped them off and, with a flourish, pulled several other items from the shopping bag: a roll of insulated wire, soldering gun, a tube of conducting gel, and two playing-card-sized copper electrodes.

"Hurting her is easy," Wilder said. "Beneath your talents."

Ignoring him, Cowling used the soldering gun to affix a yard-long piece of wire to each of the two electrodes, then twisted the other ends of the wires around the output terminals of a brick-sized power transformer next to Patti's head.

"Let her go," Wilder pleaded. "I'll play if you want to get nasty."

"Oh, you're gonna play, all right."

Cowling coated the underside of the electrodes with conducting gel, taped one to Patti's right arm and the other to her left thigh. She stirred from semiconsciousness and Cowling smiled at her. Singing to himself, he plugged the transformer's electrical cord into the timer.

"Sixty hertz, hundred 'n' ten volts, moderate intensity of ten amps, a healthy girl like Patti ought to last maybe five minutes before the current boils her brain and short-circuits her heart."

Patti howled inside the tape across her mouth and bucked wildly against her restraints.

"Please, for Christ's sake," Wilder cried. "You want me to beg, okay, I'm begging . . . Cowling! Don't . . ."

Cowling put a circle of thin steel cable around Wilder's neck. It looped around itself in a slipknot that constricted like a choke-chain when pulled. He carefully measured Wilder's arm and the excess cable at the end of the noose, then clamped it to the worktable. He switched the Makita to reverse and removed the bolts from the restraints holding Wilder's head, neck, chest, and left arm, but the steel cable around his neck afforded him only about six inches of movement.

"Here's the deal, Captain America. I'm going to leave you kids alone. Truly; I have a meeting to attend. Conditioned-response scenarios don't work unless the subject knows there are genuine rewards or penalties.

Yours are simple: in thirty minutes current will flow to the transformer. If you can reach the wire to the electrode on her leg and disconnect it, bravo, you save the day. I'll let her live."

"Bullshit."

"Absolutely *not* bullshit! Ten milligrams of Rohypnol before I take her to the ER will eradicate all memory of the last month of her life, let alone this evening. They'll simply think some overjuiced undergrad date-raped her; it happens all the time. On the other hand, if you fail . . . well, I hope you like seared tuna."

He folded the slack in the electrode's wire in half and playfully wagged it. Wilder lunged for it and the steel cable around his neck cinched tight, gagging him before he could reach the wire. Noting how far Wilder could extend his arm, Cowling took the hammer from under the workbench and drove a nail in Patti's bench just beyond Wilder's reach. He looped the wire around the nail, and stood back to admire his handiwork.

"Man, I could win me the Science Fair with this one!"

Cowling kissed Patti on her bloodied lips, climbed the steps, and left. She struggled in a manic fit to get free.

"Patti, it's okay," Wilder said, "I'll get it off you, I promise . . ."

He strained to reach the electrode wire, but each time the cable around his neck cinched like a garrote. His fingertips were only three inches from the wire. He stretched toward it, the cable getting tighter and tighter, until he almost passed out. He used his free hand to adjust the cable around his neck, then tried again and again. The sensation of choking overcame him and each time he briefly had to stop. Then Wilder noticed Patti's violent movements were shifting her heavy workbench, even if only by millimeters. It hadn't been bolted down like his.

"Patti! Listen! Throw your weight toward me. Move your table closer. Do you understand?"

She nodded her head and tried to shove herself toward him, but she weighed so little that the workbench barely moved. Wilder strained toward the bench and gagged as the cable repeatedly cut into his throat. It felt as if he'd been trying for hours. Finally, he got his fingertips around the edge of Patti's bench and the cable cut tighter into him. He jerked the bench toward him, nearly strangling himself with each pull. It began to move, a hair's width at a time.

The timer clicked on. Electricity flowed to the transformer and

Patti's body spasmed as the current coursed through her. Wilder lunged for the wire. The cable around his neck threatened to sever his head, but he curled his index finger around the wire and pulled. It tore loose from the electrode, stopping the flow of electricity. Patti lay as if dead for a moment, then took in an enormous breath and began sobbing.

Wilder flipped the loose piece of transformer wire up and over the soldering gun Cowling had left on the far side of Patti's workbench. He carefully dragged the soldering gun across the workbench . . . closer . . . closer . . . until he got his hand around it. Although he did not want to do what had to be done next, Cowling would be back at any moment.

He laid his head against the bench to maximize the slack in the cable around his neck and gingerly slid the tip of the soldering gun under it, then pressed the tip against the cable as hard as he could while squeezing the trigger switch. The heat from the tip quickly radiated around the circumference of the cable loop. His skin sizzled beneath the hot coil, but he kept the pressure on. The cable went white-hot and the glow expanded outward in both directions along its length. Screaming, Wilder pushed harder.

The cable snapped. He could sit up. He reached his arm under the workbench and felt around for the hammer. Finding it, he pried up the bolt on the strap holding his other arm. He almost dropped the hammer as a wave of disorientation and hallucinations hit him. With his other arm free, he pulled Patti's bench closer and got to work. She'd stopped crying and seemed practically catatonic.

"Cowling's been drugging me. If I lose it, it's up to you to get help. Okay? Patti?"

She nodded. She was a lot tougher than she looked. Wilder got her arm loose and she pulled the tape from across her mouth.

"Fuckin' prick wacko, I'm gonna kill him!"

She grabbed the hammer and clawed at the remainder of her restraints. Once free, she started on Wilder's. He helped as best he could, though his mind was racing out of control somewhere at the far edge of the known universe. Two straps left. Wilder and Patti froze at the sound of the door unbolting, then worked double-time on the restraints.

Cowling stopped momentarily, halfway down the steps, gaped at the two empty workbenches, then bounded down the rest of the way. Wilder, hiding behind the stairs, yanked Cowling's ankles and sent him sprawling onto the floor. Cowling came after him in that superstrong, unrelenting

Terminator way he'd seen with the other Mad Yuppies and in Woomera. Wilder threw a box of glass beakers at him, stumbling backward as Cowling lunged at him.

Then Patti stabbed Cowling in the lower back with the hot soldering gun. He screeched and yanked it out, pulling its cord from the hanging electrical socket. A shower of orange sparks rained down as the insulation inside the box broke away. A workbench, soaked with chemicals over its years of use, ignited and low blue flame fanned out across its surface, spreading to the packing material and crates piled against it. Cowling moved toward Patti and Wilder hit him across the face with the hammer, knocking his jaw grotesquely out of alignment. Wilder grabbed the TV/VCR and tried to pry Cowling's videotape out of it, but without power it would not eject. Cowling pounced on him and Wilder brought the TV down with all his strength, screen first, just missing Cowling's head. The tube imploded into a billion shards of glass.

Everything in the room was now burning, including the wooden steps leading outside. Holding the remains of the TV/VCR, Wilder tried to reach Patti, cut off from the steps by the flaming workbenches and crates. Still protecting his secrets, Cowling grabbed the machine away from him. Wilder pushed through the flames, dragging Patti toward the steps. He could barely walk, ill from exhaustion, the drugs, and the smoke.

Then he felt the cool, moist, nighttime grass against his face as he collapsed on the lawn. The Old Chem building burned spectacularly behind him. He hugged the ground, hopelessly drug-sick, convinced he would spin right off the earth if he let go. He decided there would be no peace for him other than death, so he released his hold on the lawn. He shot into the night sky like a sky diver in reverse, falling upward, ever faster, until he reached the vacuum of space. His body blasted apart into a trillion pieces and his atoms spun themselves into a sparkling, luminous funnel and corkscrewed toward the sun. They touched off a supernova, swallowing all existence, and Wilder surrendered to the ecstasy of perfect silence.

Twenty-seven

Wilder struggled to the surface of consciousness and awoke to a festival of pain. His entire body stung, ached, throbbed, and burned. He opened his eyes and thought he surely must still be hallucinating—Laura and Kate were smiling down at him.

"You're awake!" Kate shouted. "You've been sleeping for*ever!*"

"Well, twenty-seven and three-quarters hours," Laura said. "Not that anyone's been counting."

Wilder pulled Kate close and kissed her forehead. She wrapped her arms around his neck and began to cry. He buried his face in her hair and held her tight, then looked up at Laura, his cheeks streaked with tears. Crying as well, she squeezed his hand. Brent and Cindy came into view. Wilder felt a deep gratitude for being alive, and for the presence of those who meant so much to him.

A nurse wearing an Air Force uniform rushed in to check Wilder's vitals.

"How'd I get home?" he asked.

"Airplane," Brent said. "Not that you needed one. You could've *floated* back in your condition."

Dr. Jeb Adams, Tom Herrold's replacement at the Malcolm Grow Medical Center, followed the nurse into the room.

"Okay, folks, I need to talk with Matt for a moment."

Wilder tried to sit up, but could barely get his head off the pillow. "Brent, wait, stick around . . ."

Brent looked at Dr. Adams, who nodded. Kate, Laura, and Cindy left the room while Dr. Adams examined Wilder.

"How bad is it?" Wilder asked.

"Physically, you have two bruised ribs, some second-degree burns, dehydration, a myriad of bumps and abrasions. What most concerns us are any lingering effects of the drugs, especially the LSD."

"Such as?"

"ER at Rexford administered twice the standard dosage of niacin-amide to counteract the hallucinogenic, and it also took additional shots of chlorpromazine to get you to sleep. Such resistance to treatment can indicate organic damage to the brain—lysergic psychosis."

"How will you know for sure?"

"Given we're having this conversation, the prognosis is good. Most cases the patient remains in a permanent state of altered consciousness."

"I've seen that very thing," Brent said. "I lived in a frat house during college."

Dr. Adams smiled. "I hear ya." He looked at Wilder. "Your job is to rest and let us keep an eye on you, okay?" Wilder nodded, and the doctor left.

Brent pointed at a huge flower arrangement on the table near the window.

"Get-well wish from your new best friend." Brent paused for dramatic effect. "Ethan Nichols."

"What are you talking about?"

"The Professor's pert and underaged girlfriend is suing the snot out of the university. She'll be okay, but her lawyer's been real graphic about what happened in Cowling's Chamber of Horrors."

"How's that make Nichols my pal?"

"He wants you to help corroborate Cowling had been acting without university knowledge."

"Well, first they can give me his computer. There's a database of thirty people who were involved in a test of some mutated drugs—Gail and everyone else on the perp list, including six who haven't snapped yet."

Brent shook his head. "Computer's gone. Cowling's office was destroyed in the fire, along with the rest of the chemistry building."

"Maybe he kept off-premise backups."

"The university looked, no luck. And it'll be a while, if ever, before Cowling's able to tell 'em anything."

"He *survived?*"

"Yep. He's comatose. They've got no idea if he'll ever come out of it."

"Cowling had films of the people in the test group. I saw it, and I recognized somebody else. Burton Marsh."

Brent stared at his friend for a moment, then sighed. He'd seen Marsh on TV just that morning. The President was hardly a drooling loony.

"Matt, c'mon. Cowling gave you a *shitload* of acid."

"It wasn't a hallucination," Wilder insisted. "I *saw* him—twenty, twenty-one years old, under the influence of the stuff like the others. Cowling even told me how fucking excited he was, waiting to see what the President would do."

"Can anyone else identify Marsh?"

"It was a secret test, even to the other participants."

"The tape?"

"Melted in the TV. There's more. Cowling went on this political-mystical tirade. Said he's been supplying the TAA with a similar drug, giving the Khaldun their weird abilities."

Brent nodded, amazed. "So there's your Woomera connection . . ."

"Yeah. But listen: Cowling told Batu about Marsh."

Brent stood up. "Jesus! What are we supposed to do with all this?!"

"First, find absolute proof of the President's condition. Now that we know what's causing it, maybe we can find something in the medical or autopsy reports of the others that'll also show up in his med records."

"Whoa, slow down. Our only duty is to inform Colonel Chang."

"We can't discuss this with *anyone*! I don't trust channels. OSI's had at least four cases fucked with: Woomera and Travis infiltrations, my Rexford investigation, and Joval. If there's a leak and Marsh finds out we know about him, it could set him off. That's how it worked with the others: They were triggered when confronted by a threat. Only safe course is bringing the information to the folks who can remove him from office."

Although everything Wilder said made sense, Brent still couldn't quite imagine running with this themselves.

"Except for impeachment, only the VP and a majority of the cabinet can remove a President," Brent said. "They tell the Senate president pro tem and the House Speaker he's unfit, the VP becomes acting President. You think some monkeys from the OSI are gonna convince a dozen Marsh appointees to toss him out of office?"

"Give Ballard and Frost the proof, let *them* line up the cabinet."

"Just like that? Three weeks before a major military operation?"

"Yeah."

Brent said nothing, trying to think of alternatives, but none came to mind. He wasn't fully convinced Wilder had seen what he claimed, but the consequences were too dire not to give him the benefit of the doubt.

"Okay, let's do this one step at a time. For now, we'll keep it just between us. But I gotta think the rest of it through. We'll talk later."

Wilder nodded, fair enough. He wondered how much his friend really believed him. And if he did, how long it'd be before Brent did what any smart officer would do: get this hot potato out of his lap and into someone else's.

Although more drugs were the last thing Wilder wanted in his system, he needed to get back on his feet. Braced by a fistful of painkillers and stimulants, he left the Malcolm Grow Medical Center eighteen hours after regaining consciousness. Dr. Adams screamed like hell, but Brent pulled rank and okayed it.

From home, Wilder called Dr. Dharwadkar, the Malcolm Grow pathologist who'd autopsied Gail, and asked him to reexamine her tissue samples for anything even remotely unusual. The pathologist said he'd get to it as soon as his schedule allowed.

"Humor me," Wilder said. "It's not like the stiffs will care if you're late."

"All right, all right, I'll call you tomorrow."

"Tonight."

Then he called Laura to ask if she had any friends in television news—he wanted to borrow any tapes of presidential segments aired in the past couple of weeks. He said nothing of what he knew about Marsh, only that he wanted to catch up on the news. Laura obliged, but wondered why he'd become a political news junkie all of a sudden.

Later that afternoon Brent stopped by. Since their discussion he had vacillated from belief to disbelief. He had unshakable faith in Wilder's integrity, but grave doubts about anyone's ability to separate reality from fantasy during a catastrophic hallucinogenic experience.

While Kate played in the backyard with Mrs. Lindstrom, the housekeeper, Wilder had taken a short nap, more painkillers, and now sat on the floor by the TV, watching the stack of tapes sent via messenger by a producer at C-SPAN. He studied Marsh carefully, running each segment two or three times. He stopped to make note of a commentator's observation that the President, one of the most publicly accessible chief executives in recent memory, had made almost no public appearances during the past few weeks. Unless lobbying for support of Operation Swift Sword he never left the White House or met with reporters. Still feeling sore and weak, Wilder got to his feet and crossed to the dining room table, strewn with papers and books.

"Check this out." He handed Brent some pages of yellow legal pads he'd filled with notes. "You literally cannot overdose on LSD, which is why I'm not dead. Aside from its mind-altering properties, it has barely any effect on the body. The key word, however, is barely. It does cause a degree-or-so rise in temperature, elevation in a muscle enzyme called creatine phosphokinase, and an increase in the production of uric acid. It can also cause trace bleeding in the upper gastrointestinal tract."

"Okay, professor . . . so what?"

"I asked Julie Nelson's and Jonas McKee's doctors to pull their charts. Julie had every symptom except the GI bleeding, and McKee had 'em all, just as if they were under the influence of a drug taken thirty years ago. I've got calls in to the docs treating the other perps, but I'm dead certain they'll tell me the same thing."

"If Marsh had those symptoms, don't you think his doctor would notice?"

"Yeah, but according to the experts I talked to, he wouldn't worry about anything except the GI bleeding. None of the other stuff is serious because it's usually transient."

Brent sighed. "It's not conclusive."

"It's a piece of the puzzle."

"Look, give it a rest for tonight. General Dryden heard you were out of the hospital, and asked if you could meet him on the runway, twenty-three hundred hours. Some prototype hypersonics are arriving en route to the theatre of operations: the Centurion and a couple of UCAVs. I'll tell him you're not up to it."

"No, don't. I'll grab another nap beforehand. I'd really like to see that stuff."

Wilder and Dryden, the Andrews base commander, watched as a massive Lockheed C-5 transport plane taxied to the hexagon-shaped Air Force One hangar at the southwest end of the Andrews runway. Moments later, the Air Force One team, who have higher clearance than regular ground crews, rolled the F-77 Centurion and the UCAV uninhabited aircraft down the rear loading ramp and towed them inside the hangar, the most secure site on base.

It occurred to Wilder that next to the presidential 747s, the Centurion looked like a mouse beside two elephants. But what a mouse: Its low, SST-like nose, indented cockpit, swept-back, retractable wings, and near-black stealth skin were dramatic—no, *otherworldly*—in the nighttime shadows. The crew backed the aircraft into a corner where a temporary enclosure had been erected and Security Forces would stand twenty-four-hour watch.

Dryden smiled to himself. Wilder was staring at the Centurion with lust in his eyes.

"That is one choice airplane," Dryden said.

"Oh, *yeah*," Wilder replied.

The fact he could no longer fly created a deep ache in his heart, as bad as it had been in the darkest moments after Iraq. With hypersonics, aviation was taking a fabulous stride forward, and it devastated him to be left behind.

While perfunctorily reviewing security procedures with Dryden, the ground crew, and the sentries, Wilder's mind wandered back to the Marsh problem. He could think of no way to investigate the President's behavior without talking to the people close to him. Good luck finessing that one. He considered Laura's acquaintance with the First Lady . . .

"Amy darling, it's Laura calling. Say, just between us chickens, has your hubby, the President of the United States, recently lost his marbles?"

Not likely.

Wilder returned home at one A.M., finding Mrs. Lindstrom asleep in the guest room. He returned to watching the C-SPAN tapes. It saddened him to know the country would lose Marsh, one way or another. He admired the President and felt privileged to have spent some private time with him. He fast-forwarded to the press conference three weeks ago, on June 27, where Marsh showed the footage of Batu Khan's decapitations in the dissident Ukrainian village.

"Bobby, good to see you back on the beat," Marsh said on the TV.

"Good to be back, Mr. President," the reporter replied. "Please thank Mrs. Marsh for the flowers and kind note."

"I will. At least we know security hasn't forgotten you—letting you in with an expired press pass."

The reporter twisted the plastic White House security pass clipped to his jacket, looked at it, and shrugged. The other reporters laughed.

Wilder watched the exchange again. It sure seemed as though the President's eyes went from the reporter's face, down to his pass, then back up before making the comment about it being expired. He couldn't very well track down the reporter and question him—it would be much too risky to spark anyone's curiosity at a national newsweekly. He called Brent, waking him, and told him what he'd seen. Brent was underwhelmed. "Maybe he knew about the expired pass or saw it beforehand. A lot easier to believe that than he read twelve-point typeface from thirty feet away."

"I talked to Dr. Dharwadkar," Wilder said. "Gail's autopsy showed a small elevation in uric acid and creatine levels—"

"Forget about all that," Brent said. "I checked into pulling the President's medical records. They're absolutely off-limits, even to the OSI."

"*Shit* . . ."

"Look, Matt, maybe it's better to call Chang, tell him what you believe and give him whatever you've got to back up your claim."

"Just give me till Monday before doing that."

"What for?"

"In case I get an inspiration."

"*Inspiration?* Don't talk like that, it scares me."

To give Wilder a little extra time to recuperate, Laura took Kate to a theatrical production of *Peter Pan* at Georgetown University the next afternoon. But laid out on the sofa in her living room, racking his mind for what to do next, Wilder didn't find a moment's relaxation.

When Laura returned home with Kate, Wilder offered to call for takeout, but Laura insisted on making dinner.

"Humor me. I love to cook and seldom get the opportunity."

Laura understood the Washington Field Office would have ever-increasing responsibilities as the commencement of Operation Swift Sword loomed closer. Two of the three Air Force bases under the WFO's jurisdiction were key debarkation points to Europe. Also, a TAA-backed terrorist attack on the nation's capital was a very real threat. The injuries Wilder suffered at Rexford had bought him a respite, but soon, and for the foreseeable future, he'd be too busy to see her very much.

After the best New York cut Wilder ever tasted, he let Kate play with the vacationing neighbor's cat while Laura went over to feed it. Sitting together on the back porch swing, watching Kate and the cat, he considered telling Laura about Marsh. He certainly trusted her, but decided it would be cruel to burden her with such knowledge, especially given her fondness for the First Couple. She would find out soon enough.

When it got dark they moved inside and Kate soon fell asleep in the den. Laura and Wilder stood together looking at her.

"If there's anything more beautiful in this world than a sleeping six-year-old," she whispered, "I've never seen it."

Wilder picked up Kate's shoes. But when he stood up, Laura was covering her with a quilt.

"No sense waking her, Matt. She'll be fine here."

Wilder's pulse sped up several notches. As much as he'd wanted to, he hadn't expected to spend the night. Laura turned off the living room lights and took Wilder's hand to lead him to her room. He stopped at the foot of the stairs, pulled her gently toward him, and kissed her. Her full, soft lips tasted slightly of something familiar. Vanilla, perhaps? No, simply her essence. Her arms moved around him, her body conforming to his. As she relaxed into him her breath quickened and Wilder felt her heart beating against his chest. He felt its echo, as well, low in her abdomen. They looked at each other for a long moment. Nothing needed to be said.

Laura kissed him again. This time her lips parted and her tongue lightly encircled his mouth. Wilder marveled at how clichés are so often true: The sensation radiated through him like electricity. Given how closely he'd held his emotions before now, the openness and vulnerability he now showed made her trust him completely. Wilder paused to regard her face again, and noticed his fingers were moist. So were her eyes. She wiped them and tried to laugh.

"Well, what do you expect? I cry at romantic movies."

"I do, too. Tell anyone, you're a goner."

There was a touch of shyness in Laura as she undressed in the bedroom, which made Wilder yearn for her even more. He presumed she'd have a fabulous body and it exceeded all expectations. He pulled off his shirt and pants, moving slowly from the soreness of his injuries. Laura sat on the bed, fumbling with her bra. He knelt in front of her and helped her undo it, slipped the straps off her shoulders, then slowly tipped her back onto the bed to kiss her again. He moved more gracefully than Laura would have expected for a man his size and strength. More gently, too.

Laura saw the large, angry bruise on his side from Cowling's hammer blow, and she shifted slightly so he could lean his weight on his other side. She could tell he was keeping the full force of his passion in check, letting her set the pace. She pulled him close, wanting him, now. She cried out as he entered her. Wilder paused, kissing her face, her eyes, her shoulders while she caught her breath. After a few moments, she clutched him, wrapped her legs around him, and jammed her mouth against his. Wilder let himself go, making love to her with all the emotion he'd suppressed for so long. Their desire for each other, their movements, even their breathing were perfectly synchronized. Laura came again. She couldn't believe it.

Wilder didn't stop this time and Laura didn't want him to. All the while they made love she rode at the brink of yet another orgasm. She let it intensify as his thrusts quickened and increased in power. Finally, she felt Wilder throb inside her as he ejaculated. This triggered in Laura the orgasm she'd been resisting, and she clung to him as it shuddered through her.

They lay together quietly, and Laura sighed. She wanted to tell him how she felt, but a sudden self-consciousness struck her.

"It's strange. Making love to you seems easier than saying the words."

"Forget the words if they make you uncomfortable."

"No, it's stupid. Some preprogrammed fear of rejection kicking in."

"That's one fear you can scratch." He looked at her. "I love you. You don't love me back, I'll become one of those mumbling subway guys with a bag of your books, showing your picture to strangers."

243

Laura flashed her killer smile. She couldn't remember ever being happier.

"I love you." Saying it felt wonderful. "I love you, I love you . . ." She wanted to shout it, skywrite it, get a tattoo that spelled it in a Valentine heart. She laughed. "Don't mind me, the giddiness and euphoria should pass in, oh, about six or seven decades."

Wilder pulled her close and kissed her. "I can live with a little giddiness until then . . ."

Twenty-eight

T he next morning, Wilder used Laura's computer to do a Lexis-Nexis search, and found a piece in the *AMA Journal* about the doctor in charge of Marsh's yearly physicals—a Navy internist named Boyer. According to the article, the originals of the presidential medical files were kept up in the White House Infirmary. Dr. Boyer, however, kept copies of the most recent exam report and labwork in his private office, locked away in a manner specifically approved by the Secret Service.

An hour later, Wilder squeezed into a packed elevator in Building Nine at the National Naval Medical Center in Bethesda, Maryland. Sunday morning, a favorite time for visiting, brought thousands of civilians and military dependents onto the sprawling Center campus. He got off on the deserted fourth floor and listened at the door to Housekeeping. Inside the empty room, he helped himself to a freshly laundered doctor's smock. Something felt missing, so he grabbed a brushed metal clipboard from the table. Perfect. He took the elevator to the seventh-floor administrative offices and knocked on Dr. Boyer's door. No answer. He stood facing the quiet hallway so he could watch for anyone approaching and slipped two thin, steel tools out of his wallet. Using the lockpicking skills he'd learned as part of his OSI training, he gained entry in forty-five seconds. Once inside the outer office, he repeated the process to open Dr. Boyer's private office. It had more earth tones than the great outdoors: Navajo-pattern area rug, adobe-colored walls, rough-hewn desk and coffee table. He searched the office, finding a locked compartment built behind a hinged bookshelf, and inside that a fireproof, four-drawer filing cabinet. Using a flashlight and small mirror to check behind and under for alarm or sensor wires and found none; he then began picking the cabinet's cylindrical-key lock.

Unknown to Wilder, however, an invisible biometric coating on the face of the drawer sensed movement and activated a tiny wireless transmitter hidden inside the cabinet. In the OPS-I building of National Security Agency headquarters, Fort George G. Meade, one of Marsh's ExOps received an intrusion alert. Using a principle similar to the Fingerloc sensor on Wilder's notebook computer, the biometric coating read the infrared energy radiating from Wilder's face and transmitted a rendering of its outline. An NSA computer began matching it against the millions of digitized and stored photo IDs, driver's license pictures, and mug shots, starting with Dr. Boyer's. Since it didn't match, and only Boyer had the authority to access the cabinet, the ExOp alerted the security office at the Naval Hospital of the break-in.

Struggling with the difficult cylindrical lock for almost three minutes, Wilder glanced over his shoulder and noticed a shadow through the translucent outer door glass. The shadow tried the door, found it locked, and quietly opened it with a master key. Two six-foot-five, barbell-pumped Shore Patrol officers, pistols drawn, inched into Dr. Boyer's office and looked around for signs of disturbance. One noticed the round base of the floor lamp had been moved slightly from the indentation it made in the carpet—the electrical cord had been yanked from the base, leaving bristling strands of bare copper.

In Boyer's private bathroom, Wilder tied the wire to the radiator and climbed through the window, rappelling down onto the ledge one floor below. He shuffled Harold Lloyd–style along the ledge and climbed into another window just as the SPs poked their head out the window above. Coming back inside on the sixth floor, he found himself in a deserted Magnetic Resonance Imaging suite. He cracked the door leading from the nursing room to the hallway. Spotting another pair of SPs, he slipped back inside and backtracked, but then saw yet another SP. They intended to corral him in the suite. He really didn't feel like hurting the Navy security men, nor did he want to get arrested. Watching the SPs enter and unholster their pistols, it occurred to him he wouldn't have to do either.

Hiding in the crawl space behind the control consoles, he tossed a pen through the door leading to the scan room. When the clatter attracted the SPs, Wilder waited until all three were next to the scanner, then pushed a row of switches on the console to activate the MRI. The immense magnetic coil inside the scanner began circling the examination portal with a loud, rhythmic thumping. The powerful magnetic field generated by the scanner tore the pistols from the SPs' hands, pinning them against the side of the scanner and attracting their other equipment as well—walkie-talkies, handcuffs, Mace, belt buckles, badges, watches. The SPs stumbled toward the scanner, struggling to get their Sam Houston utility belts off. It occurred to Wilder they had that same helpless, confused expression as Wile E. Coyote when one of his Roadrunner traps backfired.

Wilder ran down the hall toward the fire escape doors. A pair of scrub nurses finishing their coffee break saw him shove his white smock in a trash can, glanced at each other, and stepped in front of the fire escape doors to block his way.

"Hey there, fella. Who are you?"

Wilder grinned. "Exterminator. They got a rat problem, third floor."

"I think we got a rat problem right here."

The taller nurse turned to her friend. "Call security." Then, to Wilder, in an I-mean-business tone: "Don't move."

He started for the doors. "Love to oblige, but I've—"

She decked him with a jackhammer right to the jaw. Wilder sat up on the linoleum, shaking his head.

"Jesus, lady . . ."

"I said, don't fuckin' move!" Her voice was as powerful as her fist.

Wilder sighed and pulled his Sig from a pancake holster on his belt.

"I'd never hit a woman, ma'am. But I *would* shoot one."

The nurse didn't call his bluff, so he got to his feet and pushed through the fire escape doors. A moment later the SPs, freed of their utility belts, burst out of the MRI suite and the nurses pointed at the fire escape stairwell.

"Down there! He's got a gun!"

One of the SPs dialed security and told them to send armed officers to the ground floor of the fire escape. Wilder, however, never got that far. He ran downstairs to the fifth floor, circled the building to the public elevators, and blended in with the visitors leaving the hospital.

Stan Woodruff closed the Oval Office door and glanced at the grandfather clock beside it. Four o'clock. He'd planned on having a quiet

Sunday dinner with his wife and the kids. Then the President had called, ordering him to the White House immediately. Marsh handed him a red folder containing a picture of Wilder and a copy of his Air Force service record.

"Sir?"

"This son of a bitch tried to steal my medical records this afternoon. ExOps made a positive match from a biometric film."

Woodruff had no clue Marsh had been using the ExOps on his own. The President had every right to do so, of course, but chief executives *never* dealt directly with covert agents.

"Wilder . . ." Woodruff said. "He's the OSI agent involved in that business at Rexford University, isn't he?"

"One and the same. Amy and I had the bastard here as our *guest* a couple weeks ago. He's Laura Bishop's goddamn boyfriend!"

Marsh studied Woodruff. Wilder, the investigator who connected Cowling with Mad Yuppie Disease, now trying to steal the President's medical records . . . what significance would the secretary of defense give to it? Fortunately, if Woodruff had any suspicions, he didn't show them. Marsh sensed no tremor in his voice, no smell of fear.

It did occur to Woodruff that Wilder could be seeking a connection between President Marsh and Professor Cowling, but he didn't believe for an instant he'd find one. The Mad Yuppies were violently insane. Woodruff had known Marsh for two decades, and the President, by all indications, had been behaving no differently than usual. Woodruff, self-ishly, was more concerned about being out of the loop with the ExOps. He presumed himself, as secretary of defense, privy to all the President's intelligence reports. What other information did Marsh receive without his knowledge?

"Where's Wilder now?" Woodruff asked.

"He entered the Andrews main gate at three-thirty P.M. Order the Air Force to pick him up, then pass him to our people. I want to know what the hell he's up to. Whatever it is, I doubt he's operating officially."

Marsh intensely hoped this to be so. His insides cinched with re-pressed rage. He couldn't, *wouldn't* step down. He had too much left to do.

"I'm sure you're right, sir. Says here he's got a history of extreme behavior."

"Well, if he's unstable I want him locked up," Marsh said.

"If he should resist capture?"

"Bring him in by any means necessary."

While Kate cleared the table, Wilder rinsed the dishes and put them in the dishwasher. He was back to zero: no proof of Marsh's condition beyond what he'd learned in Cowling's lab. Every minute mattered, but he felt completely stymied, desperate for any way to move forward. Finishing with the dishes, Kate looked at him. "You seem sad, Uncle Matt."

Well, sweetheart, the most powerful man in the world is about to become violently insane and our deadly enemy, the second *most powerful man in the world, knows all about it.*

"Guess I miss Laura. Want to play Frisbee?"

They went out onto the front lawn. Most of their neighbors were out on their porches, socializing, playing ball. The major across the street struggled to unhitch a ten-foot-long, two-wheeled boat trailer from his Chevy Blazer, so Wilder walked over to help him, then returned to the Frisbee game. As he leapt in the air to retrieve one of Kate's wildly inaccurate throws, he noticed a blue-and-white Security Forces car turning onto Cedar Drive and stop at the intersection north of them, a block away. He tossed the Frisbee back to Kate. Another security car drove up Cedar from the south, also stopping a block away, so he stepped into the street and looked past the houses at the end of his cul-de-sac. Between them, through the trees, he made out movement: a security officer on foot.

A two-hundred-decibel alarm went off in Wilder's head and he walked casually back to his yard. "Kate, honey, c'mon in the house for a moment."

Inside, he sat on the sofa so he could look at her eye to eye, but he didn't know where to begin. A horrible reality struck him: No matter how hard he fought to make everything right, he had little hope for success, meaning they could lose each other forever.

"Listen to me, sweetheart. I have to leave for a while, right now. I'll call Brent and Cindy, tell them you're comin' over."

"What's wrong?"

Wilder struggled for the words to explain. "There's a situation I'm very worried about. No one else knows about it, and since it's a secret, some people won't understand what I'm doing about it."

"Will they try to hurt you?"

"Absolutely not, I promise. And once everyone else understands what's happening, it's all gonna be okay again."

"When?"

"Soon. I love you so much, Katie . . ."

"Please hurry back." She hugged him and tried not to cry. It agonized Wilder to see how much he'd shaken her up.

He dialed Brent and heard a sharp click on the line—the phone was tapped.

"Hey, Kate left her Malibu Barbie there. She's coming over for it."

Kate glanced at the coffee table, where Malibu Barbie sat in her pink-and-white convertible. She'd never heard her uncle lie before.

"Sure. We'll start looking around for it."

"She's on her way. Watch out for her, okay?"

Brent caught the edge in his friend's voice. "Matt?"

"Sorry, got something on the stove."

Wilder hung up and went back outside. The security officers were now only a couple hundred feet away. The neighbors gawked from their yards, wondering what was going down. With a nervous glance back at her uncle, Kate ran toward Brent's house, one street over. Watching her go, Wilder fought back tears.

The security officers approached carefully. They knew Wilder; his arrest order had shocked them and they were smart enough to be afraid of him. He calmly crossed to the house next door and opened its garage door. The security officers moved double-time; an engine coughed to life inside the garage and Wilder came roaring down the driveway on a 1959 BMW motorcycle.

Slowing the bike momentarily, he grabbed the front of the two-wheeled boat trailer on the major's driveway, hooked its hitching ball into the bars of the bike's luggage rack, and hauled it toward the houses at the end of the cul-de-sac. Behind them was a playground and the eight-foot-high chain-link fence—overgrown with vegetation and topped with concertina wire—that encircled the entire base. He jumped the curb onto the lawn between the two houses and the lone Security Force officer leaped out of the way, stumbling into a Jacuzzi. Wilder nearly skidded out of control as the motorcycle's wheels spun in the tree-bark chips on the playground, then hit the brakes next to a redwood picnic table. He jammed the front of the boat trailer against the side of the table, its nose pointed up toward the fence. Backtracking and turning around, he opened the throttle and sped toward the boat trailer. Running to catch him, the other security officers tried to shoot out his tires, then watched with slack-jawed amazement as he aimed his wheels for the two-inch-wide aluminum railing in the center of the trailer. It formed a lift-ramp, allowing him to zoom airborne over the perimeter fence.

With a lot of that luck Brent often marveled at, he came down hard on the wide shoulder of Branch Avenue and stayed upright. He leaned hard against his momentum and turned the bike to keep from skidding into the road. Merging into the traffic, he disappeared into the flow of taillights heading into downtown Washington.

Twenty-nine

Laura, sprawled on the sofa reading, walked to her office to see who could be sending her a fax at eleven forty-five Sunday night. She took from the machine a note in Wilder's handwriting:

Check Hotmail account ContactLaura-1116006. Password is author of your fore-edged book.

She hurried to her computer to access the free Hotmail e-mail service and logged onto the account Wilder had just created: *ContactLaura-1116006* / password *Daniel Defoe*. She found another message:

Meet me P Street Beach, 12:30 A.M. There are two brown sedans outside—government agents surveilling you. Take bicycle through backyard to next block, ride in circles until certain no one following. Your phone, personal e-mail account probably monitored, too.

Frightened, she pulled on jeans and a sweatshirt, tied her running shoes, and took her bicycle down off the wall. The Beach, only a few blocks from her house, was actually a grass field next to Rock Creek, just below the P Street Bridge at the eastern edge of Georgetown. Its nickname came from its popularity as a place to sunbathe. She followed Wilder's instructions, zigzagging around the deserted neighborhood for twenty minutes before riding down to the field. Wilder emerged from the dark trees bordering the creek bank a couple minutes after Laura arrived. He knew by now his pursuers would've recruited the FBI and city cops to search for him under some trumped-up charge, and he hoped they hadn't issued a shoot-to-kill order.

Laura ran over and hugged him. "Jesus, Matt, you're scaring the hell out of me. What's going on?"

"President Marsh was one of Cowling's test group."

Stunned, Laura stepped back and shook her head, not wanting to believe him. Wilder told her all about seeing Marsh on Cowling's videotape, about his conversation with the Professor, and how the tape, his only tangible evidence, had been destroyed in the fire at Rexford.

"Marsh must suspect something," Wilder continued. "Air Force Security tried to arrest me tonight. They're obviously watching you in hopes of catching me. I don't think you're in any danger if you maintain normal appearances. If anyone confronts you, say we're not speaking anymore. Tell 'em I drink, smacked you around, whatever—just make it convincing."

He explained his concerns about passing information about Marsh up the chain of command, wanting instead to go directly to the House Speaker and president of the Senate. Then he told her about Cowling supplying the Khaldun with his compound, and that the Professor had informed Batu Khan of Marsh's condition.

The level of detail in Wilder's story, and the passion with which he told it, soon convinced Laura of its truth. Horrified, she stared at the dark creek.

"I dread to think how," she said, "but Batu is sure to take full advantage of this. You have to get some proof about Marsh, quickly."

"That's the problem, I've got nothing. I even tried to steal his medical records from Bethesda."

"*What?!*"

"Yeah, that's how they're onto me."

The conversation had become so surreal that Laura simply forged ahead.

"How about corroboration from someone close to him?"

"I doubt anyone in the White House knows anything's wrong. I've seen how adeptly the others hid their condition, right up to the moment they snapped."

Laura nodded, feeling hopeless and depressed. Neither of them spoke. Then something occurred to her, an idea almost too frightening to verbalize.

"Maybe he let his guard down during a private moment."

"What are you thinking?"

"Remember the big noise in the press about Marsh and Batu Khan's agreement not to record their VS meetings?"

"Yeah, yeah, fosters honest exchange . . . as if world leaders suddenly turn honest when the cameras are off."

"I don't think they're ever off. You heard what he said in the VS Room that night: He personally controls the video machines. I'm certain he tapes *everything* happening in there."

"Conjecture."

"Remember the taping equipment inside the credenza? Most chief executives, including this one, have no need to carry a wallet, key chain, or spare change. Yet we saw Marsh has the key to that credenza in his pocket. If there's one trait all modern presidents share, it's an overwhelming desire to document their presidency. Until the existence of Nixon's tapes was revealed, even his closest advisers didn't know he recorded their conversations. Now it's a given, people tend to forget about it. Including, I'm sure, the President himself."

"Okay, he keeps the key with him. And he *was* pretty weird about it. But I think they'd notice me trying to pickpocket the President, Laura."

"*I'll* get the tapes."

Her attempt at offhandedness made Wilder laugh.

"Forget it. Too risky."

She shivered in the damp, cool air. "Let's avoid our first fight and agree I'm going to try."

"No. If you were caught they'd lock you up and throw away the *room.*"

"It's worth the risk. We know on at least one occasion the President lost control of his emotions in the VS Room. Mrs. Marsh kidded him about the hole he'd put in the wall with his fist. What if the episode were more serious than just a flash of temper? What if it happened more than once?"

Wilder had to concede the tapes could be important. However, Laura might as well be saying the solution to their pesky poverty problem lay in all that nice gold in Fort Knox.

"One thing bothers me," Laura said. "The only way to get into the White House is through Mrs. Marsh. I'd hate lying to her while trying to get her husband removed from office."

"If it happens quietly, before he does anything horrible, you'll have done the woman and the country a hell of a favor."

Laura took Wilder's comment as tacit approval of her plan, which terrified her.

"God, Matt, what am I supposed to do, ask if I can come by to look at the flatware?"

". . . And this one, rimmed in amaranth, is from the Monroe service, made in France by Dagoty et Honoré." Standing in the China Room, a red-themed sitting room near the South Portico on a sunny Monday morning, Amy Marsh handed Laura a dinner plate. Laura nodded and pretended to study it.

"Mrs. Benjamin Harrison began the collection in 1889," Amy continued. "Mrs. Theodore Roosevelt greatly expanded it, and stopped the practice of giving away or selling damaged pieces. Even today they're broken and scattered in the Potomac River, per her instructions."

Laura scribbled notes on a legal pad. Under any other circumstances she'd be fascinated, but she was so nervous she barely heard anything Amy said. That morning she'd called the First Lady's personal secretary to say *National Geographic* had just asked to gather some last-minute information about the White House china collection for a pictorial. She'd expected a low-level staffer to show her the damn plates, but when Amy heard about her visit she wanted to show Laura the china herself.

As Amy talked, Laura's mind kept returning to the lock-picking lessons Wilder had given her on the furniture at an always-open office supply store. Then she'd practiced for two hours using her desk lock, similar to the kind on a credenza, until she could open it in a few seconds.

Amy paused for a moment, noticing Laura's flushed face and shortness of breath. "Laura, honey, are you all right?"

"Yes, sorry. Cramps from hell."

Amy finished showing Laura the china at twenty-five past twelve. Laura thanked her effusively and excused herself, saying she had a lunch date in the building with her friend Jerry Fisher, the *Washington Post*'s White House correspondent, at twelve-thirty. In actuality, she'd set the lunch for one o'clock. Laura walked quickly upstairs to the State Floor and crossed over to the West Wing. Since she came from the private residence area and wore a high-level security badge, she could move freely around the White House corridors. She walked with brisk determination, hoping it would mask her raw terror, then slowed as she approached the VS Room, located at the far side of the hallway from the Oval Office. She could hear her heart pounding, and her hands were so sweaty her palm-print had soaked into her yellow legal pad. I'm in the fucking White House, Laura thought, about to steal from the President of the United States.

She opened the door, prepared to say she got lost if she encountered anyone inside, but found the room deserted, the lights low, and the video wall in blue standby mode. She closed the door and leaned against it, reviving her nerve. After a moment she crossed to the credenza, crouched down next to it, and steadied her arm against the door as she inserted the lock-picking tools. Just as Wilder said, it had the same metal-disk tumblers as on her desk. After the longest minute of her life, she got it open.

Last time she'd seen inside the credenza, several tiny DV videocassettes were stacked next to the video recorders. Now they were gone. She just stared for a moment, incredulous, then turned on the recorders and pushed the eject buttons. Empty. Frantic, she felt around inside the cabinet, behind the machines, all around the bottom shelf. No tapes. She looked around the room for other places they might be, but there were no obvious storage areas. Laura couldn't believe she'd taken this risk for nothing. She froze, hearing voices in the hallway outside. When all became quiet again, she forced herself to concentrate on relocking the credenza—the only thing worse than leaving empty-handed would be getting caught. She slid the lock-picking tools into the cylinder, but everything Wilder had taught her flew from her head. After struggling with it for a couple minutes, she gave up. She had to get out of there.

Laura sat in a stall in the women's room near the pressroom, willing herself to calm down. The frustration and disappointment were unbearable. Although lunch with Jerry Fisher would be critical to maintaining appearances, she wished she could leave the White House immediately.

Fisher, a tall, gregarious African-American, leapt from behind his desk as Laura entered the pressroom. She held up her hand before he caught her in his signature bear hug.

"Not too close. I'm coming down with a summer cold."

"Come on, Bishop, don't even think of bailing on lunch."

"No, I'm not, but I can only stay for a few minutes."

Shoppers, tourists, and the local lunch crowd swarmed Union Station's mall and restaurants. Downstairs, commuters stood in long lines to buy tickets in the Amtrak station. Wilder sat inside one of a row of old-fashioned wooden phone booths in the ground-floor lobby, keeping the jointed door open far enough for the booth's interior light to remain off. He couldn't use his cell phone or pager—by now his pursuers would've cloned their electronic identification codes to eavesdrop on their transmissions—so he'd told Laura to call him here at two-fifteen, an hour from now. He hated that his fugitive status effectively removed him from the action, and especially hated waiting, so he connected Laura's notebook computer to the pay phone with an acoustic coupler and checked the VICAP database. No new criminal incidents that might relate to Cowling's test group had been reported. He next called California to see if Professor Cowling had awakened from his coma. He hadn't. Wilder reread some e-mail messages Laura had exchanged on his behalf with Brent that morning via the Hotmail account. In them, Brent related how Colonel Chang had grilled him about Wilder's activities. However, suspecting the arrest order came from the President, Brent had denied all knowledge of Wilder's motives.

Wilder slipped Laura's computer into an oversized mailing envelope, donned a pair of sunglasses and a Redskins baseball cap, and stepped out of the phone booth. He figured he'd better get something to eat while he had the chance. Crossing the lobby, he noticed a D.C. transit cop twenty-five feet away. The cop unconsciously betrayed his interest by immediately turning away when Wilder glanced in his direction. Then he keyed the walkie-talkie on his belt and spoke into the microphone clipped to his lapel.

Even with an APB, it seemed very unlikely to Wilder a transit cop could make him in a packed railroad station—whatever agency Marsh was using to hunt him must have technology classified even to the OSI. Though he'd been wary of his beeper and cell phone, he'd felt safe dialing into his Internet Service Provider—a normal trace could get no farther than the ISP node's general identifier, not the precise telephone number from where he'd accessed it. But in this case he presumed, correctly, that Marsh's men had intercepted his log-on code and used some special method to pinpoint his location to the phone in Union Station.

He saw another cop pick up his movements, so he stopped at a water fountain and watched them in the reflection in a glass display case. They approached with caution, meaning he'd been characterized as dangerous. He walked normally, arms loose at his sides, wishing it weren't the good guys tailing him, and wandered toward the long lines at the Amtrak counters. The cops grew nervous as he bobbed in and out of their view and they began to close in. Wilder entered a notions shop and stood behind a newspaper rack. He peered around the corner; one of the cops was approaching the door. Then providence smiled. Wilder spotted a teenaged boy, probably a runaway, stuffing packs of cigarettes into his pockets. The shop clerk, a bored Vietnamese woman busy with a customer, was oblivious to the theft. Wilder yanked the kid behind the rack.

"Easy, I'm doing you a favor." With an iron grip on the kid's neck, he picked him up so he could look around the side of the rack. "See the cop over there? He's been following you." The kid had no trouble believing him. Wilder took off his hat and sunglasses and put them on the teenager.

"Get out of here. Move."

The kid glared suspiciously at Wilder. "Why you helpin' me?"

"My fuckin' old man was a cop."

The teenager ran across the train station. Since he and Wilder both wore light-colored shirts, the hat and glasses were enough for the cops to mistake him for their quarry. He almost made it to the main doors when a half-dozen transit cops surrounded him, guns drawn. Wilder backtracked toward the train gates, hoping to slip across the tracks and grab a taxi on North Capitol Street. He pushed through the Metroliner commuters on the platform and hopped down into the track bed.

One of the cops crossing the tracks saw Wilder, glanced at a faxed copy of his military ID photo, and spoke into his radio. Within seconds a police chopper appeared and hovered a hundred feet overhead. Two SWAT sharpshooters hung out the copter doors. One had a .22/.250 sniper rifle, the other a six-barrel, .762mm motor-driven machine gun. Apparently, they'd been ordered to bring him dead or alive, with the former no doubt preferred. The machine-gunner fired first. Several short volleys sent Wilder diving for cover under a parked locomotive, then the sniper kept him pinned down with a succession of highly accurate, single shots hitting the gravel inches away. He lay there for a moment, seething with frustration. Getting killed or engaging in a protracted standoff with cops wasn't going to accomplish anything, so he took out his cell phone and dialed 911.

"Nine-Eleven emergency . . ."

"Yeah, hi . . . this is Matt Wilder. Right, Wilder. Tell everyone at the train yard I'm tossing my pistol. Soon as that sniper takes a rest I'll come out. And ma'am, remind them this call's on tape . . ."

It never looks good to paste an unarmed man giving himself up.

Thirty

President Marsh didn't feel like having a VS meeting with the British prime minister, even though Patrick Kendall was just about his only remaining ally regarding the TAA.

"Patrick, sorry I'm late . . ."

Marsh sat down in the VS Room and put a pile of papers on the coffee table. Kendall, a ruddy blond from the west of England, greeted Marsh warmly. Marsh, however, didn't reply. Instead, he stared at the doors on the VCR credenza, which were slightly ajar, then instinctively touched his pants pocket for the key. The prime minister stopped talking and watched as Marsh got up, crossed to the credenza, and crouched down to examine it. He slipped a pen through the handle to pull a door open without smudging any fingerprints.

"Burton, is anything the matter?"

Marsh drew in a long breath. Mixed in with the odors of dust, furniture polish, warm electronic units, the wood, stain, and glue of the credenza he perceived something mildly sweet, like the scent of a freshly picked flower. He recognized it instantly, and it took intense self-control not to howl with rage. Marsh turned to the VS screen, suddenly remembering Kendall.

"Sorry, have to get back to you."

Marsh turned the outgoing signal off. The British prime minister, still visible on the screen, called Marsh's name a few times. An aide came into view, and together they fiddled with their controls, trying to bring the White House back on-line. The President grabbed the telephone receiver and one of the White House operators answered.

"Get me security."

Under a yellow half moon, Batu Khan and Chu'tsai rode their stallions across a pasture at the base of a valley, a mile wide and ten miles long. The highland air in the Hentiyn Nuruu Mountains of northeastern Mongolia was cold at two-thirty in the morning, even in summer. A half-dozen Khaldun Horsemen, Batu's personal escort, rode behind at a respectful distance. As Batu stopped and dismounted, the Khaldun commander rode forward to take the reins of his stallion. Chu'tsai stayed on his horse, smoking. He leaned forward, casually, cowboy style, arms crossed on the horn of his saddle. No one spoke.

All eyes turned toward the far end of the pasture. A huge shape slowly emerged from a triple-wide train tunnel. Head-on, the shape looked like a total eclipse: a dark black circle surrounded by a fiery, orange glow. Then it changed direction and moved across the pasture: a long, black, metallic cylinder like polished obsidian, with flames spewing from the engines at its rear. It taxied toward Batu on oversized tires, especially designed for the flat pastures of Mongolia, adapted to this environment just as the space shuttle had been designed to land on the Mojave salt flats. As the craft came closer its great size became apparent—230 feet long and 60 feet high, similar in size to the hull of a 747, though it had no portal windows and only smooth protuberances where wings and tail fin should be. Then the protuberances slowly expanded, and like a folding fan a tail fin rose up out of the fuselage and locked into position. Two pairs of overlapping wings unfurled, shortest at the front and longest in the back, extending straight out for maximum lift during take-off and subsonic flight. Like the F-77 Centurion, it could fly as slow as a biplane, then its wings would sweep back incrementally as it accelerated, the two pairs connecting in a delta shape at supersonic speeds and recessing almost flat against the hull at hypersonic speeds.

Batu's heart pounded with pride and excitement. At last, he rejoiced, the Day of Glory was upon them, as well as the maiden voyage for his new command ship, the *Altun Ordu.* Her name meant Golden Horde, honoring the Mongol army that overran western Asia and eastern Europe in the thirteenth century under the first Batu Khan. A hatch opened on the smooth fuselage and a staircase unfolded. Batu paused to kneel and pray before ascending into the *Altun Ordu,* profoundly aware of the historical significance of the moment. He smiled at the uniqueness of the scene: an aircraft more advanced than anything that had ever flown, appearing magically upon an ancient, moonlit pasture, his shaman and six faithful horsemen there to bid him farewell. A tableau perfectly illustrating his destiny as his people's link to their glorious past and their brilliant future.

As Batu prayed, Chu'tsai remained silent. He could not help but get swept up in Batu's fervor since the VS meeting with Marsh, and he believed it would be successful, but recently he'd found himself unable to sense the future or discern its outcome. This bizarre change in his powers deeply concerned him.

Batu smiled at him and shook his head. "I know you'd prefer I stay on the ground, but I can't, especially this time. I'm not like Marsh; I don't command my warriors over the telephone! Conflicts may be fought on the battlefield, but they are won or lost *here*"—he tapped his forehead— "in the minds of the opposition. My direct participation gives focus to their fears, which a faceless war machine can never do no matter how effective it is. Do I have your blessing?"

Chu'tsai dismounted and embraced his friend. "You have the highest blessing, as always, Batu, in all you do." He watched Batu board the *Altun Ordu* and take off; then he remounted his horse to wait for his own transportation to arrive.

Concurrent with the *Altun Ordu*'s departure, five new hypersonic, fighter/bomber penetrators took off from a hidden air base north of the Aral Sea in Kazakhstan, 2,800 miles from Batu's pasture. Batu had christened their design Temujin, after Genghis Khan's name at birth. From yet another underground hangar a hypersonic transport, Yesugei, also took wing. Named in honor of Genghis's chieftain father, she had a less streamlined design than a Temujin, being twice as wide and four times longer than her fighter sibling. All seven aircraft headed north, with the *Altun Ordu* in the lead.

Jerry Fisher delivered a lame punch line to Laura and two White House staffers at their table. They laughed and Laura glanced at her watch— one-forty P.M.—then looked up as the others' laughter came to an unnaturally abrupt halt. Two Secret Service agents stood behind her, one male, the other female, both wearing gray suits and expressions to match.

"Miss Bishop, please come with us."

Laura tried not to appear as frightened as she felt.

"Me? What's going on?"

"Now. Please."

She reached for her purse, but the female agent took it, tucked it under her arm, and led Laura out of the dining room. Fisher and the others exchanged surprised glances. They'd never seen the Secret Service so businesslike within the confines of the White House. Laura, feeling faint, walked along in silence, running the possibilities and rehearsing her denials. Had she left fingerprints in the VS Room? Did someone see her go in? Thank God she hadn't taken anything. The agents stopped at the VS Room, knocked softly, and then opened the door. The female agent handed Laura her purse and gestured for her to go inside. She stepped in the room; the agents remained in the hall and closed the door behind them. The room was darker than before.

"I'm a little confused, Laura."

The President of the United States stood up and offered her a whiskey glass with a shot of bourbon in it. She shook her head.

"Take it. You're all flushed. Your heart sounds like it's going to jump right out of that clever little blouse. Are you frightened about something?"

"Yes, sir, I sure am. The Secret Service interrupted my lunch, escorted me up here without explanation . . . it's pretty intimidating."

Marsh handed her the glass and she took a sip of the liquor. She knew enough about the symptoms of Cowling's test group to understand Marsh could all but read her mind. He stepped closer, took her security badge between his fingers and looked at it, his face only a few inches from hers. He studied her intensely. His need to know her motives barely outweighed the intense urge roiling within him to hurt her.

"Let me explain my confusion: I'm informed you're visiting us on a writing assignment. You met my wife in the China Room. According to her, the two of you went nowhere else."

Laura cringed, miserable about Amy ever thinking she'd taken advantage of their friendship.

"Don't worry, Amy doesn't know anything. This can be our little secret—if you're honest with me. I'd like to think of us as friends. We are friends, right, Laura?"

"I certainly feel that way about you and Mrs. Marsh."

Marsh's anger made it difficult to focus, but he had to structure his questioning carefully. What she said, how she said it, what she'd omit would all help determine how much if anything she knew. Also, he didn't want to create a problem with her if one didn't exist.

"Tell me exactly what you did from the moment you walked through the VS Room door a little while ago to the moment you left."

Laura decided to keep her lies as small as possible. "I came in . . . just looked around . . . I had a few minutes before my lunch appointment; I was curious to see the room now that it's all finished. I know I shouldn't have been wandering around without an escort—"

"What were you looking for in the credenza?"

"Credenza?"

Marsh came close to striking her. Laura felt a chill as his eyes went dark and cold, like a shark's.

"You unlocked it. Where'd you get the key? *What were you looking for?*"

"I was only here for a moment. I didn't unlock anything. I wasn't looking for anything!"

"I have the only key and the credenza was locked this morning. It is now open. You were the only one in this room. Please don't make it difficult. Nothing is missing, that's not the issue. Take me into your confidence and this embarrassing situation remains between us. If you don't, I'll have to believe your intentions were to harm me, to harm the presidency. I'll be forced to bring others in, people who *will* get the truth."

Despite her terror, Laura spotted a weakness in Marsh's threat: He wants to keep this quiet more than she does.

"Sir, I welcome the opportunity to get to the truth. Let me talk to those other people."

Marsh's rage came dangerously close to overwhelming him. Laura stood frozen with terror, expecting at any moment he would slam her through the wall.

"Who do you think you're fucking with? If I say you tried to stab that letter opener through my heart, it's over. You'll be this year's Squeaky Fromme. Talk to me, *now*! Did Matt Wilder send you here?"

"Matt?"

"Answer me! *He* sent you here, didn't he?!"

Laura could barely think. She searched for some way to calm the President down; her denials only further infuriated him. She stepped back, flopped down onto the sofa, and began to cry.

"I don't see Matt anymore."

"You're a liar."

"It's true," she said, crying harder. "He . . . he hit me."

Marsh stared at her. "Okay, keep talking, what were you doing?"

"I opened the cabinet with a lock pick. It was easy; I learned how to do it on the Internet."

"What were you looking for?"

"Videotapes."

"Why?"

Laura sniffled, then composed herself. "I wanted to see you talking to Batu Khan. Like you'd promised I could . . ." She held her eyes to the floor.

"Those conversations weren't recorded, Laura."

"With all due respect, Mr. President, give me a fucking break."

Marsh said nothing. Her confession made sense; he'd forgotten about his offer, later withdrawn, for her to observe his VS meeting with Batu Khan. Naturally such an opportunity would be insanely tantalizing to someone like Laura. He just hadn't imagined she'd have the gall to help herself when he reneged. He felt enormously relieved, but wanted to make her suffer a while longer, if for no other reason than for giving him such a scare. Before he could, however, Curt Levinson rushed in. He barely noticed Laura as he spoke to the President in an urgent whisper.

"Sir, Woodruff wants you to dial extension eight-twelve."

Only certain Executive Office phones had access to extension eight-twelve—the direct line to the secret radar-monitoring facility at Svalbard Station. Marsh punched in the number and listened for a moment. What he heard enraged him.

"When? How many? Heading? I don't care, give me the goddamn specifics!" He looked at Levinson and gestured toward Laura. "Get her the hell out of here!"

One eye on the President, Levinson gestured for Laura to come with him. As she stood up she acted on impulse, picking up her purse from the bottom, causing its contents to spill onto the floor in between the sofa and a sideboard. She crouched down, flustered, and flung everything back into it except for her cell phone. With her back to Marsh and Levinson, she quickly speed-dialed the number of her vacationing neighbors, and slid the phone under the sofa. She stood and Levinson led her out of the VS Room, toward the Marine Guard at the elevator.

"I'd be overstepping my bounds if I asked what's wrong?" Laura asked, trying to sound nonchalant.

"Let's just say the President really loses his cool when folks don't do their job." In actuality, Levinson had no idea what was happening. He'd never even heard of extension eight-twelve and he was goddamn chief of staff.

"So, no big crisis?"

"Only for the guy getting his head handed to him." He asked the Marine Guard to escort Laura to her car, then he hurried back to the VS Room.

Not wanting to interact with civilian law enforcement, the ExOps ordered D.C. Metro Police to return Wilder to Andrews AFB so they could pick him up there. Base Commander Dryden, Brent, and four security officers met the SWAT chopper when it landed behind Hangar One. Wilder, frustrated and impatient, his hands cuffed in front of him, shot Brent a let-me-do-the-talking look.

"Someone's coming to get you," Dryden said to Wilder. "I don't know who or why, but orders came from Secretary Woodruff himself. Look, if this is an Air Force matter, I should know about it."

Wilder checked his watch: two-fifteen P.M. By now Laura would be trying to call him at the Union Station phone booth to let him know if she got any tapes.

"Sorry, sir, I can't say, but I can assure you the problem is outside the Air Force."

At the brig, a single-story, six-cell building near the main gate, the Security Forces sergeant-in-charge informed General Dryden his office needed him back at once. While the four security officers stood cautious guard just outside, the sergeant locked Wilder in one of the otherwise empty cells.

"Sir, if you could come with me . . ." he said to Brent.

"I need five minutes, sergeant," Brent replied, pulling rank.

The sergeant grumbled and closed the door. Wilder paced his cell, trapped and intensely frustrated. He had to find a way to escape, but doubted he'd have much luck with five armed men stationed outside.

"Laura's at the White House, trying to steal Marsh's Virtual Summit tapes," he told Brent. "She thinks they might contain something incriminating."

Brent shook his head, stunned. He'd only met Laura briefly at the Malcolm Grow Medical Center, and hadn't figured her to be as insane as Wilder.

"Jesus, you're a bad influence on people."

"It was her fucking idea, and I'm worried sick about it. But if she uncovers anything, help her get it into the right hands. It's up to you two now."

Brent nodded.

"You'd better leave before those guys get here," Wilder continued. "Don't let 'em know we've been talking. And listen, if I should have a sudden heart attack in captivity or, you know, choke on a ham sandwich, take care of Kate for me. Tell her how much I love her."

"I got a better idea. Stay healthy until we get through this."

Laura walked through her town house door, relieved to see the surveillance cars were gone. Marsh must've believed her story about breaking up with Wilder and why she wanted the tapes. Still, just to be certain, she crossed to her neighbors' house through the backyard and let herself in through the rear door. It had been almost thirty minutes since she'd left the White House; the microcassette tape in her neighbors' answering machine, recording what her phone heard in the VS Room, had reached the end. Snapping it out and rewinding it in her handheld Lanier recorder, she felt as scared now as when she'd been with Marsh—sooner or later her phone would be found. With luck its battery would run down so no one could be sure it had transmitted anything. She'd also left a lipstick and a fountain pen with it, to make it look like one of several things she'd missed when gathering the contents of her spilled purse.

Clicking the Play button, she heard Marsh grilling someone over the phone: "How many? From where? What heading?" Then she heard a knock at the VS Room door. She could not recognize the voice at first.

"Stan, what the hell's going on here?" Marsh asked.

"I don't know. That's why I wanted you to talk to Svalbard directly."

Stan ... Stan Woodruff, secretary of defense, Laura thought. She heard another knock at the door.

"Standby!" Marsh called out. And then, in a lower voice, "Shit, that's Levinson."

"Well, sir, given what's happening, it's time to bring the senior aides into the loop. If we have to mobilize—"

"No. It's premature do anything just yet, not even share this information."

"But sir, we're looking at a time frame measured in minutes!"

"I'll let you know when I'm ready to take action. Open the door for Curt." Then Laura heard Marsh pick up the phone, dial a three-digit number, and say "Patch the display through to the VS screen . . ."

Thirty-one

A highly detailed, color, three-dimensional rendering of the earth had appeared on the VS screen as Levinson entered the room. Seven yellow lines emanated from various places within the TAA. At the tip of each line, like the head of a tadpole, an oval bore numbers indicating altitude and airspeed. They inched northward, with the one starting from the Hentiyn Nuruu mountains slightly in the lead, and all had just reached Russian airspace. Marsh stood with his back to the VS screen, his brow furrowed in concentration. Everything about the escalating situation angered and confused him: the appearance of Batu's new planes, the mystery of their destination or intention, and, worst of all, the realization he would have to make fast, clear-eyed decisions. He still had enough self-awareness to fear his anger and paranoia could cloud his judgment, especially since those emotions were intensifying by the moment.

Woodruff crossed to Levinson and pointed to the aircraft indicators on the graphic display.

"Several minutes ago, Batu Khan launched seven hypersonic, second-generation stealth aircraft. They appear to be five small fighters, a command craft, and a transport."

"TAA hypersonics?!" Levinson said, moving closer to the screen. "Where are these images coming from?"

Woodruff looked at the President, feeling he should be the one to explain. "Sir?"

It took Marsh, still lost in thought, a moment to respond. "Yes; what?"

"The origin of our data?" Woodruff said.

Marsh pondered the question, then smiled. Enormous self-satisfaction about the apparent success of his counterintelligence program suddenly supplanted all his worries.

"Last year we learned several of our design and propulsion facilities had been infiltrated," he said. "At first we planned to plug the leaks, closing the proverbial barn door after the horse ran off. But instead I decided to let them continue spying while we manipulated the stolen data. Working with key defense contractors and a special team recruited from the NSA, we fed the infiltrators tainted technical information about our stealth material. I don't understand the science . . . Stan, you tell him."

"We included a hidden isotope signature in the formula for second-generation stealth materials. The formula is identical to ours, just as stealthy to all known radar, except for one molecular difference. Then we installed a radar downlink at an abandoned monitoring station and tuned it to perceive that isotope. You're looking at the real-time image coming from that station."

"We had no idea until just now whether Batu's engineers swallowed the false formulas, let alone built any aircraft!" Marsh added "The wily little bastard fed us phony information, too. Our best intelligence sources assured us the TAA's hypersonics program has been a colossal failure."

"We had a residual effect in mind as well," Woodruff said. "Any investment Batu made in hypersonics would diminish the resources and expertise available for developing nuclear weapons."

"Who else is seeing this readout?" Levinson asked.

"The ExOp tech at Svalbard Station and us. No one else," Marsh said.

Woodruff crossed to the phone and picked it up. "I'll have Mancini move us to a higher alert condition."

"Absolutely not!"

Instantly angry again, Marsh grabbed the phone from Woodruff and slammed the receiver down. The situation was moving too fast and he didn't want to do *anything* before he could think it through. He remembered the cryptic comment Batu had made during their VS meeting about his not lasting in office, and all the paranoia about Batu possessing intimate knowledge about him returned in an intense, sickening rush. He feared that however he responded, he would play right into Batu's hands. He hit upon a rationale to buy himself some time:

"Look, we went to a lot of trouble to get the ability to detect those planes," he said. "Changing our alert status would tell Batu we're aware of them."

"I understand wanting to protect this capability, Mr. President, but a passive stance . . ."

Marsh tried, unsuccessfully, to mask his fury at Woodruff's dissension. "Any indication we can see his aircraft blows an enormous tactical advantage! What's your hurry; we don't even know where they're heading!"

Woodruff shot a nervous look at Levinson. He found the President's strange logic and volatility very unsettling. Levinson agreed with him about the danger of waiting, but he feared contradicting the President, so he withheld his comments until they could be certain of the TAA fleet's destination.

Marsh dialed extension eight-twelve to reach the ExOp at Svalbard Station, then clicked on the speakerphone.

"It looks like the planes are converging," he said impatiently. "When the hell can you give us a destination?"

"Sir, until they're lined up on a common vector, all we can determine with any certainty is they're on the Great Circle Route toward the North Pole and points beyond."

The euphemism "points beyond" annoyed the President. They had a map of the world right in their faces. Past Siberia lay the permanent ice of the Arctic, then Greenland and the Northwest Territories. Marsh seriously doubted they were headed for Canada. He clicked off the speaker box and Woodruff sat next to him.

"Sir, unless they pull an about-face, it's clear those planes are heading toward U.S. airspace. Past experience with Batu Khan would instruct us to anticipate the worst. We *must* prepare an airborne and missile defense, in the event of—"

"No. I understand now. He's gonna overfly the continental U.S. to see if we react. What better test of his stealth capabilities? I won't let him intimidate me into revealing we can see him. This information does not leave this room until I say so."

"We can warn the Joint Chiefs without making any perceptible change to our readiness status," Woodruff said.

"Goddamn it, Stan, it's an easy concept to grasp: We wait. No one needs to know anything right now."

Woodruff didn't push it any further, but he stole a look at Levinson.

Neither understood the President's agenda, but they certainly knew why he wanted to keep this information from the Joint Chiefs. Mancini and the others would go ballistic if they learned TAA warplanes were approaching the continental United States. And since members of the military had almost unlimited latitude for taking defensive measures on their own, without specific orders from the commander in chief or anyone else, Marsh would have to fire the bunch of them if he wanted to maintain his current course of inaction.

Inside her neighbor's house, Laura stopped the tape. She found it almost impossible to believe what she'd just heard. Her hands shaking, she dialed the Union Station pay-phone number and a man answered on the first ring.

"Yes?"

"Matt?"

"I'll get Agent Wilder for you—may I say who's calling?"

Laura hung up. Shit. She didn't need anyone to draw her a diagram: Wilder had been captured. She looked at the clock. Two twenty-five P.M. Her knowledge of what happened in the VS Room via the tape was about a half-hour delayed. By now, Marsh and the others must know exactly where the TAA planes were headed.

She called the Washington Field Office at Andrews and asked for Brent. His secretary said he was out of the office but she'd page him and patch him through. While waiting, Laura played the tape at double-speed, skimming through moments of silence and irrelevant talk. She slowed the tape to normal speed as the President used the speakerphone to answer a call from the radar tech at Svalbard:

"The aircraft have settled into a low-earth orbit of 150,000 feet and a cruising speed of mach five," the tech said over the speakerphone in the VS Room, "and we've made tentative assumption about their destination. They're approaching the Pole on a course that will take them, once they enter our hemisphere, directly along seventy-seven degrees west."

"Son of a bitch!" Levinson said. "They're coming to Washington!"

Marsh looked away from the others in order to hide any visible sign of the panic he felt. His mind ran at light speed, almost beyond his control, a jumble of thoughts and emotions swirling around one another.

"How long before they arrive?" he asked.

The tech did the calculations. "At current speed and heading, factoring reentry, they'll arrive over Washington at four forty-five local time."

Marsh clicked off the phone. Sitting, he leaned his head against his closed fists. He had to focus, take control. Withdrawing deep inside himself, he slowed his breathing and banished all extraneous thoughts. After a moment, something clicked. He achieved a perfect, transcendent clarity of mind, and his blinding rage turned to ecstasy in a breathtaking moment of inspiration. Circumstance was handing him an unprecedented opportunity, and never in his life had he felt more capable of exploiting it.

"Sir, are you all right?" Levinson asked.

"Absolutely." He looked up and had a small, calm smile on his face. "Listen to me: Those planes will fly right over our heads. If we panic we play into his hands. There could come a day when the knowledge we're protecting right now—our ability to track his Air Force—will help preserve the security of this nation."

"Excuse me, sir, but who's to say they're not carrying enough bombs to destroy this city?!" Levinson asked.

"Nothing is going to happen! Even Batu Khan knows better than that. I know what I'm talking about, I've dealt with the bastard, so stop questioning me!"

Laura stopped the tape again as Brent came on the line.

"Laura, I'm at the Andrews brig. Matt's been captured." He glanced through the door leading to the outer office, where the increasingly suspicious Security Forces sergeant and his four officers stood with their hands resting on their side arms.

"Is he all right?" she asked.

"Yeah . . ." Brent saw no reason to worry her by mentioning the guys on their way to pick Wilder up.

Laura summarized her confrontation with Marsh and how she'd taped twenty-five minutes of conversation in the VS Room.

"Christ on a crutch, Laura." He spotted a wall phone about ten feet from Wilder. "I'm gonna try to get Matt on the line."

Ducking under the small window in the cell-area door so the sergeant couldn't see him, Brent stretched the wall-phone receiver wire across into Wilder's cell.

"Laura, I'm on . . ." Wilder said.

"We have to get this tape to someone, right now," Laura said. "Seven TAA stealth fighters are flying toward Washington. They're invisible to all the early-warning systems except one, which is under Marsh's personal control, and he's refusing to inform the Joint Chiefs or anyone else."

Wilder and Brent looked at each other.

"Are you *sure?*"

"Of course! Here, listen."

She fast-rewound to play back a few sections, including the radar tech describing the aircraft's heading, position, and ETA. Wilder stood dumbfounded, listening to the President describe his program of letting Batu Khan's men steal tainted classified information.

"Woomera . . . Andrews . . . Travis . . ." Wilder said, wide-eyed as the truth hit him. "No wonder they pulled the cases. We weren't supposed to catch those guys!" Despite his astonishment, he had no time to dwell on it.

"Have you heard the whole tape?" he asked Laura.

"All but the last few minutes. I'm fast-forwarding to where I left off. Maybe Marsh is right and it's only a flyover."

"You'd test your stealth capabilities with one fighter, not seven," Wilder said. "Brent's gonna meet you on the east steps of the Capitol, soon as you can get there. If this isn't proof Marsh is insane, I don't know what is."

Brent shook his head. "Congress has recessed for the summer—"

"Senator Ballard is in town; I saw him on the news this morning," Laura said. "I don't know about the Speaker."

Brent looked at his watch. "ETA four forty-five. Shit, we got a bit more than two hours. I'm on my way."

Laura hung up and hurried down her neighbor's back steps, holding the Lanier up to her ear to listen to the remainder of the thirty-minute-old recording. A word the President said stopped her dead. She rewound the tape and played it again.

"Lipstick . . ."

"Sir?"

"Can't you smell it?"

Her heart pounding, Laura heard rustling close to her hidden phone.

No one in the VS Room spoke for a moment, then the President of the United States shouted, "Fucking *bitch!*"

The sound abruptly ended.

She turned off the Lanier and walked in a daze across her backyard. Passing the driveway, she saw one of the tan sedans with government plates screech to a stop in front of her town house and two ExOps get out. One waited on the sidewalk while the other walked quickly toward the house. Laura locked eyes with him, then ran away, hopping her neighbor's garden wall. He spoke into a radio microphone; the other ExOp jumped back into the sedan while the one on foot gave chase.

Pedestrians jammed the sidewalk along Wisconsin Avenue, forcing Laura to run along the roadway between the traffic and the line of parked cars. She looked over her shoulder. The sedan slowed momentarily at the intersection, but the ExOp on foot was gaining fast. Up ahead, a car door opened in her path—a pair of tourists getting out of their rented Ford Taurus. With the ExOp only a few yards behind, Laura ripped the keys from the tourist's hand and hopped into the driver's seat. As he let out a surprised yell and lunged for her, Laura yanked the door closed and locked it. She mouthed "sorry," started the Taurus, and made a jackrabbit jump into traffic.

The ExOp on foot waved the sedan over and jumped in. Terrified, Laura watched in the rearview mirror as it recklessly cut through traffic to catch her. She had neither the nerve nor the skill to stay ahead for much longer. She hung a left between oncoming traffic onto M Street, another onto 31st Street, and raced north to P Street toward the park where she'd met Wilder in the middle of last night. It seemed like a hundred years ago. The sedan cut in behind her and bumped her to force her over. Momentarily losing control she swerved into the wrong lane, turned onto 20th Street, and ran the light across Massachusetts. A tangle of cars slowed the sedan down; by the time it got through the intersection Laura had disappeared. Then the ExOp in the passenger's seat spotted the Taurus, its driver's door open, idling near the Q Street entrance to the Dupont Circle Metro station.

Laura stared down at the longest descent in the Metro system—two steep, end-to-end escalators leading to the train platforms almost two hundred feet underground—then looked back and saw the sedan pull up outside. Digging in her purse, she crossed to a homeless woman sitting on the concrete floor, cushioned by layers of blankets. She shoved a twenty-dollar bill in the woman's hand and pulled one of the dirty blankets from under her. While running to the escalators, she folded the blanket into a thick square. A flat, stainless-steel separator ran in between the up and down escalators. It looked like a long kids' slide and to keep it from being used that way it had sharp, diamond-shaped steel bumps every couple of feet along its length. Laura sat at the top of the separator, put the blanket under her ass, and slid down. The ExOps came so close to catching her that one of them grabbed a few strands of her hair.

The blanket protected Laura from the steel bumps as she slid rapidly down. Behind her the ExOps bounded down the escalator steps, elbowing people out of their path. Fifty feet from the end of the escalator, Laura dug her heels into either side of the separator to slow herself down. She slid off the bottom of the escalator, half falling toward the ticket kiosk next to the turnstiles. The attendant ducked as she slammed into the glass; his fright turned to outrage when she hopped the turnstile and dashed onto the train platform. Wiping some blood from her nose, Laura tried to fade into the crowd. She saw the ExOps show their badges as they climbed over the turnstiles, then the line of recessed floodlights alongside the southbound tracks flashed to announce arrival of the train. She dodged behind a group of noisy high school kids as the train pulled in, pushed through the doors as they opened and hurried toward the rear of the train. The ExOps got there as the train began to move. One spotted her through the window and, running alongside the train, leveled a nine-millimeter pistol at her. Laura dove out of the way as two rounds neatly penetrated the Plexiglas window. Passengers panicked at the sound of the shots and she ran into another compartment, lost in the hysteria.

Hearing some voices approach, Wilder stepped onto the cot in his cell to look outside through the tiny, barred window. He'd never felt so frustrated or useless. The door opened and the Security Forces sergeant led two men into the cell area. The sergeant took a pair of handcuffs off his Sam Houston belt.

"Sir, I'll have to ask you to stand with your back against the bars, arms held together."

Wilder obliged; the sergeant reached through the bars, cuffed his wrists behind his back, and gave the key to one of the men. Wilder looked them over. They were wearing Dockers, navy blue blazers, and ties loosened at the collar like real estate agents.

"Shit, if I'd known you guys dressed so sharp, I'd have joined the NSA instead of the OSI."

"Walk," one said. They flanked Wilder, each gripping one of his arms, and led him outside toward the flight line. He lightly bumped his shoulder against each man to determine what they were packing and where, and he felt a shoulder holster hugging Lefty's ribs. As they approached Hangar One, Wilder heard an idling helicopter, then its tail rotor came into view when they rounded the building. It's now or never, he thought. He stepped down hard on Righty's foot. Annoyed, Righty reoriented himself to get out of his way and Wilder moved sharply back, breaking Righty's grip. He leaned into Lefty, who still had a hold on him, and landed a powerful sideways kick to Righty's knee. Righty's knee bent perpendicular and snapped; he screamed and collapsed to the tarmac. Wilder used his shoulder to shove Lefty against the side of the hangar and kneed him twice in the groin. Lefty gasped and his legs gave out.

Lying on the tarmac, Righty cradled his broken knee, rolled onto his back, and pulled his pistol. Wilder kicked it out of his hand and threw himself on top of him, cracking Righty's head against the ground. He slipped his handcuffed hands around his thighs and strained to pull his feet over and through the handcuff chain. Lefty unholstered his pistol and steadied his aim. With his handcuffed hands now in front of him, Wilder dove onto Lefty before he could fire. He wrestled the pistol away and jammed its barrel into Lefty's mouth.

"Key."

No answer. Wilder didn't have time for a lengthy interrogation.

"I'm gonna count to one."

He cocked the hammer and pushed the gun barrel down Lefty's throat. Gagging, Lefty patted the inside pocket of his sports coat. Wilder knocked him out with the pistol and fished out the handcuff key. He removed the cuffs and put them on his former captors, looping the chain through a U-shaped water pipe bolted to the back of the hangar, then took a cell phone from a plastic holster on Righty's belt and patted him on the head to say thanks for everything.

Wilder ran across Arnold Avenue toward the Burger King parking lot. Walking quickly between the rows of cars, he glanced inside each one until finding the keys in a Security Forces sedan. His destination, Building 5016, stood at the end of a deliberately convoluted route and he had to circumnavigate a half-dozen structures before he reached it: the Air Force One hangar. He hoped news of his fugitive status hadn't spread around the base; it would be nice to do this the easy way. He parked the Security Forces car out of sight of the entrance, walked toward the hangar, and greeted the two-man guard detail. They didn't seem very interested in him—a good sign—as he crossed under the President's identical blue-and-white 747s. The temporary enclosure for the prototype F-77 Centurion stood at the southernmost edge of the pentagon-shaped hangar. A pair of special Security Forces guards stood at attention as he approached.

"Good to see you back on-line, sir."

"Good to be back."

Wilder looked around as if expecting someone and frowned.

"How come this aircraft's not in position yet?"

"Sir?"

"Jesus H. Christ! The President will be here in about five minutes! She's supposed to be on the runway! Where's the support crew?"

The guards looked at each other as their careers flashed, or more accurately flushed, before their eyes.

"But, sir . . . are you *sure* about that?"

"About as sure as I'm gonna shoot your insubordinate ass if you don't roll the doors open!"

Wilder opened the inner door leading to the prototype and the guards unlocked and activated the motor-driven openers on the exterior doors. Wilder pulled himself up onto the Centurion's wing, peered into the cockpit, and grabbed the metal Zero-Halliburton suitcase on the seat. He snapped it open to confirm a lightweight pressurized suit and fishbowl helmet were indeed inside, then hopped into the cockpit.

"Sir, we'll get the ground crew to tow 'er out!"

"No time; step back!"

Wilder looked at the controls—they were several technology generations newer than the F-117A he'd flown over Iraq, but all recognizable thanks to his extensive reading about the aircraft and her systems. The instrumentation and controls were LCD panels and touch-screens, with a projection of key data in the heads-up display. He powered up and the panels came to life in a checkerboard of colors. The hypersonic engines sounded different from the jets he was used to—they were quieter, lower pitched. Tickling the throttle, he moved the Centurion forward onto the runway, motioned the guards closer, and shouted over the engines:

"One more thing, guys"—he pointed Lefty's pistol at them. "Pop the clips out of your side arms. Toss them to me."

The guards did as they were told. It wasn't necessary, but Wilder knew it would save their butts if they could say he stole the plane at gunpoint. Taxiing south to the far end of the main runway, he dialed Brent's cell phone number on Righty's phone. Brent answered on the fourth ring.

"Spaulding."

"I only got a few seconds, so let me do the talking—"

"Matt!?"

"Listen, with second-generation stealth, full invisibility depends on electronic countermeasures and a command craft controlling the jamming drones. If I knock the command craft out, their planes should show up on our radar. Won't light 'em up like a video game, but at least our guys will see *something* coming. I figure if I follow longitude seventy-seven west, I'll run right into the formation."

The whine of hypersonic engines in the background made it obvious Wilder wasn't just theorizing. Before Brent could ask any of the thousand questions he had, Colonel Chang took the cell phone from his hand. They were in the colonel's office, with an armed Security Forces officer standing at the door. Chang hadn't been convinced by Brent's earlier claim of ignorance about Wilder's activities, so when Brent tried to leave the base in a major hurry, Chang decided to reel him in.

"Wilder," he said into the phone, "it's Chang . . ."

"Sorry, sir," Wilder replied, "no time to explain." He hung up.

Brent hadn't explained either. Colonel Chang glared at him.

"If I'm not convinced in sixty seconds there's a rock-solid reason for this insanity, I swear to Christ I'll have him shot down."

Brent didn't doubt it.

"May take a bit more than a minute, sir, so bear with me."

Wilder reached the end of the runway, turned the Centurion around, and stopped. Pushing the cockpit canopy open, he jumped down onto the tarmac with the Halliburton suitcase and began donning the ultralight space suit and clear helmet. It was a tight fit—Wilder wore a forty-four long and the suit was about a forty-two regular. He climbed back into the cockpit and saw a line of vehicles speeding down the runway toward him, so he pulled on his gloves, twisted their wrist-rings tight, and closed the canopy. He pushed the throttle forward, creating the most intense acceleration he'd ever felt, and the Centurion become airborne in five hundred yards, screaming over the heads of his pursuers at close to mach one.

To avoid colliding with any other planes, he stayed below a thousand feet through the National Airport control zone. Then, breaking the sound barrier over Rockville, Maryland, he pointed the Centurion's nose skyward and shot up to 45,000 feet. Cruising northward, far above commercial traffic, invisible to all known radar, Wilder eased into a cruising speed of mach three and turned the two-way radio off; there'd be plenty of time to get his ass chewed if and when he landed. At a mere twenty-two miles a minute he put the aircraft through a few standard maneuvers to get a feel for how she handled, to familiarize himself with the controls, and to acclimate himself to the thrill of flying again.

Glancing down, he noticed several rows of unlit LCDs low and to the left of the main instrument array—the indicator panel for the missing flight-assist computer. The engineers were still testing the neural net, so it had not yet been installed. Several other components were also missing, including the onboard radar. With a nudge of the stick, the dual-mode ramjet/scramjet engines shot the Centurion to 85,000 feet, then 100,000, then 150,000. The sky went from blue to purple to the blackness of space, and with insufficient oxygen for the air-breathing jets the hydrogen-fuel engines took over. At practically the height of the space shuttle it became a whole new kind of flying for a former fighter jock. He banked to the right to look down on the blue expanse of the Hudson Bay and the deep green provinces of Ontario and Quebec. Photographs and TV never did the view justice. It took his breath away.

He ran the navigational math in his head: with Batu's formation traveling at mach five and the Centurion at her dizzying maximum speed of mach twelve, they were approaching each other at 4.2 miles per second and would rendezvous in fifteen to eighteen minutes over the northern end of Baffin Island. Since he would not be able to see the TAA aircraft on his instruments, he would need to be close enough to make visual contact. Finding them wouldn't be too difficult, however. If they were on a true heading along longitude west seventy-seven, the extreme precision of modern global positioning navigation guaranteed them to be within a few meters, east or west, of their chosen course. The Centurion would be invisible to TAA sensors as well. But in order to remain undetected once in visual range, Wilder resorted to a technique dating back to the flying aces of World War I. He veered off his true-north heading and climbed to 180,000 feet. He would hunt them with the sun at his back, using its glare to obscure his presence.

In the *Altun Ordu*, Batu Khan walked along the rows of control stations and Tactical Information Terminals. He wore a pressurized pilot's suit with the helmet off and his *shalwar qamiz* draped across his shoulders, kept in place with strips of Velcro. Occasionally, he would deliberately neglect to make positive contact between the floor and his magnetic boots and allow himself to float weightless for a moment. He could barely contain his excitement. This will be a Day of Glory the world will never forget, he thought.

Already, the *Altun Ordu* performed beyond expectation. She cruised in the twilight between atmosphere and space with the Temujin penetrators and Yesugei transport following twenty miles behind and twenty thousand feet below her. A dozen unmanned drones flew in front of her in a three-hundred-mile semicircle. The drones resembled thick, metal starfish measuring four feet across, with the same obsidian skin as the *Altun Ordu*, sensor lenses on each of their five pointed tips and emitter cones on their top and bottom. Their instruments included cameras and sensors for forward reconnaissance, wide-band electromagnetic emitters for radar jamming, and a core of high explosives—if necessary, they could be flown into enemy ground targets or aircraft with the destructive power of a two-thousand-pound conventional bomb. Batu had named them Duuas, after a stanza in the epic poem *The Secret History of Mongols*:

> . . . *Their grandsons were two brothers,*
> *Duua the one-eyed and Dobun the Clever.*
> *In the middle of Duua's forehead was one great eye.*
> *With this eye Duua could see a place so far away*
> *it could take three days to reach it.*

He smiled, thinking about his ancestors and the essential Mongol tactics of controlling the high ground and personally conducting the battle from that position. How proud they'd be of this craft, of this mission, of him. The Day of Glory would incorporate another principle of warfare applied with great success by the khans of old: The bolder your strike, the more the enemy will consider you too dangerous to counterattack.

Chu'tsai radioed to report he would soon arrive at an airfield near the TAA town of Talovka, five miles from the Russian border, to begin his part of their adventure. Batu could sense the nervousness in his friend's voice, but it did not sway his faith in Chu'tsai's ability to successfully oversee the key activities in perhaps the most audacious act of war in history.

"I wish you could see the *Altun Ordu* in action," Batu told him. "She exceeds my wildest fantasies."

Chu'tsai's worries about the magnitude of their plans still nagged at him, so Batu's reference to wild fantasies made him uncomfortable.

"I need your promise you'll stick to the one agreed-upon target, Batu. Especially since we'll have no way of knowing whether the attack will have its intended effect."

"It'll work, all right. As Cowling told us, Marsh is most likely to snap when facing a direct threat. My only regret is not being able to watch the arrogance wiped from his face."

Thirty-two

At two fifty-five P.M., Laura jogged up the steps of the Capitol South Metro station and emerged in the afternoon sunshine, half-expecting an entire Army division to be waiting to arrest her. She knotted her hair in a bun in an attempt to be less conspicuous, flagged a cab on New Jersey Avenue, and took it to the Capitol Building. At the main entrance she looked around for Brent, then crossed to the security desk.

"Has an Air Force officer named Brent Spaulding checked in with you?"

The Capitol Police guard, a clean-cut black kid of twenty named Babich, flipped through his visitor log and shook his head. Laura waited ten interminable minutes, then decided she must go it alone. She went back to the security desk.

"Please call Senator Jonathan Ballard's office and say Laura Bishop must speak to him immediately. It's a matter of the gravest urgency." Laura knew the phrase sounded melodramatic. Babich clearly thought the same thing, as he stifled a smile while dialing the phone.

A pretty legislative assistant from Ballard's old Brooklyn neighborhood led Laura to the senator's private office. He had the best suite on the Hill; Laura remembered seeing him on TV, saying it wasn't so long ago a black man like himself would not have been allowed to use the drinking fountain outside the door. Ballard smiled and shook Laura's hand. Her message from downstairs had certainly piqued his curiosity. As she sat on the sofa, facing a postcard view of the Mall and Washington Monument, she noticed one of her books on the coffee table.

"If you could inscribe that to my grandson, Derek, I would indeed be grateful."

"Of course."

Ballard noticed her hands were shaking as she took the Lanier tape recorder from her purse and put it on the table. She glanced at the door, wishing Brent would show up.

"Senator, I have a tape for you to hear. First I'll tell you the backstory to give it context. Due to my principal source's inability to join us, I must relate some of it secondhand. I can vouch for his integrity, however, and the firsthand evidence on the tape corroborates his story."

She briefly outlined Wilder's investigation of the Mad Yuppie killings. How he'd traced all the perpetrators to Rexford University, then to Professor Cowling, and how, when being tortured by Cowling, he'd learned about his secret test of a mutated LSD compound. There'd been thirty people in the test group, excluding Cowling himself, Laura said, with twenty-six accounted for.

"Senator, I'm here because I know the identity of one of the unaccounted-for test subjects. It's the President of the United States. What's worse, as part of some strange political agenda, Cowling informed Batu Khan of the President's condition."

Ballard leaned back in his chair. "Can you prove these extraordinary allegations?"

"Special Agent Wilder saw film of the test group taken in 1973," Laura said. "Burton Marsh was one of them." She skipped over the part about Wilder being under the influence of a hallucinogenic at the time. "As you know, he attended Rexford as an undergraduate that year."

"Along with about nine thousand other people. Where is this film?"

"Destroyed in the fire that consumed the Rexford chemistry building."

"I see. And where's Agent Wilder? This is a tale best told in the first person."

"Well, sir . . . I'm not presently in touch with Agent Wilder." Telling Ballard the Air Force had Wilder locked up in the Andrews brig would hardly bolster his credibility.

Ballard sighed. He found her claims almost impossible to believe and considered ending the conversation right then.

"Tell me about this tape of yours."

Laura dreaded relating this part of the story. But only by being honest about how she obtained the tape could she convince Ballard of its authenticity. Taking a deep breath, she told Ballard of her attempt to steal Marsh's VS tapes and how she left her portable phone in the VS Room. Ballard stared at her, dumbfounded. The pretty midwestern author sitting before seemed the least likely person imaginable for such escapades.

"I made the tape a bit more than an hour ago," she concluded. "The events they're discussing are still unfolding."

She ran the portion of the tape where President Marsh told Levinson about the detectable flaw in the TAA planes and the Svalbard radar station known only to him and Secretary of Defense Woodruff. She skipped ahead to the ExOp calculating the range and position of the TAA planes, and then to Marsh's insistence that no one in the U.S. government or military be informed. Finally, she played the moment Marsh smelled the lipstick and discovered her phone.

Ballard's expression of incredulity faded just a little, but didn't disappear.

"No, can't be . . . the Burton Marsh I know always has sound reasons for his decisions."

"That's the point, this isn't the Marsh you know," Laura said. "This insidious madness means he's capable of anything, especially during a crisis. We think Batu has sent his aircraft toward Washington specifically to take advantage of the President's volatility."

"This whole story is outrageous! Burton Marsh is one of the finest presidents ever to have served!"

"Please, Senator," Laura said, "I have no ulterior motives. It isn't political or personal; I'm very fond of Mrs. Marsh, and the President, too. But surely he could alert our military commanders without revealing our radar capability to the TAA."

"I'm sorry, Miss Bishop, but all you've got is hearsay about a discussion between Mr. Wilder and Professor Cowling, a missing film, and an alleged recording of the President in a private meeting that was at best made illegally. At worst, despite your claim it was recorded this afternoon, it could've been made a month or a year ago, or pieced together from several conversations. Still, I don't think you're deliberately trying to undermine the presidency, and I'll go so far as to concede that you believe what you're telling me . . . not that your belief makes it true—"

Ballard's intercom buzzed. Annoyed, he picked up the phone. "Thought I said I wasn't . . . No, put him through."

Laura appreciated the interruption—it would give her a moment to figure out how to convince Ballard. Obviously, she hadn't had much luck so far.

"Yes, Charles, hello," Ballard said.

He listened for almost a minute, muttering only the occasional "un-huh," or "I see," while his expression grew ever more dismayed. "Have you discussed this with anyone else?" he asked. "That's good. This must be conducted according to procedure and in utter secrecy. Best thing you and yours can do right now is sit tight, as difficult as that might be." With a sigh and a "thank you," he hung up and turned to Laura.

"That was Colonel Charles Chang, the OSI regional commander. He said he'd detained Agent Spaulding, which is why he did not meet you here."

Laura didn't like the sound of *detained.*

"I know Charles quite well," Ballard continued. "His integrity is beyond reproach. He told me he has information corroborating your story and that I should accept whatever you say with full assurance of its veracity."

Thank you Colonel Chang, Laura thought.

"He's made the difficult and, in my opinion, proper decision not to inform his superiors in the Air Force of these allegations until I've spoken to the President's cabinet. God forbid such concerns about President Marsh prove to be true, but I'm afraid we must behave as though they could be, and avoid all possibility that he could learn of our suspicions. After all, should he actually suffer from this horrible condition . . ."

"That's why Agent Wilder wanted me to bring this information directly to you."

"Yes, Agent Wilder . . ." Ballard shook his head. "Charles asked me to tell you Wilder escaped the Andrews brig and took off in a prototype hypersonic fighter in pursuit of the incoming planes."

Laura's breath caught in her throat. "Jesus, he'll end up killing himself!"

Her reaction told Ballard she had a personal relationship with Wilder.

"I'm sorry." He buzzed his assistant on the intercom. "Tell Judy to set up a conference call with Glendon Frost and Vice President Taylor. Frost isn't in town, so try his home number in Pennsylvania. No answer, or the Missus doesn't know where's he's at, call his girlfriend's apartment. Don't give up till he's on the line. Then I want everyone in the President's cabinet on another conference call, ready to be patched in when I say so. I don't care where they are, what they're doing; tell them they're waiting on me, the Speaker, and the VP. They're not to tell anyone we're calling, just relax till we get on. Now, write this down, I don't want you forgetting anyone: State, Treasury, Defense . . . no, scratch Woodruff, he's not available. Justice, Interior, Agriculture, Commerce, Labor, Health and Human Services, HUD, Transportation, Energy, Education, and Veterans' Affairs."

Ballard hung up and turned back to Laura. "Even with Colonel Chang's assurances, I'm not making any final judgments here. It's my responsibility to share this information with certain individuals as prescribed in the Constitution. It's their job to decide whether there's sufficient concern to consider invoking their powers under the Twenty-fifth Amendment."

Laura handed the Lanier to Senator Ballard. As they stood up, she noticed he seemed much older than she'd first thought.

At first, the Duua drone looked like a small black satellite silhouetted against the bright earth below, then Wilder realized what it was and quickly arced around to let it pass. Seeing the Duua encouraged him—it meant he'd found the correct heading and, more important, that the TAA indeed used jamming drones to augment their stealth capabilities. He slowed down to mach six and checked the charging status of the Centurion's speed-of-light weapons systems. Hypersonic velocities made it too difficult to target and fire conventional munitions such as air-to-air missiles, so the plane carried an array of prototype, high-power microwave cannons—three emitters set forward, two aiming to the rear, and one aiming downward. Wilder had set the capacitor storage system to charge when he took off, so he expected it to be at full-power status by now. Stunned, he saw the HPM only had a nineteen percent charge.

A status check of the weapons systems revealed the problem: Only five of the twenty HPM power capacitors had been installed. Enough to fire a few bursts to test the emitters, but certainly not enough to blast the TAA control craft out of the sky.

Wilder had no time to beat himself up for not noticing this sooner—glancing outside, he saw a ghostlike silhouette at one o'clock, thirty degrees down. The *Altun Ordu*. He slowed the Centurion again to match the command craft's speed, came around to keep the sun at his back, and scanned for escort fighters in the star-speckled blackness of space above and the bright, hazy blue of the atmosphere below. Seeing none, he couldn't help pausing for a moment to admire the *Altun Ordu*, with its obsidian-colored fuselage and fan-jointed wings swept back like a hawk's in a dive. Without his HPM weapons he needed a Plan B, but came up with nothing except flying into the *Altun Ordu* kamikaze-style, a very unappealing option. Then he noticed the oxygen-generating cylinders under the skin of his space suit, and Plan B appeared fully formed in his head.

With the sun at his shoulder, he moved closer to get a better look at the *Altun Ordu*'s configuration. Fortunately, she had no windows on her flanks; only the cockpit had a direct view outside. The sun's glare would obscure him to within a thousand yards. If he could move into position in a split second, without overshooting and ending up in their line of vision on the other side, he could cruise literally inches from her without being detected.

The *Altun Ordu*'s design was so aerodynamic she appeared to be a solid piece of metal, making it very difficult for Wilder to find his objective—a hatch or entryway. Finally, he took it on faith that like every other aircraft her size, she had a service panel somewhere on her underbelly. He zipped the Centurion directly behind and below the *Altun Ordu*, then inched forward beneath her. A third of the way along he spotted a faint, three-foot-square seam with a recessed air-hatch handle so tightly integrated with the hull that it was almost invisible.

The next step depended on the Centurion's autopilot having the same programmable quirk as several other prototype fighters Wilder knew about. He checked to see if it would interface with the sensor arrays; it did, so he filtered out all data except the proximity sensors and set the autopilot to maintain a steady fifteen-foot distance from the *Altun Ordu*. Although not really meant for such use, Wilder hoped the autopilot would hold, otherwise the Centurion would splat against the bottom of Batu's command craft like billion-dollar roadkill.

He flipped on the autopilot and felt the Centurion go rigid with the computerized control, then he carefully checked his flight suit. He'd put it on recklessly fast and didn't want to find out the hard way that a boot or a glove hadn't fully sealed. Digging Lefty's pistol out from under the seat, he secured it to his suit with a Velcro strap. In space, Wilder thought as he opened the Centurion's canopy, no one can hear you say "Oh, fuck . . ."

He half expected a rush of air or some other tangible indication of his great speed, but felt nothing in the stillness of space. He unclipped his seat harness and pressed his feet against the bulkhead beneath the rudder controls, so he wouldn't float out of the cockpit, and looked up at his goal: the small, recessed twist-handle in the *Altun Ordu*'s service hatch. Without a space-walk tether, Wilder had exactly one chance to push off from the Centurion, float fifteen feet through empty space, and grab hold of that handle. The underside of the *Altun Ordu* was smooth as glass. If he missed, he'd slide along its length and tumble into its white-hot rocket exhaust. Or he'd float helplessly away until his orbit decayed, which, at this relatively low altitude, would happen almost immediately. With those cheerful thoughts in mind, Wilder steadied himself with the edge of the canopy. His first impulse was to jump hard and fast, but he remembered astronauts saying the worst thing about weightlessness was overdoing it, losing control. So he stepped lightly, just enough to guide him in the right direction.

There is something instinctually terrifying about losing contact with all other masses, because it is so unprecedented in human experience. Wilder floated as his own tiny satellite for a little over ten seconds. His hands, awkward and clumsy in their gloves, stretched to grasp the handle. He bumped into the hull of the *Altun Ordu* much harder than he expected and clawed at the handle, a six-inch-wide circle with a straight bar across it. He could feel himself spinning and sliding, overshooting his mark, and he tried to hug the wide, smooth hull to slow his movement away from the handle. Just before bouncing off into empty space, he twisted his foot around and lodged the tip of his boot underneath the handle. His drift stopped abruptly and he floated upside down beneath the hatch. Wilder let his body go limp to avoid any movement that would knock him loose from his tenuous hold. He swung his body around, positioned himself perpendicular to the hull, then carefully drew his knees to his chest and reached again for the handle.

The space suit would not let him crouch down tight enough to grab it, and he didn't want to release his toehold on a solid object, but having no choice he slipped his foot out and lightly tapped the handle as he did. It sent him into a high-diver's somersault spin, and as his head came around to the *Altun Ordu* he grabbed for the handle. This time he got his left index finger under it. Working all his fingers into the handle, he steadied himself against the hull and turned it a quarter of the way counterclockwise. The green light beside it went off, a red one came on, and the hatch door opened. Wilder ran his fingers along its edges, searching for the magnetic sensor that would warn the cockpit crew the hatch was open. Feeling a half-inch metal lump in the otherwise smooth hatch lip, he held Lefty's pistol alongside the magnet to deactivate it. With any luck, the cockpit alert cut off so quickly it would be disregarded as a false alarm. Wilder swung himself into a small airlock, closed the hatch behind him, and used some emergency oxygen tanks to pressurize the airlock without engaging the regular controls.

Thirty-three

"**W**hat the hell . . . ?" Secretary of Defense Woodruff said, looking at the VS screen.

Marsh, who'd been preoccupied on the phone with the ExOps trying to locate Laura and the neighbors whose number she'd called, turned to face the screen. Three new pairs of yellow lines appeared on the map over the TAA. One pair originated in the town of Talovka and headed northwest; the others traveled due west from the towns of Agartu and Saykhin, also less than ten miles from the Russian border.

Another line on the phone rang, extension eight-twelve, and Marsh clicked over to it. "What the fuck's going on?" he asked.

"Six more TAA aircraft have taken wing, sir: three penetrators and three small transports, traveling in pairs, low and subsonic. They appear destined for the Russian interior."

"Keep us posted," Marsh said, frowning, and hung up.

"Russia? What for?" Levinson wondered.

Marsh had no idea, although numerous possibilities raced through his head. He didn't want to talk about it. He had too much on his mind already: the transmission from Laura's cell phone; Batu's planes approaching; and, most of all, steeling himself to take his transcendent plan all the way to its completion. He tossed his jacket onto a chair and loosened his tie.

"It makes complete sense," the President said. "He's overflying Moscow, too. Confirming they can't see his new planes either."

Woodruff ran his finger along the planes' routes. "Sir, I don't think they're going to Moscow. Follow the lines: They're heading toward these cities along the Volga River: Saratov, Kamyshin, and Volgograd."

"So? They're nothing but farming and industrial centers," Levinson said.

"According to yesterday's Shell Game report, the Russians moved at least one SS-twenty-five mobile launcher to each of those cities within the last seventy-two hours," Woodruff replied.

"You're hypothesizing, Stanley," Marsh said, but he wondered if the secretary of defense might be right.

"Even if there's only the remotest possibility of Batu Khan making a try for those weapons, we have to warn the Russians, offer them air and intelligence support," Woodruff continued. "Batu's forces have less than a hundred miles to go, they'll be there in ten minutes!"

"I'm no more willing to demonstrate our surveillance capabilities to the Russians than I am to the TAA," he replied. "Not until I'm absolutely certain there's an overwhelming reason to do so!"

"We've always feared such a move by the TAA; the Russians will be caught entirely off guard!" Woodruff said.

"It's true, Mr. President," Levinson said. "If Batu is not stopped today, we run the risk of dealing with him as a nuclear power tomorrow."

"All right, that's enough!" Marsh glared angrily at his chief of staff. "I have no intention of allowing the Trans-Altaic Alliance to become a superpower, but I won't interfere until I'm certain of his intentions."

"What if we find out too late to do anything?"

"I know what I'm doing!" The President sat on the sofa but then, increasingly agitated, he shot back to his feet. "Fucking Russians didn't lift a finger to sponsor the U.N. resolutions against the TAA! Instead of supporting my deadline for withdrawal and joining a coalition against Batu, they said I overstepped my authority, have no business policing their part of the world. As far as I'm concerned, they deserve whatever happens to them."

Levinson and Woodruff stood dumbstruck, simply not believing the President of the United States could harbor such beliefs.

At three-fifteen P.M., Senator Ballard's assistant opened his office door to let Laura in. She had been pacing the hallway for fifteen minutes. Although it seemed an eternity, she now worried too short a time had passed for the cabinet to agree to take action. Senator Ballard rose when she entered. He held a worn, pamphlet-sized copy of the U.S. Constitution. Earlier, while waiting for his conference call to come together, he'd reread the first paragraph of Article Twenty-five, ratified on February 10, 1967:

> *Whenever the Vice President and a majority of either the principal officers of the executive departments or of such other body as Congress may by law provide, transmit to the President pro tempore of the Senate and the Speaker of the House of Representatives their written declaration that the President is unable to discharge the powers and duties of his office, the Vice President shall immediately assume the powers and duties of the office as Acting President. . . .*

Ballard gestured for Laura to sit down.

"The Speaker and I conferred with Vice President Taylor and eight cabinet secretaries, the most we could locate on such short notice. Nonetheless, eight of fourteen is sufficient to make a majority. I related your allegations, without editorial comment, and I played some excerpts from your tape."

"And the response?"

"General agreement the allegations are troubling and warrant careful consideration. Everyone found Secretary of Defense Woodruff's unavailability particularly frustrating. We'd hoped he could comment on the feasibility of the TAA actually having the kind of aircraft discussed on the tape. So, rather than remove him from a meeting with the President and risk jeopardizing the secrecy of our inquiry, we settled instead for the opinion of the chairman of the Joint Chiefs, General Mancini. I asked him, hypothetically, to gauge the possibility of an undetectable penetration of American airspace by TAA warplanes. He assured us all current intelligence indicates they do not possess such capability."

"But you heard the tape," Laura said, "it's all so secret Marsh's own chief of staff didn't know about it!"

"Miss Bishop, these are proceedings of profound gravity. The cabinet members need tangible proof of imminent threat to justify invoking the Twenty-fifth Amendment in less than an hour. Without it, prudence demands they examine the issues in a more appropriate time frame. Especially since they also lack conclusive proof of the condition from which you allege the President suffers."

"Sitting on his hands while denying his senior advisers crucial information seems like proof enough to me, sir."

"Look, the secretaries and the Vice President believe honest, well-intentioned individuals have raised troubling, if unsubstantiated, concerns about the psychological well-being of the President. They will investigate those concerns in a sober, cautious fashion. They did agree to stand by for the next hour should anything occur that would change their decision."

Laura felt bitterly disappointed; yet if she were in the cabinet, she'd probably reach the same conclusion. She picked up the Lanier tape recorder on Ballard's desk.

"Maybe if you let General Mancini listen to the tape instead of considering a hypothetical situation he'd have a different opinion."

"Constitution's real clear about it: Anything to do with judging the President's fitness to serve is strictly a civilian affair, not military. It's limited to the Vice President and fourteen other people in the Executive Branch. That recording is now privileged material as part of their investigation."

He held his hand out, expecting Laura to return the Lanier.

"I'm sorry, Senator. If you don't want Mancini to hear this, you'll have to call Security."

"Don't force me to do something as distasteful as have you arrested. I don't care how certain you are of the President's incapacity. It is not for you or me to decide."

Ballard stepped slowly toward her. Laura glanced over at the door, weighing whether or not to make a run for it. Ballard shook his head.

"You wouldn't get twenty feet before they stopped you."

He stepped closer and took the Lanier from her hand.

"I'm sorry. Good afternoon, Miss Bishop."

Laura ran down the stairwell to the main lobby and crossed to the guard station. The Capitol Cop who checked her in, Babich, looked up from *Car & Driver* magazine.

"Is there a place I can make a phone call in private?"

Babich pointed to the Security office at the end of a short hallway. Without the tape Laura could never make her case to General Mancini, but she had one other person she could turn to.

The inside door of the *Altun Ordu*'s airlock led to a small, isolated equipment room below the main cabins. Floating weightless, Wilder oriented himself into a vertical position using handholds on the wall, then removed his helmet and clipped it to his belt, keeping it close should a hasty departure be necessary. He heard no sound except the muffled rumble of the engines and, somewhere up above, hushed voices. He cracked open a sliding door, looked around, then went through to the next compartment, also deserted. Spotting another airlock on the wall, he peered through thick glass on the door into a large open area—a hangar for several spare Duua drones and a small hypersonic fighter. The fighter, one of the new Temujin penetrators, had the same deep metallic black coloring as the *Altun Ordu* and the same unique fanwing design. At rest, its wings were closed, so it looked more like a missile than an aircraft. It had no markings other than a stylized rendering of a shooting star on its hull.

With any luck, Wilder would not need to go near the occupied cabins above. He would find the equipment that transmitted controls to the drones somewhere in the unoccupied decks below, disable it, and make the TAA planes appear, however faintly, on American radar. Since the drones flew in front of and below the command craft, he figured the transmitter would be near the front landing gear. As a bonus, he'd try to cripple the command craft itself and send it plunging into the atmosphere after he returned to the Centurion.

He wriggled into a maintenance passageway, a triangular crawl space flush against the hull and crisscrossed with steel support beams. Pulling himself rapidly along on the beams, he headed toward the nose of the aircraft. As he passed the hangar area the passageway opened up into a hold, six feet high and as wide as the hull of the plane. Three rows of squat, desk-sized black boxes lined the open area and the sharp, burnt-metal-and-ozone smell of ultra-high-voltage equipment hung heavy in the air. Wilder recognized them as huge versions of the high-power microwave capacitor cells in his Centurion. A deep transformer-like hum emanated from them, and he felt a prickly electrostatic charge. Signs in several languages warned of the danger of proximity to charged capacitor cells. Unfortunately, to get where he wanted, Wilder had to go right through them. Gliding midair carried too much risk of accidental contact with a cell, so he walked slowly between them, holding himself steady with his feet on the floor and his hands on the ceiling. He had to stay exactly in the middle of the rows between the cells; power would arc through the air into his body if he came too close. Intent on his task, he missed a glint of movement ahead.

One of Batu Khan's Khaldun Elite, a huge man in a gold robe, lunged at him, swinging a shiny steel scimitar at his midsection. Wilder pushed off from the floor back toward the power cells and the scimitar hit a crossbeam with a clang and a spark. He clung to the ceiling with his hands and feet, wary of the power cells, but the Khaldun launched himself scimitar-first toward Wilder. He was oblivious to their danger and Wilder could see why at once: The Khaldun had that eerie, serene, Cowling-induced smile on his face.

Wilder rolled across the ceiling to avoid the blade, then grabbed the big man's wrist with one hand and his throat with the other. As they struggled face-to-face, choking and gouging, Wilder stared at the Khaldun's long, braided Fu Manchu mustache, tied at the tips with goat-hide thongs. Absent gravity to dampen their struggles, they bounced wildly around the top of the hold. Each time the scimitar strayed down toward the power cells, an arc of electricity threatened to jump to it.

Wilder bent back one of the Khaldun's fingers, breaking it. The scimitar floated out of his hand, then Wilder pressed his thumbs into the Khaldun's Adam's apple. The Khaldun kicked at him, trying to break free; fortunately, the awkward state of weightlessness negated much of the Khaldun's amazing strength. They drifted closer to the power cells and Wilder felt his hair crackling from the static charge. Suddenly, a second powerful pair of hands grabbed him—the fight had attracted another Khaldun Elite. Their iron grasp made struggling completely futile.

The Khaldun took him up to the main cabin, floating him between them as they walked carefully along the passageway toward Batu's quarters. They made sure each footstep made contact with the metal floor surface—no one wanted to drift awkwardly into the air in His Excellency's presence.

The guard in front of the felt-flap doorway to Batu's quarters had an AK-74U machine gun clipped to his belt, but held in his hand a weapon posing far less danger of puncturing a spaceplane's hull—a steel crossbow. He gestured for the two Khaldun to bring Wilder inside. The one who fought Wilder bowed, put his hands behind his back and snapped his broken finger back into place, fearful Batu would notice his injury. Batu, livid, waited in the center of his quarters, arms crossed, feet planted on the floor.

"Stand him up! Let me see him!"

The Khaldun rotated Wilder upright, and he grinned at Batu and his colorfully garbed guards.

"Little early for Halloween, ain't it, guys?"

Batu took the sword from the second Khaldun's scabbard and handed it to him.

"If he speaks again, except to answer a question, cut off his hand. Sit him down."

The Khaldun grabbed Wilder by the helmet-ring of his space suit, shoved him down onto a three-legged stool bolted to the floor, and lap-belted him to it. If Wilder hadn't been in Batu's private sanctum he wouldn't have believed it existed. A round space fifteen feet in diameter, its walls and ceiling draped with green felt, it held all the contents of Batu's *ger*: his cot and table, electronics cabinet, even the hand-painted map of the TAA and the meteorite that streaked across the Siberian sky on the night of his birth. The only additional touch was a huge, sealed, two-hundred-gallon tropical fish tank built into one of the walls. Chu'-tsai had laughed for an hour when he saw it in the *Altun Ordu*'s design plans, knowing exactly why Batu wanted such an outrageous extravagance: *Star Trek*'s Captain Picard had a fish tank in his ready room on the Starship *Enterprise*.

Although Wilder had heard Batu personally conducted battle operations, it still came as a surprise to be face-to-face with the son of a bitch.

"How did you get on my aircraft?" Batu demanded. He presumed Wilder had stowed away back in the mountains. "*Why* are you on my aircraft?"

Wilder looked at the Khaldun holding a sword over his wrist. "Easy with the blade there, Sparky, I'm answering a question." He turned to Batu. "How much tax money you sink into this new air force of yours?"

"No one in the Trans-Altaic Alliance pays taxes! There is a tithe to the Empire. All citizens contribute with enthusiasm, pride, and love."

"Well, your enthusiastic hundred billion dollars or so didn't buy what was advertised: second-generation stealth."

It took all Batu's control not to slit Wilder from chin to groin with his dagger. Wilder's glibness and lack of fear infuriated him, but Batu clenched his jaw and let him continue.

"We've been tracking all seven planes since they took off. We saw them converge on the seventy-seventh parallel and we know they're heading to Washington."

"You've been listening to our flight plans."

"Sorry, pal, I just got here. You were pretty good, stealing aircraft and engine designs and making us think your development programs were failing. But our guys were better. They made sure the information you got was a little bit tainted—that's why our radar can see your composite airframes. Might as well have neon signs on their wings saying Eat at Joe's."

As Wilder hoped, Batu tried to mask his amazement while growing angrier by the moment.

"Marsh is gonna be thrilled when they shoot this tub out of the sky and he learns you were on it. Think how popular he'll be. They'll be adding his face to Mount Rushmore by next Tuesday."

Since no American radar except the one under Marsh's control could see Batu's planes, and since Marsh refused to intercept them, Wilder figured telling Batu otherwise seemed to be the one way to cause him to second-guess his plans. Alter them. Make a mistake.

Batu studied Wilder carefully. Why would he admit the Americans knew they were coming? Did he think he'd make the TAA warplanes turn around and go home?

"You're a liar and Marsh is a coward! He struts and lectures on television every night, yet he cannot look me in the eye!"

"He was probably trying not to laugh, knowing you believed all that shit your drug-pushing pal Cowling told you. In fact, we've *all* been having a good yock about how gullible you people are."

"I know of nobody named Cowling . . ."

Like hell, Wilder thought. Batu looked like he'd been kicked in the balls at the mention of the name. As with the TAA stealth capabilities, Wilder hoped to make Batu start doubting himself in case any aspect of his plans depended on Marsh's condition.

Batu struggled to remain poker-faced while thinking it all through. Cowling's story about Marsh could *not* be part of an American disinformation plot. The Professor had e-mailed them a compressed MPEG video of the young Marsh participating in the test, so they'd seen it with their own eyes. And Cowling had a forty-year history of countercultural beliefs; he'd supported the TAA's goals from its inception.

But if anything else Wilder said were true, how much of the actions already under way would change? Not much, Batu decided. Especially his plans in Russia.

"So. You came all this way to freely tell me I'm a fool and your President is expecting us?"

"No, actually, I'm here to fuck up your day . . ."

Wilder kicked the Khaldun holding the sword, then pulled the softball-sized iron meteorite from its wooden stand and threw it at the fish tank, five feet away. The glass shattered, and two hundred gallons of water, fish, sand, and aquatic plants gushed out. The weightless water coalesced in the air into thousands of various-sized spheres, from larger than basketballs to tiny droplets. The whole room suddenly seemed under water. The more Batu and his Khaldun Elite pushed the floating liquid away from their faces, the faster it broke apart into smaller globules and choked the air. It felt like being inside an enormous lava lamp.

Holding his breath, Wilder unclasped his lap belt and sprung toward the Khaldun with the sword. He knew if either Khaldun got hold of him, they could literally break him in half. Quickly twisting the sword around in the disoriented man's hand, he ran him through the abdomen with it, wrested it loose, and zoomed for the door. The other Khaldun lunged at Wilder, who slashed him across the neck. A stream of red liquid orbs spewed from the wound, intermingling with the floating water. Batu kicked off from the floor and grabbed Wilder's leg. Locked in battle, they drifted to the ceiling and became tangled in its draped felt folds. Batu slashed at Wilder with his dagger, putting a tiny slit in the arm of Wilder's space suit. When he tried to bring the blade down into Wilder's throat, Wilder held it back with the flat side of the sword. Batu was amazingly strong—the dagger tip cut into Wilder's skin and little dots of blood streamed out. Wilder got his foot against Batu's chest and shoved him away. Batu tumbled backward, rolling along the felt-draped ceiling.

The guard outside the door pushed through the curtains. Wilder emerged from the cloud of weightless water and the guard fired a short metal arrow at him with his crossbow, narrowly missing him. Wilder buried the sword in the guard's chest and grabbed the small AK-74U machine gun off his belt. Pulling himself along the ceiling, he worked his way toward the front of the *Altun Ordu*. By the time he reached the cockpit, the flight crew expected him. Hiding behind the bulkheads separating the cockpit from the main cabin, the copilot began closing the airtight emergency hatch to keep Wilder out, while the pilot fired at him with his crossbow.

A flashing red light and Klaxon went off as the air hatch between the cockpit and main cabin began to slide closed. Wilder held himself steady against the cabin wall with his feet and, aiming carefully, fired the machine gun through the closing air hatch at the windshield. The special glass could withstand hypersonic speeds or the point-blank impact of one shot, but not fifty in the exact same spot. It chipped under the shower of bullets, then a hairline web of cracks appeared. With a snap and a tornadolike whoosh of air, the glass fractured. The pilot and copilot were sucked outside, the sound of their screams cut off when they hit the vacuum of space. Wilder clung to the bulkhead to keep from getting sucked into the cockpit through the still-closing emergency air hatch, then it closed and the rush of outgoing air ceased in the rest of the aircraft.

Wilder slammed a fresh magazine in the machine gun and felt the aircraft begin to drift and shimmy. By eliminating any way to enter the cockpit without depressurizing the entire plane, he'd doomed the *Altun Ordu*. Soon she would nose down toward Earth, her low, fragile orbit transforming into a death spiral. He had to prevent Batu from escaping in the small fighter stored below.

The realization of the *Altun Ordu*'s fate—and their own—spread through the crew. Everyone stayed at their stations. Theirs would be a glorious death, in service of their khan. Khaldun Elite, meanwhile, implored Batu to hurry to the Temujin in the hangar.

"Find the American first. I want his death before I leave!" Pushing a technician aside, Batu keyed the microphone at a console. He warned his pilots, following in the Temujin penetrators and Yesugei transport, they might be visible to American radar. He ordered them to follow their flight plan, as there would be no further direction from the *Altun Ordu*.

Chu'tsai, listening half a world away, hailed Batu on a private channel and asked what happened.

"I'll tell you everything over lamb and *koumiss* when we celebrate our victory tonight." Too enraged to talk any further and eager to find Wilder, Batu clicked off.

Moving through a narrow space behind a panel of electronics, Wilder heard Batu's voice nearby. He backtracked and tried to get close enough for a clear shot, but a technician spotted him and shouted to the Khaldun surrounding Batu. Two gave chase, firing at Wilder with their crossbows, so he climbed down into the control rooms below the main cabin. Crossing to the airlock on the wall, he peered through the window into the hangar holding Batu's Temujin. A cluster of techs were flight-prepping the craft while four Khaldun guarded it. One spotted Wilder in the window and alerted the others. They rushed the airlock; Wilder sought cover but couldn't find any. A line of razor-sharp metal arrows chewed up the floor inches from him. He clipped the machine gun to his belt and flew across the corridor, just ahead of the arrows, toward the control room and the outside hatch. With the Khaldun close behind, he unclipped his helmet from his belt and put it on, then climbed down into the airlock leading to the exterior hull. He sealed it and, inside the airlock, punched the "depressurize" button just as three Khaldun entered the room above him. They tried to open the inner door. Too late. The outer door on the hull opened and Wilder dropped down into empty space. It appeared as though he'd made a clean escape, until he noticed a small, foggy spray of oxygen leaking from the nick Batu had made in his space suit.

In accordance with the latest attempt at national sobriety, all the bars in the Russian city of Kamyshin closed at midnight. Several men stumbling home along the narrow, riverside streets stopped singing and looked up as they heard a low aircraft approaching. They watched in amazement as a Yesugei transport passed slowly overhead, dropping one Incursion Tube over the docks and two more over the central city. Forty Khaldun Commandos and twelve Khaldun Horsemen emerged from the ITs. Flying in the transport, designated Yesugei-K to differentiate it from the one heading for Washington, the Yesugei-W, Chu'tsai rushed from one situation screen to another, excitedly barking orders into his wireless headset, directing the movements of the men below. The Khaldun first destroyed the main telephone switching equipment and jammed all radio and cellular frequencies. Another team secured the entrance to the docks, while others commandeered the tower and an enormous Russian AN-24 Ruslan transport plane at the airport, twelve miles from town. At the docks, they incinerated a makeshift barracks housing the Russian soldiers responsible for guarding the missiles; concurrently, the lead Khaldun team blasted their way into the riverside warehouse with automatic weapons and grenades, facing only a handful of surprised Russian soldiers. Just as Woodruff had predicted, the same scene played out in two other cities along the Volga: Saratov to the north and Volgograd to the south. In moments, the powerful Khaldun had neutralized the Russian forces.

The blitz cut off all electricity and the Khaldun lit flares to illuminate the warehouse. Two Transporter-Erector-Launchers, dark, hulking, ugly monsters on fourteen tractor-sized wheels, sat in the center of the otherwise empty space. They stood taller and wider than a train locomotive, almost a block long, painted in camouflage colors. Each carried a three-stage RS-12M intercontinental ballistic missile mounted horizontally on a hydraulically operated launcher, 70 feet long, 5.9 feet in diameter, and weighing 99,670 pounds, tipped with a single 550-kiloton nuclear warhead. Two pairs of TAA engineers strapped themselves to the side of the launchers. Following the Soviet breakup, the United States and other Western countries had set about hiring key people from the USSR's nuclear missile program to keep rogue powers like Iran, Iraq, and the TAA from employing them. This removed most of the nuclear physicists from the open market, but not the mathematicians and engineers who had created the guidance systems. These same men working for Batu had a decade ago helped design the electronics for the SS-25s. Now, rather than trying to break the Permissive Action Link's 128-bit encryption algorithms, the engineers had built duplicate PAL circuitry and preprogrammed it with their own launch codes and targeting information.

While the engineers worked, the Khaldun started the twelve-cylinder, Shumerlya-made diesel engines on the TELs and drove them out of the warehouse. One headed for the Kamyshin airport, where they would load the missile onto the AN-124 Ruslan transport, the aircraft the Russians themselves used to move the TELs during their bimonthly shell game, and fly it to the TAA. The other TEL lumbered slowly toward the residential sections west of the city. Batu had chosen its destination, the blockwide, cobblestone Borodin Plaza, for several reasons: Being enclosed within narrow streets in the most densely populated area of town it would complicate any attempt by the Russians to retake the missile by force, and it had a clear view of the southwestern sky. Also, his engineers would need the transit time for the delicate task of swapping the PAL circuitry.

The engineers radioed Chu'tsai, reporting that the process of removing the original circuitry had begun. The difficult part would be in replacing it without tripping the disabling device, installed to prevent such tampering, which would render the missile unusable. Despite this danger, however, they assured him the missiles would be under their full control by the time they reached their destinations.

Thirty-four

Wilder had only seconds to get into the Centurion and repressurize its cockpit before his air supply dropped lethally low—the hole in his suit threatened to rip wide open, just like the windshield of the *Altun Ordu*. To make matters worse, the *Altun Ordu* began slowly spiraling as her orbit decayed, with the Centurion circling her like a moon a scant fifteen feet from her underside. Wilder crouched against the hatch and prepared to leap back toward the Centurion, but the bright Earth and the black sky flip-flopping in and out of view made him dizzy and disoriented. Keeping his eyes fixed on the Centurion's open canopy, he gently pushed off. He floated across open space and scrambled for a handhold as he impacted the front of the cockpit. The pressure loss was so severe in his suit that he came close to blacking out, and his arms and legs felt like lead as he struggled to pull himself inside.

Once in his seat, he closed the Centurion's canopy and the cockpit slowly began to pressurize. Punchy from oxygen deprivation, he fumbled to maneuver away from the *Altun Ordu* fast enough so that her wings wouldn't come around and swat the Centurion like a mosquito. He waited until they were properly oriented in reference to the Earth then disengaged the autopilot, switched to manual control, and hit the throttle. The Centurion shot ahead of the spinning *Altun Ordu*, just missing her left wing as it spun past.

He flew back up toward the sun, anticipating that Batu Khan would order a few of his fighters to break formation and hunt him down. Instead, Batu himself emerged from the *Altun Ordu*'s hangar in his Temujin penetrator and flew at him. Wilder cut into an evasive arc and shoved the stick forward. Combat flying without the flight-assist neural net, he thought, should be a *real* hayride. Batu took off in pursuit, now appreciating Chu'tsai's insistence that he practice in simulators and air tunnels. The hypersonic Temujin compared to his old MiG was like a Ferrari compared to a motor scooter.

Batu couldn't bear to glance back as the *Altun Ordu* entered the exoatmosphere in a spinning free fall. A cone-shaped stream of everhotter air appeared at her nose. Her black skin glowed like molten metal in a forge. First her graceful, delicate wings succumbed, turning orangewhite and crumbling away from the fuselage in pieces. Then her body began to disintegrate. As she streaked ever faster toward the earth, a blinding, cometlike cowl of flame obscured her death.

As hard as the Temujin tried to overtake the Centurion, Wilder kept ahead of him. An audible alarm and a heads-up indicator told him Batu's weapon-aiming sensors were sweeping the Centurion. Wilder went into a dive just as Batu fired his HPM cannon and saw the concentrated energy beam as it streaked over his head, distorting the view of the stars behind it. He planned to dodge the fire, either until Batu got tired of chasing him or until he ran down the Temujin's power capacitors. Then he could inflict some damage with what little juice he had in the Centurion's HPM cannons. Relieved at how readily his Red Flag flight-combat training came back, he feigned to the left several times, always trying to keep Batu out of his blind side. Again Batu fired, missing the Centurion by only a few feet.

Wilder banked and turned, climbing past the Temujin, and Batu stuck with him through an intense, ultra-high-speed game of dodgem. After a few passes Batu noticed the particular pattern to Wilder's movements—the American always tried to keep him to the right. He fell back, letting Wilder put some distance between them. Then he accelerated full throttle, tipped his wings as if going to the right, and cut across to the left. Wilder went into a power-dive—a split-second too late. The outer edge of the energy stream from Batu's HPM cannon irradiated the underside of the Centurion. The energy wave rocked the plane; every electronic system spiked and shut down, then the engines coughed to a stop. Batu saw the Centurion's engine exhaust ports and instrumentation go dark and she went into an out-of-control, end-overend spin.

Wilder resisted the impulse to wrestle her out of the deadly spin. His only hope of survival was playing possum—letting his aircraft fall toward the atmosphere like a lump of lead. Batu watched with great satisfaction as the Centurion plummeted. In moments she would suffer the same fiery fate as his *Altun Ordu*. He turned as something momentarily blocked the sun—the other four Temujin penetrators and Yesugei transport catching up to him. The Yesugei pilot radioed Batu and gently reminded him of their tight schedule. Batu, his mind back on the mission, ordered his pilots to follow him to a new heading and altitude in order to avoid detection. With one last glance at Wilder's out-of-control Centurion spinning from sight, he took his place in front of the formation and they streaked away.

Standing near the VS Room door, the President eyed Woodruff and Levinson suspiciously. He hated having them there; he knew they were analyzing and judging his every word and gesture. Despite this, he'd ordered them to stay, ostensibly to monitor the progress of the TAA flyover, but in actuality because he didn't trust them to keep their mouths shut about it.

Levinson and Woodruff stared ashen-faced at the yellow lines on the three-dimensional globe, still heading due south along the west seventy-seventh parallel. At this rate Batu's planes would be over Washington in an hour. Unlike the TAA aircraft, Wilder's Centurion contained no flaw in its stealth material and carried its electronic countermeasures onboard, so it remained invisible even to its creators' radar. Also, on the VS screen they could see one TAA Yesugei and its Temujin escort now circling each of the three cities along the Volga River. Woodruff took no pleasure in his prediction coming to pass. Rather, he and Levinson watched anxiously for any sign of a Russian response. Both men had been friends with Marsh for over twenty years, leading them to the same conclusion: He must have a damn good reason for his behavior. If it were only a little outside the norm they'd chalk it up to bad judgment. But this was so unlike anything he'd ever done they could only assume he would pull a rabbit out of his hat at the very last minute and dazzle them. Except the last minute fast approached and there were no rabbits in sight.

"Sir," Woodruff said, "take a look at this." Annoyed, Marsh crossed to the screen.

"One of the planes approaching us just disappeared," Woodruff told him. Indeed, Marsh now saw only six yellow lines instead of seven. The phone rang and extension eight-twelve lit up. Marsh put the ExOp tech on the speaker box.

"Mr. President, we lost tracking on what we believe was the TAA command craft."

"We noticed. Find it."

"It appears the aircraft burned up in the atmosphere. There was a very brief signature on regular radar. They're reporting it as a meteor."

"What happened?"

"We have no idea."

"Figure it out and get back to me."

One less plane now approaching should've been good news, but it made Marsh nervous. He didn't like mysteries; he just wanted to run down the fucking clock until the planes arrived in Washington so that everything could get started.

"I have the strength," Marsh thought to himself, then turned away from the others, rattled, as he realized he'd said it out loud.

Levinson, noticing the President sweating, turned the VS Room thermostat down a few degrees. Woodruff turned his attention back to the TAA activities in Russia.

"Let's presume Batu is planning a commando action. His forces are surely on the ground by now. If they follow their usual procedure of crippling the telephone system and jamming the radio spectrum, it might be hours before anyone outside the affected areas knows of the invasion. We could see what's happening if we moved a camera satellite over the Volga . . ."

The suggestion infuriated the President. "So NORAD can transmit the data to Air Combat Command? Which part of my order to suppress this goddamn information didn't you understand?!"

Woodruff decided to try another tack.

"Let's at least look at our Asset Overlay. Should it become necessary, it certainly can't hurt for you to know exactly what we've got to work with."

Marsh almost declined, then decided it would keep Woodruff and Levinson busy for a few minutes without cost, as the Asset Overlay could be activated by computer without outside intervention or knowledge.

"Whatever. Go ahead."

Woodruff punched his password code into the VS Room remote and the real-time locations of all U.S. military assets in the Mediterranean, Mideast, and Western Asia regions appeared on the VS screen as an overlay on the existing map. He and Levinson moved closer to study it. Most planes, ships, and men were grouped in Istanbul and the Incirlik air base near Adana, Turkey, in preparation for the August 12 offensive against the TAA. They saw various ships en route to the area, and augmented force levels in several outlying bases. Looking at the map only increased Levinson's frustration.

"Even if we had the appropriately equipped forces and a workable time frame, it'd be pretty goddamn awkward to send aircraft or ground forces into the heart of Russia to fend off an invasion of their country."

He glanced over at the President, who stood with his back to them, facing the video controls above the VCR credenza, mesmerized by the small video monitor built into the panel. It displayed the map and radar image from Svalbard, and he repeatedly used a pair of buttons to zoom in on the approaching planes, check their progress, and then zoom back out to the full view of the globe.

"Sir?" Levinson said. "Please, reconsider and call the Russians. Tell them what's happening."

After a moment, Marsh turned to him. But before he could reply the phone rang. He scowled and picked up the receiver.

"If he says it's so damn urgent put him through." While listening, Marsh's expression clouded with anger.

"That's nonsense, absolutely without merit," he said into the phone. "Let me make this clear and unequivocal: No matter what you see or hear, real or rumored, no one is to take any military action whatsoever without the President's direct authorization. Now, I'm not saying there exists any imminent reason to consider use of the military, I'm just saying I need everyone on our team to work with me, not second-guess me. There is certain information I cannot yet share with you, is that understood?"

Marsh hung up and his face contorted with barely suppressed rage and paranoia.

"Mancini just told me he's heard *rumors* about the TAA having some special new aircraft." He grabbed Laura's cell phone from the sideboard next to the sofa and threw it. It smashed against the wall only inches from Woodruff's head.

"She's talking to people!" Marsh shouted. "Did either of you know of her plan to spy on me? Curt, did she say anything to you when leaving?"

"No, sir, absolutely not," Levinson said.

Marsh moved threateningly toward him. "Lie to me and it's over. Not just your career, I'll rip your fucking heart out! Think carefully: Who are her allies? Who is she talking to? Answer me!"

Levinson backed away, so frightened by the President's raw hostility that he couldn't speak. Disgusted, Marsh turned away and dialed the Secret Service office in the White House.

"Find Laura Bishop. She was last seen in the Dupont Circle metro station about an hour ago. Inform the FBI and D.C. police she made an attempt on the President's life."

The haze of superheated air around the Centurion glowed hellish red as she increased speed in her free-fall reentry. Wilder waited three minutes—enough time for Batu to assume he was dead. If he didn't get control of his aircraft and restart her engines, he soon would be. Batu's HPM blast created a cascade failure in all the Centurion's electronics, and Wilder's one chance at survival was to manually reboot the main computer, then bring the subsystems back on-line in exact hierarchical order. Trying to remember the details from his reading about the Centurion's subsystems, he removed the faceplate from one of the instrument panels. First, he would need to restore power. Of the Centurion's three redundant methods for creating auxiliary electricity, two—the solar power panels and chemical storage batteries—had been fatally overloaded. The remaining option, the Ram Air Turbine, hadn't been designed for use at hypersonic speeds, so Wilder knew when extending the RAT that it would soon burn to nothingness in the hot reentry.

The RAT locked in place and some meters and lights came to life— for a short time he'd have enough auxiliary power to reset the computers. He slid out the modular circuit board for the master system, pulled its micropin power connectors, counted to five to let any residual charge dissipate, then reconnected them. A series of relays clicked and several small LCD panels blinked awake. While the computer ran through its seemingly interminable self-test and parity-check cycles he glanced impatiently out the window at the ever-brighter halo of burning air around him. Once it finished, he slid the board back into place and repeated the process for the engine control subsystem and the fuel control and flight control boards. Each time he forced himself not to rush—if any system came on-line without a full reset or in the wrong order, he'd have to start all over.

The instrument lights flickered as the RAT began crumbling under the intense heat outside. Without it, he would be unable to restart the engines. He slammed the last circuit board back in place, pushed a row of buttons to direct the RAT's power to the starter, and prayed the reintroduction of hydrogen fuel into the white-hot engine chambers wouldn't cause an explosion. With a slight jolt the armature holding the RAT broke away from the fuselage, but the engines began turning under their own power.

Wilder carefully nudged the throttle to regain stability and ease the Centurion's nose up, trying to assume the right combination of thrust, position, and resistance to get the aircraft back atop its own shock wave, literally like a surfboard on the ocean. This would normally be handled by the neural-net flight assist, and Wilder sorely wished it had been installed. He felt around for the precise flight attitude . . . gently . . . mustn't overshoot it.

The rumbling suddenly calmed. The cloak of fire surrounding the aircraft disappeared, as if a huge blast furnace had suddenly turned off. Wilder once again had control of his aircraft. He reactivated environmental control and came around to a due-south heading, streaking into the stratosphere at twelve times the speed of sound.

The Sixth Space Warning Squadron sat atop Flatrock Hill in Cape Cod, Massachusetts, home to one of four Precision Acquisition Vehicle Entry/ Phased Array Warning System (PAVE PAWS) radar sites in the United States. The main building, a five-story triangle, held a phased-array radar consisting of oval sensor fields covering the two sides of the building facing northward. Junior Surveillance Technician Sergeant George Hotchkiss began running a diagnostic check on the main and redundant computers controlling the PAVE PAWS radar.

A few moments ago a group of tiny, faint, unidentified signatures had unexpectedly appeared and he wanted to confirm they were the real thing, not a computer glitch. The PAVE PAWS system served primarily to detect a sea-launched ballistic missile attack and to supply such information in real time to the North American Aerospace Defense Command and the Space Surveillance Center at Cheyenne Mountain, Strategic Air Command, and the National Command Authorities. When Defense Command called, as surely they would, Hotchkiss wanted to be able to assure them the SWS systems were all functioning properly.

At the nearby Bayshore Tavern on Route 46, six fishermen at the bar flirted with a pair of cute bank tellers, and Don Henley's "Boys of Summer" played on the jukebox. Lt. Major Bruce Newman sat at a table, alone, licking the salt off the rim of his margarita glass and nibbling on a blue-corn nacho chip. He hated his assignment at the Podunk Sixth and longed to get transferred back to a real Air Force base. Oh, well, at least he had the rest of the afternoon off. Newman groaned as his cell phone rang. Christ, what crisis is it now, more pigeon shit on the phased array? Pine needles in the rain gutters of the uplink bunker?

"Sir, it's Hotchkiss."

"Go ahead, Sergeant."

"We picked up a cluster of unidentified signatures over Quebec, Canada, approaching our airspace."

"What kind of signatures?"

"That's the thing. Systems indicate they're no bigger than a bunch a sparrows!"

"Goddamit, Hotchkiss, why in the hell would we give a rat's ass about a bunch of sparrows?!"

"Well, Major, sir, they're coming in at twenty-six hundred miles an hour."

The information regarding Batu's incoming planes moved instantly to the NORAD Space Surveillance Command and the office of the Joint Chiefs. General Mancini, livid that enemy aircraft had come so close without the military's knowledge, and enraged at the President's dishonesty, picked up the phone to call Secretary Woodruff's office. Although he had the authority to immediately implement all defensive measures available to the military short of a nuclear strike, his gut told him to get more information about the President's bizarre behavior before proceeding. He stopped dialing when he heard through his live link to Cheyenne Mountain a radio voice hailing Air Combat Command.

"ACC, this is USAF Centurion . . . over."

Word had earlier gotten around the Air Force command loop from Dryden, the very upset Andrews base commander, that Wilder had commandeered the prototype Centurion aircraft. No one except Brent and Colonel Chang had any idea why Wilder had done such a thing, and true to their promise to Senator Ballard they denied all knowledge of his motives when asked by General Mancini.

"Go ahead, Centurion . . ." the brigadier general at the ACC said. "Wilder?"

"Yeah—" Wilder began.

A different voice cut in. "Wilder, this is General Mancini. What in the hell are you—"

"Sir, can you get us on a private connection?"

Mancini ordered the ACC to patch him directly to the Centurion through a digitally encrypted combat frequency.

"PAVE PAWS should've picked up six TAA penetrators by now," Wilder said. "Do not—I repeat—do *not* inform the President you know of their existence. He knows they're coming and will order you to let them approach. The President is . . . no longer fit to serve. Senator Ballard and Vice President Taylor should know this by now and will be working the problem."

"My fucking God," Mancini said. He muted his microphone and ordered his assistant to get the Vice President on the phone.

"Also, Batu Khan is piloting one of the fighters heading toward Washington," Wilder continued. "It's black, with retracting fanwings and a shooting star on her fuselage just below the cockpit."

In fifteen seconds he'd hit Mancini with one hell of a lot of information to digest.

"Repeat last, Centurion, you're talking about Batu Khan *himself*?"

"Yes, we had our hands around each other's throats less than a half hour ago. It's a long story, but I lost him."

"Do you know if the enemy planes are carrying weapons of mass destruction?"

"No, sir, the fighters have high-powered microwave weapons, but I saw no air-to-air or air-to-ground missiles. There's also a small transport plane, rear loading, inappropriate for bomb delivery."

"If they're not on a bombing mission, did you have any indication what they're planning?"

"No, but Batu is aware the President is dangerously unstable. He might believe some sort of attack on Washington would set him off, but for what ultimate purpose I don't know."

Mancini sat dumbfounded. The more Wilder told him the worse it got.

"I tried to make him doubt the accuracy of the information about the President," Wilder said, "but it probably wasn't enough to make him change his plans. Look, I'm missing a lot of instrumentation up here. Can the ACC give me a fix on the penetrators' location?"

"Cannot oblige, Centurion. I'm informed they disappeared from our screens a few moments after they appeared. And none of our space-based assets are positioned over the continental U.S."

In other words, only the PAVE PAWS radar stations, on the ground, were currently monitoring the continental United States. Radar perceives targets on a direct line of sight: Flying at near zero altitude, any aircraft farther than twenty-six miles from a ground-based array is hidden from detection below the horizon because of the curvature of the Earth.

"General," Wilder said, "the terrain might help us out. I lost them over the Hudson Straits. If I were Batu I'd drop down to tree level, cut though the lowlands across Labrador and Quebec. It would make a hellacious sonic-boom footprint if they're still hypersonic, but the sound would be geographically isolated by the surrounding hills. Find out which towns are getting their windows blown out and the ones who aren't, and we got him within twenty, thirty miles."

"Stand by, Centurion. Will return with that information as it's ascertained."

Mancini signed off with Wilder and relayed instructions for dozens of ACC personnel to start calling cities and towns throughout Quebec Province. He next ordered Telemetry Intelligence, a highly classified land-and-satellite-based data eavesdropping system, to begin tracking the area for encrypted, digitally compressed burst messages used by combat aircraft to communicate with each other and their command base.

Mancini's assistant broke in to say he had Vice President Taylor on the phone. Mancini told Taylor about the incoming penetrators; the Vice President simply said "thank you" and hung up.

Closing his office door in the White House, Taylor sat behind his desk and stared at the framed color photograph of President Marsh on the wall. It took him a moment to reconcile himself with what must happen next. He removed a piece of vice presidential stationery from the drawer, wrote a few lines on it, then telephoned Senator Ballard.

"Mancini says they've picked up the TAA warplanes on the EWS," Taylor said.

"Good Lord."

"I've drafted a short statement. It's coming through on your private fax; tell me if you think it's sufficient."

Ballard pulled the paper out of the machine on his credenza:

To Senator Jonathan Ballard, President Pro Tempore of the United State Senate, and The Honorable Glendon Frost, Speaker of the United States House of Representatives.

Sirs:

We the undersigned hereby declare Burton Henry Marsh presently incapable of discharging the powers and duties of the office of President of the United States.

Taylor had signed it, dated it, and printed his name under his signature.

"I felt it would be more forthright to put it in longhand," he said.

"Yes, I'd agree. And what you've written is fine."

Ballard told his secretary to get the House Speaker and the cabinet members back on the conference call at once. Taylor tried to keep his mind on the details; otherwise he feared the bigger issues would overwhelm him.

"How can we get everyone together in time?" he asked.

"The Constitution specifically uses the word *transmit* in reference to the written declaration. I'm only an old civil rights lawyer, but I think it'll be acceptable to daisy-chain the letter via fax: get one secretary to sign it, forward it on to the next. If we get at least eight signatures, the last person can fax it to Frost and your office at the White House. I'll meet you there and we'll present it to the President."

Taylor's stomach knotted. He never expected a Vice President's most important and terrifying duty to call, especially under such bizarre and perilous circumstances.

"God help me, Jon, I don't know if I'm ready to be President, let alone the possibility of being at war within an hour."

Thirty-five

From his Yesugei-K over Russia, Chu'tsai checked in with his engineers working on the SS-25 missiles, then radioed Batu to inform him the replacement of the PAL circuitry and progress to the launch sites were proceeding on time.

"Promise me you'll stay back when the others arrive in Washington," he said. "If anything should happen to you, all our efforts are for nothing."

"You worry about our goals there. I'll be ready when destiny calls."

Despite Batu's assurances, Chu'tsai grew more concerned by the moment. "It was risky enough for you to be on the *Altun Ordu* when you reached the U.S.; now you're in a fighter, close to the action, and without a redundant communications system. Respect your vulnerability, and that of our greater purpose."

Chu'tsai resisted his desire to say anything further. It frustrated him that Batu did not give their goals in Russia, staggering in their magnitude, his undivided attention. But ever since they began planning their Day of Glory, Batu's personal animosity toward President Marsh had kept him more interested in what Chu'tsai considered to be their secondary objectives in Washington.

In his Temujin, Batu glanced over at a red, sealed plastic envelope dangling from a chain attached to his instrument panel.

"Who will be the first in position?" he asked.

"The team in Kamyshin."

"Which target have you assigned them?"

"Forty-one ten/twenty-nine twelve. The Volgograd team has thirty-six two/thirty-seven."

"Perfect. We will proceed at oh two hundred as planned."

Batu clicked off and smiled. He'd have plenty of time to relish his actions in Washington, and then, with his famous flair for the dramatic, he'd administer the coup de grâce from Russia.

As Wilder had anticipated, enormous sonic booms had rattled certain areas of Quebec as Batu's formation streaked through the hilly terrain. The Centurion sped to Batu's projected coordinates at orbital altitude to conserve fuel, then streaked into a wave-rider reentry. Without the neural-net flight-assist computer it took intense concentration and a delicate touch to keep the aircraft stable while descending almost vertically and leveling off at 2,500 feet. Cutting through the hills further narrowed the possible location of Batu's penetrators, and Wilder soon spotted their contrails. He used the Centurion's telescopic viewer to study Batu's six-plane formation. Batu flew in front, just above the ground. Two other Temujins, identical to his but for the shooting-star logo, flanked him at his tail. The Yesugei-W flew behind them with the last two Temujins pacing it for protection.

To Wilder, the ground below was a complete blur and the view ahead approached with breathtaking rapidity, like a movie run at a hundred times normal speed. He glanced at his airspeed gauge—he and the TAA planes were traveling at almost mach four—then switched on his partially powered HPM cannon, even though twenty percent capacity had little chance of doing lethal damage to an aircraft. Descending to the altitude of the TAA formation, a mere three hundred *feet* above the ground, he turned on the Centurion's Obstacle Avoidance System and hung back. Batu's formation would soon emerge from between the hills and fly over the broad mouth of the St. Lawrence River. There'd be room to maneuver out there. He keyed his radio mic.

"General Mancini, this is Centurion. I've made visual contact with the enemy."

"Affirmative," Mancini said, "proceed at will. There's nothing we can do from this end. I've ordered the Washington Military District commanders to have their pilots suited up and ready to go, but they can't go airborne without the President knowing we're aware of the intruders' presence."

"Roger that, sir."

Both Wilder and Mancini were painfully aware that even if the President allowed the military to do its job, Washington, D.C., had few fixed air defenses. A violation of American airspace simply wasn't supposed to happen, so no one had seen the need to surround the nation's capital with permanent antiaircraft or antimissile batteries. Also, the United States had never before faced an enemy with such a marked technological advantage. Of all the planes in the inventory, only the newly delivered F-22 Raptor had supercruise, the ability to fly supersonically without afterburners. Even that came up woefully short compared to the hypersonic capabilities of Batu's Temujin penetrators, and no American planes had speed-of-light weapons installed. Unfortunately, Wilder realized, the task of stopping the TAA penetrators from reaching Washington had fallen solely to him.

"Signing off for now, Centurion," Mancini said. "Telemetry Intelligence is decoding the TAA radio transmissions and I just received the first transcript."

Marsh rapidly paced the VS Room, lost in his own thoughts. He caught Levinson staring fearfully at him and he stopped pacing.

"What are you looking at?!" Marsh growled.

Levinson didn't reply. He flopped into a chair, heartsick and confused, and looked down at his hands. Secretary of Defense Woodruff glanced over at him, wishing to hell they had thirty seconds alone. He understood enough about electronic countermeasures to suspect the loss of the TAA command craft had made Batu's other planes partially visible to standard radar. At first, he couldn't decide whether telling the President would make him more or less reasonable, but ultimately his instincts told him to keep quiet. He prayed that General Mancini would somehow realize Marsh knew about the approaching aircraft and had deliberately misled him.

The phone rang and Marsh, expecting it to be either the ExOps searching for Laura or those manning Svalbard station, clicked on the speaker box.

"Mr. President, it's General Mancini." As much as the chairman of the Joint Chiefs distrusted Marsh, he had new information that had to be given to the commander in chief of the armed forces.

"I thought I made it clear to quit bothering me," Marsh said, and he reached over to disconnect the call.

"Sir, listen to me! We've just received hard intelligence Batu Khan's forces in Russia have taken control of five SS-twenty-five nuclear missiles," Mancini said. "Three are to be flown to the TAA, and the other two are to be launched from Russia against the American forces amassed in Incirlik and Istanbul."

The news hit the VS Room like an incendiary bomb.

"Where did you get this information?" Marsh asked.

"Telemetry Intelligence is decoding radio transmissions between the TAA penetrators approaching Washington and their counterparts above Russia, and also from Batu's ground forces in the Russian city of Kamyshin. There is no mistaking their meaning: They made specific references to the longitude and latitude of our bases, and they plan to launch at six P.M. Washington time."

Marsh clenched his jaw. Although the news shocked him as much as the others, he willed himself to mask his emotions.

"Less than two hours?! You're certain of the time?" Woodruff asked Mancini.

"Yes, sir. They've determined it based on the ETA to their launch locations plus the time necessary to raise the missiles to firing position and activate the control systems."

Woodruff had to sit down; among the servicemen stationed overseas were his oldest son, a niece, and a nephew.

"What's to stop them from launching earlier?" Levinson asked.

"Ballistic missiles don't direct themselves in flight. To find their target they must know exactly where on the face of the Earth they started from. Since Batu's people preprogrammed the replacement circuitry, the SS-twenty-fives cannot be deployed from anywhere but the predetermined locations."

Marsh erupted, but not about the specter of a nuclear attack on American forces.

"Everybody shut up! Mancini, who authorized this surveillance?"

"I did, sir. Given the circumstances, any discussion regarding—"

"My instructions were explicit! No one was to do anything without my approval! Who else is involved? Who else?!"

"Sir," Levinson said gently, "forget about all that. We have an unprecedented peril to contend with—"

Marsh ignored his chief of staff and raged on:

"You deliberately disobeyed me! I can't be responsible for the outcome if I don't have complete control of the situation! General, you're relieved of duty!"

Marsh punched a button on the phone to disconnect the call.

"Sir, please . . ." Woodruff said. "The chairman of the Joint Chiefs had every right to take those actions! We need him to—"

"I don't *care* about his rights, he fucking *betrayed* me! Call the Pentagon, have the Marine Guards escort him out of the building. If you have a problem, you can tender your resignation now!"

Levinson shot a look at the Secretary of Defense to silence him. With no way to immediately remove Marsh from the top decision-making position, it became critical to keep him calm and reasonable.

"The crisis in Russia supersedes all other issues," Levinson said. "We're your senior advisers; it's our job to give you our counsel."

Woodruff took his cue from Levinson and murmured his agreement. As Levinson hoped, it made Marsh feel less threatened and he calmed down a notch.

"Sir, it might be possible to jam the TAA transmissions, keep Batu's men at the missile sites from receiving the order to launch," he suggested.

Woodruff shook his head. "Even if we had an AWACS directly over central Russia, which we don't, it's practically impossible to interfere with digital burst radio transmissions. It's a waste of time discussing anything that's not a hundred percent certain to prevent the launch of those missiles."

He looked at the Asset Overlay showing American military forces in the region. "We have two options. One, give the Russians full intelligence support and pray they can somehow take back control of the missiles in time, which is highly unlikely. Two, which I recommend, could come from right here." He pointed at an oval on the Asset Overlay showing a nuclear-powered attack submarine, the USS *Philadelphia*, sailing beneath the Black Sea, fifty miles off the coast of northern Turkey.

"The *Philadelphia* is 780 miles from Kamyshin, meaning her Tomahawk cruise missiles could be there in about eighty-five minutes. Two per target, each carrying a high-explosive payload armed for an altitude burst, they'd kill everyone manning the SS-twenty-fives without risking nuclear contamination from a ruptured warhead."

"Conventional payloads or not, we can't unilaterally fire missiles into Russian cities!" Levinson said. "At the least, we'd better fucking warn them!"

"Karzhov's people lost control of their assets, what else can he expect us to do?" Woodruff turned to the President. "It's our best option. If you order the strike now, the Tomahawks will get there forty minutes before Batu's attack commences."

Marsh once again became lost in his own world. As his thoughts coalesced in his mind he had to be careful not to speak them aloud, for the barrier between his interior and exterior voices seemed to be fading away. After a long moment, he looked up at Woodruff.

"Get the vice chief of staff on the phone."

Breathing an enormous sigh of relief, Woodruff did as ordered and Marsh took the receiver from him.

"Jim, this is the President." A moment ago, he seemed at the brink of emotional meltdown. Now, for the benefit of the vice chief of staff, he sounded calm and fully in control. "I'm relieving General Mancini of duty, effective immediately. I am aware of the actions of Batu Khan's forces in Russia and of his aircraft approaching the United States, and no one is to respond in any way to those situations without my direct authorization. I'm sure you're all extremely concerned, but I guarantee the problems are not what they seem."

Woodruff and Levinson looked at each other, horrified. They'd expected the President to order the cruise missile strike.

"You have to trust me," Marsh continued. "My strategy is based on information that I cannot share with you just yet. Failure to follow my specific directions will have catastrophic results. If one American aircraft takes wing without my approval I will be forced to have it shot down; if one missile is launched the ship firing it will be sunk. I need your solemn assurance my orders will be followed to the letter, especially with regard to the Eastern Hemisphere: No one, no matter how well intentioned, can even consider attacking positions inside Russia. Agreed?"

The moment he hung up, both Woodruff and Levinson began protesting.

"*Quiet!!*" Marsh roared.

He glared at his advisers, daring them to utter another sound. His eyes went gray and flat—*inhuman,* Levinson thought. The President, his oldest and closest friend, had become a complete stranger to him.

Marsh turned his back to them and sat in perfect stillness. This latest development hadn't changed his mind about anything, it simply took his intentions to a dizzying new height.

Speeding out of the Senate parking garage, Senator Ballard merged his Continental into the heavy traffic on Pennsylvania Avenue. Thousands of government employees were pouring from the Classical Revival–style buildings in the Federal Triangle to get a jump on the weekend. Meanwhile, Taylor reconvened the conference call with the cabinet secretaries and informed them of General Mancini's news. He said his declaration would come to each of them in turn with no time for debate: They were to sign it or not, then in either case forward it to the next secretary via fax. He emphasized all eight had to sign, otherwise it would lack the Constitutionally mandated majority to put it into effect.

Ballard crossed 15th Street to Hamilton Place, drove onto the White House grounds through the little-used West Gate, and entered the West Wing through the employee's entrance. He knew that while vice presidents have two offices—a large, formal one in the Old Executive Office Building and a smaller one in the White House itself—like most of his predecessors, Taylor used the one in Old Exec only for ceremonial purposes.

Taylor and Ballard sat in the West Wing office, furnished with modest, nineteenth-century English mahogany and a framed oil painting of his wife and two children, waiting for the declaration to return from its rounds. Ballard looked out the window, half expecting to see the TAA penetrators swooping out of the sky, then the fax machine clicked on and started printing. The men watched impatiently as the printed page slowly began to emerge. The handwritten declaration looked ratty from multiple generations of faxing, but was still legible. He counted the signatures as they appeared—two, four, five, seven . . .

Eight.

Approaching American airspace, Batu's Temujin moved to the center of his formation in order to be flanked and protected by the other aircraft. Approaching the Gulf of St. Lawrence they sped up to mach five, unaware of the Centurion following ten miles behind. Wilder weighed his options: either wait for a clear shot at Batu himself or go in now and try to reduce the number of TAA planes. Choosing the latter, he set the HPM beam for three-foot-wide coverage and accelerated, flying so near to the water he could practically taste the salt. As he approached, the rear Temujin's proximity sensor began blaring and its pilot radioed a warning to the others.

"Behind us!"

Wilder passed quickly overhead and swept along the rear Temujin with a few million BTUs of focused microwave energy. Although his partially powered HPM cannons were insufficient to damage an aircraft without a sustained, extremely accurate hit, he knew a direct blast through the enemy's cockpit canopy would be enough to heat-plump the pilot like a goddamn ballpark frank. Indeed, the inside of the canopy splattered with red as the pilot's head and chest blew apart and the Temujin spun out of control, crashing into the Gulf.

Outnumbered and outgunned, Wilder immediately pulled into a tight turn, up and away from the formation at a dizzying mach eight. He came and went so fast that Batu, in the lead, saw nothing except a flash of gray behind his shoulder and the fiery impact of the rear Temujin on the water below. Startled and angry, he looked around and adjusted his instrumentation in hopes of locating their attacker, but the Centurion had vanished like a phantom.

"Tighten the formation and stay alert," he radioed to the others. "Increase the gain on your proximity sensors."

Obscured from their direct sight by the glare of the sun, cloaked from their radar by the Centurion's true second-generation stealth, Wilder paced them from high and to the west. Okay, he thought, that was the easy one. Next time they'd be expecting him. Up ahead, Batu reorganized his formation into a T shape to compensate for the lost Temujin and maximize his and the Yesugei-W's safety. Since the American had approached from below, Batu dropped altitude to 150 feet. No one would dare fly any closer to the earth. Not at this speed.

It took enormous self-control for Secretary of Defense Woodruff to stay calm, but if he didn't raise his voice it was possible to speak without the President becoming agitated and defensive.

"Sir, please, we stand to lose twenty-five thousand Air Force personnel based at Incirlik and billions of dollars in aircraft and matériel. Plus two dozen ships harbored at Istanbul and eighty thousand sailors and marines. That's the destruction of a sizable percentage of our warfighting capability, never mind an avalanche of telegrams to American families!"

Levinson's heart went out to Woodruff, knowing one of those families would be his. Marsh sat on the sofa with his head bowed, and he didn't respond to Woodruff's pleas.

"I know you don't want that," Woodruff continued, "so please help us find a satisfactory solution. If you call Karzhov, we can at least make a pretense of giving the Russians a stab at reacquiring their nuclear weapons before we deploy our Tomahawks."

Woodruff looked at Levinson, whose concerns about Batu's pending attack now outweighed his worries about a Russian reaction.

"Unfortunately, Stan's right. If we want to neutralize this threat with any degree of certainty, we *will* have to use our cruise missiles. We'll just have to hope there's minimal collateral damage or civilian casualties."

"Each second matters," Woodruff said, looking at the VS screen. "The Tomahawks need eighty-five minutes to reach their targets. In four minutes they won't have sufficient time to get there before Batu launches the SS-twenty-fives. *Please*, sir . . ."

"That's enough! Your opinions don't matter! You don't have the capacity to grasp the bigger picture—"

Marsh stopped mid-sentence; he heard the elevator at the end of the hall opening and the footsteps of two people approaching. He switched the VS screen to blue with a remote control, then there was a knock at the door. Woodruff and Levinson looked at each other. They hadn't heard anything. How did the President know to mute the view *before* the knock?

Livid, his paranoia raging, Marsh crossed to the door. Only someone high up the food chain could get past the Secret Service agents stationed outside, and he didn't want any more of his people ganging up on him, not this close to success. Still, he couldn't very well barricade himself inside the VS Room. No, let them come, a hundred men couldn't sway him from his path.

Opening the door to find Taylor didn't surprise him, but seeing Ballard did. He couldn't control the president pro tem of the Senate the way he could his staff. At once he smelled Taylor's nervousness.

"We're in a meeting here."

"I'm sorry, this can't wait," Taylor said.

Marsh noticed a letter-sized envelope in Ballard's hand and had to fight back the urge to snatch it from him and open it. Taylor glanced at the others—Secretary of State Woodruff and Chief of Staff Levinson looked *scared.* He'd rehearsed his speech in his head; now, facing the President, his friend, he didn't know how to begin, so he decided to give Marsh one last chance to redeem himself.

"We're aware of the incoming planes. You must mobilize the military, contact the Trans-Altaic Alliance, and demand they cease any attempt to violate American airspace."

Marsh considered responding with a flat denial until he saw Taylor's eyes find the shell and smashed innards of Laura's cell phone scattered on the carpet. He wished he had her within his grasp just then; he'd fucking disfigure her, right down to the bone. It infuriated him that she'd gotten to the top people so quickly.

"We heard the recording made from that phone," Taylor continued. "Also, the enemy aircraft whose existence you denied to the Joint Chiefs have become visible on our radar."

"I don't need to explain or justify anything, Adam. Not even to you."

"Tell him the rest of it, Mr. President," Woodruff said.

"Shut up, Stan—"

"About the pending nuclear attack on our forward forces—"

"I said *shut the fuck up!*"

Frightened, Woodruff stepped back a few paces and did as the President ordered.

Taylor looked at Levinson, who nodded grimly. Woodruff's words were true.

"Christ, Burt, what are you thinking?!" Taylor asked.

"I'm thinking of what's best for this nation, as you all should be."

"Batu Khan's forces are about ninety minutes away from firing Russian SS-twenty-fives at our people in Incirlik and Istanbul," Levinson said for the newcomers' benefit. "What's best is preventing their attack while it's still within our power to do so!"

"It's my decision, nobody else's!" Marsh said.

"What *is* your decision?" Ballard asked. He had a sick feeling, realizing Laura had told him the truth about Marsh's mental state.

"I'll tell you when the time comes," Marsh replied.

"The time is *now!*" Woodruff said, his voice rising. "In two minutes our response window closes!"

"I told you to shut up!" Marsh shouted. He took Woodruff by the arm and shoved him into a chair. Woodruff cried out—Marsh's grasp was so strong that it loudly snapped the bone above his elbow. The others in the room could hardly believe what they were seeing. Levinson crossed to Woodruff to help him.

"Sir! His arm—"

"He'll live," Marsh replied, cutting him off.

Taylor had seen and heard more than enough. He took the envelope from Ballard. "Sir, a majority of members of the cabinet and I have informed Senator Ballard and Congressman Frost that we believe the President is no longer able to discharge the duties of his office."

He used the third person because otherwise it was too painful to say the words.

"Give me that," Marsh grabbed the envelope, unfolded the fax, and read it. "Only eight signatures?"

"They were all we could contact on such short notice."

"Not one fucking ally among my own people. . . ."

Sweating, his hands shaking, he tore off a piece of paper from the notepad on the coffee table and wrote a few lines:

To: The Senate and House of Representatives
From: The President

Contrary to the Declaration executed today by the Vice President and certain members of the Cabinet, no inability exists on my part to serve as President.

He signed the note and shoved it into Ballard's hand. "See you in the Senate chambers. Now sit down, I've got work to do."

Ballard shook his head—he'd expected this. The Twenty-fifth Amendment, like the Constitution as a whole, concerned itself foremost with the balance of power. Paragraph Two of the Amendment stipulates in the event of anything other than a catastrophic incapacity, the President can challenge his removal:

. . . When the President transmits to the President pro tempore of the Senate and the Speaker of the House of Representatives his written declaration that no inability exists, he shall resume the powers and duties of his office. . . . Thereupon Congress shall decide

the issue, assembling within forty-eight hours for that purpose if not in session.

Although he and Taylor feared Marsh would turn the Amendment back on them, they hoped the President would not want to take the issue to Congress.

"All you've done is buy yourself a couple of days, sir," Ballard said, "and set the stage for a grotesque public spectacle. In the end, Congress will vote in support of the cabinet's declaration. Frost and I will see to it. If you step down now, we'll say it was for medical reasons. Adam can assume the duties of Acting President until this crisis is behind us."

Marsh took a breath, barely controlling the compulsion to strangle the old senator. It would be so *easy*.

"There is no crisis. I'm in control of the situation. As I said: two days, Senate chambers. Until then, I don't want to hear another word about it."

Taylor crossed to the door. "Damn it, *I'll* call the Joint Chiefs; they'll deal with this insanity with or without you!"

"Stop!" Marsh bellowed, startling Taylor so badly he literally stopped midstride. Then, in a slightly calmer voice: "Step through that door, Adam, and I'll have the Secret Service bring you right back. In handcuffs and a gag across your mouth, if that's how it has to be. That goes for the rest of you as well. I'm still the President."

Taylor stood with his hand on the doorknob, glaring at Marsh. Finally, he let his hand fall to his side. Unless someone put a bullet in the President's brain there wasn't a damn thing they could do.

The assertion of his authority made Marsh feel better. In his mind, and aloud, too, he repeated a phrase several times: "the big picture, remember the big picture." However satisfying it would be to lash out at his tormentors in the room, he knew it would cost him his power and position. And he was still lucid enough to resist his violent compulsions, especially now, being so close to showing the world the righteousness of his vision.

He clicked the video mute off and the three-dimensional image returned to the VS screen. Ballard and Taylor hadn't realized Batu's aircraft were already so close to Washington.

"What about Batu Khan?" Taylor asked. "For weeks now I've listened to you argue for a war against the man and all he stands for. I know the country's been slow to come around, but take it from someone who would rather do anything but go to war, your words were true. Sometimes fighting is the only way. How can you deliberately stand by and let him do this to us?"

Marsh, suddenly eager to explain, spoke in a soft, urgent voice, as if imparting some cosmic revelation. "What goes through your minds when you look around this city, at its buildings and monuments? When I learned enemy warplanes were approaching this hallowed place, naturally my first impulse was to protect it at all cost. Then I thought about the meaning of those monuments. They honor sacrifice, dedication, bravery; ideals American citizens scarcely comprehend. Suddenly it became clear to me: Our people don't deserve such monuments anymore.

"Until that moment my petty hatred for Batu Khan had blinded me to the truth: He's *irrelevant*. There will always be men like Batu. The names and the faces change, but the darkness within mankind will continually find an instrument to express itself. The real cancer is not this or the next Batu Khan, it's apathy. It's those in this country who argued against my policies, who encouraged the enemy by allowing them to doubt our resolve. I'm giving America a great gift, the ultimate demonstration of inaction and its consequences, and it will strengthen her forever."

It took Taylor a moment to reply. "We won't let that happen, Burt."

"You have no choice. I'm in command, and I doubt the four of you could kill me before the Secret Service came in and blew your brains out. And as for stopping me, forget it. Haven't you ever noticed? There are no fail-safes in the system to prevent someone from doing *nothing*."

"The military can and will act defensively, on its own authority. They don't need to wait for you to come to your senses," Taylor said.

Marsh looked at his watch and shook his head. "The wait is over. As of fifteen seconds ago we have no conventional weapon capable of reaching the Russian targets in time. I know it's painful, but this nation will be infinitely better for it."

Thirty-six

Wilder took his second shot at Batu's formation just after it crossed into U.S. airspace at the northeastern tip of Maine. Flying over a flat meadowland at mach three, he came up behind them in the narrow sliver of space between the formation and the ground. Crop dusters flew higher—the underside of the Centurion nearly touched the grass. He slipped under the Temujins flanking Batu, then popped up directly behind him. Batu's proximity sensor sounded and he reflexively shot upward before Wilder could fire at him. It took the other TAA pilots a moment to realize what happened, then one flew up to ride Batu's tail and protect him while the other veered off to chase the Centurion.

As he rapidly gained altitude, racing after Batu, Wilder activated his rear-facing video viewer and turned on the grid overlay. He avoided his pursuer's HPM fire by keeping himself in a direct axis with Batu's Temujin, which made shooting at him too risky. By referencing his front and back views, Wilder continuously compensated for the pursuer's attempts to get Batu's Temujin out of his line of fire.

Batu, meanwhile, turned to get a look at his enemy. Ever since seeing the Centurion in space he'd worried about how many hypersonic fighters the United States had pursuing them, but hadn't suspected this Centurion to be the same aircraft he'd blasted while in orbit. He screamed into his headset at his pilots:

"Get on either side of him! Fire crossways!"

The pursuing Temujin sped up while the one pacing Batu pulled alongside the Centurion. Wilder had only seconds in which to take a shot at Batu, so he surged forward. With extraordinary reflexes and even better instincts Batu rolled away from the Centurion's HPM beam just as Wilder fired at his cockpit. As the Centurion paced him overhead, Batu caught a glimpse of the black scoring his HPM cannon had etched on the Centurion's underside during their orbital dogfight. He screamed with fury, realizing Wilder had survived.

With Batu no longer in front of him, Wilder's vulnerability forced him to retreat. By the time he could get back on Batu's ass, the guys on *his* ass would blow him out of the sky. The two Temujins stayed with him despite intense acceleration, so Wilder suddenly moved into the right one's path. The surprised TAA pilot veered to avoid a collision, losing his weapons lock on the Centurion. The other pilot fired wildly before he, too, would have to retarget. Wilder banked into a tight evasive turn and the HPM blast meant for him hit the right Temujin. It exploded midair only a hundred feet away, bombarding the underside of the Centurion with white-hot chunks of shrapnel.

Wilder struggled to control the Centurion through the shock wave from the explosion. The stick felt sluggish—some of the fly-by-wire lines were severed by shrapnel penetrating the fuselage. Then his rear-facing display went dead from fragments smashing its lens. A warning light flashed, indicating the Centurion's HPM emitters had also stopped functioning. He tried to reactivate them, but they did not respond. Another alarm went off as the ultra-high amperage flowing to the HPM's secondary power systems began feeding back and overloading the main capacitors, so he quickly took the entire system off line to keep the capacitors from exploding. The damage had rendered him effectively weaponless in an aircraft with diminished maneuverability. Bitterly frustrated, he limped toward a bank of clouds to take refuge.

Batu returned to his decimated formation and ordered the pilot pursuing the Centurion to keep searching. But however much he yearned for Wilder's destruction, he forced himself to stay focused on his goals in Washington, now only twenty minutes away.

The Khaldun at the wheel of the SS-25 Transporter-Erector-Launcher drove slowly through the narrow, winding streets of suburban Kamyshin. The rumbling of the immense TEL woke people along the route, but those who bothered to look out the window saw what appeared to be a four-jeep Russian Army escort surrounding the TEL and went back to bed. Over the years, the government had done far stranger things than move a nuclear missile through a neighborhood of apartment buildings.

Strapped to the side of the vehicle just under the missile, the two TAA ballistic engineers had used hypos of nitroglycerin to blast open the steel panel locks covering the Permissive Action Link circuitry, which controlled missile arming and guidance. Batu's senior engineer, a former employee of the Moscow Thermal Technology Institute, knew the circuitry well—until 1994, he'd worked on the team that built that very component for the Russians' missile program. Peering through a pair of illuminated jeweler's magnifiers he replaced the circuit board, one connector at a time, with a duplicate. The replacement board's nonvolatile memory had been preprogrammed with alpha-bravo codes, now in Batu's possession, to unlock the fail-safe device and instruct the missile to launch at the coordinates programmed into the replacement.

The new PAL circuitry powered up and the senior engineer radioed the news to Chu'tsai: The SS-25 would be ready to fire the moment they raised the missile to firing position in Borodin Plaza.

In the VS Room, the Vice President turned from the screen as Woodruff, clutching his fractured arm, moaned softly.

"The doctor should look at Stan's arm," Taylor said to the President.

"When this is over," Marsh replied coldly.

Levinson, pacing the room, glanced at the clock. It was four thirty-five. In ten minutes Batu's planes would arrive over Washington; in less than ninety the TAA would launch the stolen missiles at a large percentage of the American military. He wondered if he could kill or incapacitate the President, a man he loved like a brother, without being heard by the Secret Service agents just outside the room. It would have to be him—Woodruff certainly wasn't able, Ballard was too old, and Taylor couldn't very well assume the presidency if he killed his predecessor himself. Marsh stood calmly near the VS controls, watching the screen but also watching the others in the room, so he caught a quick moment pass between Levinson and Senator Ballard. He said nothing because what transpired pleased him—Ballard had indicated with a subtle shake of his head not to try anything foolish. Ballard had good reason: He'd read about Cowling's test group, and if Marsh was at all like the others he'd have many times his normal strength and a volatile, potentially homicidal temper.

Woodruff shifted around in his chair, trying to ignore the pain. "I'm sure it's occurred to the rest of you so I might as well say it out loud. The window is closed for conventional subsonic weapons, but one option remains: an ICBM can reach any target in Russia in twenty-eight minutes."

"We might've been able to get away with destroying a few city blocks in Russia, but not a nuclear attack!" Levinson said.

"Karzhov would do the same if the tables were turned," Woodruff replied. "The purpose of those weapons is to protect American lives and interests; however horrible their deployment may be, the stakes are now too high not to. We have no other options."

All eyes went to the President, because only the commander in chief has the authority to order the use of nuclear weapons. Woodruff glared hatefully at him.

"A half hour ago we could've accomplished the same thing with conventional missiles, minimal collateral casualties, and little risk of Russian retaliation. God*damn* you, sir, for forcing this choice upon us."

Marsh's face twisted with rage. He shot to his feet and crossed to Woodruff, who cowered in his chair, genuinely afraid the President would kill him this time.

"Are you *threatening* me?!" Marsh hissed. "You fucking cockroach, don't ever speak to me like that! You should be on your knees, thanking me . . ."

The VS Room door opened, startling everyone because no one had knocked first. Amy entered, with a small smile fixed on her face. She glanced momentarily at the VS screen but did not react, nor did she acknowledge anyone else or the extreme tension in the room. She kept her eyes on her husband.

"Burt, I need to talk to you for a moment . . ."

Marsh, so absorbed in his plot and convinced of his own invincibility, had completely forgotten about her. He grabbed her arm.

"Not now; you can't stay here! I'll call for a Marine copter to take you to Fort Ritchie."

Amy didn't respond to his panicked tone, she simply nodded in agreement. "Fine, I'll go right away. When will you be joining me?"

"Soon. I have a few things to wrap up." Despite Marsh's concerns about making her leave, it soothed him to see a trusted face. Lost in thought, he ran his fingers through her hair and smiled. "I have so much to tell you about. You're going to be so proud . . ."

The President sounded like a child seeking approval from its mother. Amy's breath caught in her throat, but then she smiled back at him.

"I'm sure I will be. I always am."

Everyone stared at Amy and her husband, the strange moment frozen in time, then Taylor stood up. He couldn't let the First Lady go without telling her what was happening, and Marsh couldn't stop him from speaking. Maybe she could still reason with the President. But at the last moment Taylor's instincts kept him quiet for a moment longer. He stood motionless, watching Amy carefully—*surely* she knows something is wrong. Ballard, standing next to him, began to speak, but Taylor touched his arm to silence him.

"Sorry, sweetheart, you have to go," Marsh said. "I'll be along."

She nodded. "I understand . . ."

Marsh leaned over to kiss her, then stopped short. He noticed an almost-imperceptible quiver in her smile, a moment where her gaze didn't meet his and he heard her heart pounding, belying her calm exterior. He smelled something utterly foreign to the woman he'd known for thirty years. Fear.

"I love you," she whispered, then squeezed her eyes shut.

An expression of stunned surprise crossed President Marsh's face and he stepped quickly away from his wife. He glanced down at his pants leg and saw a hypodermic syringe buried to the hilt in his thigh. He looked at Amy. The pain of his cabinet's betrayal was a thousandth of the agony he now felt at hers.

"*No!*"

Yanking the hypo out he lunged toward Amy, but had to steady himself against the wall. He went for her again, intent on punishing her—the one person he truly trusted had robbed him of seeing his greatest triumph. Taylor pulled her aside and stepped in between them, but Marsh's legs would not obey him and he stopped walking. Nor could he speak, although the chilling expression of pure hatred on his face articulated the depth of his final madness far more graphically than words. He directed the full force of his powers against the narcotic flowing to his brain, struggling to stay conscious, maintain control, but finally he succumbed. Taylor and Levinson grabbed his arms and eased him gently down onto the sofa. His eyes darted wildly about, then slowly began to close; his head bobbed twice in a final gesture of resistance, then he was still.

Amy turned to Vice President Taylor, her voice cracking with emotion. "Dr. Whitaker prepared that hypodermic at my insistence. My husband will remain unconscious for at least twenty-hour hours."

"How did you know?" Senator Ballard asked.

"Laura Bishop called. I've sensed for weeks Burt wasn't . . . right, but it came and went, so I'd rationalize it away."

Amy had understood everything the moment Laura mentioned Professor Cowling. Marsh told her when they were first married about volunteering for Cowling's test group and how he'd unknowingly taken mutated LSD; he'd been worried if it ever came out it would harm his political future. Over the years Amy forced herself to forget the conversation, but it had echoed the past few weeks.

"God, I'm so sorry!" she said. "It's my fault he went this far . . ." She came close to breaking down, but pressed on. "Did the cabinet vote to remove him from office?"

"Yes," Taylor said.

"Did he countermand their declaration?"

Ballard handed her the note Marsh had written. She tore it up and put the pieces in her pocket.

"That document never existed. Are we all in agreement?"

Everyone nodded.

"Jon, I believe as a former federal judge you're still empowered to administer the Oath of Office. I've written it down, in case you don't know it verbatim." She handed him a sheet of paper, then looked again at Vice President Taylor. "Burt always had the greatest faith in you, Adam."

Adam Edward Taylor raised his right hand and took the Oath of Office for the presidency of the United States. Amy Marsh and Curt Levinson stood beside him, serving as witnesses. Then, as Amy brought White House physician Dr. Whitaker into the room to check Marsh's vitals, President Taylor put everyone to work.

"Stan, tell European Command in Vaihingen that Incirlik and Istanbul are under imminent threat, and take them to DEFCON 1. Get our interceptors airborne over Washington, then reinstate General Mancini and find out everything he knows about the situation. Inform the Joint Chiefs, National Security Council, and the Secret Service that President Marsh is incapacitated. They'll need to hear it directly from you, Mancini,

Jon, and the cabinet, too; there can't be any question as to the chain of command. Curt, tell the operator to get Karzhov on the line."

Taylor glanced over at the VS screen. "Our Air Force hasn't a chance in hell against hypersonic warplanes. Start moving the staff down to the Situation Room. Alert D.C. Metro Police, the FBI, and the National Guard of a possible air attack, then have Secretary of State Burroughs get word through the Greeks to the TAA: Any action against American interests or personnel will be viewed as an act of war. We will respond without hesitation and to the fullest measure. Jon, call the Speaker and tell him he's next in line to the presidency."

While everyone set about their tasks, President Taylor took a deep breath and picked up the phone beside the VS controls. "Have them bring in the football."

In moments a uniformed warrant officer and an armed, two-man escort knocked quietly and entered the room. Even now, more than a decade after the end of the Cold War, a team of warrant officers on the President's staff stood at the ready around the clock, carrying the alphanumeric codes authorizing the use of nuclear weapons. Holding a hard-shell attaché case handcuffed to his left wrist by a two-foot-long steel chain, the officer placed the case on the sideboard behind the sofa.

"Open it," Taylor said.

"*Sir?!*"

Senator Ballard stepped forward and showed the officer the signed declaration. "Mr. Taylor is President now, son."

The officer read the declaration carefully and looked around the room—Mrs. Marsh, the secretary of defense, and the White House chief of staff nodding their agreement; Dr. Whitaker tending to Woodruff and an unconscious Marsh. He saluted the new President and dialed the combination lock on the case.

"There is no one in this room less inclined toward the nuclear option than I am," Taylor said. "But barring a miracle in the next few minutes I see no other choice to save the lives of a hundred thousand American servicemen and millions of civilians in Adana and Istanbul."

"And what of the Russian lives this will cost? Or the risk of retaliation?" Ballard asked. Although he didn't say anything, it surprised him how quickly his friend seemed to have lost his lifelong reticence toward conflict.

"This isn't a theoretical exercise, Jon, and we're working within a time frame of minutes and seconds, not hours or days. We have our people and warfighting capability to protect; we must move this process forward while at the same time searching for a way not to exercise it. I'll see what we can do about the Russians once I talk to Karzhov. That's the best I can do."

Levinson stepped closer to the President. "You should get downstairs to the Situation Room."

Taylor glanced over at Amy, who was kneeling beside her husband and the doctor.

"Is there anything I can do?" Taylor asked softly.

"I just want to get him somewhere safe," she replied.

"I'll see to it, if you could spare me for a moment," Levinson offered.

Taylor nodded, and noticed the chief of staff's eyes were wet with tears.

Woodruff, waving off any additional care from Dr. Whitaker beyond a sling for his arm, finished briefing the Commander in Chief of the U.S. European Command in Vaihingen then dialed a single digit to connect with the Senior Controller at Strategic Air Command in Omaha.

"This is Secretary of Defense Woodruff. I'm with the President and he has authorized the release of nuclear weapons. Repeat: the National Command Authority is authorizing the release of nuclear weapons. Stand by to receive target coordinates and authorization codes."

Taylor took the hard plastic envelopes from the warrant officer, but hesitated breaking them open. The simplicity of the process had never really struck him before: Mankind's most devastating capability put into effect by one person reciting a handful of random letters into a telephone.

"Strategic Command reports they'll have ICBMs from Francis E. Warren retargeted to each of the Designated Ground Zeros within five minutes," Woodruff said. "What alert status should we assume stateside?"

"Give me your assessment of what the Russians might do."

"Ideally, nothing; they'd recognize their responsibility for losing control of their missiles, we'd placate them with increased economic aid, maybe even help them pass off the attack as a nuclear accident."

"Is that what you expect?"

"No. Karzhov is more frightened of the ultra-nationalists and the old-line Communists in his government than of us. An unanswered nuclear attack on their country would surely force him from office, probably get him shot and start a civil war. Besides, any country's deterrence to attack is based as much on its willingness to strike back as its ability to do so. Given the Russians' hatred for their postsuperpower status, I fear that alone would compel them to take the hard line."

"Meaning?"

"There's a very real possibility they could hit us with what they'd consider a measured response: destroy three similarly sized American cities and dare us to escalate after, in their minds, the score had been settled. At best, sir, you must be prepared for them to *threaten* such a thing."

"That's insane!"

"Unfortunately, it's not. It's simply about deterring you from killing their people. May I speak frankly?" Woodruff asked. The President nodded. "Your reputation for being . . . militarily disinclined will precede you. Karzhov will be particularly dangerous because he'll believe if he's tough enough he'll prevent you from launching."

"Understood," Taylor said. "Keep this situation secret from all civilian authorities, but move our stateside missile, Command Centers, and Air Combat bases to DEFCON 2."

Thirty-seven

Washington appeared through Batu's telescopic display at four-forty P.M. A golden luminosity from the late-afternoon sun gilded the distant city's white monuments. Batu excitedly took in the view, then signaled the formation to slow to subsonic speed and split up: He and the Yesugei-W circled in a holding pattern over Virginia while two of the Temujins flew ahead.

Concurrently, at eleven-forty P.M. local time in Greece, the phone rang at the CBS Athens Bureau and a sleepy field producer answered.

"Bureau desk . . ."

"I have a message from His Excellency Batu Khan for the American people that must be aired at once. He has chosen your network for this great honor." The man, who spoke in heavily accented English, gave her the satellite transponder code from where the transmission could be received.

"Wait, what's this about?"

The man hung up. While a tech aligned the uplink, the producer called the managing editor of the news division in New York. Batu's demand for free access to the American airwaves outraged the managing editor, until he heard it was an exclusive.

Ninety seconds later a musical fanfare and a snazzy BREAKING NEWS graphic preempted the local programming nationwide. The message had been taped that morning, Ulan Bator time. Batu sat cross-legged on the floor of his *ger*, dressed in his *shalwar qamiz*, and he spoke directly to the camera:

On April fifteen, 1986, American F-111 jets invaded the night skies above the sovereign nation of Libya. Not on a mission of territorial gain, nor the subjugation of her people. The bombers came to show Libya's leader his vulnerability to the wrath of his enemies. That his cities, his house, his family, he himself were within their destructive reach. In later years, your country also rained destruction upon Iraq, Bosnia, and others. I have learned much from studying the American people and their culture, and I have the greatest love and admiration for you. However, I have been forced to take action by your arrogant President, who imposes his will with bombs and missiles from afar, complacently believing geography exempts him from harm. In my conversations with Burton Marsh, I asked only to be accepted as a friend. He has rejected that course for our two great peoples, so the responsibility for all that follows lies solely with him."

And the screen went black.

Traffic in both directions on the four-lane road in suburban Maryland slowed to a crawl and people stopped to gawk, oblivious to the horns blaring behind them. A few pulled over and got out of their cars to join the neighborhood kids watching from the embankment: Wilder had landed his damaged space plane in the parking lot of a half-completed shopping mall and taxied her out of view beneath a freeway overpass. Still wearing his sky-blue space suit, he stood on the shoulder of the road, assessing the damage to the underside of her fuselage. Working inside a small, blast-damaged panel, he located the severed fly-by-wire cables and spliced jumpers across them. Skinning wires with a sharp fragment of metal and one's teeth ain't no way to work on a $500 million aircraft, he thought, but it seemed to be working. The HPM emitter lenses were a different story. They'd been shattered when the Temujin exploded, and he could not salvage enough parts to cobble together one functioning emitter. Enormously frustrated, he climbed back into the cockpit. He may have his maneuverability back, but he still had no weapons; the odds, which were bad enough before, were now impossible.

"Better get up the hill before I start the engines," he warned the kids.

The kids scrambled out of the way. Wilder closed the canopy and radioed in the news of his incapacitated weapons to General Mancini.

"I'll keep after them, sir. I'm still able to distract 'em, maybe even inflict some damage."

He taxied across the median onto the empty parking lot and accelerated into a nearly vertical takeoff. In seconds the Centurion disappeared into the clouds.

Fearing the pending arrival of Batu's planes as well as Marsh's ExOps, Laura had remained in the Capitol building. At the phone in the lobby she called upstairs to Senator Ballard's office only to learn he'd left the building unexpectedly. She then tried to call Colonel Chang's office at Andrews, but several times she got an "all circuits busy" message. Finally she connected and asked for Brent.

"We haven't heard anything about Matt," he quickly told her. She could hear urgent voices and commotion in the background, and Brent sounded scared. "No time to talk," he said. "Batu's threatening to nuke our overseas forces; we've just gone to DEFCON 2 here, DEFCON 1 over there."

Brent clicked off and Laura, stunned, hung up the phone. The U.S. military hadn't been at DEFCON 2 since the Cuban missile crisis in 1962, and never at DEFCON 1, so Batu's threat must be serious indeed. She wished she had some other way to get further information.

Babich, the Capitol cop at the main desk, glanced over at Laura and smiled to himself at her concerned expression—must be more of that "gravely urgent" stuff. Returning to his magazine, he noticed a fax had ejected from the machine under the counter and he looked disinterestedly at it. Much to his surprise it had Laura's passport photo on it, along with an APB for her arrest issued by the Department of the Treasury, Secret Service Division. The charge: attempting to kill the President of the United States. Babich stood up and unsnapped his holster. Just then, another Capitol cop hurried across the lobby toward him.

"You're not gonna *believe* what was just on the tube, man—"

"Later, watch the desk." He handed the other cop Laura's APB and then walked toward her.

"Miss Bishop?"

Spooked by Babich's suddenly all-business attitude, Laura bolted through the door. He took off after her, and at the top of the steps grabbed her by the waist.

"Lady, you're under arrest." Holding her with one arm, he keyed the walkie-talkie on his belt with his other hand. "Unit Seven, call the Secret Service, tell 'em I got the woman they're lookin' for, Laura Bishop."

Before Laura could protest, she stopped struggling and looked up in the sky. The two black, streamlined Temujins from Batu's formation flew slowly into District of Columbia airspace five hundred feet from the ground, their fanwings extended for maximum lift, heading directly for the White House at no more than a hundred miles per hour. As they approached, four batteries of newly installed Patriot-II missiles on the roof of the executive mansion spun around and locked onto them. Laura and Babich watched dumbstruck from their virtual front-row seats across the Mall as two Patriot-IIs streaked across the sky. The first Temujin destroyed both missiles midair with his HPM cannons. The second Temujin buzzed across the top of the White House, irradiating the men at the Patriot controls before they could fire another volley. The first Temujin joined the offensive and together they fired wide-angle blasts across the mansion and grounds. Men on foot, in vehicles, and in guard posts on the White House grounds died instantly under the concentrated energy streams. Laura and Babich joined in the instantaneous stampede into the Capitol Building for cover.

Apart from the whine of the low-flying Temujins and the electric crackle of HPM fire, there were none of the sounds associated with battle—no screaming bombs, no earthshaking explosions. Thus, President Taylor and his staff in the subterranean Situation Room knew nothing of the Temujins' arrival and assault above them until a half-dozen Secret Service agents burst from the private elevator to set up a defensive perimeter. While Taylor talked to General Mancini on the phone, Woodruff and Levinson watched and rewatched a tape of Batu's brief television message, searching for clues as to his intentions for Washington. Mancini, at least, gave them one bit of positive news: his belief, garnered from his conversation with Wilder, that Batu's aircraft were not carrying weapons of mass destruction. Then Levinson gestured for everyone to be quiet: The operators had Russian president Karzhov on the phone.

"Sir, this is Adam Taylor. President Marsh has stepped down due to an incapacity, and I have assumed the office of the presidency. There are some people on the line with me who will confirm this: Secretary of Defense Woodruff; Chief of Staff Curt Levinson; Senator Jonathan Ballard . . ."

Batu's Temujin and the Yesugei-W remained in their holding pattern while the other penetrators finished neutralizing the White House defenses. Then, as Batu excitedly crossed the Potomac, he decelerated and activated a video system to record him in the cockpit and the view from the Temujin's nose camera. He adjusted his heading slightly, allowing the camera a clear depiction of his approach to the White House, then removed his oxygen mask and helmet so they wouldn't obscure his blond hair and striking Eurasian features.

"In all the world," Batu crowed to the camera and to posterity, "there are but a handful of men with the power to visit war upon the very heart of the American capital. No one before me has had the courage to do so, and even if they'd dared, no one but Batu would bring it here *himself*. . . ."

Suddenly, his radar blared a warning: Two F-22s and twenty assorted F-16s and F-18s from Langley Air Force Base were swarming toward them. The U.S. interceptors surrounded the TAA aircraft, trying to compensate with numbers for what they lacked in speed and firepower, and fired volleys of Sidewinder missiles. The Temujins, however, destroyed most missiles with their HPM cannons or leapt instantly from biplane speed to hypersonic speed to easily outmaneuver and outrun the missiles, leaving them to spin harmlessly toward the Atlantic.

Batu and his pilots went on the offensive and it was a turkey shoot: Even the F-22s were no match for speed-of-light weapons and extraordinarily maneuverable, hypersonic aircraft. As their numbers dwindled, some remaining American pilots even tried to ram the Temujins midair, but the TAA pilots dodged aside and blasted them with HPM fire.

In minutes, the wreckage of almost two-dozen American aircraft lay burning on the White House lawn, the Mall, atop nearby buildings, and in the streets. The sudden, violent air battle and the rain of burning debris sparked mass panic in the crowded downtown quadrant. Motorists abandoned their cars and joined the crush of pedestrians searching for shelter.

Energized by the excitement of battle, Batu yearned to see Marsh's reaction. Surely he must be huddling, angry and frightened, in the mansion below. If this direct and personal attack did not make the President self-destruct as Professor Cowling had promised, nothing would. And then, amid all the confusion from the White House assault and the president's madness would come the total destruction of all American forces amassed against the TAA.

He returned to narrating his Day of Glory for the camera: "This is not indiscriminate terrorism, some cowardly truck bomb. The Americans brag of putting a man on the moon. I will do them one better: I will put the very symbol of the TAA, our magnificent Khaldun Horsemen, inside the White House itself!"

Batu knew such a striking image would be one of the most memorable of the new century, as eternal as the images of the first mushroom cloud or the Nazi rallies at Nuremberg.

The Americans had never made provision for such an assault on the White House. Its defenses had been designed to deter large vehicles on the ground or in the air. Men on horseback or on foot could simply slip in between the concrete barriers, facing nothing more than a handful of Park Service rangers, Secret Service agents, and D.C. Metro cops protecting the mansion's entrances.

On cue, the Yesugei-W transport throttled back above the Naval Observatory in Georgetown to extend its wings and decelerate, then it banked into a tight arc across the Tidal Basin in front of the Jefferson Memorial and headed north toward the White House. Inside her, end to end, were three Incursion Tubes, each holding four Khaldun Horsemen and their stallions. In order for the men and their highly trained animals to survive liftoff and weightlessness, an intricate system of special restraints bound them to the padded walls and floors of the ITs. The slow-flying Yesugei-W's rear cargo doors opened and the first Incursion Tube began to roll out above the Executive Mansion grounds.

Suddenly, the Centurion appeared in a hypersonic flash from the late-afternoon marine layer over the Chesapeake Bay. Wilder had come looking for Batu, but when he saw the Yesugei-W droning over the White House he quickly changed course and made a steep descent toward it. The transport pilot, startled, sped up and pulled into an awkward evasive maneuver; one of the crew members guiding the ITs out of the cargo doors lost his grip and fell from the back of the plane. Lowering his landing gear, Wilder smashed the wheels of his weaponless space plane into the Yesugei, fracturing the cockpit canopy. Blinded, with many of their controls and instruments damaged, the pilot and copilot lost control of their aircraft. Through his radio, Batu heard their confusion and panic.

"Get the ITs out!" he screamed into his microphone. "Over the White House!"

The Yesugei-W, however, could not stay airborne much longer, let alone remain on course. It lost altitude and veered right, skimming the roof of the National Gallery of Art. Its landing gear only half extended, the transport belly-flopped onto the grass a few hundred feet from Capitol Hill. As it skidded toward the incline the remaining ITs slid out the back. The harnesses inside the Tubes protected the Horsemen, but several of the Commandos were injured or killed before the ITs rolled to a stop. The Yesugei-W crashed into a stand of trees, barely missing the Capitol building, and exploded in an intense fireball.

So enraged he could barely control his Temujin, Batu radioed to the other Temujins: "Go after him!"

But Wilder had kicked the Centurion back into hypersonic speed and disappeared into the immense marine layer, to wait for his next chance at Batu. Batu circled the crash site to assess the damage to his forces. The handful of Khaldun Horsemen and Commandos who survived the crash-landing were climbing or riding, dazed, out of the crumpled ITs. Thanks to Cowling's drug, they were oblivious to their injuries. Two Khaldun Horsemen got their bearings and raced toward the Executive Mansion, followed by four Commandos on foot. Circling above, Batu Khan urged them on while watching their progress through the videolinks mounted on their helmets.

Two young teachers and twenty elementary school students had been posing for pictures near the Capitol when Batu's attack began, and they now huddled under the cherry trees for cover. Seeing the Khaldun swarming the area froze them with fear. Laura and Babich beckoned urgently from the Capitol doorway. Many of the kids were simply too scared to move, so Laura and the Capitol cop sprinted down the steps to help the teachers herd the kids back up the stairs. Blinding smoke and the stench of burning aviation fuel from the crashed Yesugei-W filled the area. Babich, leading the way, made a tempting target in his blue uniform, and a Temujin pilot, circling slowly overhead on a fresh approach to the White House, fired a burst from his HPM cannon. The Capitol cop pitched forward with a wet grunt as every organ in his body ruptured like an overcooked egg. The kids, narrowly skirting the line of fire, screamed at the sight of his grotesquely swollen and blistered corpse.

The Temujin pilot, distracted by his attack on Babich, didn't see the surviving Patriot-II battery fire a missile from the White House roof. The Patriot-II impacted the Temujin, obliterating it midair. Its flaming remnants rained down everywhere—on the Horseman and Commandos racing toward the White House, and on Laura and the kids. She threw herself over a group of them to shield them from the blast while two more Capitol cops ran through the smoke, fire, and debris to help bring them inside. Laura wobbled to her feet, then looked at the cops with a stunned expression and collapsed to the sidewalk. One of the cops rolled her over and found a mangled piece of burnt metal from the exploded Temujin lodged in her back. He keyed his walkie-talkie.

"We need a doctor, west entrance, Capitol Building!"

Laura reached around, trying to grab the shrapnel. "Get it out or it won't stop bleeding!"

"Try to relax; the doc's on his way . . ."

Determined to endure the most intense pain she'd ever felt, Laura went limp and let the cops carry her up the stairs to the Capitol lobby.

As expected, Russian president Karzhov immediately threatened President Taylor with a retaliatory strike if the United States launched its missiles against Russian targets. Over Woodruff's and Mancini's protests, Taylor told Karzhov he would delay the ICBM launch order until moments before the close of the deployment window in order to allow the Russians a shot at defusing the situation themselves.

The connection to Karzhov in the Kremlin remained open, but Taylor muted the sound. While everyone watched a video screen in the Situation Room showing the data from the radar at Svalbard, Woodruff lobbied the President to reconsider the delay.

"We're taking an enormous risk for what amounts to a symbolic gesture, sir, and it's surely more than they'd give us."

"It's not symbolic. If we have any chance to reason with the Russians and avoid retaliation we must convince them we've exhausted every other option."

"Our fighters are approaching the region," Karzhov said over the phone. "They will find the stolen missiles and kill those in control of them."

Taylor already knew of the MiGs' approach over the Volga because he could see their progress across the night skies via the Svalbard radar. He turned the mute off the phone.

"We're still intercepting Batu Khan's radio transmissions," Taylor said. "His planes are tracking yours and he's ordered them destroyed."

"Our MiGs can handle anything," Karzhov replied.

"The TAA aircraft are hypersonic, with speed-of-light weapons . . ."

Taylor and the others watched the screen as the TAA penetrators, invisible to the Russians, leapt to hypersonic speed and changed course to intercept the MiGs. In moments, all five MiGs vanished from the radar screen. Karzhov stopped talking for a moment; someone obviously informed him of the loss of their aircraft. After a sharp exchange in whispered Russian, Karzhov came back on the line.

"Our fighters report Kamyshin has come into view . . . all lights are off, the invaders have cut the electricity . . . our pilots have activated sensors to detect the radioactive cores of the stolen missiles . . ."

Taylor and Woodruff exchanged a look: Karzhov was trying to run down the clock by pretending his Air Force still had a chance.

"President Karzhov, sir, your aircraft are gone," Taylor said. "I'm sorry."

It took Karzhov a moment to find a response. "We have additional planes on their way!"

For once, he spoke the truth. Taylor and the others could see two groups of MiGs approaching the region from the northeast.

"They're at least fifteen minutes away," Taylor said. "Past the close of our launch window."

Furious that the Americans knew as much if not more about his Air Force than he did, Karzhov immediately switched gears.

"There will be no U.S. nuclear strike within Russian borders, do you understand?! You know so much about what is happening over here, you should've warned us when we still had the time to take back our missiles ourselves! This crisis is your doing, not ours! The moment you launch I will answer in kind!"

Taylor let him rant. This performance was as much for the benefit of Karzhov's allies and enemies in the Kremlin monitoring the call as for him. The new President glanced at the clock. Only six minutes remained to deploy the ICBMs in time to destroy the stolen missiles. He picked up the plastic envelopes containing the go-codes, broke them open, and removed the laminated code cards. Woodruff looked at Taylor, expecting him to begin reading the codes.

"Sir?"

"We may have one last option," Taylor said.

Thirty-eight

Wilder was hidden in the marine layer above Chesapeake Bay, readying another try for Batu. As he gained altitude and broke through the top of the clouds, he could see several columns of black smoke rising from the central part of the District. His radio crackled to life.

"Centurion," General Mancini said, "stand by for the President of the United States."

Wilder scowled. Burton Marsh was about the last guy on the planet he wanted to talk to.

"This is President Adam Taylor . . ."

Even in a day full of surprises, that one was a corker.

"Yes, *sir*!"

Taylor got right to the point. "Batu Khan is moments from transmitting the launch codes for a nuclear attack against American forces." He did not need to elaborate. "Do you have any possible way of stopping him?"

"Yes, sir, I believe I do. How long do I have?"

"Five minutes. General Mancini has further information; I'll put him through."

"Roger that, Mr. President."

As soon as Taylor signed off, the Situation Room erupted with dissenting voices.

"I grant you Wilder's been able to destroy three hostile aircraft, but he hasn't been able to get close to Batu and he no longer has any weaponry!" Woodruff said. "Giving him this additional time cuts too close to the response window. And even if he succeeds, Batu might have implemented a contingency plan against his own inability to order the launch."

"That's true, sir," Levinson said. "Nothing short of destroying the Russian missiles before they leave the ground will unequivocally guarantee the elimination of the threat."

The arguments did not sway Taylor. "The notion Batu would share control of nuclear weapons runs contrary to everything we know about the man, and everything we've been intercepting in their radio transmissions. Wilder's five minutes seems a reasonable gamble. The discussion is closed."

"Then you must proceed with the authorization protocols, right up to the final order to release the weapons," Woodruff said. "If Wilder fails to stop Batu, you'll need only issue a single command to launch the ICBMs."

"Agreed," Taylor said.

Wilder headed into Washington, staying so close to the ground he had to cut between the taller buildings along the route. He set the stopwatch on his Rolex and disengaged the Centurion's electronic countermeasures so President Taylor and the others in the White House could watch his progress on the VS screen. His only option for downing Batu would be ramming his Centurion into the Temujin, and he figured he'd have the chance for one, maybe two tries in the allotted time. As he soared over the Mall he spotted Batu and the other Temujin. They were flying subsonic, irradiating the area near the Capitol Building with their HPM cannons, laying down cover for the Khaldun heading toward the White House. Then, as Wilder searched for the optimum approach path, a more effective gambit than trying for a simple midair collision occurred to him. He switched the HPM weapons systems back on-line. Immediately an alarm blared, warning of a catastrophic overload in the main HPM power capacitors. With the secondary storage systems damaged and unable to absorb the enormous amperage used by the microwave emitters, the capacitors would soon become overcharged and explode. This would ignite a chain reaction in the fuel system—a known risk of carrying speed-of-light energy weapons on a small fighter—and cause the Centurion to blow apart like the space shuttle *Challenger*.

Wilder shut down all electrical systems except flight control to increase the amperage flowing to the capacitors and accelerate their destruction. He considered whether it would be better to hang back and rush Batu just before the Centurion explodes, or try to get within lethal proximity of the Temujin and hope he could stick close when Batu tried to shake him. Unable to judge exactly when the capacitors would hit critical overload, he chose the latter plan.

Wilder didn't want Batu to see the new damage to the Centurion, for then he'd know her weapons were off-line, so he rode the Temujin's tail. As he closed the distance between them, Batu banked and turned to get away, but Wilder matched his every move and tried to get closer. He glanced at his watch—four minutes remaining—then at the weapons systems overload indicator. Its green/yellow/red bar graph crossed from yellow into the red.

On the Situation Room video screen, the oval icons representing the Centurion and Temujin looked like an arcade game as they sped through the three-dimensional outlines of city buildings.

Since Wilder hadn't fired his weapons, Batu figured he must have another reason for wanting to get so close. He knew the Centurion had slight superiority in speed and maneuverability, so he resisted his instinct to fly up and away. Being in the open sky would work to Wilder's advantage. If the American desired proximity, Batu would prevent it by keeping solid objects—buildings—between them.

For the first time since arriving above Washington, he felt vulnerable. He radioed Chu'tsai, informing him of Wilder's pursuit. Chu'tsai tried not to panic, although this had been his worst fear about Batu leading the U.S. incursion.

"You must leave the area at once," he implored Batu. "I warned you of this. What if you're unable to order the missiles away?!"

"All right, I'll transmit the go-codes now. The engineers will be free to launch the moment they're in position. Patch me through to them."

Batu turned his attention back to the Centurion, inching ever closer. Cruising along Independence Avenue, Batu dropped to ten feet above street level and tried to shake the Centurion by skimming under the arched Knapp Memorial Bridge between the Department of Agriculture buildings. Wilder stayed on his tail, the tips of the Centurion's wings missing the concrete by inches. Batu cut between the Hirshhorn and Air and Space Museums and crossed the Mall. The noise and engine wash from their aircraft shattered windows everywhere as they flew between the buildings.

Three minutes left.

Momentarily flying over an open area, Batu ripped open the code envelope and stuck the launch authorization card on his instrument panel so its ten large block letters, English alpha-bravo codes, were in clear view. Then he turned to follow Pennsylvania Avenue into the crowded heart of the city. Wilder hated the notion of his aircraft exploding in such tight quarters, surrounded by civilians, but he had no choice. The Temujin zigzagged from street to street, skating just above the car tops in an amazing display of aerial dexterity. Wilder's lack of depth perception put him at an extreme disadvantage. He had to fly by mimicking Batu's maneuvers rather than by attempting to judge the minuscule distances between his aircraft and its surroundings.

Batu glanced quickly down and read two of the ten codes, "delta . . . sierra . . ." into the radio. After saying each code he strained to listen through the weak, static-filled connection as the engineers repeated them in confirmation.

Hearing this through their real-time radio interception, President Taylor grabbed the telephone connecting him to Wilder.

"Centurion, he's reading the go-codes ahead of schedule!"

"Understood!" Wilder replied. *Dancing as fast as I can . . .*

The Centurion's weapons overload alarm switched from a pulsating to a steady tone and the meter reached its maximum reading inside the red. Wilder struggled to remain close enough to Batu to guarantee the Temujin's destruction. But each time he closed the gap Batu found a way to elude him, or he would have to take evasive maneuvers from other Temujin on his tail.

Batu emerged from the space between the Marriott and the Willard Hotel and flew over Pershing Park toward the open area above the White House lawn. He read two more codes, then the Washington Monument loomed ahead and he banked sharply to the east to avoid it. Finally having some room to maneuver, Wilder sped up. The acceleration sent a spike of power from the engines to the weapons systems and he could smell the capacitors starting to burn. They were only seconds from blowing. Batu also increased speed, then arced skyward in a tight, belly-up loop. Wilder edged closer, aiming the needle-nose of the

Centurion at the Temujin's exhaust port. The Centurion would blow up any second now.

Suddenly, the alarm in Wilder's cockpit stopped sounding and the overload meter plunged into the green. A relay clicked off, blocking the flow of power to the capacitors—some goddamn brilliant engineer's redundant fail-safe had kicked in! Cursing Air Force efficiency, Wilder groped blindly for the relay switch. He found it on the weapons control board, reset it, and held it in the on position with his knee. At once, the alarm and meter resumed their prior positions. He shot forward and for a heartbeat he remembered the salt flats at Woomera, when his jet-propelled semi had pursued the Infiltrator's Land Rover. This ride made that one seem like a tricycle race. Two minutes remaining . . .

Batu circled back toward the central city, leveling off long enough to transmit another three codes. With only seconds to go before his aircraft self-destructed, Wilder shoved the stick forward. Thick toxic smoke filled the Centurion's cockpit from the burning capacitors and a new visual warning indicator flashed a bright red countdown across the heads-up display:

SYSTEM OVERLOAD IN 5 . . . 4 . . . 3 . . . 2 . . . 1 . . .

Wilder kept accelerating. He would stay aboard the Centurion until she exploded to be absolutely certain Batu didn't swerve away. He knew the President would see the two aircraft disappear from radar, confirming their destruction, and he hoped Kate would find comfort in the simple mathematics of his sacrifice: one life given to save so many others.

But instead of the expected 0 on the display countdown, the word EJECTING appeared. The Centurion's canopy blew away from the fuselage with four small explosive charges and Wilder's seat blasted straight up out of the cockpit. The abrupt acceleration snapped his head back and his chest became too heavy to breathe. *Damn* engineers—automatic pilot ejection! Another fail-safe, its existence undoubtedly buried on page 2,500 of the tech manuals.

Below Wilder, the Centurion blew apart in a spectacular flash of light and heat. Fire and debris overtook him, hammering against the metal cage beneath his seat. Then, only moments after the shockwave washed past him, his parachutes deployed.

The exploding Centurion tore apart the rear of the Temujin, blasting metal shrapnel through the exhaust ports into the engines. They seized up and stopped. Fires broke out in the circuitry and hydraulics. Batu struggled with his unresponsive controls and tried transmitting the final three codes, but the radio was dead. He tried to punch out; the ejection system and automatic canopy release didn't operate and he couldn't extend his landing gear.

Gliding on what remained of his wings, he searched for a safe place to set down. He nudged the Temujin toward a long, uninterrupted stretch of water—the Reflecting Pool before the Lincoln Memorial. He landed hard, scraping along its shallow bottom, splashing huge arcs of water on either side. The plane slid the entire length of the pool then crumpled to a stop at the base of the monument.

The fire in the Temujin roared toward the cockpit. Batu shut off the oxygen valve to slow its spread. The landing had crushed the underside of the fuselage, shoving twisted pieces of composite material up through the floor. One jammed against Batu's left leg, breaking it just above the knee. He wrenched his leg loose and manually released the canopy. The sudden rush of fresh air intensified the fire raging at his feet. He strained to grab the card upon which were printed the launch codes, but his broken leg and the searing flames prevented him from reaching it. When his flight suit began to burn he gave up, pulled himself out of the cockpit and rolled out onto the ground.

In the VS Room, the loudspeaker broadcasting the intercepted transmissions from Batu and the other TAA aircraft remained silent. The oval icon representing the Centurion disappeared from the screen when Wilder's aircraft exploded, but Batu's oval remained onscreen while landing. Taylor looked at the clock—sixty-five seconds to go. He picked up the phone connecting him to Wilder.

"Centurion, please advise status of Batu's plane . . ."

No answer. He looked over at Woodruff, holding another phone, ready to pass along the ICBM launch order to SAC.

"Sir, the Centurion is gone. Batu's plane appears to have landed—"

"Someone get me visual report on the condition of that goddamn aircraft!" Taylor shouted.

Air Combat Command couldn't oblige the President: Batu's planes had destroyed all of the American fighters in the area.

Wilder, still stunned from his explosive ejection, drifted on parachutes over the east end of the Mall. Pulling the chute lines, he twisted around to see what had happened to Batu. At the Lincoln Monument, three-quarters of a mile away, he spotted the Temujin, its canopy open, burning in the Reflecting Pool. He barely made out the tiny figure crawling up the steps toward the Lincoln Memorial. Wilder felt confident he'd accomplished his goal, but it didn't matter if he couldn't inform the President of his success. Even if Batu's transmissions went dead, the White House would need direct confirmation that the Temujin was in flames and Batu had left the aircraft.

He unbuckled part of his seat harness and leaned over, struggling to reach a tiny UHF radio inside the emergency kit attached beneath his seat. He doubted anyone at the ACC would think to monitor that frequency—UHF emergency radios were used when crashing behind enemy lines—but he had no other mode of communication. The cell phone he'd taken from Righty blew up with the Centurion and he didn't see any pay phones floating nearby.

Before he could reach the emergency kit, the last remaining Temujin zoomed at him. Wilder was still two hundred feet from the ground and absurdly vulnerable. The TAA plane leveled off, its pilot savoring the kill. Looking below, Wilder spotted the Spring Grotto, a small, tree-shaded pool at the base of Capitol Hill. Okay, he thought, if Batu can land in the fucking water, so can I. He tugged at one of his chute lines to move directly over the Grotto as the TAA pilot targeted his weapons.

Wilder unbuckled the rest of his harness, grabbed the emergency kit, and dropped out of the seat. A moment later, a concentrated beam of microwave energy turned the seat and its ejection cage into a molten tangle of metal. Wilder tucked himself into a ball to cannonball into the water. He hoped for more than a couple feet in depth, or it would *not* be happy landings. Crashing through the tree branches above the Grotto he splashed into the water. Its six-foot depth barely kept him from breaking his back on its rocky bottom.

Angry he'd missed Wilder, the TAA pilot circled around for another shot. Wilder pulled himself painfully out of the water, took cover behind an ornamental boulder, and pulled the emergency radio from its pouch. Twenty seconds remained.

"This is Wilder . . . Batu's plane is down and in flames . . . inform the President!"

In the VS Room the President nodded to Woodruff, who passed the order to the Strategic Air Command:

"We have an affirmative for release, on my mark—"

"—Stop!" Taylor shouted.

"Delay that!" Woodruff said.

"Batu's plane is down . . . He's out of the cockpit . . ."

They could hear Wilder's faint voice through their live link to the ACC thanks to General Mancini. The moment the Centurion disappeared from the radar screen he'd ordered the ACC to monitor the UHF frequency. Trusting in Wilder's training, Mancini felt certain he'd remember to use the emergency radio. Taylor, intensely relieved, could hear the ACC guys cheering through the radio. Mancini also took Wilder's word of the Temujin's downing as assurance Batu had been stopped. But Secretary of Defense Woodruff didn't share their excitement.

"Mr. President, he didn't say he'd seen Batu Khan dead or that he completely destroyed his aircraft."

"Batu stopped sending the codes," Senator Ballard said.

"He could start again," Woodruff replied. "What if he has another radio aside from the one in the aircraft?"

"We repeatedly heard them say he has no redundant communications capabilities and that the missiles cannot be launched without his specific order," Mancini said through the speaker box.

"That could've been said to mislead us."

"They didn't know we were listening."

"It's *not* a confirmed kill," Woodruff insisted.

Taylor had less than ten seconds to decide.

"No Air Force pilot would report an aircraft down if he didn't mean his mission had been accomplished," Mancini said.

Taylor didn't have time for clarification from Wilder. No time to think it through, he had to rely on his gut. Five seconds to go . . .

"Cancel the launch."

In his Yesugei-R circling above Kamyshin, Chu'tsai leaned in next to his radio, trying over and over to contact Batu and get the remaining launch codes. Then the pilot of the last Temujin radioed in, confirming his worst fears: Batu had crash-landed. Stunned, he closed his eyes for a moment's meditation. Surely he would've sensed a change in Batu's spiritual status if his friend were dead. His throat tightened with emotion as he decided Batu still lived.

"He's alive!" he said to the Temujin pilot in Washington. "Find him!"

"Sir," Chu'tsai's navigator called out, "twenty more MiGs are approaching our airspace!"

"Shoot them down!"

As his escort Temujin flew off Chu'tsai didn't bother to take evasive action, confident his aircraft's second-generation stealth would, as before, protect them from radar- or heat-guided missiles.

On the ground at the Kamyshin airport, the other stolen SS-25 approached the huge AN-124 transport plane Batu's men would use to fly the missile into the TAA. A hundred feet from the rear of the transport the TEL slowed down for its trip up the ramp and into the hull. The Khaldun climbing into the cockpit noticed a strange light in the sky, like a shooting star with a long yellow tail. It was the last thought he ever had. A Russian missile hit the nose of the transport plane, destroying its front third. Accompanied by the scream of low-flying jets, other missiles rained down on the airport, blasting ten-foot-wide craters in the runway. The explosions made an interconnected ring of holes around the TEL, stranding it on an island of macadam. So much for Batu's hope of bringing home the ultimate prize.

On the far side of the city, the other TEL broke through the east entrance to the broad Borodin Plaza, shoving cars aside as if they were tin cans. It drove into the plaza, stopped in front of the Orthodox church, and the TAA engineers, still awaiting Batu's final codes, scrambled down to confirm its exact position with a GPS receiver. Several jacks around the circumference of the TEL dug into the cobblestones and leveled the vehicle, while enormous hydraulic drives began lifting the erector arm and the missile container to a vertical position. A single Russian MiG suddenly zoomed low over their heads, gone as quickly as it came. For a moment, silence, then the plaza lit up in a spectacular fountain of fire. The jet had dropped a half-dozen canisters of napalm—hot enough to incinerate any living thing near the TEL, but not explosive enough to accidentally detonate the warhead.

Above the cities of Kamyshin, Volgograd, and Saratov, the Russian interceptors spread out, two for each of the six TAA invaders. Chu'tsai, still trying to raise Batu, looked up from the radio and saw the MiGs flying right toward his Yesugei. Guided by real-time data now supplied to them by the American radar at Svalbard Station, the Russian pilots could target their air-to-air weapons on the heretofore invisible TAA aircraft. Watching two missiles streaking toward him, Chu'tsai understood why he'd stopped seeing the future earlier that evening—there was none to be seen. The explosions tore apart his aircraft, and he survived just long enough to feel the burning air of his last breath broil away his lungs.

Wilder radioed the location of Batu's downed aircraft and climbed out of the Grotto, searching for a quick way across the Lincoln Memorial through the tangle of gridlocked, abandoned cars. The city seemed deserted. Everyone still remained in hiding. Among the smoldering pieces of wreckage strewn nearby Wilder noticed some pieces of the Centurion. Suddenly, an injured Khaldun Horseman charged him, scimitar held aloft, his robes charred and tattered. Wilder fired at him with the AK-74U he'd taken from the *Altun Ordu,* but the bullets didn't penetrate the Horseman's armor. He took careful aim and shot him in the face, flipping him out of the saddle.

Clutching his broken leg, a machine gun slung across his back, Batu crawled up the steps into the Lincoln Memorial. Honest Abe stared down at him from his massive chair and below, a platoon of National Guardsmen moved cautiously toward his downed aircraft. One of them caught a glimpse of his yellow *shalwar qamiz* behind a marble column and signaled to the others. Batu fired a burst at them, so they took cover behind his Temujin and called for backup. The Guardsman captain gestured for his men to split up and approach the memorial from outside Batu's line of fire.

Batu knew he was hopelessly trapped, so he reached in through the collar of his *shalwar qamiz* and pulled out a Triton. He would not let that sanctimonious prick Burton Marsh parade him around in chains. Looking up at the statue of Lincoln made him think of his brother, Mikhail. How they'd watched *Mr. Smith Goes to Washington* together, two little Siberian boys enthralled as Jimmy Stewart found strength and inspiration at this very place. For Batu, ending up here brought the opposite emotions. His failure to launch the Russian missiles or get his Horsemen inside the White House filled him with a crippling grief. His only hope lay with the possibility his men had gotten at least one of the SS-25s across the Russian border into the Trans-Altaic Alliance. Although he would not be there to enjoy it, his vast empire, forged by the sheer strength of his will, would finally be a true superpower.

Batu put one end of the Triton in his mouth. Just before he pulled it apart, a shadow passed overhead and a sweeping blast from the remaining Temujin's HPM cannon killed the Guardsman platoon instantly. Moments later, landing gear extended, the Temujin rolled to a stop in the shallow water of the Reflecting Pool. The canopy opened and the pilot, a Mongolian barely twenty-one years of age, leapt from the craft and ran to him. Tears ran down the pilot's face.

"They're dead! All of them! Everyone in Russia!"

"Chu'tsai?"

The pilot nodded. Batu hung his head and began to weep. The loss of his friend cut more deeply than the unraveling of his Day of Glory. After a moment, the pilot helped him to his feet.

"Get me to the plane."

The pilot nodded, understanding he must sacrifice himself to save Batu—the Temujin had only one seat. Batu paused at the top of the monument's steps and looked around. No other American forces had yet arrived. He and the pilot had a moment alone, and an idea came to him for how to make the most of it. He slipped his *shalwar qamiz* off his shoulders and handed the garment to the pilot. The pilot, knowing what Batu wanted of him, didn't hesitate. He draped the garment over his flight suit and Batu took the dog tags from around the pilot's neck.

"Do you have a family?"

"Yes, Batu. A baby girl."

"I'll see she's taken care of."

"Bless you."

Batu gestured to the base of the statue to show the pilot where he wanted him, then limped a safe distance away while the pilot sat on the floor and put the Triton between his teeth. He paused, frightened, so Batu moved closer to him.

"I love you," he said.

The pilot smiled and snapped the Triton apart. As it exploded, Batu closed his eyes and let the pilot's blood splash over him. It was like a baptism, imbuing the Emperor of the Trans-Altaic Alliance with faith reborn. Even with his devastating losses, as long as his people remained this strong, such a day could never be called a failure.

Several open-topped Army National Guard troop trucks sat in front of the Capitol. Two Guardsmen carried Laura, lying on a makeshift stretcher made from a door, to one of the trucks to take her to the hospital. A Guardsman at the bottom of the hill called out to his captain and pointed at the wreckage of the Centurion burning on the grass nearby, its unique design apparent even in pieces.

"Sir, it's one of ours!"

Wincing in pain, Laura sat up and looked at the Centurion, seeing the USAF and the Stars and Stripes on the fuselage. Gasping, she feared the worst until she noticed the seat had ejected from the cockpit. She asked for the binoculars hanging around the Guard captain's neck and scanned the area, then a huge smile spread across her face as she spotted Wilder galloping across the Mall on a white Khaldun stallion.

Just before Wilder reached the Reflecting Pool, the Temujin turned around for a takeoff. He couldn't quite tell through the glare on the canopy—did the man in the cockpit have a shock of white-blond hair? The plane taxied through the little water left in the pool and Wilder emptied the AK-74U's clip at the Temujin while it zoomed over his head, although he had scant hope of doing any damage.

Bounding up the stairs to the Lincoln Memorial, Wilder found a half-dozen D.C. Metro Police standing over the headless, handless body at the base of the statue. A huge red semicircle had backsplashed on the marble behind it and an enormous amount of blood soaked into the *shalwar qamiz*, practically obscuring its yellow color. As the cops excitedly radioed in the news of Batu's death, Wilder crouched down next to the body. Although it seemed compact and strong like Batu's, it didn't quite match his recollection of the man.

Wilder turned at the sound of a honking car horn as the National Guard truck sped toward him; he saw Laura lying in the back, clutching the side of the truck so she could sit up and look for him. He ran down the stairs three at a time, jumped into the back of the truck, and gasped at the blood soaking through her bandages.

"Get her to an ER!" he shouted to the Guardsman behind the wheel.

The truck drove on the shoulder, around the abandoned cars on 23rd Street, and Wilder knelt next to Laura, more frightened than he'd ever been.

"What happened?" he asked.

"I'll be okay." Amazed to find him earthbound and safe, she didn't care about her injuries. "If you'd gotten killed up there, I never would've let you live it down."

Wilder kissed her, and his heart soared higher than any plane could ever take him.

Epilogue

Two hours after the attack, Amy Marsh broke the news to the public about her husband leaving office. She said only that President Marsh had suffered a head injury during the assault on the White House. The new President, Adam Taylor, spoke after she did. He urged the stunned American people to focus not on the assault on Washington or the theft of the Russian missiles, but on how to make sure such things would never happen again.

Amy put her husband in a sanitarium in New Hampshire. She chose it for its airtight privacy and because she could live in a cottage on the grounds. The doctors kept Marsh on a combination of Thorazine and Stelazine merely to sedate him, as they held little hope for recovery. During his few wakeful hours per day he sat quietly in his room, his only communication being his repeated refusals to see his wife. Rumors about the real cause of the former President's incapacity soon erupted on the Internet, and the news organizations tried repeatedly to uncover any information about him. But the handful of people who knew what really happened, Wilder and Laura included, all believed the truth to be too destructive and without benefit. Compelled as well by their fondness for the Marshes, they agreed among themselves to an unbreakable code of silence. The irony of this was not lost on Wilder. Uncovering the truth had almost killed him, but now he would do his damnedest to keep it hidden.

Three days after assuming the presidency, Adam Taylor invited Wilder to the White House for a private meeting, no reporters or staff, to thank him for all he'd done. Wilder, however, felt miserable his job had been incomplete: He hadn't captured or killed Batu Khan. President Taylor, like everyone else, wanted to believe the headless body at the Lincoln Memorial belonged to the leader of the TAA—Batu had yet to resurface and prove them wrong—but Wilder disagreed. He'd fought with Batu on the *Altun Ordu* and felt certain the body belonged to someone else.

Taylor nodded and changed the subject. He and his staff had been considering various options for responding to the attacks on Washington and Russia; at that moment, Wilder's insistence that Batu had escaped made him decide which one to go with.

Right after the meeting with Wilder, President Taylor approved massive air strikes against the secret locations in the TAA from which Batu's Temujin penetrators had taken off, and any other places deemed vital to his ability to wage war. The sorties continued nonstop, day and night, for a week. American, Russian, British, Canadian, Israeli, Saudi, Jordanian, Indian, Italian, Australian, and, finally, even French planes dropped more explosive tonnage on military targets across the vast Trans-Altaic Alliance than during World Wars One and Two combined. The bombing ceased when Batu's generals, their forces in disarray, pulled all TAA personnel from Georgia and the Ukraine in a frantic exodus. Losses: four Allied planes downed, and an estimated 8,000 TAA casualties. The TAA inflated that figure to 350,000 and, in an irony that surely would've amused Burton Marsh, filed a charge of war crimes against the American government with the United Nations.

The Supreme Leader of the Trans-Altaic Alliance remained in hiding throughout the American-led attack. Though he took great satisfaction in Marsh's departure from the presidency, Batu knew his empire had gained nothing from its incursions into Washington and Russia except the enmity of a formerly apathetic American public. The world learned he was alive when, from his *ger* somewhere in the wilderness, he broadcast a scathing denouncement of the U.S. retaliation and reasserted his control of his empire. The TAA, which without a leader seemed close to unraveling from the intensity of the air strikes and the world's condemnation of its actions, immediately stabilized under the strength of Batu's personality.

President Taylor, understanding that American indifference had played a large part in emboldening Batu, sent him a letter via the Greek ambassador. Its full text read:

Sir:

Like my predecessor, I will govern this nation by following my conscience and not the polls. That said, please be aware that ninety-seven percent of the American public approved of the airstrikes against the Trans-Altaic Alliance. Among the other participating nations, the numbers were the same.

We are watching you.

Adam Taylor.

To Brent's great amusement, no one in the Air Force ever mentioned to Wilder any of the details of his escapades, such as stealing the Centurion at gunpoint.

At Rexford University, Wilder helped oversee a joint FBI/OSI task force as they computerized the chemistry department's enrollment records from 1966 to 1980 and traced all former students' current whereabouts. But before the project's completion, in various parts of the country three more citizens in their fifties snapped and committed extreme acts of violence. This brought the total, including President Marsh, to thirty—the same as the number of records in Cowling's database. In each new case the FBI prevailed upon the local authorities and families to help obscure from the media any possible interrelation to the others, and everyone who knew about the still-secret test group hoped it meant the last of the Mad Yuppies. Wilder, however, still had his doubts. What if Cowling had conducted more than one group of tests? Were there more potential time bombs out there?

For a brief moment it seemed possible to get definitive answers to these questions when, in his hospital room, Cowling's eyes suddenly popped open. But despite all efforts by the FBI, his doctors, and his psychiatrists to prevail upon him, he refused to cooperate. Prison officials moved his burn-treatment equipment into a special maximum-security cell; since he became uncontrollably violent if anyone tried to tranquilize him and he wouldn't eat his food if his medication had been ground into it, the doctors simply stopped drugging him. Which was fine, except for the other inmates' complaints about his frequent, twelve-hour stretches of nonstop screaming.

The first day of fall came on a Sunday, seven weeks after Batu Khan's aborted Day of Glory. Late-afternoon shadows crept across the small lawn behind Laura's town house and an autumn crispness filled the air. Wilder and Laura sipped Coronas in her backyard while he waited for the grill to heat. The shrapnel wound in her back was healing neatly, thanks to excellent reconstructive surgery at the George Washington University Medical Center. Brent stood at the table, mixing margaritas and making a salad. Kate and Cindy tossed a Frisbee. They'd made a secret bet about how long it would take before the guys cried uncle and asked for help with dinner. Kate's money said ten minutes or less.

She'd recently returned to school—first grade already! Her teachers tried, gently, to help the kids put the recent events in perspective and understand why some of their fathers, pilots of the American interceptors, would never come home. Little evidence remained of the physical damage to the White House and central Washington. Batu Khan's injuries to the national psyche, however, would take much longer to heal. Many observers compared it to the country's collective melancholy in the months following John F. Kennedy's assassination. America mourned the abrupt end of the Marsh presidency, while struggling to accept the realization that her borders were no longer beyond the reach of enemy forces.

Laura turned as she heard the phone ringing inside. "Who on earth could that be?"

She went inside to answer it and Wilder returned to a conversation with Brent about the man who would surely remain everyone's favorite topic for months to come, Batu Khan.

"The media keeps saying his biggest mistake was misjudging us," Wilder said, putting the steaks on the grill. "But I'm not so sure he did. His real miscalculation was going too far too fast. If he'd stolen the missiles and just *threatened* to use them, it probably would've forced us to pull our troops back."

"I don't give a husky one whether the Batu Khans of the world misjudge us or not," Brent said. "The real danger is us misjudging them, and making policy based on false assumptions. We can't view the rest of the world through the prism of our own culture and values. Just because we're not comfortable with . . . hell, I don't know, pick an atrocity . . . it doesn't mean some other fella won't do it twice before breakfast and find enormous satisfaction in it."

Wilder smiled. On certain subjects, Brent made him sound down-right easygoing. While waiting to turn the steaks, they joined in the Fris-bee game with Kate and Cindy. A couple minutes later, Laura came back outside with a bemused expression on her face.

"Let me guess: another reporter wanting inside information about the former President," Wilder said.

"Worse. Some people wanting to produce a miniseries: *The Amy Marsh Story*."

"Yeah, I got that same call myself," Wilder replied. "I hung up on them."

"I told them Mrs. Marsh showed extraordinary bravery during the crisis last month," Laura said, "and violating her privacy would hardly be the way to reward her. *Then* I hung up on them."

"Never mind that," Brent said. "How much did they offer a big, fa-mous writer like you for your participation?"

Laura hesitated, uncomfortable about discussing money. "Well . . . a half-million dollars."

Brent looked at Wilder and started laughing.

"What's so funny?" Laura asked.

"They only offered Matt fifty grand!"

"Oh . . ."

She didn't know what else to say, so she took a sip of Wilder's beer. He laughed along with Brent and held her hand.

"Gotta say, I love you so much right now it hurts," Wilder told Laura.

Like the song says, hurts so good.